D0363874

IN THIS GRAVE HOUR

By Jacqueline Winspear

Pardonable Lies

Messenger of Truth

An Incomplete Revenge

Among the Mad

The Mapping of Love and Death

A Lesson in Secrets

Elegy for Eddie

Leaving Everything Most Loved

A Dangerous Place

Journey to Munich

In This Grave Hour

The Care and Management of Lies

IN THIS GRAVE HOUR

A Maisie Dobbs Novel

JACQUELINE WINSPEAR

Allison & Busby Limited
12 Fitzroy Mews
London W1T 6DW
allisonandbusby.com

First published in Great Britain by Allison & Busby in 2017.

Copyright © 2017 by JACQUELINE WINSPEAR

The moral right of the author is hereby asserted in accordance with
the Copyright, Designs and Patents Act 1988.

All characters and events in this publication,
other than those clearly in the public domain,
are fictitious and any resemblance to actual persons,
living or dead, is purely coincidental.

All rights reserved. No part of this publication may be reproduced,
stored in a retrieval system, or transmitted, in any form or by
any means without the prior written permission of the publisher,
nor be otherwise circulated in any form of binding or cover
other than that in which it is published and without a similar
condition being imposed on the subsequent buyer.

A CIP catalogue record for this book is available from
the British Library.

First Edition

ISBN 978-0-7490-2180-1

Typeset in 11/18 pt Sabon by
Allison & Busby Ltd.

The paper used for this Allison & Busby publication
has been produced from trees that have been legally sourced
from well-managed and credibly certified forests.

Printed and bound by
CPI Group (UK) Ltd, Croydon, CR0 4YY

Dedicated to
Irene, Joyce, Sylvia, Joseph, Ruby, Charles, and Rose
Our family's World War II evacuees

In this grave hour, perhaps the most fateful in our history . . . for the second time in the lives of most of us, we are at war.

– KING GEORGE VI, 3RD SEPTEMBER 1939

PROLOGUE

London, Sunday 3rd September 1939

Maisie Dobbs left her garden flat in Holland Park, taking care to lock the door to her private entrance as she departed. She carried no handbag, no money, but had drawn a cardigan around her shoulders and carried a rolled umbrella, just in case. There had been a run of hot summer days punctuated by intermittent storms and pouring rain, leaving the air thick and clammy with the promise of more changeable weather, as clouds of luminous white and thunderous graphite lumbered across the sky above. They reminded Maisie of elephants on the march across a parched plain, and in that moment she wished she were far away in a place where such beasts roamed.

Her journey was short – just a five-minute walk along a leafy street towards a Georgian mansion of several stories: the home of her oldest friend, Priscilla Partridge, along with her husband, Douglas, and their three sons. The youngest, Tarquin, had been sent to Maisie's flat earlier with a message for her to hurry, so they could listen to the wireless together – as family, united, at the worst of times. For without doubt, Maisie was considered family as far as Priscilla, her husband, and their boys were concerned.

Despite the warmth of the day, Maisie felt chilled in her light summer dress. She slipped her arms into the sleeves of her cardigan as she walked, transferring the umbrella from one hand to the other, conscious of every movement.

Where was she the last time? Had she been so young, so distracted by her new life at Girton College, that she could not remember where she was and what she had been doing when the news came? She stopped for a moment. It had been another long, hot summer then – the perfect English summer, they'd said – and she wondered if, indeed, weather had something to do with the outcome, pressing down on people, firing the tempers of powerful men until they reached a point of no return, spilling over to upend the world.

The mansion's front door was open before she set foot on the bottom step.

'Tante Maisie, come, you'll miss it.' Thomas, now eighteen years of age, stood tall, his hair just a shade lighter than his mother's coppery brown. He was smiling as he beckoned Maisie to hurry, then held out his hand to take hers. 'The wireless is on in the drawing room, and everyone's waiting.'

Maisie nodded. It seemed to her that each day Priscilla's boys gained inches in height and increased their already boundless energy. And though he was the eldest, Thomas could still engage in rambunctious play with his brothers. They'd always reminded Maisie of a basket of puppies on those occasions when she saw them in the garden, teasing one another, tugging on each other's hair or the scruff of the neck. But Thomas was also a man. Today, of all days, his passing boyhood filled her with dread.

'Maisie – come on!' Priscilla hurried into the entrance hall, brandishing a cigarette in a long holder. She reached out and linked her arm through Maisie's. 'Let's get settled.'

As they stepped into the drawing room, Douglas Partridge managed a brief smile and a nod as he approached. 'Maisie. Good, you're here.' He drew back after touching his cheek to hers, and held her gaze for a second. Each saw the pain in the other, and the effort to press back the past. She nodded her understanding. Memories seemed to collide with the present as they joined Priscilla and the boys, along with the household staff – a cook, housekeeper, and Elinor, the family's long-serving nanny, no longer needed but much loved.

'I thought we should all be together,' said Priscilla as the housekeeper moved to pour more tea. The wireless crackled, and the company grew silent. Priscilla shook her head – no, no more tea – and motioned for the housekeeper to take a seat, but she remained standing, a hand on the table as if to keep herself steady.

Douglas reached towards the set to adjust the volume.

'Here we go,' he said.

Maisie noticed Douglas glance at his watch – he wore it on his right wrist, given the loss of his left arm during the Great War – and was aware that she and Priscilla had cast their eyes towards the clock on the mantelpiece at exactly the same moment, and Timothy had leant across, lifted his older brother's wrist and looked at the dial on his watch, touching it as if to embed the moment in his memory. It was eleven-fourteen on the morning of 3rd September 1939.

The wireless crackled again: static signalling the coming storms. At quarter past eleven, the voice they had gathered to hear – the clipped tones of Neville Chamberlain, the Prime Minister – shattered their now-silent waiting.

This morning the British Ambassador in Berlin handed the German Government a final note stating that, unless we heard from them by 11 o'clock that they were prepared at once to withdraw their troops from Poland, a state of war would exist between us.

I have to tell you now that no such undertaking has been received, and that consequently this country is at war with Germany.

As the speech continued, all present stared at the wireless as though it held the image of a person. Maisie felt numb. It was as if the cold, slick air of France had remained with her since the war – when, she wondered, would they begin referring to it as 'the last war'? – and now the terrible, biting chill was seeping out from its place of seclusion deep in her bones. She glanced at Priscilla, and saw her friend staring at her sons, each one in turn as if she feared she might forget their faces. And she knew the deep ache of loss was allowing Priscilla no quarter – the dragon of memory that war had left in its wake; a slumbering giant stretching into the present, starting anew to breathe fire again. Priscilla's three brothers had perished between the years 1914 and 1918.

Now may God bless you all. May He defend the right. It is the evil things that we shall be fighting against – brute force, bad faith, injustice, oppression and persecution – and against them I am certain that the right will prevail.

Douglas, who had remained standing throughout the speech, leant forward to switch off the wireless.

Priscilla touched the housekeeper on the shoulder and asked for a pot of coffee to be brought to the drawing room. The cook had already returned to the kitchen, reaching for her handkerchief and dabbing her eyes as she closed the door behind her. Elinor had followed with a muttered explanation that she 'had to see to' something; no one heard what it was that had to be seen to.

'Papa . . . what do you think of—'

'Father, Mother, I think I should—'

'Maman, shall we—'

The boys spoke at once, but fell silent when Douglas raised his hand. 'It's time we men went for an invigorating, excitement-reducing walk around the park just in case the day spoils and the rain really comes down. Come on.' And with that, all three of Priscilla's sons left the room, ushered away by their father, who held up his cane as if it were the wing of a hen chivvying along her chicks.

Silence seemed to bear down on the room as the door closed.

Priscilla's eyes were wide, red-rimmed. 'I'm not going to lose my sons, Maisie. If I have to chop off their fingers to render them physically unacceptable to the fighting force, I will do so.'

'No, you won't, Pris.' Maisie came to her feet and put an arm around her friend, who was seated next to the wireless. She felt Priscilla lean in to her waist as she stood beside her. 'You wouldn't harm a single hair on their heads.'

'We came through it, didn't we, Maisie?' said Priscilla. 'We might not have been unblemished on the other side, but we came through.'

'And we shall again,' said Maisie. 'We're made of strong fabric, all of us.'

Priscilla nodded, pulling a handkerchief from her cuff and dabbing her eyes. 'We Everndens – and never let it be forgotten that in my bones I am an Evernden – are better than the Herr-bloody-Hitlers of this world. I'd chase him down myself to protect my boys.'

'You're one of the strongest, Priscilla – and remember, Douglas is worried sick too. You're a devoted family. Hold tight.'

'We're all going to have to hold tight, aren't we?'

Maisie was about to speak again when there was a gentle knock at the door, as if someone had rubbed a knuckle against the wood rather than rapping upon it.

'Yes?' invited Priscilla.

The housekeeper entered and announced that there was a telephone call for Maisie, though she referred to her by her title, which was somewhat grander than plain Miss Dobbs.

Maisie gave a half smile. 'Who on earth knows I'm here?' she asked, without expecting an answer.

'Well, your father would make a pretty good guess and come up with our house, if you weren't at home. I daresay they've been listening to the wireless too, and Brenda would have wanted him to call. You'll probably hear from Lady Rowan soon too.'

'Oh dear,' said Maisie as she stepped towards the door. 'I do hope Dad's all right.'

In the hall, she picked up the telephone receiver, which was resting on a marble-topped table decorated with a vase of blue hydrangeas.

'Hello. This is Maisie Dobbs. Who's speaking, please?'

'Maisie, Francesca Thomas here.'

Maisie put her hand across the mouthpiece and looked around. She was alone. 'Dr Thomas, what on earth is going on? How do you know this number? Or that I would be here?'

'Please return to your flat, if you don't mind. I have some urgent business to discuss with you.'

Maisie felt a second's imbalance, as if she had knelt down to retrieve something from the floor, and had come to her feet too quickly. What was the urgent business that this woman – someone in whose presence she had always felt unsettled – wanted to discuss on a Sunday, and in the wake of the Prime Minister's broadcast to the nation?

Francesca Thomas had spent almost her entire adult life working in the shadows. In the Great War she had become a member of La Dame Blanche, the Belgian resistance movement comprised almost entirely of girls and women who had taken up the work of their menfolk when they went to war. Maisie knew that with her British and Belgian background, Thomas was now working for the Secret Service.

'Dr Thomas, I am not interested. Working with the—' She looked around again and lowered her voice. 'Working with your department is not my bailiwick. I am not cut from that sort of cloth. I told Mr Huntley, quite clearly, no more of those assignments. I am a psychologist and an investigator – that is my domain.'

'Then you are just the person I need.'

'What do you mean?'

'Murder, Maisie. And I need you to prevent it happening again. And again.'

'Where are you?'

'In your flat. I took the liberty – I hope you don't mind.'

CHAPTER ONE

As Maisie hurried from Priscilla's house, fuming that Francesca Thomas had violated her privacy by breaking into her flat – a criminal act, no less – an angry, deep-throated mechanical baying seemed to fill the air around her. It began slowly, gaining momentum until it reached full cry. A woman in a neighbouring house rushed into the front garden to pull her children back indoors. A man and woman walking a dog broke into a run, gaining cover in the lee of a wall. There were few people out on this Sunday morning – indeed, many had remained indoors to listen to the wireless – but those on the street began to move as quickly as they could. Maisie watched as each person reached what they thought would be a place of safety – running towards the sandbagged underground station, to their homes, or even into a stranger's doorway. Shielding her eyes from the sun, she looked up into the sky. Nothing more threatening than intermittent clouds. No bombers, no Luftwaffe flying overhead. It was just a test. A test of the air-raid sirens situated across London. She looked at her watch. Twenty to twelve now. People began to emerge from their hiding places, having realised there were no metal-clad birds of prey ready to swoop down on life across the city. It was nothing more than practise – as if they needed practise for war.

Taking the path at the side of the property, Maisie approached her flat by the garden entrance. Dr Francesca Thomas was seated on a wicker chair set on the lawn. She was smoking a cigarette, flicking ash onto the grass at her feet. The French doors were open to the warmth of the day, and Thomas leant back as if to allow a beam of sunlight to bathe her face. Maisie studied her for a few seconds. Thomas was a tall woman, well dressed in a matching costume of skirt and jacket, the collar of a silk blouse just visible and the customary scarf tied around her neck, the ends poked into the V of the blouse, as a man might tie a cravat. The scarf was scarlet, and Maisie suspected that if it were opened up and laid flat, a pattern of roses would be revealed. Her thick hair, now threaded with grey, was cut above the shoulder and brushed away from her face. It was a strong face, thought Maisie, with defined black eyebrows, deep-set eyes, and pale skin. She wore a little rouge on her cheeks, and lipstick that matched the scarf.

Francesca Thomas did not look up as Maisie approached. Her eyes remained closed as she began to speak.

'Lovely garden you have here, Maisie. Quite the sun trap. Those hydrangeas are wonderful.'

Maisie sat down in the wicker chair next to her visitor. 'Dr Thomas – Francesca – you didn't come here to talk to me about the hydrangeas. So, shall we go inside and you can tell me what was so important that you had to break into my house and hunt me down.'

Thomas shielded her eyes with her hand. 'Yes, let's go in.'

Maisie came to her feet and extended her hand, indicating that

Thomas should enter the flat first. She paused briefly to look at the French doors. They appeared untouched, though no key had been used to open them.

'I won't ask how you broke in, Francesca – but I will get all my locks changed now.'

'Never mind – most people wouldn't have been able to break into the flat. I'm just a bit more experienced. Now then, let's get down to business.'

The doors to the garden remained open. Francesca Thomas made herself comfortable on the plump chintz-covered sofa set perpendicular to the fireplace, while Maisie took a seat on the armchair facing her.

'Maisie,' Thomas began, 'you will remember that during the last war many, many refugees from Belgium flooded into Britain.'

Maisie nodded. How could she forget? Over a quarter of a million people had entered the country, fleeing the approaching German army, the terror of bombing and occupation. Most had lost everything except the clothes they stood up in – homes, loved ones, neighbours, and their way of life – everything they owned left behind in the struggle.

'At one point, over sixteen thousand people were landing in the coastal ports every single day,' Thomas continued. 'From Hull to Harwich, and on down to Folkestone. It went on for months.'

'And yet after the war, they left so little behind,' said Maisie. 'When they left, they might never have been here in England – isn't that true?'

'Yes. They were taken in, and in some areas there were even new towns built to house them – they had their shops, their currency. And after the Armistice, Britain wanted the refugees out, and their own boys home.'

'And I am sure the Belgian people had a desire to return to their country too.'

'Of course they did. They wanted to start again, to rebuild their communities and their lives.'

'But some stayed,' said Maisie.

'Yes, some stayed.' Thomas nodded, staring into the garden.

Maisie noticed that Francesca Thomas had not said 'we' when referring to the Belgians, and she wondered how the woman felt now about the heritage she had claimed during the war. In truth she was as much British as she was Belgian. Maisie wondered if in serving the latter she had mined a strength she had not known before, just as Maisie had herself discovered more about her own character in wartime. She rubbed a hand across her forehead, a gesture that made Thomas look up, and resume speaking.

'There are estimates that up to seven or eight thousand remained after the war – they had integrated into life here, had married locally, taken on jobs, changed their names if it suited them. They didn't stand out, so there was an . . . an integration, I suppose you could say.' Thomas gave a wry smile.

'But life is not easy for any refugee,' said Maisie.

'Indeed. They went from being welcomed as the representatives of "poor little Belgium" to their hosts wondering when they would be leaving – and often quite vocal about it. And although there were those villages set up, they were not places of comfort or acceptance in the longer term. But as I said – most refugees went home following the war.'

'Tell me what all this has to do with me, and how you believe I can help you.'

Thomas nodded. 'Forgive me, Maisie – I am very tired. There has been much to do in my world, as I am sure you might understand. I begin to speak about the war, and a wash of fatigue seems to drain me.'

Maisie leant forward. Such candor was not something she had experienced in her dealings with Thomas. She remembered training with her last year, before her assignment in Munich. Thomas had drilled her until she thought she might scream 'No more!' – but the woman had done what she set out to do, which was to make sure Maisie had the tools to ensure her own safety, and that of the man she had been tasked with bringing out of Munich under the noses of the Nazis. Now it was as if this new war was already winning the battle of bringing Thomas down.

'I want you to do a job of work for me, Maisie. This is what has happened. About a month ago, the fourth of August, a man named Frederick Addens was found dead close to St Pancras Station. He had been shot – point-blank – through the back of the head. The position in which he was found, together with the post-mortem, suggested that he was made to kneel down, hands behind his head, and then he was executed.'

'So he could well have seen his killer,' said Maisie. 'It has all the hallmarks of a professional assassination.'

'I suspect that is the case.'

'Tell me about Addens,' said Maisie.

'Thirty-eight years of age. He worked for the railway as an engineer at the station. He was married to an English woman, and they have two children, both adults now and working. The daughter is a junior librarian – she's eighteen years of age, and the son – who's almost twenty – has now, I am informed, joined the army.'

Maisie nodded. 'What does Scotland Yard say?'

'Nothing. War might have been declared today, but it broke out a long time ago, as you know. Scotland Yard has its hands full – a country on the move provides a lot of work for the police.'

'But they are investigating, of course.'

'Yes, Maisie, they are investigating. But the detective in charge says that it is not a priority at the moment – it's what they call an open-and-shut case because they maintain it was a theft and there were no witnesses, therefore not much to go on – apparently there was no money on Addens when his body was discovered, and no wallet was found among his belongings at the station. And according to Scotland Yard, there are not enough men on the ground to delve into the investigation.'

'What's his name?' asked Maisie.

'Caldwell. Do you know him?'

'Yes. I know him – though we've not crossed paths in a few years.' Maisie paused. 'What about Huntley's department, or the Foreign Office? Surely they must be interested in the outcome of this one.'

'Chinese walls and too much to do – you know how it is, Maisie.' Francesca Thomas came to her feet and stood by the door, her gaze directed towards the garden. 'I want you to investigate for me. I trust you. I trust you to keep a calm head, to be diligent in your work, and to come up with some answers.'

'I don't do this kind of work for nothing, Dr Thomas.' Maisie stepped towards the bureau in the corner, took a sheet of paper and pen, and wrote down a series of numbers. She handed it to Thomas. 'These are my fees, plus I will give you a chit to account for costs incurred along the way.'

Thomas looked at the paper, folded it, and put it in her pocket. 'I will issue you with an advance via messenger tomorrow, and I will also send you addresses, employment details, and any other information I have to hand on Addens. I take it you will start immediately.'

'Of course.' Maisie allowed a few seconds to pass. 'Dr Thomas – Francesca—' She spoke the woman's name in a quiet voice, so that when Thomas turned it was to look straight into Maisie's eyes. 'Francesca, are you telling me everything?'

'A Belgian refugee – one of my countrymen – who made England his home and lived in peace here, is dead. The manner of his death begs many questions, and I want to know who killed him. That is the nub of the matter.'

Maisie nodded. 'I will expect your messenger tomorrow – at my office in Fitzroy Square.'

Francesca Thomas picked up the clutch bag she had set upon the sofa. 'Thank you, Maisie. I knew I could depend upon you.' She left by the French doors; seconds later Maisie heard the gate at the side of the house clang shut.

She stepped into the walled garden. Beyond the brick terrace and lawn, she'd planted a perennial border to provide colour from spring to autumn. The hydrangeas admired by Thomas had grown tall and covered the walls, their colour reflected in an abundance of Michaelmas daisies. She strolled the perimeter of the garden, deadheading the last of the season's roses as she went. This was ground she knew well – investigating a death in suspicious circumstances was home turf. But two elements to her brief bothered her. The first was the matter of a designed execution. Such acts were often planned when the perpetrator considered the victim to have committed an unpunished crime – and if not a crime, then an error for which forgiveness could not be bestowed. Or perhaps the man with the bullet in his skull had seen something he was not meant to see. And in those cases, the person who carried out the assassination might not be the person harbouring a grudge.

The second element that gave Maisie pause was that she believed Thomas might not have been as forthcoming as she could have been. In fact, she might have lied when she had told Maisie there was nothing more to tell. *I want to know who killed him, that is the nub of the matter.* The words seemed to echo in Maisie's mind. Indeed, she had a distinct feeling that there was much more to the nub of the matter – after all, during the telephone call which Maisie had taken at Priscilla's house, Thomas had suggested that murder might happen again. *And again.*

'Well, the balloon has well and truly gone up now, hasn't it?' Billy Beale lifted the strap attached to a box containing his gas mask over his head and placed it on the table. 'Morning, miss. Sorry I'm a bit late—' He looked at the clock on the mantelpiece. 'More than a bit, this morning. The trains were all over the place. Army on the move, that's what it is – seen it all before, more's the pity.'

Maisie had been standing by the floor-to-ceiling window, holding a cup of hot tea in her hand, when her assistant entered. She walked across to his desk. 'Not to worry – I've not been here long myself, only enough time to make a cup of tea. Sandra's late too.'

At that moment the door opened and Sandra Pickering came into the office, placing her handbag, a narrow document case, and her gas mask on her desk.

'I'm so sorry – you would never believe—'

'We've been in ages, Sandra – what kept you?' asked Billy, a glint in his eye.

'Take no notice of him,' said Maisie. 'We've all had the same trouble this morning. There's the army mobilisation, and there are still a good number of children being evacuated.'

Sandra shook her head. 'I've had enough of this already – I forget my gas mask half the time, and when you walk down the road there's those big barrage balloons overhead, and you feel as if it's the end of the world. Oh, and since the announcement yesterday, they're adding to the sandbags around the Tube stations too. And they've been sandbagged for months now, all ready for this.'

'Those balloons certainly block out the sun,' said Maisie. She looked at Sandra and Billy in turn. 'Get yourselves some tea' – she nodded towards a tray set upon a low table close to the windows overlooking Fitzroy Square – 'and then join me in my office. I want to go over work in hand, and we've a new case. An important one too.'

'A murder, by any chance?' asked Billy.

Maisie nodded as she stepped across the threshold into her office. 'Oh, yes, Billy – it's a murder.'

'Good – something to take my mind off all this war business.'

When Maisie Dobbs, psychologist and investigator, moved into the first-floor office in Fitzroy Square almost ten years earlier, it had comprised one large room, entered via a door situated to the right at the top of the broad staircase that swept up from the main entrance. The Georgian mansion had originally been home to a family of some wealth, but the conversion of the property to offices on the ground and first floors, with flats above, had taken place some decades earlier, as industry boomed during the reign of Queen Victoria. Billy's desk had been situated to the right upon entering the office, with Maisie's alongside the ornate fireplace – though a temperamental gas fire had long since replaced coals. When Sandra began her employment with

Maisie to assist with administration of the business, another desk had been squeezed in close to the door.

A series of events and a crisis of confidence had led Maisie to relinquish her business in 1933. Billy and Sandra had found alternative employment, and Maisie travelled overseas. When she returned to England in late 1937, it was as a widow, a woman who had lost the child she was carrying on the very day her husband was killed in a flying accident in Canada. That he was testing a new fighter aircraft was known by only a few – as far as the press was concerned, Viscount James Compton was an aviator, a wealthy but boyish man indulging his love of flight, looking down at the earth.

Drawn back to her work as an investigator, Maisie discovered the former office in Fitzroy Square was once more available for lease – but it was not quite the same office. In the intervening years a considerable amount of renovation had been carried out on the instructions of the interim tenant. There were now two rooms – a concertina door dividing the front room from an adjacent room had been installed, so when a visitor entered, Billy's desk was still to the right of the door, and Sandra's situated where Maisie's desk had once been positioned. But to the left, a second spacious room – the office of a solicitor during her first tenancy – was now Maisie's domain, with the doors drawn back unless privacy was required. Today the doors were wide open. Maisie's desk was placed to the left of the room, with a long trestle-type table alongside the back window, overlooking a yard where someone – a ground-floor tenant, perhaps – had cleared away a mound of rubbish and was endeavouring to grow all manner of plants in a variety of terracotta pots.

As they stepped into Maisie's office, Billy took a roll of plain wallpaper from a basket in the corner – a house painter friend of

Billy's passed on end-of-roll remnants – and pinned a length of about four feet onto the table. Maisie pulled a jar of coloured crayons towards her and placed a folder on the table in front of her chair, opening it to a page of notes.

'"Frederick Addens, age thirty-eight, a refugee from Belgium during the war."' She sighed. 'The last war, I suppose I should say.' She paused. 'He was found dead in a position indicating some sort of ritual assassination – though according to information given to our client by the police, they suspect the murder is a random killing motivated by theft.' She pushed a sheet of paper towards Billy, who leant in so that Sandra could read at the same time. 'As you can see, he was a railway engineer, working at St Pancras Station.'

'One of them blokes you see diving onto the lines when the train comes in,' said Billy, his finger on a line of typing. 'Blimey, I've always thought that was a rotten job, down there where the rats run, all that oil, and that loco must be blimmin' hot when it's just reached the buffers. I tell you, I always wondered what would happen if the train started rolling and they hadn't given the engineer time to get back onto the platform.' He shook his head.

'I think the guard checks, Billy,' said Sandra.

'What about our friends at Scotland Yard, miss?' asked Billy. 'What have they been doing about the case?'

'They've pretty full hands at the moment – and though our client does not say as much, I suspect she believes there is an attitude of "victim not born here, so investigation can wait" on the part of the police. That might not have been my conclusion, but the fact remains that any investigation is not moving at a pace considered satisfactory by the client, so she has turned to me.'

'She?' asked Sandra.

Maisie slid another sheet of paper towards Billy and Sandra. 'I've worked with Dr Francesca Thomas in the past – she is a formidable woman, and trustworthy in every regard.'

'Where do we start?'

'The first element of the investigation to underline is that we must move with utmost respect for the safety of Dr Thomas. It is not something she has had to request of me – she assumes our confidence, which of course we accord all our clients. But I would like us to be even more vigilant than usual. Dr Thomas was a member of La Dame Blanche during the war, and—'

'La what?' Billy interrupted.

'La Dame Blanche was a Belgian resistance movement supported by the British government, comprised almost entirely of women – from schoolgirls to grandmothers. But with regard to Dr Thomas, I should add that she is more than capable of taking care of herself. We can assume she's not currently sitting on her hands waiting for something to happen.'

'Best not to get on the wrong side of her, then,' said Billy.

'Not if you value your throat, I would say.' Maisie reached into the jar of crayons. 'Anyway, as I said, I just wanted to mention that we need to be even more careful than ever. Right, let's get started on the case map, shall we? I'm expecting a packet of additional documents from Dr Thomas this morning – it should arrive at any moment, I would imagine. That will help.'

Maisie wrote the name of the deceased on the paper, using a thick red crayon, and drew a circle around the words 'Frederick Addens'. There was something childlike in the process, as if they were in primary school, beginning an innocent drawing. She smiled.

'What is it?' asked Billy.

Maisie looked up. 'I was just thinking of Maurice,' she said. 'He always comes to mind when I start work on a new case. Not just because he was my teacher, but almost everything he said contained a lesson.'

'He taught you about case maps, didn't he?' said Sandra.

'Yes, when I first became his assistant. And it's such a simple thing, really. Putting down every thought, every consideration, on a large sheet of paper to better see threads of connection. But he always used thick wax crayons in many colours – he said colour stirs the mind, that work on even the most difficult of cases becomes akin to playing. And because a case map is an act of creation, we bring the full breadth of our curiosity to the task.'

'Instead of being old and stuck in our ways.'

'Something like that, Billy.'

'We'll have to get used to seeing nothing but stuffy old grown-ups, won't we?' Sandra reached for a green crayon. 'I walked down the street this morning to catch the bus, and it was so quiet – no children playing as I passed the school, no girls out with the long skipping rope, no boys kicking a ball about. It was as if the Pied Piper had been through and taken the lot of them – and the army were moving into the school! But no children in the streets.' She looked at Billy. 'What's happening with yours, Billy?'

Billy shrugged. 'It's not so much Margaret I'm worried about, but the boys. Our little Billy's not so little any more – eighteen soon, he is. And Bobby, he's sixteen, doing well in his apprenticeship at the garage, and full of himself – I sometimes wish we'd never named him after my brother; he's all hot-headed and knows everything. And look where that got his uncle.' He turned to face Sandra. 'My brother lied about his age to enlist after a girl shoved a white feather in his hand,

and he ended up under a few feet of soil in a French field. That's where it got him – and to think he could have just walked away and ignored the stupid girl.'

The bell above the door to the office began to ring, cutting into the mood of melancholy seeping into the conversation.

'Not a moment too soon. Sandra, that will be the messenger we're waiting for. Would you—'

'Right away, miss.'

Sandra stepped out of the office. As her footsteps echoed away to the front door, Maisie reached out to lay her hand on Billy's arm. 'You're the father to two young men now, Billy. Love them as you've always loved them, be the good father you've always been.'

'It's Doreen I worry about more than anything – she's all right now, been on an even keel for a few years. But if something happens to one of those boys . . . I dread to think of it, really I do, miss. I don't want her to lose her mind again – terrible thought, that is.'

Maisie nodded, looking up as Sandra returned to the room, and handed her an envelope. 'Here you are, miss. It was all I could do to get him to give this envelope to me – I thought he would just barge up here, but I assured him I worked for you and I wasn't a spy! I had to sign an official docket for him, to say I'd received the papers. He was very polite though, and nicely turned out – mind you, working for an embassy, you'd expect him to be. And his English was perfect.'

'I'm sure Dr Thomas has very high standards for her staff.' Maisie picked up a letter opener, unsealed the envelope, and began to lift out a sheaf of papers. 'Sandra, would you have a go at getting the names of some of the associations set up to look after Belgian refugees during the war? Just in London, Kent, and Sussex for now. We're going to need names, and more background information. And Billy –

30

you've been an engineer, so I think you should talk to the staff at St Pancras in the first instance. Find out about Addens, his work, how he mixed with his fellow workers, that sort of thing. Try to find out if he seemed a little more flush with money than usual. And did he seem in any way different in the weeks before he died? Usual procedure at this point. I'll go over to speak to his wife, perhaps the local pub landlord, and anyone else – without seeming too curious, I hope. I want us to understand the geography of the man's life, and then we can start digging deeper. Oh, and I'll be paying a visit to Detective Chief Inspector Caldwell, if I can see him today.'

'Detective *Chief* Inspector? That little gnat's a *chief* inspector?' Billy's eyes had widened.

'Now then, Billy. Let's be respectful, shall we?' Maisie paused. 'Though I know what you mean – it came as a bit of a shock to me, the "chief" bit. And before we all leave, let's just go over those cases in hand – we'll need to keep all the hoops spinning.'

They discussed the case of missing jewellery – not the sort of assignment Maisie would usually take on, but the client had been referred by Lady Rowan. Billy reported on a case regarding a wife who doubted the fidelity of her husband, and the trio conferred on another case concerning the whereabouts of a wealthy widow who appeared to have vanished, but who Maisie – having located the woman – knew very well just wanted to get away from her manipulative adult sons.

As Billy left and Sandra began a series of telephone calls, Maisie stood by the windows in the main office and watched her assistant make his way across the square. She could see from the way he carried himself that he was glad to be starting out on a bigger case. The dodgy wills and missing valuables were only engaging to a point; Billy always liked to sink his teeth into a more substantial assignment, one they were all working on together. But she knew he was troubled too, with one boy of enlistment age, another approaching it, and a wife with a history of mental illness. She would have to keep an eye on him. And on Sandra too. For if she was not mistaken, her newly married office administrator was expecting a child – and given her comments this morning, Sandra was fearful of what the future might hold for her firstborn.

For her part, Maisie knew that each day had to be taken as it came, and to do her work she must be flexible, to move the fabric of time as one might if sewing a difficult seam, perhaps stretching the linen to accommodate a stitch. She had learnt, long ago and in the intervening years when she was apart from all she loved, that to endure the most troubling times she had to break down time itself – one carefully crafted stitch after the other. If consideration of what the next hour might hold had been too difficult, then she thought only of another half an hour. She had explained this to Priscilla, once, and her friend had asked, 'What's the longest time you could bear, Maisie?' And she had whispered, 'Two minutes.' But at some point the two minutes became five, and the five became ten, and as time marched on she was able to imagine a day ahead and then a week, until one day, almost without realising it, she could plan her life, could look forward to time laying out the tablecloth as if to say 'Come, take what you will, be nourished and know that you can bear what might be on your horizon, the good and the ill.'

Now, on this day, some twenty-four hours after a new war had been declared, she wondered if she might have to begin reining in the future once again, with her thoughts only on the next hour, and the hour after that. She stepped back to the table and leafed through the folder of papers. As she read through the notes, the nagging feeling returned that Dr Francesca Thomas had not been entirely open with her regarding some aspect of the assignment. Or was it that, despite her regard for Thomas – the nature of her past, her bravery, and her ease with secrecy, subterfuge and danger – Maisie had never quite trusted her, despite her own assurances to Sandra and Billy?

Picking up her hat and document case, Maisie left the office – only to return to collect the gas mask she had left behind.

CHAPTER TWO

Twenty-five Larkin Street, in Fulham, was just beyond the World's End area of Chelsea. Maisie travelled by underground railway to Walham Green Station, and walked to Larkin Street. Having been born in Lambeth and engaged in work that took her from the poorest streets to the most exclusive crescents in London, Maisie had no fear of a slum. Though now a woman of some wealth, for the most part she dressed in an unassuming manner. Her clothes were good but plain, and it was not her way to flaunt her status in any perceptible fashion. Thus she walked with ease through an area so called because King James II – who rode regularly along the King's Road in his day – had described the region as being at the end of the world.

For Frederick Addens it had been a world that had saved his life, following his escape from the German army occupying Belgium. According to the notes furnished by Thomas, Addens had entered Britain aboard a fishing boat that came aground just outside

Dymchurch. Some twenty people had made the crossing in storms plaguing the English Channel – it was not a long journey by any means, but for refugees fleeing an enemy, it might as well have been a million miles. Addens was almost sixteen when he at last reached safety, the same age as the century. He was married two years later, to an English girl, Enid Parsons, a young woman three years older than her new husband. Her first sweetheart, the boy she had loved since childhood and thought herself destined to marry, had perished in August 1916, in one of the many battles fought along the Somme Valley in France from July to November that year.

Maisie slowed her pace. How had it been for the young couple, both grieving for what had been lost, yet embarking on a new life together? She understood loss, understood how it could leach into every fibre of one's being; how it could dull the shine on a sunny day, and how it could replace happiness with doubt, giving rise to a lingering fear that good fortune might be snatched back at any time. Yet they had raised a son and a daughter, and now Enid Addens – a woman just a little older than herself – was enduring the brutal death of her husband, and perhaps the departure of her son to another battlefield. Maisie wondered how she would ever be able to speak to the woman, to question her about her husband's murder. The truth of the matter, that she might stir the woman's heart with her enquiries, almost made her turn back to the office. And then she remembered the trust placed in her by Francesca Thomas, and she knew she had it within her to gain the widow's confidence. Detective Chief Inspector Caldwell's less compassionate approach, on the other hand, might have cost him valuable time and information.

Arriving at the rented terrace house, Maisie appraised the property where Frederick Addens had lived with his family. It was clear they had endeavoured to keep a clean home in a grubby area. Unlike those on either side, number 25 had received a fresh coat of paint in recent years, probably work carried out by Addens and his son. What was his name? Ah, yes, Arthur, named for Enid's brother, who had died on the very same day, in the same battle, as her sweetheart. The girl was named Dorothy, and called 'Dottie' by the family. She bore her grandmother's name. Maisie wondered why there was no hint of Addens' relatives in the naming of their children.

The path had been swept and the tiled doorstep looked as if it received a generous lick of Cardinal red tile polish every week. Someone had tried to grow flowers in the postage stamp of a front garden, but the blooms were patchy. Maisie approached the front door and lifted the knocker, rapping three times. The drawn curtains at the side of the bay window were tweaked back, indicating someone was at home. She rapped twice more. Footsteps approached, and after a lock was turned and a chain withdrawn, the door opened, but only enough to allow a young woman with fair hair and bloodshot eyes an opportunity to size up the caller.

Maisie smiled, her manner exuding kindness. 'Hello, you must be Miss Addens. My name is Maisie Dobbs. One of your late father's compatriots has asked me to visit you and your mother.'

'I don't understand,' said Dorothy Addens.

'I'm calling on behalf of someone who knew your father in Belgium. I am an investigator, and I believe Scotland Yard might have missed a few details regarding the circumstances of your father's death.'

The young woman waited a few seconds, as if considering the request put to her by the unexpected caller. 'Just a minute,' she said. 'And I have to shut the door on you. Sorry.'

'That's all ri—' Before Maisie could finish the sentence, the door closed. She heard footsteps receding on the other side, and Dorothy Addens calling, 'Mum. Mum, there's a woman to see you, from Belgium.'

Two minutes later, Addens returned, opening the door as Maisie was looking up at the barrage balloons overhead. 'They're an eyesore, aren't they?'

'Horrible. But I suppose they make us all a bit safer,' said Maisie.

'They didn't keep my dad safe, did they?' Addens' tone was sharp, then softened. 'Sorry, Miss Dobbs – it was Miss Dobbs, wasn't it? We're all very upset around here. My mother's had a terrible time of it, what with my brother joining the army to top off everything else. Come in. She said she'll see you. But please don't stay long – she's very tired.'

'Of course.'

Maisie followed Dorothy Addens along a passageway into the kitchen at the back of the house. From the doors to the right, leading to a parlour and dining room, to the kitchen overlooking a narrow garden planted with vegetables, the house was like so many she had visited, and like thousands in towns across the country. They had been built to meet the demand for housing during the exodus of workers from the country in the middle of the last century: people beckoned by a promise of opportunity as the boom in industry powered by steam, steel, and petrol seemed poised to render agriculture yesterday's business. Each house in Larkin Street comprised three floors, and Maisie suspected the top-floor rooms might be rented to lodgers.

'Mum, this is Miss Dobbs.' Dorothy Addens pulled out a seat for Maisie and took the chair next to her mother, who sat with her elbows

37

on the oilcloth cover spread across the table, twisting a handkerchief over and over in her hands.

With a grey, lined face and hair scraped back into a bun at the base of her neck, Enid Addens could well have passed for a grandmother. Maisie remembered seeing her own reflection in a mirror after James was killed, and she wondered now if she had appeared so worn, so beaten by circumstance.

Frederick Addens' widow looked up at Maisie. 'You know my husband?'

Maisie noticed how Enid had used the present tense. The knowledge that her husband was dead had not yet seeped into the deepest part of her heart. Speaking of him as no longer being in her world likely felt akin to a knife thrust into her chest. Maisie coughed, laying a hand against the fabric of her jacket, close to her own heart – the cough had deflected attention from the pain she felt when she observed the woman's distress. She did not want to slip.

'I know someone who has asked me to look into the circumstances of your husband's passing, Mrs Addens.' Maisie opened her bag, took out a calling card, and placed it in front of the woman. 'I am by training an investigator. I assist my clients in situations where questions remain regarding something untoward that has happened. My client is from Belgium, and wants to ensure the person responsible for your husband's death is found, and so came to me.'

'Someone killed my father, Miss Dobbs – if the police can't find out who did it, then how can you? Eh? I don't want you coming here to upset my mother, even if you have the best of intentions.'

Enid Addens laid a hand on her daughter's shoulder. 'Now then, Dottie. You're the one getting upset. I'd like to hear what the lady has to say. Be a good girl and put the kettle on – make us all a nice cup of tea.'

Dorothy Addens scraped back her chair and stepped across to the stove.

'And open that back door, love,' added her mother. 'What with this weather and that stove, it's like a bakehouse in here.'

'It is close, isn't it, Mrs Addens? Would you mind if I took off my hat and jacket?' asked Maisie.

'Not at all, please – we don't stand on ceremony in this house.' Enid looked up at Maisie, her eyes filling with tears. 'I don't know what will become of us, without Fred.'

Maisie took a breath. Yes, she would entrust the woman with something of herself. She would touch her hand, tell her a little about her past, encourage the sharing of a confidence.

'I know what it is to lose your husband, Mrs Addens. My husband was killed a few years ago. It takes time to recover yourself – and I still grieve for him.'

Enid's stare seemed to dare Maisie to look away, as if she were measuring the depth of Maisie's sadness to see if it matched her own. In time she spoke again. 'So, you're an investigator and you want to find out who killed my husband. I will answer your questions as best I can. Dottie, bring the tea and you sit down too – your memory's better than mine.' She looked up at her daughter as Dottie placed cups of tea in front of her mother and Maisie. Enid turned to Maisie. 'She'll be back to work tomorrow – she's already taken too much time off on account of me. We need the money, though the railway had a whip-round for us, so we won't be short for a while, and my son will be sending money home.'

Maisie reached into her bag and brought out a notebook. 'Mrs Addens, can you tell me about your husband's last morning? It was at the end of the first week of August, wasn't it?'

'Yes, it was a Friday the fourth of August. I remember it, everything about that day now. It's as if the news made everything sort of big – do you know what I mean?' She looked at Maisie, as if to see if she shared the experience.

Maisie nodded. 'I know very well what you mean, Mrs Addens – I could describe even the smallest detail about the day my husband died. It's branded into my memory.'

'I'd been working in the shop – I've a job at a haberdashery shop up on Fulham High Street, part-time. I hadn't long been home, and was sitting down having five minutes to myself with a cup of tea to listen to the news on the wireless, and the police came to the door. I remember, I was thinking about that General Franco – they were saying how he had just declared that he would only answer to God and to history, and he'd set himself up as the ruler of Spain. And after all they've gone through, I thought to myself, now they've got a dictator in charge. Makes you wonder what's going to happen to us.' She looked away, fixing her gaze on the garden.

'My father was interested in what goes on in the rest of the world, Miss Dobbs.' Dorothy Addens lifted a cup to her lips. 'So we all have opinions in this house.'

Maisie smiled, understanding that the younger woman felt the need to underline her credentials. She wanted Maisie to know that, despite the area in which she was born, she, Dorothy Addens, was an intelligent woman, the daughter of a man who understood the importance of educating oneself.

Maisie turned back to Enid. 'What happened then – what did the police say?'

'There was a man from the railway police with them, and someone from the railways board. It was a right little crowd on my doorstep. I thought straightaway that my husband had been killed by a train – one of Frederick's mates was killed by a loco a few years ago, and another scalded to death by steam. I wondered what had happened. And I couldn't move. I was stuck to the threshold, but the railway policeman took me by the arm and led me into the parlour, and he sat me down and said that Frederick had been murdered. All these men were sitting in my parlour looking even bigger, uncomfortable perching on the edges of the chairs, while this Detective Chief Inspector told me what had happened. Frederick had been killed outside the station, down an alley not far away. They don't know what he was doing there, because he didn't knock off work until six on a Friday, as a rule – unless he had overtime – and it happened at four, or so they think. They told me he had been shot.'

'And who identified the body?'

'One of his mates, a fellow he worked with. Mike Elliot. I couldn't go to see my husband, on account of what they said were the circumstances, but Dottie – she came home while they were here – she said they were covering it up. And she said it to their faces, told them that the reason we couldn't see her dad was that it was so bad and they didn't want to tell us the truth. She can be a terror, can Dottie – if she's put out, she can get very uppity, and she was uppity with the police. Takes it all in here, you see.' Enid Addens tapped her chest with her hand as she looked at her daughter.

'Mum! I'm all right. Just tell Miss Dobbs what she needs to know – you don't need to ramble about me.'

Enid gave a half smile. 'She wouldn't have cried in front of them, so her temper started up. That's how it is with some people. Friend of mine had a dog who was a right growler, showed his teeth to anyone

41

who came up to him, but it was as if his wires had been crossed when he was a pup – that growl was a purr, and all he wanted was a pet. Well, she growled at the police until I sent her off to make a pot of tea. I tell you, Miss Dobbs, I could hear that girl crying her eyes out in the kitchen, and I knew that all she wanted was someone to comfort her – and I couldn't do it because it was as if I was paralysed in my chair. The railway policeman – he was a big fellow, looked like a family man – he went out and I heard him say, "That's it, love, get it out of your system, you have a good cry."'

'He came where he wasn't wanted. If you remember, Mum, I sent him off packing back to the parlour.' Dottie reached into the pocket of her summer dress and pulled out a packet of cigarettes.

'Go outside if you want to do that, Dottie. I have enough trouble with the flue on that stove, without you smoking up the kitchen.'

Dottie Addens pushed back her chair and flounced out to the back garden, where Maisie could see her light her cigarette and inhale deeply. She held her head back and blew out a series of smoke rings.

'I'm sorry about that. She's normally such a good girl – has some spirit, but she idolised her father. He always said she reminded him of himself, when he was younger – well, it must have been much younger, because he was married to me at eighteen.' Enid Addens rubbed her upper arms, tears welling in her eyes again. 'He was so young, really, but a man already. He knew what he wanted, and he wanted a wife and a family, and to be settled – that's what he wanted, and he chose me, so I was a very lucky woman. I thought I'd lost my chance, and then Frederick came along.'

Maisie brought her attention back to Enid. 'Mrs Addens. I'm used to meeting people in these difficult situations – I would be just like

42

Dorothy if I'd lost my father.' She paused for a second. 'Can you tell me what else the detective said?'

'He asked lots of questions – he was like a gun, firing off one shot after the other. He wanted to know if Frederick had friends, who his friends were. He wanted to know about the darts team at the pub – really, that was the only thing Frederick did outside the family; darts practice on a Friday night at eight, and then a match of a Sunday. He'd be back in time for a quick bite to eat and we'd work in the garden – we did that together; we loved the garden, small though it is. We never had our dinner until later in the evening on a Sunday. It was one thing that Frederick was firm about. He said he wanted his Sunday dinner like they did it when he was a boy – in the evening, not in the middle of the day, when afterwards all you do is sleep. No, he liked to have something to show for his day, Frederick. And seeing as he'd left his own country behind to come here, it was the least I could do for him – put a Sunday dinner on the table at the time he liked it, though it wasn't how I was brought up.'

'Did your husband ever talk about anyone who had upset him in any way – perhaps a fellow engineer, or someone on the darts team? Or someone who he'd disagreed with, something like that?'

The woman shook her head. 'No. I mean, there might have been a niggle here and there – we all have them – but nothing serious, nothing lingering.'

'How about friends from Belgium? He came over with others, didn't he?'

'No, no one that I can remember. I even asked him about it, and he said his wife and family were his best friends, and that his first family – that's what he called them, his first family – were all gone

43

anyway.' Enid Addens was quiet, kneading her handkerchief. 'I know that when he came away from Belgium, he had seen some terrible things. Houses being shelled, people running from their homes, and the Germans coming in. It was as if he wanted to just push everything to the past, where it belonged. He came here to start anew, he said – and what was gone, was gone. You couldn't bring it back, and he said that he didn't want to.'

Maisie allowed some seconds to pass before pressing with her next question. 'Do you know why your husband was not with the Belgian army, during the war? I know he was young, but he could have passed for older, I would have thought.'

'He said he tried to join, but there was his age, and the doctor said he had a heart murmur into the bargain, though he never had any heart trouble that I was aware of. He never had cause to go to the doctor here about it.'

Maisie could see Enid's eyes becoming glazed, as if she were unable to focus. And soon the tears returned. 'It's hard, isn't it, speaking about them as if they're gone, and then not gone? You just can't get the words right; they're here and then they're not here. And you realise, you've just had a day, then a week, and then a few weeks that they are never going to see again, and you can't talk to them about those weeks because they aren't here any more.'

A shadow fell across the floor where a shaft of sunlight had been gleaming.

'I think that's enough, Miss Dobbs. My mother's very tired.' Dottie came back into the kitchen and put an arm around Enid's shoulders. 'You should go upstairs, Mum, try to get some shut-eye for a bit. I'll make something nice for dinner.'

Maisie stood up, put on her straw hat and placed her jacket over

44

her arm. 'You're quite right, Miss Addens. Your mother is very tired and should rest.'

'I'll see you out,' said Dottie.

Maisie caught the young woman's eye. 'Thank you.'

When they reached the doorstep, Maisie turned to Dottie. 'Do you have any idea who might have borne a grudge of some kind against your father? Someone who he could have slighted, even inadvertently?'

She shook her head. 'My father was a gentleman and a gentle man, Miss Dobbs. I have gone over this in my mind, because I would love to lay my hands on the throat of whoever killed my father.'

'Did you notice anything different in your father's behaviour in the weeks or days before his life was taken? Anything at all?'

Dottie Addens shook her head, a smile grazing the edges of her lips. '"Before his life was taken." That's rich – as if someone just came by and calmly took the life out of him, leaving only a shell. No pain, no terror, nothing unsanitary, just ran off with his soul. No, Miss Dobbs – before my father's brains were shot out of his head across the pavement, I hadn't noticed a thing. He was as kind as always, as considerate and funny as always, and as tired as always.'

Maisie was quick to respond. 'Any more tired, perhaps, than usual?'

Dottie Addens shrugged, the vertical lines between her eyes gathering. 'He might have been. But then, he did a tiring job, and it's been hot. He always said his job was harder in summer than in winter, and it's been a sultry few weeks.'

'Granted.' Maisie paused. 'You know, Dottie, if you want to channel that anger – and believe me, I know the destructive power of anger – then let your eyes and ears work for me. If you think back on anything – anything – different about your father's actions, mood, or behaviour, then come to me. Nothing is so small as to be insignificant.'

'I've got to help my mother now.'

Dottie Addens held Maisie's gaze for a second, then closed the door, leaving Maisie on the doorstep.

Maisie stepped away from the house, but before setting off in the direction of the underground station, she looked back and considered the many houses that seemed so ordinary on the outside – yet inside their shells lingered untold human sadness. 'May they know peace,' she whispered, and went on her way.

The Crown and Anchor, not one hundred yards from Frederick Addens' house, looked less than inviting. Maisie knew, though, that she should take the opportunity to talk to the landlord. It was clearly what her father would have called a 'drinking pub' – tough around the edges, one where the women would be welcome in the saloon bar but not in the public bar; different entrances for different sorts. Even before she opened the door with the stained-glass window etched with the words 'Saloon Bar', she could smell the blended aroma of beer and smoke.

She stepped inside. There was no one in the bar, though she could hear conversation coming from the public bar; the two were divided by a narrow wall and double doors, which would be opened to allow a bigger celebration – the winning of a football match, or a wedding party.

'Help you, miss?' asked the landlord as he mopped along the shining wooden bar with a damp cloth.

'A shandy, please, sir.'

'Right you are, miss.'

As Maisie stood watching the landlord, beads of sweat across his balding head, his sleeves rolled up and an apron tied across his middle, she considered her conversation with Enid and Dorothy Addens. That Dorothy Addens was a protective and loving daughter was without question. That Dorothy idolised her father was evident. But there was something; a flicker of emotion Maisie had seen in her eyes, not only when she was questioning her mother, but when Dottie shut the door as Maisie left the house. It was barely visible, like a dust mote caught in a sunbeam, a feeling that the daughter had some knowledge about her father that she was keeping to herself.

'There you are, miss. That'll wet your whistle.'

Maisie reached into her bag for her purse and paid for the shandy. She took a sip and declared it just what she needed. 'I wonder if I could ask you a question or two about one of your customers.' She took a card from her bag and laid it before the landlord, adding, 'I work independently and I am helping a friend of Mr Addens – a friend from long ago who is not happy about the length of time it's taking to find out who was responsible for his death.'

The man took up her card and squinted at her name. 'Bloody eyes – can't see a thing without my glasses, and my glasses are never where I want them.'

'My name's Maisie Dobbs. I'm an investigator. Would you mind very much if I asked you a couple of questions?' She took another sip of the lukewarm shandy.

'Let me just make sure the rabble next door are topped up. The men in there all came off a shift an hour ago, and one of them's getting hitched – well, he says he is. I'll believe it if I ever see him walk up the aisle!'

Maisie sat on a stool, and looped the handle of her bag over the hook for women's handbags under the top of the bar. She did not take out her notebook – she would have to remember everything until she was on the Tube back to the office.

'Now then, what can I tell you about Fred?' The landlord returned to the saloon bar, took up a fresh dry cloth from a hook on the wall, and began to wipe it across the counter between them, as if his hands needed to keep moving. 'Terrible business. Terrible. Nice bloke, very nice – wouldn't hurt a fly – so I don't know why someone would hurt him. Probably knew he had his pay packet on him, being a Friday. And him having to come over here to stay alive in the war. I was in Belgium, and I saw what the people went through.'

Maisie did not interrupt, though it was clear the landlord was going to ramble on. Maurice had always taught her that there were times when it was best to let people talk even if the chatter meandered away from the route she would like the conversation to take. 'You never know what gems might fall out of pocket while they're on their own merry-go-round,' he had cautioned.

'I mean, I witnessed it myself. A long line of families walking towards the docks. They had horses loaded up, they had handcarts filled to overflowing with everything they owned. Little children hunched over with sacks; poor little mites. They were going one way, and we were going the other, straight into the German army. And it went on. Mind you, talk about brave – those people had it here.' He took his fist to his chest, just as Maisie had reflected Enid Addens' feelings when she touched her chest to signify her broken heart. 'They pulled together, and then they had to fight too – women and children, boys – I know what happened. That's why I liked Frederick – we all did, us old soldiers who'd been over there. We knew what it took for

48

him to get here, and then make a go of it. And he's a worker – hard bloomin' work too, six days a week on the railway, come rain, shine, and snow. Hot and cold. Bloomin' good darts player too – could get a double top without even squinting at the board. Bull's-eye was easy for him. I mean, some of them are so off-kilter when they throw the feathers, you'd have to duck if you were out there on the street! And he was a good sport.' The man seemed to choke up. 'We miss him. Something rotten, we miss old Frederick.'

Maisie asked if Frederick Addens had ever argued with anyone. *No.* Had he seemed changed lately? *No.* She asked if he had been seen with anyone not known to the regulars, anyone of note. *No.* She asked what the man knew of Addens' life before he came to England, if they'd ever spoken of it over a pint. *No, Frederick never talked about it.* She asked if Addens had lately seemed distracted, perhaps more fatigued or worried than usual.

'Miss, I don't know if you've been keeping up, but there's a war just been declared, and we all knew it was on its way because we've been preparing for it since March. There's them bloody barrage balloons up over London, there's barely a child on the streets because they've all been sent away, and it looks like old Adolf is going to do his level best to blow us to bits and then march in here and take over. Everyone's been tired for months, everyone's worried, and if – like Frederick and me – you've been at the sharp end of it before, then you're not going to be sleeping easy in your bed, now are you?' He paused, his mood altered as he picked up Maisie's glass, still half full. 'Another?'

'No, thank you, sir. You've been most kind, and I appreciate your help. As I said, I am trying to find out who might be responsible for the death of Mr Addens.'

The landlord sighed. 'Don't mind me, love. I'm sorry. It's this weather bearing down, like you're being suffocated.' He shrugged. 'It's just that there's us who know what war really means.'

Maisie set a coin on the bar by way of a tip. 'I know, sir. I was a nurse. I was there too. And I was wounded and saw my friends killed.'

'Then you'll know why our Frederick was tired, why he looked a bit pale. He's seen it all before, and he could see it coming again.'

CHAPTER THREE

Maisie tried to get comfortable on the underground train as she considered the conversation with Enid Addens and her daughter. But it was an off-the-cuff comment by the pub landlord that remained with her. *He's seen it all before, and he could see it coming again.* It was true though, that's what some people were saying: they'd never trusted that Hitler, the appeasement was all a load of hot air, and that we'd better not believe any newspaper if it told us the war would be all over by Christmas – that's what the politicians said the last time and then look what happened. But Maisie wondered if Frederick Addens had seen something more coming – had he known his life was in danger? And from whom? A bullet to the back of the head hardly suggested an act of revenge by a disgruntled office clerk, upset because the train back to Purley was running late.

Maisie left the Underground at Charing Cross. She might have chosen Embankment Station – it would certainly have shaved a few moments off her walk to New Scotland Yard – but tunnels first sealed during the Sudeten crisis of 1938 were now blocked again. The Sudeten crisis, when Adolf Hitler's armies moved to claim Czechoslovakia for the Third Reich, had inspired fears that Britain would be next, and the proximity of the station to the Thames rendered it vulnerable to flooding if it were bombed – and it was predicted this new war would be played out in the air, if the blitzkrieg upon the ordinary citizenry on behalf of Franco during the recent civil war in Spain was anything to go by. Maisie felt ill every time she remembered the German and Italian aircraft lowing in the distance, and then coming in close for repeated bombings, with the terrifying Stukas, their sirens wailing as they swooped down. She had volunteered as a nurse in Spain, in part to exorcise the loss of her husband and unborn child while tending the wounded men and women who fought for freedom from oppression. It wasn't only Frederick Addens who had seen terror coming.

New Scotland Yard's distinctive ornate red-brick building designed by Norman Shaw loomed into view, its spires, turrets, and chimneys, together with its strategic place on the Victoria Embankment, conspired to intimidate all who crossed the threshold. She entered the building and asked a policeman at the enquiries desk if she might see Detective Chief Inspector Caldwell. She gave him her calling card. The man raised an eyebrow, and directed her to be seated on an uncomfortable wooden bench, then picked up the telephone receiver in front of him. She watched as he nodded, smiled, and replaced the receiver. He looked up and beckoned to Maisie, his curled finger summoning her to the counter.

'Detective Sergeant Able will be down in a moment. He'll escort you up to see Inspector Caldwell.' He pointed towards the seat again. 'He won't be another five minutes.'

Maisie thanked the man and stepped away. She did not sit down, but instead walked back and forth along the corridor, her first thought dedicated to the unfortunate Detective Sergeant Able, who, if she knew anything about the banter within the Metropolitan Police, probably had a hard time of it, given his name – she suspected he must be a good sport to work with Caldwell. By the time she had turned and reached the desk, the detective sergeant was waiting for her.

'Miss Dobbs? Detective Sergeant Able. Please follow me.'

Able was wearing a tweed jacket with elbow patches and trousers of light grey wool. His shoes were polished to a military shine, though his tie was askew, and from what she could see of his white shirt, he was a man who lived alone and had only a passing acquaintance with an iron.

'I've heard a lot about you, Miss Dobbs – it is all right to call you Miss Dobbs, isn't it?' Able did not wait for a reply, but went on, as if nervous in Maisie's company. 'I mean, Inspector Caldwell said you have another name, with a title, but he said not to use it. I hope he's right, Miss Dobbs.'

'He's right, and thank you for asking, Sergeant Able. I would imagine he told you I would get stroppy – he likes that word – if you used the title. But I wouldn't bite your head off. It's just better for my work to be plain Miss Dobbs.'

They left the staircase and turned into a corridor. 'Inspector Caldwell was telling me about that case you worked on a few years ago – the army bloke who'd killed someone, murdered him in a dugout in the war. He said you just went in and faced him down.'

Maisie smiled and looked up at the young detective sergeant. 'My, that is praise coming from your guv'nor! How is he?'

'I've not worked with him for long – I was in uniform before I got the job.' He paused just before they turned into a room with a scattering of desks. 'Mind you, the lads say he's got a lot more amenable since his promotion.'

'That's encouraging,' said Maisie as they entered the room. 'Ah, speak of the devil.'

Caldwell had emerged from his box of an office and was walking across the room towards Maisie. 'Miss Dobbs.' He held out his hand, smiling. 'I know you're not here on a social call, but let me say it is very nice to see you again. Mind you, I have a feeling this warm glow might not last very long – you're not here to have a quick chat, I take it.'

'Hello, Detective Inspector Caldwell. You look well,' said Maisie. She sized up Caldwell, who seemed to have developed something of a paunch since she last saw him – perhaps too many liquid lunches at the pub, compounded by late dinners due to his working hours. His jawline was less taut, and he had lost some hair, leaving his widow's peak more pronounced. However, his blue eyes seemed to sparkle as he grasped the opportunity to offer a quip or two.

'Not the very best time to be in our trade, is it? Give me another day or two, and I might not be so full of joy. It's too hot, there's too many people coming into the country, there's too many people getting themselves into a spot of bother, and now you turn up – come on, let's repair to what you could loosely call my office. You can tell me all about what's brought you to my door.' He turned to his assistant. 'Able, do you think you might be able to ably make a cuppa for the good lady and myself? You know how I take mine, and milk, no sugar, for the lady, oh ablest of Ables.'

'Right you are, sir.'

Once seated with the half-paned door closed, Maisie removed

her white summer gloves. 'I suppose poor Sergeant Able would have the rise taken out of him wherever he worked – the constabulary is probably no worse than a bank or a factory.'

'Wait until he gets into the army. Mind you, I'm going to try to keep him – protected job, and all that – but we're bound to lose some to the war. Then he'll be Private Able, and heaven help him. Those lads will have him up a tree before he knows it. Now then, what can I do for you? I don't need to tell you, I haven't got all day.'

Maisie explained her connection to Dr Francesca Thomas, though she did not mention her by name, instead referring to her 'client'.

Caldwell pinched the top of his nose and blew out his cheeks. 'I could have laid money on it being the Belgian you were here about. I know it sounds very dodgy – bullet to the back of the head, obviously made to kneel down – but we've come to the conclusion that the man who murdered Addens was just your more theatrical sort of thief. Addens had just picked up his pay packet – his mates had seen him put it in his back pocket – so all the villain of the piece had to do was come up behind him, stick a gun in the back of his head, get him to kneel down, take the money out of his pocket, pull the trigger, and run.'

Maisie nodded. 'Hmmm. I knew there was a suspicion of theft, but I didn't have details about the amount of money he had with him.'

'Now you do. And if you haven't—'

'But something doesn't sit well. Why on earth would someone then kill Addens? I mean, get him to kneel down, take the money – but all he had to do, the man with the gun, was tell Addens to stay where he was and not move. He didn't have to kill him.'

'Times are hard, Miss Dobbs – well, for some of us they are—'

'Oh dear. Just when I thought you'd changed, you go sarcastic on me.'

'Sorry about that – slip of the tongue.' Caldwell leant forward. 'But just imagine it, Maisie – I can call you Maisie, can't I? Just imagine it – this Frederick Addens works blooming hard down in the pit of the railway platform, he gets his wages on a Friday afternoon, just before knocking-off time, and the next thing you know a tyke is taking the hard-earned cash – money he probably needed to keep a roof over the family's head and food on the table. And Addens was a big bloke. As a young lad he'd come over here on a boat in the war and made a life for himself through nothing but hard work. I wouldn't have banked on him staying put for one minute – he would have got up and tackled that thief down, gun and all.' He sighed. 'To top it all, no one saw the perpetrator, no one heard a shot – well, you wouldn't, with the racket around St Pancras. No one knows who might have killed him. We lost anything we could get our teeth into before it even happened.'

'What do you think about the killer?' asked Maisie.

He shrugged. 'I'd put money on another foreigner. Someone willing to take a chance, who hasn't any feeling for killing a person – someone who's had it a bit rough. Having said that, he could come from Hackney, for all I know – there's people who've been starving on our own streets, these past few years. At least this war is going to give a few more people jobs. I mean, put them in the army, put food in their bellies, and give them something to do. Give them guns for good reason, and perhaps they'll stop making the policeman's life a misery – with a bit of luck.'

'May I see the post-mortem report? And how about statements from the men Addens worked with, or people he knew around World's End?'

Caldwell sighed. He leant back in his chair and reached into a cabinet to leaf through a series of files. Pulling out one thick buff-coloured folder, he placed it on his desk.

'I'm going to see if Able has gone to India for the tea, and I'm going to accidentally leave this report here on my desk. Lean to one side while you're being nosy, won't you – I don't want my blokes out there seeing a civilian woman letting her curiosity get the better of her because I've been silly enough not to put confidential reports in a safe place.'

Caldwell left the room, closing the door behind him. As Maisie shifted her chair and reached for the folder, she heard his voice boom across the office. 'Anyone know where Able has managed to lose himself this time?'

She took out her notebook and began to transcribe the most pertinent points from the reports. Though the case had not been written off by Scotland Yard, it appeared it wasn't exactly open to new information. She closed the file, placed it on the desk in front of Caldwell's chair, and turned to leave. Opening the door into the office where Caldwell's men worked, she saw the detective walking towards her, weaving in between the desks.

'You're going to have to get a cup of char at a caff on the Strand, Miss Dobbs. Able is probably lost in a corridor somewhere. Sorry I couldn't help you any further. But always nice to see you.'

As Maisie was thanking Caldwell, Able hurried towards them. He was bearing a tray laden with two cups of tea and a packet of digestive biscuits. 'I ran around looking for some biscuits, fresh, not all limp from the heat. It took me longer than I thought.'

'Miss Dobbs is just leaving, Able. I'll take the tea – you show her out. I could do with two cups anyway.'

As Maisie made her way towards the underground railway at

Charing Cross, she reflected on the notes she'd taken in Caldwell's office, in particular a page detailing the type of weapon used to kill Frederick Addens. According to the report, it was a Ruby pistol. She was not an arms expert, but she knew the Ruby was used widely by forces from different countries during the Great War, and that it was popular with the French and Belgian armies. And she had seen many carried by soldiers in Spain. On the one hand, the gun was plentiful, so it was not surprising that one might find its way into circulation in England. It had its faults, but she remembered that as she took one away from a wounded soldier in Spain, he'd called after her to tell her to keep the gun so that she could protect herself. The weapon, he added, could be used by anyone, even a novice.

While Sandra typed a report and invoice for another client, Maisie considered how she might broach the subject of her assistant's health – she was looking for a means to encourage Sandra to take care, not to push herself. The trick was to begin the conversation without letting on that she suspected Sandra was pregnant. She was just about to speak when the telephone rang. Sandra reached for the receiver, and recited, 'Fitzroy five-three-two-o,' the new number assigned to the line when Maisie leased the office again.

'Oh, yes, good afternoon, Your Ladyship,' said Sandra to the caller. 'Yes . . . indeed. I'll pass you over.'

Maisie looked up at Sandra, who mouthed 'Lady Rowan' as she leant forward with the receiver.

'Hello, Rowan, how are you?' said Maisie. She had for the past year become used to addressing her mother-in-law by her Christian name.

'Beside myself, my dear. Just beside myself. We have evacuees, and I am not sure what to do with them. I mean, I know what to do with them, but we have two boys, very boisterous, and I think Cook is about to walk out.'

'I see. Not to worry.' Maisie had an immediate grasp of the situation. 'I believe I know who can deal with this problem. Have the boys started school yet?'

'Their teacher is billeted nearby, and they've been given rooms to hold classes in the village hall until the local schoolchildren are evacuated – ridiculously, the local school are evacuating to Wales, which seems utterly unbelievable to me. Julian says it's because we're on a strategic path to London, whatever that means – and if there's danger, why on earth London children are considered more expendable than the local children is beyond me. To add to our chaos, apparently the billeting officer is bringing a little girl who no one else wants, for some reason, and no one seems to know her name – I fear a monster might be arriving on my doorstep. Then of course they will all have to move anyway – a couple of military liaison people came from the Canadian embassy to Chelstone today to discuss officers being billeted here at the house. It transpires there is to be an encampment just outside the village. Of course, one doesn't mind at all – but the children will have to be rebilleted, and all this moving around must be terribly upsetting for them, so no wonder they're being awfully difficult. Having had a growing boy myself, I am certainly a match for them – you know me, I will not brook nonsense – but it's the staff. They are not used to this sort of . . . sort of wild behaviour around the house.'

Maisie had been holding the receiver away from her ear, but she brought it close to speak.

'Here's what I'll do, Lady Rowan. I will telephone my father and ask him to come to Chelstone to sort them out. Could you have George collect him in the motor car? He'll get them organised in no time – a few jobs to do in the stables, and grooming the horses, that will wear them out. In the meantime, I've an idea. It sounds as if you are going to have a houseful when the Canadian officers arrive, so I will get Brenda to go up to Dower House to prepare a room for the boys. We'll put the little girl in the small box room, though we'll put a pretty counterpane in there to jolly it up for her. I do need beds though.'

'I'll have beds sent up – they're old staff beds, cast iron so not terribly attractive, and they'd been kept in one of the barns. Thank goodness no one sought to dispose of them. They've new mattresses – Mrs Jenks ordered them when we knew we were going to have evacuees – so they're perfectly good for children. And I'll have her send linens and blankets, though heaven knows no one has needed a blanket for days.'

'All right – and look, as soon as I can get away, I will, but I'm very busy at the moment. I'll do my best to leave on Thursday. But let me telephone my father and Brenda first – I don't want them to have too much on their plates, so we'll have to see what the teacher can do to help. I expect she's overwhelmed too. Could Cook spare that lovely girl from the village who comes in to help her? If she could lend a hand with the boys in the morning – putting up breakfast – and then help with supper in the evening, I don't see why we won't be able to muddle through.'

'Yes, of course, you're right, Maisie. But I worry about the small girl. They don't even know her name – apparently she's said nothing, and the billeting officer says she was lost on the train, probably in the melee at the station. They think she should have been with the lot from Dr Barnado's, who were going to another town. They're trying to find out.' Rowan sighed. 'The billeting officer, Jane Smethers, told me the child refuses to speak and will not let go of the little case she carries everywhere – she just pulls back if anyone attempts to take it from her. Miss Smethers told me she'd had enough of the games, and was going to just snatch it from her when her guard was down, but I told her, "For goodness' sake, allow the child some dignity and privacy." Really, one should not bully a child.'

'All right, before this situation gets out of hand with the billeting officer, I'll speak to Brenda. I know she'll see to it and get everyone on an even keel. It's asking a lot of them to leave their bungalow to come to the Dower House, but perhaps it won't be for long. And perhaps this little girl will be more at ease with other children around, and when the dust settles a bit. Anyway, there's plenty of room at the Dower House – after all, the last family who rented had four children.'

'She sounded a bit upset,' observed Sandra, when Maisie was finally able to extract herself from the call.

'Oh, no, don't be fooled. My mother-in-law was loving every minute of it. It sounds as if it's the distraction she's needed to lift her from the melancholy that at times assails her. Rowan rises to the occasion when the chips are down – she's enjoyed putting an evacuee billeting officer in her place, and I think she is rather looking forward to having Canadian officers at the house. They won't know what's hit them. But I had better telephone my father – he will be more than able to sort out a couple of unruly London lads. He'll have them exhausted in no time. Priscilla has always said the key to disciplining boys is in wearing them out physically so the birds in their brains fly in formation. And she does a pretty good job.'

'And what was that about a girl?'

'Not sure. Brenda will let me know, and doubtless it will all be sorted out soon anyway. Apparently the little thing just lost her group and probably her identification label, so no one knows who she is. And if she's not speaking, it's because she's overwhelmed, poor love – as soon as they find someone she knows, I am sure all will be well. But we can take her in for the meantime.' Maisie looked up as the door opened to reveal Billy wiping his brow with a handkerchief.

'That St Pancras Station was blooming boiling today. I thought I would sweat myself silly.' He closed the door behind him.

'Why don't you have a cup of tea, Billy – hot drink to fight the heat. I just have one telephone call to make, then we can discuss what we've all found out today.'

Frankie Dobbs laughed when Maisie described the situation at Chelstone Manor. 'Not to worry, love,' he assured Maisie. 'I'll sort out the boys and Lady Rowan. They're just boys who need the law laying down without anyone losing their temper. And we'll take care of the little half-pint until they find out where she belongs.'

'Thanks, Dad – I knew I could depend on you. But take care, won't you?'

'Oh, I will – it'll perk me up a bit, setting the lads right. Once they've learnt to muck out the stables and groom a horse, they'll wind their necks in. Nothing like a big horse to sort out a big mouth! And at least there will be no cavalry coming round to take the horses this time, not like it was before. Perjured myself, I did, to keep those horses.'

'I know – remember, I was the one who had to whip up the egg whites so it looked as if we had horses going down with a terrible disease and foaming at the mouth!' Maisie heard her father laugh, and laughed with him. She told him that she would see him on Thursday, and replaced the receiver before calling Billy and Sandra into her office. Soon they were seated alongside the table by the window with the case map pinned out, and Maisie recounted the events of her morning.

'So, he was murdered by what they're calling a Ruby,' said Billy. 'What I want to know is, how they can be sure that's what it was? After all, the Ruby is really a copy of a Browning. Mind you, them ballistics boys know their job, so the likes of me won't argue with them.' He paused, shaking his head. 'But I don't know, it's not as if there are a lot of guns about, not on the streets. Knives, yes, and there's no shortage of thieves circulating, but they're more likely to have a knuckle-duster or a flick knife – from what I've seen in my time, anyway.'

'I'm doubtful about the theory that it was a particularly aggressive theft – unless the thief was a novice and more fearful than a seasoned criminal. There were no other markings on the body, only the gunshot wounds. None of it sits well at the moment.' Maisie paused. 'Billy, what about Addens' workmates?'

Billy flicked open his notebook. 'First of all, the police were right – he'd just been paid, had been given his wage packet, and the other lads saw him put it in his back pocket.' He tapped on the notebook with a pencil. 'But he still had another few hours of work to go – he'd taken on some overtime, what with all the

extra trains coming and going, due to the . . . due to the war.'
Billy cleared his throat. 'So they'd all wondered what he was doing
going off outside the station.'

'That point never emerged in the notes held at Scotland Yard,' said
Maisie.

'Could he have gone for a smoke? To get some fresh air, or—'

Billy laughed, cutting Sandra off. 'Fresh air at St Pancras, Sandra?
He'd have a long walk for that, clear out to Yorkshire!'

'Did anyone see him leave?' asked Maisie.

'None of his mates that I met.'

'According to Addens' wife, and to notes I saw at Scotland Yard,
he had a good friend by the name of Mike Elliot. Did you come across
him?'

'No, but I'll find him,' said Billy.

'What about newspaper boys outside the station?' said Sandra.
'They see more than anyone, I think.'

Billy blushed – he'd made an obvious omission. Sandra raised an
eyebrow, as if enjoying revenge for his comment about fresh air.

'Good point,' said Maisie. 'Billy, could you go back tomorrow and
talk to the tea ladies, to the newspaper boys, anyone regularly outside
or who notices people coming and going.' She added notes in red wax
crayon to the case map.

'Sandra, how about you – anything of interest?'

'I found out about several refugee associations, and it seems
that a Frederick Addens registered with one, but must have gone
to another for assistance, as they only had minimal information.
Apparently he'd arrived as a young man – just a boy, really.
According to their records, there had been an older brother and
a father in Belgium, both in the infantry and killed in the war.

Addens escaped Belgium with his mother. She caught pneumonia on the journey and died in hospital – in Folkestone – not long afterwards. So the lad was on his own. They knew he had been working for the railways in Belgium, so that's probably how he managed to get a job on the railway here as an apprentice engineer. I did a bit more calling round, and managed to talk to someone in the office on the Southern Railway, and she kindly went into their old records. It turns out that Enid had been a conductor on the trains, so he probably met her there.'

'I didn't know that,' said Maisie, tapping a pencil on the table. 'I don't like these important missing details – they might not be crucial, but still, I like to have as many cards on the table as possible.'

'The railways wouldn't have kept running during the war if it hadn't been for the women who worked on the trains, and the young apprentices,' said Sandra. 'That probably kept Addens in a job, and out of our army.'

'Billy, any signs of discord with the men he worked alongside?'

'No, they seemed a genial lot. And they were all still shocked about what had happened. Not one could think of any reason for Addens to have been killed – which is why it comes back to the money.' He scratched his head, more from habit than easing an itch. 'But what I don't get is this: how come the Addenses were so hard up? I mean, I know a lot of people are very hard up, and it's not as if many are that flush . . . but they had two grown-up children working, and I daresay giving up money for their keep every week. And another thing – they'd probably lived in that house a few years, and I bet the rent hasn't gone up much. All in all, they should have felt a bit better off because the boy had started work at, what? Fourteen? And that girl went on to do a secretarial course, and then her librarianship, all at night after she left school at fourteen too.'

'Then money must have been going out somewhere else,' said Maisie. 'I think I will have to go back to see the family – perhaps when the daughter isn't home. She's returning to work this week. But Mrs Addens was distraught about money when I saw her – and I thought it a bit odd then, for the same reason, Billy. And she also told me the railway workers had started a whip-round for the family, so they had some more money coming in.'

At that moment the telephone on Maisie's desk began ringing. Sandra leapt up to answer it, placing her hand on her middle as she lifted the receiver. Billy looked at Maisie and raised an eyebrow. Maisie widened her eyes and put her finger to her lips.

'Miss, it's Inspector Caldwell – says he would like to speak to you.'

Maisie frowned. 'I only left him a little while ago.' She stood and reached for the receiver. 'Inspector, to what do I owe this call?'

'You're going to thank me, Miss Dobbs. You're going to thank me because you'll know something important before your client, whoever he is.'

Maisie felt a shiver across her neck, along the line of the scar she'd sustained in the Great War. It was as if someone with a cold hand had run a finger against her skin from one ear to the other.

'Go on, Inspector. You have my attention.'

'Albert Durant. Age thirty-eight. Banker working in the City. Lives in Maida Vale – nice mansion flat with no family, no dog, no budgie. Found in an alley round the corner from the bank where he works. Same specs as our Frederick Addens. A bullet in the back of the skull whilst kneeling down, according to our friendly pathologist.'

'And you're going to tell me he was a Belgian refugee, aren't you?'

'Bit of a sharper type than Addens – working in a bank and all that. Came over . . . let me see, yes, 1916. Just before the Somme, I would imagine. Anyway, it looks like our thief has his eye on the same sort of target.'

'If it is theft, Inspector.'

'Oh, it's theft, all right. This one had a bundle when he walked out – had just taken it from his account to go around the corner to another bank, according to the clerk who worked alongside him. Said he always maintained it wasn't good to keep all your eggs in one basket, even if it is the bank you work for.' He laughed. 'Nice if you have the eggs in the first place, if you ask me.'

'Is there anything more you can tell me, Inspector?' said Maisie, ignoring his comment.

'Come along for another cup of Able's weak tea first thing tomorrow, and we two can have a chat. You never know what I might be able to leave on the desk while I wander out to find out if he's gone searching for digestive biscuits.'

'Thank you, Inspector.'

'And you know how it goes, Miss Dobbs, don't you? Share and share alike.'

'I may have a few details of interest to you.'

'That's what I like to hear. Tomorrow at nine? No good doing anything now – I mean, rushing around isn't going to bring him back, is it?'

Maisie shook her head. 'Tomorrow at nine, then. And I will make a telephone call to my client now.'

She exchanged pleasantries with Caldwell and replaced the receiver.

'Another one?' asked Billy.

Maisie nodded. 'I'll have to call Dr Thomas immediately.'

The telephone began to ring as Maisie finished her sentence.

'Shall I?' Sandra pushed back her chair. Maisie shook her head and picked up the receiver.

'Maisie—'

'Dr Thomas – we should meet. I know about Albert Durant.'

CHAPTER FOUR

Maisie sat in her walled garden after work, comfortable in a wicker armchair, a glass of wine on the table next to her. Another chair on the other side of the small matching wicker table was empty, awaiting a visitor.

The following morning, Billy would return to St Pancras Station. Sandra would not be at the office – her work was only part-time, two or three days per week, dependent upon cases pending. The rest of the week she spent working at home for her husband's publishing company. She had previously been employed in the company's offices, however the couple decided to adhere to convention – it might not have gone down well with other staff had she continued working at the office following her marriage. That Maisie was re-establishing her business and needed help with administration had been something of a blessing for both of them, though Maisie wondered how long Sandra might continue working. Yet she felt nothing but joy for Sandra, who had known much sadness in her life, and was now happy in her union.

The gate at the side of the house rattled, and as Maisie looked up, Francesca Thomas emerged from the path into the garden. She wore a light jacket and skirt costume in a shade Maisie thought should be called 'hazelnut' – it was a linen blend in a cream colour that seemed to veer towards brown. Thomas had tied a dark green scarf at her throat – the customary disguise to hide the scar she kept from the world – and carried a pair of olive green gloves in her hand, along with a brown leather document case of a type that seemed as if it should be used to carry sheet music. A fashionable Robin-Hood-style hat of nut brown felt with a green band sat atop her head, and a gas mask in its distinctive square box hung by a strap from her shoulder.

'I see you started without me,' said Thomas.

Maisie shrugged. 'It took me a long time to realise that I can have a measure of wine in the comfort of my home without asking permission of anyone. Would you care for a glass? It's French – just an ordinary white. It's been steeped in a bucket of water under the sink all day, in an effort to keep it cool. I've been thinking of investing in a refrigerator, but I'm not sure – I think the noise would keep me awake at night.'

'I'd love a glass of wine any way you pour it, Maisie.'

'And I have some bread and cheese, if you're peckish.'

'Thank you, Maisie. Yes, thank you.'

Maisie stepped across the threshold into her sitting room. A door to the right led to a passageway and a kitchen that was large enough for a table and two chairs. She prepared a tray with another glass, along with the bottle of wine she had opened just before Thomas arrived, and a plate with crusty bread and a wedge of cheddar. She added two smaller plates, two knives and two table napkins, plus a couple of apples from a bowl inside the kitchen cabinet. She carried the tray into the garden, setting it on the table between the two chairs.

'Fill your plate – I'll pour you some wine. And take a few bites first. We'll have a more constructive conversation if neither of us has a growling stomach.'

Thomas raised an eyebrow. 'Well, you're the trained nurse, so I had better do as you say, eh?' She picked up an apple, rubbing the skin with her napkin. 'Lovely apples – russets?'

'My favourites. There are several orchards near my house – it's in Kent, after all – and the farmer sends a boy over with a basket every Saturday morning in the season. My father has a couple of trees in his garden, and while they are still fresh, he will wrap each apple in paper, then lay them out in his shed for the winter. They keep until spring, easily. I'll be getting more this Saturday – I'll bring you some.'

Thomas thanked Maisie, placed a knob of cheddar on a quarter-slice of bread, and topped it with a wedge of apple. She took a bite and a sip of wine, and when she had finished the portion, she began to speak.

'So the police told you about Albert Durant.' It was a statement, not a question, and Maisie thought she detected a suggestion of annoyance in the other woman's tone.

'Yes. Inspector Caldwell. I might have told you that Caldwell and I have not always enjoyed the most satisfying of collaborations, but it seems he has become a much – well, a much more likable person to deal with. He allowed me access to confidential files yesterday, and his explanation for the police seemingly dragging their feet on Addens' death held water. They had little to go on – and on the face of it, it seems the attack really was a theft that became more aggressive than might have been intended.'

'Then they're not looking hard enough.'

'Francesca' – Maisie set her glass on the tray and leant forward, her hands on her knees – 'as far as we know there were no witnesses. No one to see who shot Mr Addens. We know the weapon used, but already my assistant, Mr Beale, has voiced some doubts. The police believe it was a Browning of a certain type that was copied and sold as a Ruby, which were manufactured in Spain in great numbers during the war, and supplied in the main to the French, and then – and this is interesting – to the Belgians. More to the point, it is somewhat easy for a novice to use but can also go off when you don't want it to, or fire several shots instead of the intended one. Perhaps the killer only meant to fire one bullet into Frederick Addens but was a neophyte when it came to handling a gun, and could not control the firing mechanism.'

Maisie reached for her glass and took a sip of wine. She sat back, rolling the stem between finger and thumb as she considered her words. Francesca Thomas made no attempt to interrupt. 'Frederick Addens might indeed have known his killer,' Maisie continued, 'but by the same token, the killer might be someone who knew him and knew when he would receive his wages. In defence of Caldwell's department, there is not much to chew on. I wonder why you didn't tell me about the money Addens was carrying.'

Thomas shrugged. 'I thought I had. I thought I'd noted it in the envelope of information I sent over to you.'

'We received his date of birth, details of his entry to the British Isles, his work, and his family,' said Maisie. 'We know where he worked, what he did, where he lived. But I did not know his father and brother were killed in the war. We had to discover ourselves how he came to be an engineer for the railway – and it wasn't particularly hard to find out. And I didn't know he had just been paid, therefore had money in his back pocket.'

'He was foolish – he should have known better,' said Thomas.

Maisie leant forward. 'Why? Why should he have known better? An ordinary man going about his ordinary work and on a payday receiving an envelope with a wage that would not buy a couple of nights at the Savoy. I would imagine that his mates did the same – put the envelope in the back pocket and either go home or, like Addens, go back to work for the overtime. And with the extra trains being laid on because the government has been preparing for yesterday's announcement for months, the overtime was there for the taking.'

Thomas topped up her own glass and reached across to pour more wine into Maisie's, which was still half full. 'I meant that anyone – anyone – should have known to be careful, given the greater number of refugees moving into the country in recent weeks. Especially someone who was once himself a refugee. He should have remembered how desperate people can become.'

Maisie allowed silence to descend upon the conversation – silence except for a couple of blackbirds in the garden's lilac tree, followed by the crisp domestic sounds of Thomas breaking off a piece of the bread and cutting another slice of apple.

'And now it seems Mr Durant is also the victim of theft, and killed in the same manner,' said Maisie. 'I would like to know if there was ever a connection between the two men,' she added. 'I think you might know.'

Thomas shook her head. 'Apart from both being Belgian – no. There's no connection, as far as my information is concerned. A railway worker and a banker? They might be Belgian, but let's both admit, this is England. A banker would have little to do with a man wielding an oily rag and a spanner.'

'Therefore they had never met, never heard of each other, their paths never crossed – and it was just a coincidence that these two men have been murdered. And on top of it all, you have asked me to find the killer.'

'I didn't expect there to be a second murder.' Thomas held her glass to her lips and finished her wine. She reached for another slice of bread and cut more cheese. 'I've not eaten all day – I'll have one more bite and then I must go.' She bit into the makeshift sandwich, set the remains on her plate, brushed her hands against her table napkin, and reached into her bag. 'Here, some information on Albert Durant. The police might have the same details for you tomorrow, but you should have this. He was a very clever man – his job was not exactly as an ordinary bank clerk, but one who dealt with the needs of the better-heeled customers, the sort who wanted to move money around.'

'He helped the rich get richer, then,' said Maisie.

'I suppose you could say that.'

'Are you sure there is nothing more you can add for me?' asked Maisie.

Thomas shook her head. 'Scotland Yard will have as much luck finding the killer of Albert Durant as they have Frederick Addens. I am depending upon you, Maisie. I realise my patience might be tested, but I trust you will find the killer. And my interest in this case is purely on behalf of the Belgian government.' She came to her feet, took up her document case and her gas mask, and turned to leave. 'Could you spare me one of those russets?' she added.

Maisie smiled. 'Of course.' She went into the kitchen, wrapped two russet apples in newspaper, and brought them to Francesca Thomas, who thanked her again, said she would be in touch, and then left by the side gate.

Instead of clearing the plates, Maisie picked up her glass of wine, and sat back in the wicker chair. Dusk was beginning to close in, and as she looked up, she thought the barrage balloon overhead resembled a giant sea creature beached on the sky above. Britain had been at war for one day. She wondered when it would start. When would the invasion begin? After all, that's what they said would happen: that German troops would come ashore from Dover to Penzance, that they would sail along the Thames, and they would land their aircraft on the fields of England, Scotland, Wales, and Ireland; that everyone would be heiling Hitler in Britain's very own streets. But for now everything was quiet. Quiet except for the voice in her mind, the nagging tone suggesting she pay very close attention. And the message was clear, so very clear: that Francesca Thomas – brave, fearless Francesca Thomas, who had only the year before given Maisie the tools she needed to save her own life while on assignment for the British Secret Service in Munich – was lying to her. During her initial briefing, Thomas had stated that she wanted to stop it – murder – happening again, yet only minutes ago, she said she didn't expect there to be another murder. Of course, she could have confronted Thomas on that point, could have manoeuvred her into a corner – but for now, she wanted to see how things played out.

She watched as her neighbour pulled dark blackout curtains across a lamp-lit window, hiding any sign of light and life from an enemy that might wheel down from the sky. Her own lights were off and she thought, then, what a strange life she was living, when her list for the morrow included visiting a detective, then a woman whose husband had been murdered – and afterwards coming home to draw her own blackout curtains, so the enemy could not see her.

* * *

75

'So, this new bloke, Albert Durant, he lived alone in Maida Vale – nice mansion flat, all very leafy around there, but still in London and easy for him to get to work. His wife died a couple of years ago, and they had no children. Was she English, or one of them, you know, a refugee?'

'As far as I know, Durant married an English girl too. In any case, I'll find out more when I see Caldwell.' Maisie looked at the clock on the mantelpiece. 'Speaking of whom – I should be off. Billy, I'll see you back here around twelve.'

'With a bit of luck that newspaper boy will have noticed something.'

'Yes, ask around again. There's also Addens' friend Mike – and do you still have that contact in Fleet Street?'

Billy nodded. 'Not seen him for a bit, but I know where he drinks. And they all drink, those boys – as soon as the afternoon edition is put to bed, they're down the Old Bell; your compositors, your delivery boys, your reporters. I bet you could hear a pin drop over at the *Express* come twelve o'clock, except for the typists, holding the fort.'

'Just try to get him before he's had a few too many. Find out what he knows about the Addens case.'

'As good as done, miss.'

Just as Maisie and Billy were about to leave, the telephone rang.

'Do you want to leave, so I can say you're out and not have to tell a white lie?' said Billy.

'I should answer this one. You go on, and I'll see you at noon or thereabouts. I'll lock up before I go.'

Billy nodded, touched the two fingers of his right hand to his forehead, and smiled. 'See you then, miss.'

Once alone, Maisie answered the call. It was her stepmother, Brenda.

'Maisie, dear, I don't like to bother you at work, but I thought I should give you a ring.'

'Brenda – is everything all right? Is Dad ill?'

'No, I should have said straightaway, knowing how you worry. Your father is in fine fettle – in fact, I think having to take those boys under his wing has put a spring in his step. They love Jook, and it's perked her up too, chasing a ball for them – she's not a young pup any more.'

'What about the little girl? Is she all right?'

'That's what I'm calling you about. I think you can help her, Maisie, and I was wondering if you could come down tomorrow instead of Thursday – just a bit earlier than you'd planned. Or are you too busy?'

Maisie bit her lip. 'I am a bit busy – but tell me how I can help. I thought the billeting officer was finding out where she belonged, and was planning to situate her nearer children she knows.'

'Well, that's the thing, love – they don't know. No one seems to know anything.'

'Oh, Brenda, that's not right – the child must have a mother and father. She must belong to someone. Someone knows which school she comes from, or even if she's with the orphanage children, if the poor thing doesn't have a family. They're all probably hoping someone else will do the job – they're just overwhelmed, I would imagine.'

'I don't know so much, Maisie. And I don't know how to say this, really I don't – but it could be because she's a . . . well, you know, she's a—'

'She's a what?' said Maisie. 'A little girl with no name?'

'She's a darkie. A touch of the tar brush, as the billeting officer said.'

'She's a child, Brenda. She's a poor love who has been bundled on a train, only now she's lost.'

'I know that, but the billeting officer says that's what the problem is. I don't think she's all that dark, really,' Brenda went on. 'Your father said that you were only a little bit lighter, as a child, on account of your mother's colouring. And your complexion is as white as mine now, isn't it, though you do catch the sun quickly, if you're out in it.'

'I lived in London, Brenda – and no one ever called me a darkie on account of my hair and a tendency to catch a bit of colour when the sun shines.' Maisie bit her lip. The last person she wanted to be short with was her stepmother, the woman to whom she attributed her widowed father's new-found happiness. 'I will drive down tomorrow afternoon. I'll see what I can do to help.'

'She's perfectly clean. The billeting officer reckons she can't be five years old yet, but she takes herself off to the bathroom sink every morning, closes the door behind her, and you can hear her washing herself. Yesterday I went in there after she'd put on her nightgown and gone to her bed – and she takes all her things with her everywhere she goes, bundles everything into that little case and won't let it out of her sight. Anyway, there were her underclothes, all rubbed out with soap and water, rinsed and left hanging over the edge of the bath to dry for the morning. Bless her, the poor little mite. You'd think she was a lot older, the way she's coping.'

Brenda stopped speaking, and Maisie heard her take a deep breath. She realised that making the telephone call had taken some gumption on the part of her stepmother, who was not one to ask for favours, and could deal with almost any domestic situation. Maisie suspected Brenda was more than a little concerned for the child.

'The thing is, Maisie,' said Brenda, 'you do your work and you know how to get people to talk. And this dear little girl must want someone to talk to – she can't keep all of it in, not at her age, and she's not said a word since she got here. The little mite looks so lost at times. Even Jook feels it – I can see it in her. She will go up to the girl and put her nose to her dear little hand and gets a pat for her trouble. I'd hoped she'd start telling the dog all her problems, but she might not even speak English, for all I know. That's when I thought you would be able to get her to say something.'

'I'll see you tomorrow then, Brenda. I am sure we'll find a way to help her. And I'll find out who she belongs to.'

'Thank you, Maisie. Your father said you'd be the one to bring her out of herself. He told me that once you'd had a case where a girl wouldn't say a word, but you started her talking.'

'I wonder how he knows that.'

'Dr Blanche and your father would often stop for a chat.'

'It was a long time ago now anyway. Brenda, I'll do my best to drive down tomorrow, after work. Otherwise it will have to be Thursday.'

While on the underground railway, Maisie could not get the plight of the little evacuee girl out of her mind. The child had probably been put on the train by her mother, trusting the schoolteachers to keep a keen eye on their charges. But at least the child had been fortunate to be placed in a good home where people cared for her well-being – though Maisie pitied the poor mother who had assumed her daughter was now safe in the country, well away from the slings and arrows of war. And she wondered, as the train beat a rhythm, moving from side to side as it wove its way under London, about the little girl choosing not to speak – if it was a choice. Loss of voice could have many causes – shock, pain, distress, fear. But in this case, Maisie wondered if the child was not remaining silent for another reason – to retain a semblance of power in a situation where all power was lost.

Maisie's first stop was Scotland Yard. As she exited the Tube at Charing Cross, it began to rain, with thundery clouds lumbering overhead, and a clammy warmth to the air. Caldwell was in his office waiting for her – Sergeant Able had once again been sent to bring her up to what was now Caldwell's fiefdom.

'Close the door behind you, if you're able, Able,' said Caldwell, as he gestured Maisie to take a seat on the opposite side of the desk.

'I think you've given that name of his quite a run for its money, don't you?' said Maisie.

'All in jest, Miss Dobbs, all in jest. Now then, let's have a share and share alike, shall we?'

'I wish I had something to give you in return for whatever you can give me, Inspector. You're right, this one seems cold from the time the perpetrator left the scene.'

Caldwell shook his head. 'My boys are checking a few avenues of enquiry now, but as yet there's no meat on the bone.' He pushed a sheet of paper across the desk towards Maisie. 'You know this already, I daresay – Durant was a widower, lived alone in Maida Vale, very ordinary life. Went to work, came home again, and not a lot in the way of outside interests or vices. And I do like to find a vice or two – uncover a vice, and nine times out of ten, you beat a path to the murderer.'

Maisie picked up the notes. 'It says here he and his wife liked walking, that on Saturdays they were known to take a train out to Reigate and then walk the Downs, usually having tea in a village somewhere. That's what I'd call an interest – did he continue after his wife died? After all, he was still a relatively young man at thirty-eight.'

'Oh, I don't know that his walking habits are much to go on. Murderers don't usually hang around among the cream buns and pots of Darjeeling, do they?'

Maisie began to write in her notebook while continuing to speak. 'And the weapon is the same – the examiner says it was a Ruby – the Browning copycat.'

Caldwell nodded. He was distracted by a letter he had just opened, the contents of which caused him to smile. He put the letter to one side and cast his attention back to Maisie.

'Sorry about that – yes, a Browning. Or what was it you said it could be? A Ruby? I spoke to our weapons man about it, and he said it was a possibility it could be either one, because there were more Rubys around than Brownings on this side of the Atlantic, not that it makes any difference. A gun is a gun, and we just have to find the man who's been using it.'

Maisie tapped the paper. 'All right, I have the address and I know where he worked. If I find out anything you might be interested in, I'll let you know – but as I said, I have my client to consider.'

'I think I have a right to know about that client. Your client might be the killer, Miss Dobbs – thought of that, have you?'

Maisie nodded and came to her feet. 'Yes, Inspector, I have thought of the possibility – it's one of the first things to cross my mind in a case such as this. But I have no fear in that regard.'

'And why's that? Pray tell, Miss Dobbs.'

She smiled. 'Because if my client had been the killer, no one would ever have found the body.'

Colour drained from Caldwell's face. 'I think that's it for now, don't you, Miss Dobbs? I'll get Able to see you out.'

Maisie had reached the door when Caldwell called to her. 'Oh,

Miss Dobbs – that letter I just received.' He waved it in the air, as if he were a child taunting another. 'Informal note from one of my mates in another division. Thought you would be interested in what it said. It's about Richard Stratton. Remember him? I was his sergeant for a few years, and was given my promotion when he moved on. He went to Special Branch, then threw in the towel to be a teacher of mathematics and physics at a boys' school down in Wiltshire somewhere, because he wanted to see more of his son, who was getting a free education into the bargain. And our friend Stratton was given a house in the grounds, so no rent to pay – jammy, eh? Mind you, being a widower and with it being just him on his own with his boy – who could blame him? This job's not for a man with domestic responsibilities, is it?' The grin borne of sarcasm spread wider. 'Anyway, turns out he's been lured back – special job for the government. Security. So he's on the force again, in a manner of speaking. All very hush-hush, apparently – well, I say that, but these things get around, don't they? Anyway, better get along now – you probably don't even remember him.'

'It was a few years ago, Inspector,' said Maisie. 'I'll be in touch.'

As she walked back along Victoria Embankment, then up towards Charing Cross, two quite different thoughts clamoured for Maisie's attention, both of which she tried to dismiss. The first was in connection with Richard Stratton. Of course she remembered Stratton – as Caldwell knew only too well. She and Stratton had crossed paths during several of her investigations in the past; in fact, she'd met him at the conclusion of her first case after Maurice retired. It had been obvious that Stratton was sweet on her, and she had been drawn to him, to his straightforward manner and clear head in the most difficult situations. Not for him the cheap joke or spear of sarcasm – he was no Caldwell. Stratton had placed the needs of his son before his work with the police, which surprised many, as he had been a young chief inspector, and was destined for an even more promising career ahead – especially following his transfer to Special Branch, and work on the hinterland of the Secret Service, along with Robert MacFarlane, who was now more deeply entrenched in one of the country's intelligence divisions. Yet Stratton found working with MacFarlane difficult – the Scot's brusque manner and dismissive tone had added weight to his decision to leave the police. In choosing to become a teacher, he was returning to the job he had trained for before the Great War. Now, Maisie wondered if she might encounter Richard Stratton again.

The second, more worrisome thought was one brought to the surface by Caldwell's question. *Your client might be the killer, Miss Dobbs – thought of that, have you?*

It was an impertinent comment, one designed to wrong-foot Maisie. Caldwell might be sharing knowledge with her, but it was only because he wanted her help in return. And yet the question lingered, and she wondered if her defence of Francesca Thomas might have been too quick. Because the truth was that she *had* doubted her client, and though she would defend her until proof indicated otherwise, Maisie knew that she had to keep a door open to the possibility. Francesca Thomas was a woman of fierce intelligence and unquestionable bravery – but she was also a trained killer.

Dorothy Addens was out at work when Maisie called, as she had hoped. Enid Addens answered the door, at once looking up and down the street and back into the house, as if a ghoul might emerge from the bushes and enter her place of safety.

'Might I come in for a moment, Mrs Addens?' asked Maisie.

'Yes, of course. My Dottie could be home any minute, though, and she gets very funny, what with the police coming round.'

'I thought they hadn't been here since about the time your husband died, Mrs Addens.'

The woman pulled out a chair for Maisie but remained standing, leaning against the wall in front of Maisie, as if she were afraid to settle herself too close to the visitor.

'Well, that's right. They came once, and then the inspector came again. But all the same, you have to be careful.'

'Mrs Addens, to all intents and purposes, your husband's death was at the hands of a thief, someone who knew or guessed he had his wages tucked into the pocket of his overalls. Have you reason to fear this man might find you?'

The woman shook her head, and folded her arms. 'No, of course not. I couldn't see how he could find us anyway, I mean, it's not as if Fred kept his name and address on show. And I'm sure none of his workmates knew where we lived, though they might have known about the darts team at the pub down the road – you know how men talk. He might have told them about winning a lot – which he did. I never begrudged him a half-pint at the local, though, not like some women would. He was a good man, and he worked hard – and he never came home having had too much. No, he just needed a bit of change in his pocket and to forget his work for a bit. He was a good man.'

'You met him when you worked for the railway, didn't you?'

'I did, yes.' She began picking at a hangnail, oblivious to the nervousness it revealed. 'I was a conductress, checking tickets, that sort of thing. I liked it. I wasn't stuck in one place, and I was earning money. I'd been putting away as much as I could so I could get married, for my dress and for bits and pieces for our house, if we could get one. But my fiancé was killed, in France.' She shrugged. 'Anyway, after a time I met Frederick, and we began walking out. His English was all right – I mean, I could understand him – but it became a lot better once we were courting, because I couldn't speak his language, so he had to learn mine properly. The children can still speak his language, Dorothy more than her brother. You see, when they were nippers, we had this agreement, that I would only speak to them in English and Frederick would only speak to them in French. He said that was what his family spoke when he was a boy, though Dottie says it wasn't French like they speak in Paris. Anyway, I'm going on a bit too much.' She folded her arms again.

'Mrs Addens, this is not an easy question to ask, and it will be a difficult question to answer as it might seem too intrusive, however, given my task – which is to find your husband's killer – I have to think of all the reasons why he might have been killed, over and above the money in his pocket.' Maisie noticed the woman visibly appear to retreat inside herself, moving to one side and folding her arms even tighter, as if she wanted to encircle her own body. But she continued. 'You mentioned that times were difficult for you, in terms of money. I know your husband brought in a fair wage – he was a skilled man – but it occurred to me that, since they left school, your grown children must be contributing to the household's costs. I know I brought my father money when I was first working in service, and—'

'You? You worked in service?' Enid Addens leant forward. 'You, an educated woman, worked in service?'

85

Maisie nodded. 'Where there's a will, there's a way. Look at your daughter – she left school but continued her education. She has willpower.' She regretted the off-the-cuff remark, as it had deflected attention from her question – but on the other hand, the woman's surprise might work in her favour. 'What I wanted to know was whether your husband might have had money worries. I know some people fret about money even when there is no good reason, but did you and your husband have cause for concern?'

'No cause for concern. We know most people take money from their grown children towards their keep, but we only took a little. Dottie has to be nicely turned out for work – after all, you can't have a scruffy librarian. And our son always liked to look smart too. That's how you get on, looking like the people who are better off than you, so you can earn more than them one day. My Frederick worked hard for the family, and I worked hard here to look after us all. That's how it was. And we always put some by, so we could get away down to the coast in summertime, and put good food on the table, and not scrimp and scrape for a decent Christmas dinner. Of course, I'll depend upon them more now – my son will send money home, and Dottie will give up a bit more. And like I said yesterday, Frederick's workmates have had a collection for us, and there's been someone round from the railway too. We'll have to be careful with what we've got, but we're used to that.'

Maisie nodded. 'I want to ask you one question again – was your husband fearful at all in the weeks or days before he died? Did he seem troubled?'

'No. He was his usual self. Happy. Content. Hard-working. Of course he'd agreed to the overtime, but he would always take it on if the opportunity was there – and it was often there, with the railway.'

Maisie noticed the woman look at the clock on a shelf above the stove, and she in turn consulted her watch. 'If you think of anything else – even something that seems small, insignificant, please let me know. You can send a card, or if you wish to telephone me, here's my number. There's a telephone kiosk just down the road, I noticed.' Maisie passed a card across the table.

'I think Dottie took the card you left the other day, so I'll keep this. But there won't be anything to tell. Nothing at all. My Frederick didn't know who killed him – so it's all down to the police, and I suppose you too, to find out who did.'

CHAPTER FIVE

Maisie had just reached the front door to her office when a tall young man of twenty-five or twenty-six approached. He was of slender build, and Maisie thought he was the same height as her late husband, about six feet two inches. His light-brown hair held sun-bleached streaks, as if he had been sailing in fine weather, and the blue of his eyes was of such a pale shade, it was as if they were almost transparent. He wore a charcoal-grey suit of light wool, a white shirt, and a black tie, and his shoes were plain and polished.

He bowed his head briefly by way of greeting. 'Excuse me, but might you be Miss Dobbs?'

'Indeed I am – how may I help you?'

'My name is Mr Gervase Lambert and I am from the Belgian embassy. My superior, Dr Francesca Thomas, instructed me to hand this to you personally.' He held out the large buff-coloured envelope he had been carrying under his arm. 'And if you would be so kind, I am required to obtain your signature.' He took a slip of paper from the inside pocket of his jacket and handed it to Maisie before uncapping a pen taken from the same pocket.

Maisie signed the chit confirming delivery of the envelope, and before she could thank the messenger, he was gone, hurrying in the direction of Warren Street. Maisie took the envelope up to her office, along with post she had picked up from the hall table. She placed the letters on her desk, then stepped through to the main office, where she opened windows overlooking the square so a breeze might air the rooms. A few sheets of paper flapped on Billy's desk, so she secured them with a paperweight. It was then that Maisie saw a note left for Billy in Sandra's handwriting – it must have been placed there on Monday. It was to the effect that Dr Elsbeth Masters had telephoned, and could he return her call at his earliest convenience. Maisie knew Dr Masters – she was a specialist in psychiatric care, the doctor to whom Doreen Beale had been referred in the dark months following her young daughter's death. Hearing Billy's distinctive step on the stairs, she moved away from his desk into her office. She was opening the large envelope when he entered, whistling.

'Afternoon, miss.' He ran his fingers through his hair, which Maisie noticed had become flecked with silver over the past year. 'It's another sticky one out there, ain't it? My neighbour – old boy with seaweed hanging off the gutter, says it helps him predict the weather – he reckons it'll be a lot cooler towards the end of the month, and then we're in for a chilly autumn. Right now I could do with a bit of chilly – another round of thunder and lightning to clear the air would be nice.' He drew breath, but barely paused. 'Anyway, how about a cuppa? I feel like a man just come in from the desert.'

'Lovely, Billy. Then we have work to do.'

Billy nodded and set about removing his jacket, rolling up his sleeves and taking the tray along to the kitchenette at the end of the corridor. His absence gave Maisie an opportunity to peruse the notes Thomas had sent regarding Albert Durant.

According to Thomas, Durant's English wife had died in childbirth a couple of years earlier. Ten years his junior, she'd been felled by a blood clot. The baby died with her. Maisie closed her eyes to gather her thoughts, placing one hand on her chest; the pounding felt as if it would ricochet into her ears. The loss of the child she had been carrying, delivered during an emergency operation following James' death, was not as raw as it had been – time had healed the immediate physical and emotional wounds. But if those scars became irritated by a stranger's comment or an unguarded thought, it was as if her memories conspired to drag her under in a wave of grief. She composed herself, using lessons learnt in girlhood to temper her breathing and gentle her mind. Only when she felt settled could she continue reading.

Durant was successful in his work, and had moved into the spacious Maida Vale flat with his then-pregnant wife – it appeared the property was the perfect London home for a successful man and his family. Durant was not known to engage in pastimes, though Thomas noted she had discovered that, indeed, once a fortnight he would take a train to Reigate and retrace walks along the southern flank of the North Downs, rambles that he and his wife had enjoyed until quite late in her pregnancy.

'Facing down his dragons,' whispered Maisie, as Billy entered the room, tray in hand.

'What's that, miss?' asked Billy.

'Oh, nothing – just talking to myself.'

'First sign of madness, that.' He set the tray at one end of the table. 'Right, then, let's get this down us, and we'll have the case solved in an hour, you watch.'

Soon they were seated together, the case map pinned out before them. Billy did not seem in a rush to begin; instead, he read aloud the headlines from a newspaper given to him by his Fleet Street contact.

'They've got Churchill in again. First Lord of the Admiralty, he is.' He turned the page. 'That's him off the sidelines – now let's see if he can do better than he did the last time.'

Maisie nodded, picking up a red crayon. She would not comment – her late husband had been engaged in work sanctioned by Churchill via his many contacts. In his case the contact was John Otterburn, a man Maisie hoped never to see again. She knew only too well – as did many – that Churchill had been a fierce critic of the German chancellor, and worked behind the scenes of government to prepare for a war he deemed inevitable. The member of parliament Nancy Astor might have observed that 'Churchill is finished' a few years earlier, but Maisie was aware that the portly man had been far from a political non-entity.

'And you'd better get some petrol in that motor car of yours, miss – motor spirit is going on ration soon. So you'll need to get your coupon book.'

'I wish I'd not bought the Alvis now,' said Maisie, leafing through the post.

'Oh, as long as you don't go everywhere in the motor, just save it for going down to Kent, and you'll be all right. But I hope you've got your blackout curtains up. It's a one-hundred-pound fine if you don't have them, and it's the likes of me who'll be reporting you!'

Maisie raised an eyebrow. 'The likes of you?'

'I joined up with the local Air Raid Precautions a few months ago, when they were calling for men to come forward, and for everyone to do their national service for the sake of the country. I mean, let's face it, what with everything going on since March, when them Nazis took over Czechoslovakia – and you were over there in Munich last year, so you saw a lot more than most – well, we all knew what we were in for, didn't we?' He shook his head. 'And it's not as if everyone's been that pally since the Armistice and that conference in Paris, is it? Anyway, I'm an ARP man now, ready to do a shift when I get home from work. Five nights a week after I've had my tea, I'll be out walking the streets with the old tin hat on my noddle, knocking on doors if I see even so much as a needle of light coming through. We've all got to do our bit, haven't we, miss? Them German blighters could come down out of the sky any night or day, just like we've been warned. Mind you, it's not as if they've been teeming over here to bomb us out yet, is it?'

Maisie drew breath to speak, but Billy went on, tapping his rolled newspaper on the table as if to underline his comment.

'And the German navy hasn't been slow off the mark. See what they did to that ship, the *Athena*? That's not war, that's not fair play – it's murder, what with all them passengers on board, and there was no army and no Royal Navy, but ordinary people. And it happened not far off our coast. Makes me sick.' He flung the newspaper down and shook his head again.

Maisie allowed a few seconds of silence to pass. Billy had been more vocal about matters of government of late, taking any opportunity to voice his opinions. She pushed his cup of tea towards him.

'Billy, have a look at this photograph of Albert Durant. What do you think – notice anything?'

Billy reached and took the photograph. 'Looks very official, doesn't he?'

'It's a private bank, where he worked – small, not like some of the bigger concerns. This one is more for investments. Every member of staff has his or her photograph taken for the personnel files – that's why it looks official.'

'And he looks older than thirty-eight or -nine – wasn't that his age? More like sixty-five. Mind you, I'm no oil painting, am I? I bet he saw a battle or two, that one.'

Maisie shook her head. 'According to this, he hadn't. He couldn't join the army for some reason – probably his age – and came over to England during the war with other refugees.'

Billy frowned, looking up at Maisie as he placed the photograph on the table in front of her. He was silent for a moment, as if considering how to express his thoughts.

'You know what you always say, don't you?' He reached for his cup of tea. 'About trusting your instincts – like listening to a voice inside you. Well, I've got one of them instincts right now that there's a bit of information missing on this fellow. I only have to look at those eyes, miss, and I can tell you without a shadow of doubt – and that's something for me to say, because doubt could be my middle name – but I would say he saw a battle or two, that one.' He tapped the photograph as if to underline his words. 'I'm an old soldier, and it was only when I got back that it struck me. We all know our kind, all of us who fought in the war. I don't care whether a man was on our side or the other side – if he was on a battlefield, I'd know it.'

Maisie stood up and went to her desk. She leafed through a clutch of papers until she found the envelope that had contained the earlier notes sent from Francesca Thomas. She looked into the envelope and reached in, drawing out another photograph. 'They always stick to the inside of the envelope – I meant to check again to see if she'd sent us a photograph.' The image of Frederick Addens was informal, taken with his family, perhaps in a garden, or possibly the photographer had situated himself at the park one Sunday afternoon, the better to drum up custom from couples walking with their children, mothers pushing baby carriages, and families out for the day. Maisie passed the photograph to Billy, who took it from her and squinted.

'Frederick Addens. His face is quite clear.'

'It's clear, all right,' said Billy.

'According to the notes, he wasn't sixteen when he arrived in England. Too young for service, I would imagine.'

'Hmmph! There were a lot too young for service, whichever side of the line you were on.'

'So what do you think?'

Billy sighed and turned away for a second as if to compose himself. 'Makes me wonder what my young Billy will be like, when he's my age. I mean, you try to look after them, you work hard to give them a better life than you had, and then the next thing you know, there's a nutter somewhere over there wanting to take over the world. And that really upsets the apple cart for all of us.' He rubbed his forehead and looked at Maisie. 'My instinct says, miss, that this man went to war. Of course, you could say he saw enough in Belgium, losing his brother and his father – losing everything, really – but he's got that look, that stare in his eyes. He was a boy who'd done a man's work, and I don't mean the sort of work you do under a locomotive at St Pancras Station. Speaking of which, I wish I'd had this when I went over there this morning.'

94

'What did you find out?' Maisie leant forward. 'Did you discover anything new?'

'I discovered that there was a different newspaper seller on the street – the usual bloke had to go to a funeral. And the tea lady couldn't add much, but now I've got this picture of our Albert Durant, I could nip back over there tomorrow morning and ask whether anyone'd seen him around, and whether he was asking for Frederick Addens.'

'I'd love to find another connection between these two men, so while you're at it, could you pop over to this pub and ask the same questions?' Maisie scribbled an address on a piece of scrap paper. 'I was in there yesterday – it's just at the end of the street where Frederick Addens' family lives. The Crown and Anchor, it's called. I've already been in, so I don't want to spark any more interest than necessary – and I think the landlord would remember me. You know the sort of story to make up about Durant – debts, on the run from a wife, whatever you like – but see if he'd been seen in the pub. I have to be careful with Enid Addens. She's very fragile, so I don't want to press her too hard, or the daughter will pull up the drawbridge.'

Billy went on to recount the finer points of his visit to a Fleet Street pub where he met the contact who was now a reporter at the *Daily Express*. Having left school at fourteen, Billy's friend had started work as a compositor's apprentice, before enlisting for service in 1915, as soon as he was able. Upon his demobilisation, he had returned to the *Express*, but this time as a reporter. According to Billy, it wasn't just that Stan Ditton had a way with words – he landed his stories because he wasn't afraid of much, not after the war.

'So Stan says to me, "I know about that Durant. I heard about the murder and went down there." Of course all the banks were closed on Monday on account of the war, and you know how quiet it gets in the City, after everything closes on a Friday and the men in their bowler hats go home.' Billy cleared his throat. 'Stan says it was a street sweeper who found him, in an alley just off Paternoster Row. Poor fella ran out of the alley and raised the alarm. There was a lot of blood, and the body was in bad shape, on account of the weather and how long it had been there. A copper was close by, and it wasn't long before the Murder Squad boys were on the scene and with no less than Spilsbury to inspect the body and then have it taken away for post-mortem. And you know how important he is – they were bringing out the best for the job.'

'Does Stan have any information on who the police think was the murderer? I can't say I trust Caldwell to be completely forthcoming.'

Billy shook his head. 'No. In fact, he said they were apparently muttering about it being another attack just for the money, likely done by a bloke who isn't too clever with a gun. He had a dekko in his notebook, and he confirmed that our mate Caldwell had told him, "The man we're looking for is well and truly cack-handed, and shouldn't be left alone with a wooden spoon, let alone a gun."'

'Typical Caldwell,' said Maisie.

They each continued to recount news of their morning, with Maisie making notes on the case map.

'What now, miss?'

'I would give anything to discover a link between these two men. There has to be one, over and above them both being from Belgium and both being murdered in the same manner. Billy, you poke around using those photographs. It's yeoman work, but it has to be done if we are to find a nugget to bite on. And I will look into their family lives – find out whether their wives might have been related, or even if there was some sort of thread at all between the Addens and the Durant families. Most importantly' – Maisie reached for a folder on her desk, then leant towards Billy as she opened the file – 'this is Sandra's list of associations. Each one has a name for us to contact – an administrator of some sort. I would imagine that these have been disbanded now, but there are a handful of people here that we should really speak to.' She sighed. 'I'm driving down to Chelstone tomorrow morning. It's earlier in the week than I would have liked, what with this case in progress, but there are some problems with the evacuees, and everyone seems to be losing their heads.'

'Except your dad, of course.'

'Yes, except my father. He takes things in his stride, and it seems he's already sorted out the boys.'

'I bet he's got 'em working in the stables, miss – like he did with me, when I needed sorting out.'

'It's worked for all of us at some point, Billy.' She made no mention of the 'sorting out' that Billy referred to – an addiction to narcotics as a result of being over-medicated after he was wounded during the war.

'Do you think these administrator ladies – and they're always ladies, aren't they, that get stuck in to organise refugees and the like, and people needing a home – do you think they'll remember?'

'I'm going to have to work my way through them. I'll start tomorrow morning, before I go down to Chelstone.'

'All right, miss. I've got to catch up with these other cases, or we'll be giving back the advances if we're not careful. Then I'll get back on it tomorrow morning.' Billy stood up, pushing back his chair. 'What shall I tell Sandra, when she comes in?'

'This is a tricky one, but she has the right manner to do it. Just in case I can't find out the information from these associations, ask her to place telephone calls to both the bank where Durant worked and the engineering office at St Pancras – find out if they have a place of birth on file for each of the men.'

'Well, it would be Belgium, wouldn't it, miss?'

'Yes, it would – but I want to know exactly where in Belgium. And I want to know if they came over here at the same time. I want to know if there was any way they would have had cause to meet – a social club, something like that. We might be overlapping in our searches here, but it won't do any harm – if Frederick Addens had any cause to cross paths with Albert Durant during or after the war, I want to know about it.' Maisie made some additional notes on the case map. 'And I want to know anyone else they were particularly close to – as a group, or individually.' She stepped towards her desk as Billy came to his feet, gathering his newspaper and notebook, but before he returned to the outer office, Maisie made one more comment. 'We've had seemingly unconnected but similar cases before, and something always links them. We just have to find out what it is.'

'From where I'm standing, the only thing linking these two is your Dr Thomas,' said Billy.

'I'm very aware of that, Billy. But remember, Dr Thomas is very loyal to Belgium, so any adversity affecting a Belgian refugee from the war would affect her deeply. However, if she knows and is not telling, then you can bet it's a matter of utmost secrecy – and she has been very clear regarding our need for care where the gathering of information is concerned.'

'And it could always just be a coincidence, couldn't it? And we know you don't believe in those.' Billy grinned. He knew only too well that Maisie would never discount a coincidence.

'Oh, I believe in the serendipitous moment, Billy. Just not too many at once. Remember what Maurice always used to say? "Coincidence is a messenger sent by Truth."'

'We should write that on a big piece of paper and stick it on the wall, so it's the first thing we see when we come into the office.'

'Not a bad idea, Billy. Not a bad idea.'

There were three associations at the top of Maisie's list: the Ladies' Refugee Assistance Association, which had been based close to Cambridge Circus; the London Overseas Reception Board, in Greenwich; and the South-Eastern Displaced Persons Relief Board, originally in Folkestone, but now with a small office in Tunbridge Wells. All had been dedicated to registering refugees entering Britain during the Great War, placing them in accommodation, and assisting with clothing, food, and – in the case of many – work. She was not sure what she might find at any of those addresses. The latter two, according to Sandra, had not disbanded following the war, but had been scaled down over the years. As she pointed out, though, the steady trickle of Jewish refugees from Germany over the years had become a flourishing river once again; it was said that the government was looking at placing limits on how many could be received and accommodated.

The Ladies' Refugee Assistance Association had closed in 1920, though according to her research, a Mrs Rosemary Hartley-Davies, who now lived in Sussex, was the person to speak to. Maisie decided to first tackle the office of the South-Eastern Displaced Persons Relief Board, managed by a Mr Martin Thorpe. As Tunbridge Wells was on her way to Chelstone, it would not be too much of a detour to continue to Sussex to visit Mrs Hartley-Davies.

* * *

Maisie was now well used to her new motor car, an Alvis 12/70 drophead coupe, but given intermittent showers, she kept the roof in place rather than risk a top-down drive to Tunbridge Wells the following day.

The South-Eastern Displaced Persons Relief Board was located in a makeshift office on the lower ground floor of a house not far from the new Kent and Sussex Hospital, in the Mt. Ephraim area of the town. The hospital, which had been built only five years earlier, seemed so very modern when compared to the older architecture of the town, from the Georgian Pantiles to the great number of houses and shops built during Victoria's reign. When the railway was built in the mid 1800s, a new brand of resident – the commuter – found Tunbridge Wells to be a most agreeable town and so very convenient for London. Now there were new huts in the grounds of the hospital – erected, Maisie guessed, to receive the many wounded expected if war came.

'I can spare you about fifteen minutes, Miss Dobbs,' said Martin Thorpe once they were seated in his office. He regarded her over half-moon spectacles and only sat down after Maisie had taken a chair. 'We have become very, very busy again, offering support for refugees coming from over there in Germany, Austria, and so on – but fortunately, we know the ropes.' He had spoken the words 'over there' in an imperious manner; at the mention of Germany his nostrils flared as if a plate of foul matter had been placed on the table in front of him. He wore a grey suit of some age; his tie was askew and his shirt collar seemed as if it had been turned, and not in recent weeks. He was balding, and there was a faint shimmer of perspiration across his pate.

'Thank you so much, Mr Thorpe. I understand your late mother was one of the founders of the South-Eastern Displaced Persons Relief Board.'

'Along with my wife, my mother-in-law, and several other women in Folkestone. As you probably know, refugees were coming over in their droves more or less as soon as the Kaiser's army began rolling towards Belgium and France. I was an officer in the Buffs – the Royal East Kents – and after I was wounded, I couldn't just sit about, so I helped out. Not that I was very much help at the time. Anyway, after the war there was quite a lot of work to do in terms of assisting with repatriation, and as my mother was getting on, and my work brought me to Tunbridge Wells, we decided to keep a small office going here, and were given leave to do so by the government. Frankly, not a lot of rubber-stamping went on – as long as we helped them to go after the Armistice, they let us get on with it.'

'Do you still have records of the refugees you helped?'

'In the depths of our cellarage, we do. One never knows when one might need the information, though we have been thinking of just burning the lot, now we're into another war – God help us.'

'Do you think you could find out whether you have records for either of these men?'

Maisie passed a sheet of paper to Thorpe, who squinted as he read the names. He passed a hand across his scalp and rubbed it against his upper arm, as if to remove any moisture picked up on the way. 'I'll have one of my helpers have a look for you, but I'm afraid it won't be today, or tomorrow – in fact, I don't know when we'll have the time. But as soon as I know, I could drop you a postcard.'

'Could you telephone me?' asked Maisie, offering a calling card.

'We've not a phone here, but we're getting one put in soon. Fortunately, there's a kiosk across the street – someone could give you a ring. There's a telephone up in my residence, but if I start using

101

it for this, then my bills will be most unfortunately high. I dare not allow the habit to begin.'

'I understand.' Maisie opened her handbag, took out her purse, and offered enough pennies to place a call to London.

'Thank you. It will help us enormously.' Thorpe took the proffered coins and stood up. The interview was over, and Maisie was none the wiser.

CHAPTER SIX

From Tunbridge Wells, Maisie chose a route that took her through the villages of Frant and Wadhurst, then on to Ticehurst before reaching Etchingham, just a few miles from the town of Battle. Any motor car, let alone a fast motor such as the Alvis, would have attracted attention – in every village it seemed a small gang of children stopped their playing and ran to the side of the road, waving as she passed. When she reached Church Hill, Maisie pulled over to check the address and was happy to note that she was very close to her destination. She continued on, slowing down so as not to miss the property, and soon brought the Alvis to a halt on a low grass verge outside a Georgian detached house. A stone wall limited her view of the house, though she could glimpse the roof through an ivy-covered archway above a single corroded cast-iron gate, beyond which was a flagstone path.

Leaving the Alvis, she walked along the road to another entrance which – had the ornate double gates not been locked – opened to a carriage sweep meandering to the side of the house. The mansion was clearly visible, and Maisie could see it was probably only a little larger than the Dower House at Chelstone. Retracing her steps back along the verge, she entered the grounds through the single gate.

A housekeeper answered the door and asked Maisie to wait while she presented her card to Mrs Hartley-Davies. It took only three minutes for her to return and bid Maisie follow her to a drawing room with French doors overlooking the garden. Mrs Hartley-Davies was standing just outside the drawing room, on the terrace. She was a woman of medium height, lithe in build, dressed in a sleeveless white cotton blouse, a pair of elephant-ear jodhpurs that looked as if they had seen a cavalry charge or two, and Wellington boots. She dropped a wooden trug filled with weeds at her feet. Her smile was broad as Maisie approached.

'Miss Dobbs – so lovely to receive a visitor, even one you don't know.' She threw a pair of secateurs on top of the weeds and pulled off the worn leather gardening gloves she was wearing. 'It's not often someone emerges from London to pay a visit. Especially someone of your ilk – a gentlewoman is always welcome.'

Maisie would have put Hartley-Davies' age at about fifty at most, which meant she would only have been in her mid twenties when she had been involved with displaced refugees. She believed she had already guessed why the woman might have committed so much time to volunteer work during the war, though she would wait for the reason to be revealed when they sat down to talk. Maisie suspected Hartley-Davies was a straightforward woman; there was something about her that reminded her of Priscilla.

'Let me just pull off my boots, and then I'll join you.' Hartley-Davies looked at her housekeeper, who was standing by the door. 'Coffee would be a treat, Mrs Bolton – and something to nibble. I'm starving, and it's not even lunchtime.' She looked back at Maisie. 'I'm a late luncher, so I'm afraid it's just coffee and whatever Mrs Bolton can come up with to stave off the animal in my tum.'

'Thank you for agreeing to see me, Mrs Hartley-Davies,' said Maisie. 'And a cup of coffee would be lovely.'

'My pleasure – though I was about to send Mrs Bolton back to the door with a firm refusal because I thought you might be a traveller for a company trying to sell me something. But then I saw on your card that you were an investigator, and Mrs Bolton said you were a well-turned-out woman, so I thought better of it. My curiosity was piqued. And believe me, when your day concerns nothing more exciting than a battle royale with all manner of garden pests, the arrival of an enquiry agent is thrilling!'

Her Wellingtons removed with the help of a boot jack, Hartley-Davies stepped into the room and shook hands with Maisie, inviting her to take a seat on a chesterfield set perpendicular to the fireplace, which was covered by a summery needlepoint screen. By the time they were seated, the housekeeper had returned with cold lemonade and a tray of biscuits, which she placed on the low table in front of the chesterfield.

'I thought something cold would be better for you, mu'um,' said the housekeeper.

Hartley-Davies sighed, thanked Mrs Bolton, and watched as the older woman left the room.

'It's her way – she will always give me what she thinks I need, not what I would like.' She glanced from the closed door through which the housekeeper had departed back to Maisie. 'Now, perhaps you'd tell me what this is about.' She sipped her lemonade and shivered. 'Lemons always make me do that – I love the little shock to my tongue, but it's as if a lightning strike has gone through me.'

Maisie smiled, took a sip of her lemonade, and tried not to reveal that she experienced the same reaction with lemons.

'I am investigating two crimes that might be related in some way, so I must impress upon you a need for confidence in this matter.'

'Of course.' Hartley-Davies pulled off her scarf and shook out her hair, which was the silver of someone who had lost the colour early. As if intuiting Maisie's thoughts, she lifted a few strands. 'It went this colour almost overnight in 1915 – shock of hearing my husband had been killed at Arras.' She took another sip of lemonade. 'I cannot believe that, with a war coming – and let's face it, we've all known it was coming for years now – anyone would feel like committing a crime. After all, you want to look after each other, not cause trouble . . . I would have thought. Wouldn't you?'

'Yes, I would. But it happens. There have been many dispossessed and disenfranchised people in dire straits in recent years, and sometimes desperation leads in turn to a desperate measure to obtain money. That's what the police think in this case – that two men were killed for the money they were carrying at the time. I have a client who has asked me to look into the matter . . . for personal reasons.'

'Right – so let's get to it. How on earth can I help you?'

'Your name is associated with the Ladies' Refugee Assistance Association. Could you tell me exactly what you did, and how many people you served? I'd also like to know if records are still held – or were they destroyed, or sent on to other authorities for safekeeping?'

'All right. The lion's share of the refugees came from France and Belgium, and they started coming more or less as the German army was approaching wherever they lived. If you knew any of our men who were over there, then they might have told you about seeing entire

106

villages and towns on the move, trying to get away with whatever they could carry or put on a horse and cart or a handbarrow.'

Maisie nodded. 'Yes, I understand. I was in France myself – close to the border with Belgium. I was a nurse.'

'I thought you might have been. Don't ask me why – I just think you can always tell people who've been out of the little milieu they were born to. Anyway, when the refugees came in, there was a specific procedure required to register with the authorities. And everyone was doing their best, believe me. We knew they must have all had a horrible time of it. But a group of us – we had all been at school together, and to a woman our husbands or fiancés were over in France – we decided to help out, to fill the gaps, as it were. We set up a clearing house where we helped refugees, whether men, women, children, or families. If they had no home, we found accommodation. If they needed a good meal, then we made sure they were fed – we'd taken on premises that had been empty for a while, and secured a good rate from the landlord, so we had plenty of room to offer various services. Once they were settled, we found them work, and if they needed to establish contact with someone they had known at home, then we liaised with the Red Cross, who were wonderful to deal with – plus the Germans trusted them too, so we were able to do a fair amount.'

Hartley-Davies finished her lemonade in a few gulps, and shuddered. 'That's better. Now my teeth are well and truly on edge. I suppose you might want to know how all this was funded. Well, what have you got to lose, after your beloved husband has gone to war and you're worried sick? I was never one to sit around, and I'm not shy either – so we asked for money. If I was invited anywhere, I would always make sure I told a few heart-rending tales of the flight from the Hun, or the poor state of the little children, and how we were struggling to help them. And then I would say, 'A pound or two is always welcome.' Everyone knew we were after more than a pound or two, and it's amazing what you can wheedle out of people when they are riven with guilt at not doing their bit.'

'Do you know how many you helped?'

'Hundreds. Of course, we weren't the only people doing this – and there were government departments as well. We were in touch with the other associations – some were just for men, and some helped women and families. But I would say a good few hundred passed our way, and when we closed the association in 1920, we still had money in the kitty, so we kept it in hand to help out if any stray enquiries came in. Some of our refugees ended up doing well for themselves – not afraid to try their hand at business, or work very hard for someone else. They were incredibly stoic. One of our refugees became a banker and helped with the financial side of things – not that it involved too much accounting, though it was nice to have the help.' She leant forward and took one of the biscuits. 'I almost forgot I was hungry. Anyway, that's it, really.'

For the briefest few seconds, Maisie wasn't quite sure what she might say – it was rare for such a fortuitous coincidence to be revealed so soon in a conversation.

'Mrs Hartley-Davies, was your banker a man by the name of Albert Durant, by any chance?'

The woman smiled, yet it was an unsettled smile – the sort of smile balanced between joy and shock, with an involuntary twitch at the side of the mouth. 'Yes. That's right. Mr Albert Durant. Dare I ask how you know this?'

'I am afraid I must inform you that Mr Durant has been murdered.

He is one of the men I wanted to ask you about – you see, I am trying to find out anything I can about two murder victims, who both happened to have been refugees from Belgium. Both had gone on to marry English women, and in the case of the other man, his children are now grown. Mr Durant's wife died in childbirth, as you probably know.'

Rosemary Hartley-Davies stood up and stepped towards the fireplace. She took a packet of cigarettes and a lighter from behind a framed photograph of a man in the uniform of an infantry officer.

'Excuse me,' she said, as she walked out onto the terrace. 'If I smoke this in here, schoolmarm Bolton will be after me. Believe it or not, she was my nanny when I was a girl – she may be well over seventy now, but she rules my little roost like a mother hen. I am not top dog in my own home.'

As Hartley-Davies lit up her cigarette, Maisie finished her lemonade, giving the woman time to compose herself. After a moment she joined Hartley-Davies, who was now seated at a wooden table set to one side of the French doors. An older Alsatian had lumbered from the lawn to join her. Maisie had not seen any sign of a dog when she first arrived.

'This is Emma – my best friend. She was having a little sleep under the willow tree. Emma's pushing nine now, so we're both quite settled together, aren't we, Em?' She nuzzled the animal, who looked back at her owner with the bluish-white eyes of a dog who had diminished vision. 'But do not be fooled by her. She may have poor eyesight, but she can hear very well. She won't bother you unless I seem bothered – and she knows how to show her teeth. I think she could go to fourteen or fifteen – her mother made it, and so could she. She'll be all right with you – just hold out your hand, let her have a sniff.'

Maisie held out her hand to the dog, who duly put her nose to Maisie's fingers. 'Mrs Hartley-Davies, I—'

'Yes, I know – you want to ask me about Albert Durant.' She flicked her cigarette into a flower bed. 'Might you be able to come another day? Perhaps tomorrow? I don't think I can talk about it at the moment. You see, he was such a helpful man, so very kind, I always thought, and I'm rather shocked to hear he's dead.'

Maisie came to her feet. 'I could come tomorrow. I'll drive over in the afternoon, if that's all right. My house is near Tonbridge, and it's a pleasant journey.'

'It's a bit of a distance for you, but I would appreciate the time to compose myself.' Hartley-Davies remained seated, but turned to look out at the garden. The dog lay down at her feet, lifting her head as if to provide a place for the hand of her mistress to settle.

'Of course. Thank you for seeing me, Mrs Hartley-Davies. And it's all right, I'll show myself out.'

'Oh, you won't need to do that,' said Hartley-Davies, bringing her attention back to Maisie. 'I daresay Mrs Bolton will be waiting outside the drawing-room door, ready to escort you to the gate. She's nothing if not vigilant, is Mrs Bolton. Rather like my Em – but she can see and still hear a pin drop.'

Maisie left the drawing room and, as predicted, the housekeeper was close to the door, arranging flowers in a large Chinese vase on the hall table. She put down the scissors she was using to cut stems, and wiped her hands on a cloth.

'Allow me, Miss Dobbs.' Bolton opened the front door for Maisie. 'Will you be calling again?'

'Yes,' said Maisie. 'I'll be back tomorrow afternoon – I would say around three o'clock-ish.'

'In time for tea, then,' said Bolton.

'Yes, in time for tea. I'll see you then, Mrs Bolton.'

As Maisie walked to her motor car, she considered the short but revelatory conversation with Rosemary Hartley-Davies. But it wasn't what was said that gave Maisie pause. It was a photograph. Maisie had always been drawn to photographs, could not be a guest at someone's house without lingering in front of a mantelpiece covered in framed photographs, or a series of images set on top of a piano rarely played. In case after case, she had discovered something from looking at a photograph. In this instance it was not the innocent face of a young man lost to war that had caught her eye, though she grieved the loss of the woman's husband. It was another, more informal photograph taken in a field, or perhaps the gardens of a country home, that had claimed her attention. The scene was of a team of workers, each man wielding a spade, a fork, or a hoe, with a woman standing at the centre of the group, holding a basket, as if she were delivering a picnic lunch. A child stood between the woman and one of the men. That one man – himself still a boy, really – to the left; she could have sworn it was a young Frederick Addens. And the woman, without a shadow of doubt, was Rosemary Hartley-Davies.

'She's not come home from school yet,' said Brenda, taking a seat at the kitchen table opposite Maisie, who had arrived at the Dower House – the spacious property Maisie had inherited from Maurice Blanche – shortly after three o'clock. Situated just inside the estate entrance, the Dower House had once been part of Chelstone Manor, and was once the home of Lord Julian Compton's mother until her death. Following her passing, Maurice – a long-standing friend of the Compton family – purchased the house.

'They didn't want her in the class, but I said she should join the other evacuees who've come to the village, even though she doesn't look quite old enough for school. After all, the poor little mite won't want to be stuck here with me all day, though she seems to like following your father around. He says it's like having you back as a little girl. She loves the horses – puts the boys to shame. She's fearless, even around the big hunters. Anyway, the teacher says she's catching up with the other children already.' Brenda continued her monologue, leaning towards Maisie. 'I mean, it's not as if anyone even knew if she could read or write, but she can. She knows her letters, so she's obviously been to school somewhere. And at least the teacher got something out of her. She won't read to the teacher, but Mrs Evans – that's her name – says that she can see her at her desk with a book, her finger on each word as she goes along. Her handwriting is neat, and she can answer the questions correctly – on paper – but you know, at that age it's all very simple. "What colour is John's tractor?" She'll answer "red" – the right answer. All the children have to write in their nature books every morning, listing new things they've seen, and the teacher will help with spelling. She always puts "pony" at the top, and then dog, cow, pig, and goes on to make a good list every day. But she won't answer a question, won't talk to anyone, and keeps to herself all the time – doesn't mix with the others, and they just leave her alone. At least no one is picking on her, though what with her colouring, I'd say it's only a matter of time.'

'What does the billeting officer say – any news from her?'

'Apparently she's not one of the lot from the orphanage, or from the other schools evacuated on the same train. They've been in touch with teachers evacuated on trains leaving at the same time – some going down to Sussex with their children – but nothing's come to light yet. They've even wondered if she managed to be taken to the wrong station and is expected in Ipswich or out in Hertfordshire, perhaps even down in Wales, but no answers have come back. There's been so many thousands of them to deal with, it's a wonder more haven't got lost, although hopefully they've got a tongue in their head if they have. And there's also been some questions about her birth certificate, and trying to find one for her.'

'Does anyone know her name yet?'

'She finally wrote it down for the teacher. It's Anna – for all the good knowing has done. But at least it's something to go on.'

'And she's still hanging on to her case.'

'Won't let it out of her sight. Even sleeps with it, otherwise I would have had a look.'

'Right then, time to think as if from another realm, as Maurice would have said.'

'Oh dear, I don't like it when you talk like that. I knew Dr Blanche only too well – after all, I worked for him for years – and when he talked about lateral thinking, whatever that is, I knew he was up to something.'

'This one shouldn't be too difficult. Where's Dad? Is he over at the stables?'

'Can't keep him away,' said Brenda. 'Retired a few years ago, and still helping out. And Lady Rowan encourages him. Did you know they've got a mare in foal over there? Another racehorse prospect, so they say – but who will be going to the races with a war on? What with all this talk of rationing, you can bet they'll be slaughtering horses for meat and calling it beef. There's so many horses being sold cheap from the railway companies now, and all the factories have moved over to using lorries. I read about it in the papers – excess livestock, they said.'

'Dad won't like to hear about that,' said Maisie. 'Anyway, I saw a new horsebox parked near the gates when I drove in – is it Lady Rowan's?'

'It is indeed. I reckon Lord Julian will do anything to keep her chin up – losing James, well, look what it did to her. Terrible. But she's interested in her racehorses again, so you can't blame him for wanting to keep her on the go. The thing isn't used much, because once the horses are old enough, they're in training anyway, but she likes them to come back to Chelstone for a bit of a holiday now and again – to be horses, she says.'

'Who drives it?'

'George, the chauffeur. Only now he drives the horsebox as well as a motor car. By the way, he says he'll polish up the Alvis a treat for you – he's taken a shine to that motor of yours.'

Having walked down to the stables to see her father, Maisie arrived back at the Dower House just before Anna, the evacuee girl, came home from school. Two boys burst into the kitchen, only to be cut short by Brenda.

'You can hold your horses right here, gentlemen. I want you to walk – and I mean walk – straight upstairs, change out of those uniforms into your mufti, and then you can go out to the stables to help Mr Dobbs if you like. I'll leave out a bottle of pop each, and a jam tart. All right?'

'Yes, Mrs Dobbs,' they echoed.

'I don't know why there was all the worry,' said Maisie, as she watched the boys run upstairs. 'You seem to have everything well under control, and those boys aren't too much, are they? I think Lady Rowan was just panicking, and—'

Maisie was at once aware that a small girl was standing on the threshold looking in, her eyes on Maisie. The child had jet-black hair pulled into two plaits secured with ribbons in the same green as her cardigan. A hairgrip held back a fringe that would otherwise have fallen into her eyes, and wisps had worked free around her face. She had eyes so blue they might as well have been black, and while her complexion was not that of an English rose, Maisie would not have expected it to draw undue attention. True, her skin was a little darker than most, but instead of sun-kissed, it seemed sallow. She had seen children with exactly the same colouring when she was in Spain, in the village where she had worked as a nurse during the Civil War.

'You must be Anna,' said Maisie, her smile broad, though she did not get up from her seat.

The girl put the first two fingers of her left hand into her mouth and began to suck.

'I'm about to have some tea – would you like some? I like mine milky, but I don't like sugar. How do you like yours?'

Anna sighed and looked from Brenda, who had turned away to make a pot of tea, to Maisie. She walked forward, pulled out a chair – not the one next to Maisie, but one facing her – and clambered onto the seat. She placed her small case and her gas mask on another wooden chair to her right – well away from Maisie – and kept one hand on the case.

Brenda set a cup in front of Maisie, and one before Anna, with a slice of bread and jam alongside.

'I'd better be getting on,' said Brenda. 'Make sure those boys haven't been jumping on the beds again.' She left the kitchen, closing the door behind her.

Maisie pushed the sugar bowl towards Anna, who stared at her, and then towards the door. Maisie nodded and then sat back in her chair and sipped her tea. The girl reached for the teaspoon and with one hand scooped up a half-measure of sugar, placing the forefinger of her other hand on top to ensure no grains were lost on the way to the cup. She tipped in the sugar, licked her finger, and stirred her tea, before blowing across the top of the beverage to cool it down. She put her right hand back on the case.

'Mrs Dobbs tells me you like the horses,' said Maisie. While the child was concentrating on her tea, Maisie had slipped from her neck the chain that held her wedding ring. As she spoke, she leant an elbow on the table and began absent-mindedly swinging it back and forth, as if it were a pendulum. She paid attention only to the girl.

Anna sighed, and nodded. She said not a word, but the ring had caught her eye, and she stared at it.

'Do you have a favourite?' asked Maisie.

The girl shrugged, still watching the ring.

'Shall I tell you a story about a magic horse?'

Anna's eyes widened again. She nodded, though she had begun to move her head from side to side, just a little. She rubbed her eyes.

'I think we should go into the conservatory. It's more comfortable – have you been in there? You can see for miles and miles, right across the fields. You can watch the horses in the paddocks too. Let's drink our tea and go along. It's always been my favourite place to hear a story.'

With tea finished, Maisie did not attempt to take the girl's hand, waiting patiently for her to gather her case. She followed Maisie into the conservatory, taking a seat at the opposite end of the sofa.

Maisie sat facing Anna, her left arm along the top of the sofa, as if making herself comfortable rather than reaching out towards the child. Her free hand held the chain and ring, and though she rested her elbow on the arm of the sofa, she continued to allow the gold band to swing back and forth, and was herself reassured by the movement.

'Anna, can you see out of the window and across the fields to the sky?'

The girl drew her gaze away from the chain in the direction Maisie had indicated. She nodded.

'I want you to imagine you've just seen something wonderful – a horse with wings so wide, he can fly He can fly anywhere he wants – high in the sky, or swooping down across the land. Anna . . . Anna, imagine him flying across those fields. He is big and strong, and he's carrying a very special little girl on his back. Do you know who she is?'

The girl did not look back at Maisie. She shook her head, ever watchful for the horse of her imagination.

'Oh, I think you do. Imagine this – the horse with wings is flying just over there with a very, very special passenger on his back.' Maisie paused. 'Her name is Anna.'

Anna's eyes widened as she leant forward and stared out across the fields. She smiled.

'The magic horse can take you anywhere you want, Anna. He can soar above the towns, streets, and railway lines, above the forests and meadows, and he can leap through the clouds. He has the most wonderful adventures, Anna. He will take the girl he loves anywhere.'

It was then that Maisie saw a teardrop, so clear and perfect it seemed crafted of crystal, as it trickled from the corner of the girl's eye.

'Where is he taking you, Anna?'

The child swallowed, ran her tongue across her lips. She coughed, and Maisie wondered, then, if anyone had thought to take her to a doctor, to ascertain whether there was a medical reason why she had not uttered a word since being evacuated. Now she put her hand to her mouth and choked, but eased her cough, stopping herself by swallowing a couple of times as she took up staring out at the fields again, gazing with an intensity that suggested she could really see a white horse with wings.

'Where is he taking you, Anna?'

The child coughed again. She turned around and stared at Maisie, then at her case and gas mask. She picked up her belongings, looked at Maisie one more time, and then set off out of the room.

Maisie heard Anna run upstairs, first to the lavatory, and then to the small room where a bed had been made for her. Only when Maisie heard the bedroom door close did she fasten the chain and ring around her neck once more and move to go upstairs, where she tiptoed along to Anna's room. She could hear no weeping, no sorrow being given voice, but instead she heard the child singing a song Maisie recognised – it was a child's nursery rhyme. Her mother had sung it to her when she was a child.

Ride a cock-horse to Banbury Cross,
To see a fine lady upon a white horse;
Rings on her fingers and bells on her toes,
And she shall have music wherever she goes.

Maisie closed her eyes, recalling the sweet contentment she'd felt, cradled on her mother's lap after she'd run in from school, her mother singing to her and holding her close. Perhaps that was why, in the moment, Maisie began to sing along, repeating the verse with the child.

It seemed that not a second had passed before the door was pulled back and Anna flung herself at Maisie and held on to her. Maisie bent down and lifted the child up. She said nothing, just held her, feeling her head nestle into the curve of her neck, hot tears streaming wet against her own skin.

CHAPTER SEVEN

Though Anna sat next to Maisie at breakfast the following morning, she still had not spoken.

'But at least we know she has a voice,' said Maisie to Brenda, following the children's departure for school.

After a morning catching up with her work – speaking to Billy on the telephone and reviewing her notes from the previous day – Maisie set off on her way to Etchingham to see Rosemary Hartley-Davies. As she drove along country lanes and main roads, she was giving thought to how she would present her questions – the first regarding the intensity of reaction regarding the death of Albert Durant. The second concerning the appearance of a young Frederick Addens in a photograph. Of course, the role of the association was to settle refugees, so it could have been a case of offering them work on a local farm – she might have visited the men with the intention of obtaining a photograph for the records. Or it might have been a press photograph.

Upon arrival in the village, she once again drew up to park close to the verge outside the house, and walked back to the smaller gate leading to the paved path. A sturdy padlock now hung on the gate, along with a sign cautioning against trespass. Neither had been there the day before. She turned to walk along the road, but upon reaching the second entrance, found the double gates now also secured with a padlock and chain, and another sign warning interlopers not to venture any further. Both plaques appeared home-made, as if someone had painted the message on scrap wood. As she stepped back from the gates, she heard a bell ring behind her.

'Excuse me, madam,' said a young policeman, stepping from his bicycle.

'Constable – good afternoon.' She walked back onto the lane.

'May I ask your business here, madam?'

Maisie inclined her head. 'My business, Constable?'

'This is private property.'

'I'm not on the property, Constable. As you can see, the gates are closed and locked.'

'Just checking, madam. Having to be careful, on account of an invasion.'

'Rightly so, Constable, but I don't think one woman constitutes an invasion.' She smiled. 'Anyway, is this your usual beat, or did you come here especially?'

'We received a report of strange activity in the area.'

'What sort of report?'

The constable blushed. 'Well, I saw you drive into the village, and I thought I would have a word, just to make sure. You might have been lost.'

'I see. No, not lost, and I've not seen anything strange – except the gates closed. I have an appointment to see the occupant, and now I find there's no means of gaining entry to the property. Have you seen these gates padlocked before?'

The constable frowned. 'Can't say I have. But they've probably gone away.'

'You must know everyone in the village, Constable. Do you know the owner?'

'Now the thing is, madam, the owner isn't the woman who lives here. The owner only rented it out.'

'She's lived here a long time, though, I'm sure.'

He shook his head. 'Oh, no – only a matter of six or so months, at the most. I reckon she came from London, or . . . I don't know, to tell you the truth. It's not as if anyone has to tell me, is it? But it's often people from London who come down – they want a bit of the country, then find it's too much country for them after all. Anyway, she could have come from anywhere, couldn't she?' His pallor changed, as if blood had drained from his face. 'I'd better go back to the station and report it – after all, we've just had war declared, and then this one ups and goes off, locking the gates after her. She might've been a spy – we've been told to be on the lookout, which is why I stopped to talk to you. We can't be too careful.'

'Constable, might I make a suggestion? I think we should try to gain entry to this property.' Maisie looked at the double gates, and then at the padlock and chain. She moved to the right and inspected the hinges. 'I think if we pull from here, just under this second hinge, we could lever the gate out enough to squeeze past the bushes – look, the hinges here are so rusty, they will probably give.'

'I don't know about that, madam – breaking and entering.'

'But you're a policeman – come on, give me a hand.'

The constable set his bicycle against the wall and, following Maisie's lead, pulled back on the gate. Three times they put all

122

available effort into creating enough space to enter the property, until at last, on the fourth try, the middle and bottom hinges gave way, and the gate moved back to form a triangular gap just wide enough for them to clamber through.

'That wasn't so bad, was it?' Maisie wiped her brow. 'I've known worse.'

Reaching the house, she leant towards the first window and cupped her hands around her eyes to better see within. Nothing appeared to be out of place.

'Anything in there?' Maisie asked of the constable, who was peering into the second window.

'Nothing.'

'All right, let's make our way to the back.'

They stopped to look into each window, but when they reached the French doors, Maisie slowed down. She felt her heart beat faster, and a chill crossed her bare arms. She stopped.

'You all right, madam?' asked the constable.

'Yes. Perfectly fine.' She looked up at the tall man, who at once appeared to be too impossibly young for his job. She wondered how much police work he had really seen – it seemed his daily round of the village offered little in the way of excitement. She knew that was about to change.

'Just a moment, Constable.' She gestured for him to remain in place.

Maisie approached the French doors with their many panes of glass, allowing a full view of the drawing room. Once again she cupped her hands around her eyes as she looked in. She surveyed the scene and stepped back.

'All right, madam?'

She shook her head. 'No, I'm afraid it isn't quite all right, Constable.'

'Here, let me—'

'No, it's best you don't look.' She placed a hand on his arm. 'You see, I was a nurse, in the war, and I was used to seeing some horrible things, and I think it will be a good idea if you just do as I say.' She reached into her shoulder bag and took out her keys. 'Do you know how to drive a motor car?'

'Yes, madam.' The young man's face was ashen. 'But I should—'

'Please, Constable . . . I have noticed that there are no telephone lines going to the house – I took account of it as we entered the grounds. I therefore want you to take the key to my motor car and drive back to the police station. Please get this absolutely right – you are reporting a rather brutal murder, and you and your most senior policemen must not return without the murder bag and a pathologist. This is the scene of a crime and should be secured without delay – I know how to do that in the first instance, but you will need assistance.'

'But madam—'

'You will be required to confirm my identity, so tell your superiors to call Scotland Yard and speak to Detective Chief Inspector Caldwell. Tell him you wish to establish that you have indeed been speaking to Miss Maisie Dobbs, and tell him why. That should do it.' She placed her hand on his shoulder. 'I know this all seems very out of order for you, but please believe me when I tell you I know what I am doing and I know what must be done. Is that clear?'

He nodded. 'Yes, madam.'

As he turned to leave, she called to him. 'Constable, what's your name?'

'Police Constable Sharman.'

'Constable Sharman, remember to bring the motor car back with you – ideally in one piece, with no scratches. And take account of your speed – she can go.'

'Right you are, madam.'

Maisie watched him run to the gate, and soon heard the distinctive rumble of the Alvis' engine, followed by a crunch as Constable Sharman put the motor car into gear. She stepped back to the French doors, took a deep breath, and turned the handle. The door was not locked and opened with ease. She took another, even deeper breath – it would be the last good breath she would allow herself until she left the room – and opened the double doors wide.

Maisie closed her eyes. She placed her left hand on her chest and crossed it with her right. Soon the image of a white light surrounding her body came into her mind's eye, and she knew she was protected from all that had taken place in the room.

'May they know peace,' she said in a whisper, then opened her eyes. She closed the doors behind her.

The first body was that of Mrs Bolton, who had been felled by a single bullet to the back of her head. She had been kneeling down at the time and her killer had stood behind her to take her life. Rosemary Hartley-Davies was on her back, her skull bloody and splintered. A revolver lay in her open right hand. Maisie bent down to look more closely at the wound and then at the revolver. She took note of the shape, of distinctive markings. She was no expert, but it seemed to be a Browning – or perhaps the copycat Ruby. She looked around the body, at the rug and the surrounding furniture. The blood splatter that emanated from the brain of Mrs Bolton seemed confined to the floor, as did that of Hartley-Davies. Maisie looked to one side of the latter woman's body, and noted a spray of blood. Though she could not be sure, the condition of the bodies indicated death to have been late the previous evening. Maisie was confident Constable Sharman would have recoiled from the smell. She had once told a policeman that, having smelt the inimitable fragrance of gangrene in soldiers who had languished in no man's land, she was quite immune to the smell of death.

She set her handbag on a nearby table and began to make notes. Firstly, was there a link between Maisie's visit and the murder of the two women? If so, how had the killer known who Maisie was, when she had visited, and why? Could Hartley-Davies have walked to a telephone kiosk to inform someone – and if so, where was the nearest kiosk? How long would it have taken Hartley-Davies to reach the kiosk? Why were the gates padlocked? Had Hartley-Davies put on the locks after Maisie departed? In that case, the killer either had to leap a fence, was directed to an alternative way in, or knew another means of entering the grounds. Or did the killer lock the gates after committing the murders? Maisie wondered if she had been followed on her journey to the village. No – it was so small, she would have noticed. Or had someone seen her leaving the property the day before? After all, she had a most distinctive vehicle. She wasn't sure how long it would be before the police arrived, but she had to find the woman's handbag, and an address book, if she had one. Moving from the drawing room, she searched the hall, where she heard whimpering coming from the understairs cupboard.

'Oh my – the dog!' said Maisie, running to the cupboard and unlatching the door. At the last moment she remembered to hold out her hand for the Alsatian to take her scent and – she hoped – know that she was a friend.

The dog had been cramped and emerged half stumbling from

the cupboard, her back legs bending together at the joints. At first she struggled to stand, but sniffed Maisie's hand and gave a shallow wag of her tail. Her nose went up, and she began to whine. Maisie breathed a sigh of relief that she had closed the door leading to the hall from the murder scene, for now the dog moved at an ungainly lope towards the drawing room and put her nose along the gap between the door and the floor. Her whine gave way to a howl.

'Come on, dear girl, come with me – come on, let's get some water for you.' Maisie took the dog by her collar, and though Emma did not want to leave the place where it seemed she knew her mistress lay dead – for Maisie was in no doubt that the dog had caught the scent of death even before the first shot was fired – she allowed herself to be led to the kitchen. The dog's water bowl was in a corner near a back door that opened onto the side of the house. Maisie filled it to the brim and set it down, waiting while the dog lapped away her thirst. A lead was hanging by the door, so she slipped it on Emma's collar, opened the door, and stepped outside. It took only a moment for the dog to relieve herself. Once back in the kitchen, Maisie locked the back door and left the dog to her bed and water bowl – she would find her some food later. She closed the door behind her and made her way upstairs to the bedrooms.

She was correct in her first guess as to which door led to Rosemary Hartley-Davies' bedroom. Overlooking the gardens, it was feminine without being frivolous, a room she might have chosen for herself. On the bed she found the woman's handbag. A search revealed her purse, a lipstick, comb, an invitation to the local harvest festival, and a key with a tag attached, indicating that it was for the back door. The purse inside held some money and a ticket for the opera. Maisie took the ticket. In the bedside table drawer she found an address book, and put it in her pocket. Continuing her search, she found nothing more of note in the room. She returned to the upper corridor. She wondered how far Constable Sharman would have to drive to alert his superiors, and to summon a detective. She had a feeling that, once Caldwell had been apprised of her presence at the house where two women had been murdered, he might well be on his way to Sussex.

There were three more bedrooms on the same floor. She opened the door of the first. The bed was not made up for a guest, and had only a candlewick bedspread thrown across the mattress and pillows. The room had been dusted regularly, for there was no sign of cobwebbing – it was just an empty room awaiting a visitor. The next room was smaller, and was clearly Mrs Bolton's domain. That the housekeeper's room neighboured that of Rosemary Hartley-Davies was a little surprising – servants were, as a rule, accommodated in the attic rooms. However, when Maisie was a girl working at Ebury Place, the London home of Lord Julian and Lady Rowan Compton, she had been sent to Chelstone to be the general maid, companion, and helper to the elderly Dowager. To enable Maisie to be of assistance if the octogenarian awoke in the night, she slept in a small room on the same floor, rather than a servant's quarter in another part of the house. Without doubt, Hartley-Davies had not appeared to require any assistance; indeed, as she had mentioned the day before, Mrs Bolton was old enough to be her mother. Perhaps the younger woman wanted to be close at hand should her former nanny need help.

The housekeeper's bedroom was tidy, yet filled with small ornaments and mementoes. Maisie began searching through drawers and in cupboards, finding nothing of note. She looked around the room again, and in that moment, she became still. She closed her eyes. She was missing something. There was something else . . . and within seconds she knew what it was. There was someone else in the house. It was as if she could hear their breathing in her mind, and feel it in her own lungs. Someone was in the house. She stepped into the hallway. There was only one more room on this floor. She closed her eyes, again summoning a feeling of protection, and felt herself calm. She approached the room, turned the handle, and opened the door, her first step slow and measured. She looked into the room.

'Oh,' said Maisie. She stifled a gasp.

A pyjama-clad man was tied to the bed, a handkerchief bunched into his mouth and secured with a scarf. He had only sockets where his eyes had once looked out onto the world. Maisie had seen soldiers with such wounds in the war, when the eyes had become so filled with shrapnel, there was no other choice for the surgeon but to remove them before infection set in.

'It's all right, I'm here – help is here.' She rushed to the man's side and began to loosen the handkerchief, her fingers pulling the fabric away.

'God in heaven, what's going on? Where's Rosie? And Mrs B. And who the hell are you?'

Maisie reached for a glass of water set on the bedside table, topping it up from the adjacent carafe.

'You should drink this first, then I will tell you. Come on, I'll help.'

'You could untie my bloody hands,' said the man.

'When you've had a drink and you tell me who you are. Now then, sip.' She lifted the man's head and held the glass to his lips. 'Slowly – don't gulp it, or you will be sick. There's plenty of water.'

The man nodded to indicate he'd had his fill, so Maisie drew back, returning the glass to the tray.

'My name is Robert Miller – I'm Rosie's brother. Where is she? And will you bloody untie me? I'm not the big bad wolf, you know, and from your voice I can tell you're hardly Little Red Riding Hood.'

'Calm down, Mr Miller – a lot has happened, and the police will be here any moment now.' Maisie untied the strips of torn sheeting securing Miller to the bed.

Miller reached forward and grasped her arm, twisting her flesh. 'Who the hell are you? I heard a gun, and believe me, I know a gun when I hear it. It wasn't some motor car backfiring a couple of times on the road. Where's Rosie?'

Despite his disability, Miller was strong, his grip fierce, though soon he began to fail. As Maisie reached forward with her free hand and dug her thumb into the flesh between his collarbone and his neck, he released her arm.

'Where the hell did you learn to do that?' said Miller.

'Mr Miller, please help me – we don't have much time before the police arrive, so I must be brutally honest with you regarding the situation. Your sister and Mrs Bolton have been murdered. The man who did this to you was most likely the killer, unless two people were involved.'

'Oh God, oh God, not Rosie, not Rose . . .' Miller moaned, holding his hands to his ears as if to banish Maisie's words.

'I suspect as soon as the killer found you and discovered you were blind, he knew he was safe – but he tied you and stopped you calling out to give himself time.'

'He could have saved himself the bother – takes me all day to move from this bed, and who the hell would hear me? The legs stopped working in good old 1916. Good year for getting blown to pieces, I hear.' Miller began to cough back tears.

In the distance, Maisie could hear the distinctive ringing of the bell on a police vehicle.

'The police are almost here, Mr Miller. We'll make sure you're looked after.'

'Oh God, not back to the hospital, no . . . I couldn't bear it.'

'I'm sure we can find other accommodation for you. Can I get you anything at this moment? I will have to go down when the police arrive.'

'This is embarrassing – I need help to go to the lavatory. I've my own bathroom, just over there. That's why Rosie gave me this room – because I can't exactly hobble down the corridor. I feel terrible having to ask, but I've been here all night, not knowing what was happening. My wheelchair's in the corner.'

Maisie collected the wheelchair, drew back the bedclothes, and leant across, working her left arm under the man's shoulders. 'If you've the strength to lever yourself up, I can get you there.'

Having helped Robert Miller to sit up, she lifted his legs to the side of the bed, and supported him as he moved from the bed to the wheelchair. She pushed the chair to the bathroom and helped him to stand again, and to manoeuvre himself into the lavatory.

'I'm all right from here,' said Miller.

'I'll wait outside.'

Maisie studied the room. Of course there had been no reason for the woman to mention her brother, yet by the same token there had been no sign of his presence in the drawing room – Maisie thought it would have been comforting for him to be seated close to the windows, or outside in the garden in fine weather. She knew she should not rush to judgement, but she wondered why on earth his bed had not been situated in a room downstairs. Surely it would have been far more comfortable.

'Ready when you are,' Miller called out to Maisie. He was in his chair by the time Maisie opened the door. She could see he had been weeping again, and she knew there would be many more tears.

'You're very good at this sort of thing, Miss Dobbs.'

Maisie smiled as she pulled clothing from a chest of drawers for Miller – a pair of trousers, a clean shirt, tie, and pullover.

'It's the second time today I've told someone this, but I was a nurse in the war, and afterwards for a while. They teach you how to lift and carry men – after all, you can't have nurses going down with backache every day.'

Hearing vehicles pulling up beyond the mansion, Maisie moved across to the window. The Alvis, a black police motor car, and a coroner's van were lined up outside.

'I'd better go downstairs, Mr Miller. I'm sure they'll think I did it if I'm not there waiting for them.'

'And I can tell them you didn't.'

Maisie looked back at Miller, his empty sockets staring blindly at a place above her head.

'Do you know who killed Rosemary, Mr Miller?'

He shook his head. 'No. But his hands were almost as soft as yours, and he smelt of Brylcreem, as if he'd slathered it all over his scalp. Anyway, Nurse Dobbs, you'd better go down.'

Maisie turned towards the door. 'If you want to get it right,' she commented as she left the room, 'it was Sister Dobbs by the time I'd finished.'

CHAPTER EIGHT

I t was past eight o'clock when Maisie arrived back at the Dower House. A soft late-summer dusk had begun to descend by the time she parked the Alvis, so she sat for a while in the motor car to take advantage of the waning light and the quiet, and to marshal the many trains of thought that had run through her mind on the journey home to Chelstone. Brenda had come to the kitchen window twice to see if it was indeed Maisie's motor car – most callers would have parked a vehicle at the front of the house – but hadn't ventured out to ask why she lingered. Brenda had worked for Maurice Blanche and known Maisie as his apprentice; she understood her need for silence.

She had been detained by the police at the home of Rosemary Hartley-Davies to answer questions, which she expected. She recounted the story that she'd had an appointment with the now-deceased woman and had been perplexed by the locked gates preventing access to the property. She explained that Constable Sharman had fortuitously come along, whereupon she had described her concern to him, so together they had gained entry by moving the rusted gate open. Seeing as the police had indeed checked her identity with Caldwell, there was no point in hiding the fact that she had been looking into the deaths of two former refugees and had hoped that Rosemary Hartley-Davies might be able to help her.

'Oh, yes, I remember the Belgians – had a load of them in Tunbridge Wells during the war, we did,' said Detective Inspector Wood, who had been sent to the scene along with Constable Sharman, two other policemen, and the pathologist. He was a not a young man, and it seemed to Maisie that he must be approaching retirement. He appeared tired, as if not really interested whilst going through the motions of enquiry. A young detective sergeant proved more energetic. On at least two occasions, Maisie caught Wood rolling his eyes as his sergeant expressed enthusiasm at this or that observation.

The interview was brief, though her first task had been to inform them of the presence of Robert Miller upstairs, adding that he was able to descend the stairs with help, as there was another wheelchair kept in a spacious hall cupboard. Before her interview, Maisie had returned to Miller and asked further questions. She had been curious to know why his sister had not accommodated him in a bedroom on the lower floor, given that he could just about get himself in and out of a wheelchair and was able to take care of his own basic needs – it seemed so much more work for the two women to have to help him upstairs every night.

'It was Rosie,' he said. 'She wanted me to sleep in a room close to hers, so that if I needed help, she could attend to me, and if necessary Mrs Bolton could help. And she said it was important to be normal, to come up to bed each night, and come downstairs during the day. Some days, though, I just don't feel like it, stuck out here in the country with nothing to do, nothing to show for myself, and completely unable to hold myself to account in any way at all. It's not as if I have friends to visit any more – most of them were killed in the war, though one took his own life a few years ago. He'd told me it wasn't worth living, and I sometimes ask myself if he wasn't right.'

Maisie wondered if the man's sister had not encouraged him to remain a patient, rather than helping him to become part of society once more. Other men with similar disabilities had found work – to be sure, it wasn't always the work they wanted to do, but they had company and could feel they had done something with their days. Had Hartley-Davies indulged her own need to be of service to her brother, to care for a man wounded by war?

Of course she had to alert the police to the presence of Emma. As they entered she asked them not to go into the kitchen, explaining that a very upset Alsatian was in situ. When at last she was given leave to depart the house, she asked what might happen to the dog.

'Let's have a look at the thing,' said Detective Inspector Wood.

'She's a bit older, can't see very well – though her owner thought otherwise – and her hearing appears to be fair for her age. I'll warn you, she's a big girl, and still has all her teeth.'

'That's all I need, a big dog with big teeth.'

Maisie instructed the man to hold out his hand, and as they entered the kitchen she spoke with a firm but soft voice, taking care to touch the dog first to let her know she was there.

'Blimey, that one's got a few years on her. Well, what with her owner being murdered, I might as well take her to be put down. She wouldn't be the first dog to go to her maker since Sunday – after all, there's air-raid precautions for animals, you know, and the government has said that it's best to let your dog be put to sleep. We've had a lot of enquiries about it at the station, and the local dispensary for sick animals have had people lined up all day, bringing their dogs in to be destroyed.' He paused, looking down at Emma, who now lay at Maisie's feet. 'And what with that being a German breed, it should be put down, or someone might take a potshot at the thing. I remember in 1914, just before I enlisted – I was just a young copper then – this woman came into the station in a terrible state, blood all over her, carrying her dachshund. A mob had thrown stones at it in the street and pulled it away from her. Little scrap was all but dead, and we called the vet to take it the rest of the way. But that's how it goes, when people have a temper on them and see a way of taking it out on something – or someone.' He gave a deep sigh. 'I was shocked then, still being wet behind the ears, but after a while nothing takes your feet from under you any more.'

'Detective Inspector,' said Maisie. 'I can tell you that she's not going to any veterinary to be put down, so I'd better take her with me.'

Now, at last home, gathering her bag and opening the door of the motor car, Maisie wondered if she had done the right thing regarding Emma. The dog stepped from the Alvis, raised her head, and sniffed the air.

'Emma, you are not the first dog I've brought home, so there might be a bit of trouble. Whatever you do, just try to get on with Jook – she is the number one around here.'

And the dog was not the only problem Maisie had taken on. She had left Robert Miller in the hands of the police, who planned to transport him to the local cottage hospital where he would be safe from falls and have his meals prepared and served – and he would be available for further questioning. However, if Lady Rowan agreed, as soon as he was allowed to do so by the police, he would arrive at Chelstone until other accommodation could be secured, and would stay at the manor. In Maisie's estimation, making such an arrangement was the least she could do.

In truth, she had been grateful for the presence of Robert Miller, because discussion regarding his well-being and where he might live when he left the cottage hospital distracted the police, and drew attention away from herself. Her interview had been cursory, and she'd kept in mind something that Frankie once said when bargaining for a horse. He'd let the trader think he knew little about horses, and wove a story about once buying a bad one, interjecting, with an air of innocence, observations that could knock a little more off the price every time he pointed at this or that part of the horse. When he at last held out his hand to the trader, shaking on the price he'd wanted to pay in the first place, he winked at his young daughter. 'It's often wise to let people think you know a lot less than you do,' he'd said as he led the horse back to its stabling under the dry arches of Waterloo Bridge.

'Sorry I'm late,' said Maisie, coming into the kitchen. 'Oh, Anna, shouldn't you be in bed by now?'

Anna said nothing, but Maisie thought she saw the hint of a smile on her face: a curl at the side of the mouth, and eyes that seemed less dull. The child continued to sip hot milk from a red china mug. Her small case was on the chair by her side, along with her gas mask.

Brenda lifted her chin towards the door, indicating she wanted to speak to Maisie out of earshot of the child, though they remained in the kitchen.

'We expected you earlier, so we told her she could stay up until you came home – we thought it would cheer her up.' Brenda kept her voice low. 'As soon as she walked in from school, she went looking for you – she never said, but we knew because she went straight for the library and then the conservatory, and it's only ever been you and Dr Blanche who used those rooms.'

'Oh, I'm sorry, Brenda. I wasn't able to telephone you, but—'

'Oh, my – I've only just noticed it! Whatever have you brought home?' Brenda started, placing a hand on her chest. 'That's a very big dog!'

Maisie began to explain, watching Anna as she recounted the story to Brenda – though she omitted to reveal the true circumstances of Emma's predicament, only saying her owner was troubled and therefore unable to care for the dog.

Anna had slipped from her chair and approached the dog, not gingerly, but as if she already understood the respect required to offer friendship to an animal. She was only a little taller than the dog's head, but she put her hand up to stroke the animal, who turned and licked the child's ear.

'There's still a little light to the day, Anna. Shall we take her for a quick walk down to the paddocks, let her know where she is?'

'Yes, and you'll have a chance to tell your father you've brought back another stray. He'll be back soon with Jook,' added Brenda.

Anna reached for the lead, which Maisie relinquished. And as Maisie opened the kitchen door, she exchanged glances with Brenda and nodded towards Anna's small case, which she appeared to have forgotten as soon as Emma entered the house.

The child was silent as they walked along the gravel path down to the paddocks in the grainy late-evening light. Soon Maisie saw her father in the distance, walking towards them with Jook by his side. She waved out, and when Frankie saw she had a dog with her, he called out, instructing Anna to release the lead and just let the dogs get to know each other.

'They're both old girls,' said Frankie, coming alongside Maisie and Anna. 'And while I always say it's a fight between two bitches that will go to the death, I think these two will be all right – they'll sort themselves out. And you can tell me what that big one is doing here.'

By the time they reached the back door of the kitchen, Maisie had recounted the gist of the story, leaving out the more confidential aspects of events that led to her bringing the Alsatian home. Anna walked ahead, her hand laid upon Emma's withers, while Jook remained between Frankie and Maisie.

Later, after Anna had finished her now-cool milk and gathered her case, Maisie took her upstairs to her room. She stepped outside while Anna changed into her pyjamas – already she understood the girl's need for privacy – then returned to tuck in the bedclothes. She moved to leave the room, switching off the light as she began to draw the door closed.

'Emma.' The word was uttered in a whisper, to herself. 'I love Emma.'

Maisie knew it was a pronouncement. Emma would be her dog. And indeed it was outside Anna's room that Emma slept that night, despite protestations from Brenda, who said it was bad enough having a dog in the kitchen, let alone two, and now one of them shedding hair all over the upstairs carpet.

Maisie came back into the kitchen, smiling, and was about to speak when she saw Brenda and Frankie exchange glances.

'What is it?' said Maisie.

'Let's all sit down,' said Brenda. 'I've made a pot of tea.'

Frankie sat at the head of the scrubbed, thick wooden table, with Maisie and Brenda flanking him. He spoke first. 'Brenda had a look in the girl's case – it worked, you taking her for a walk with that dog. Tell her, Bren.'

'There was a change of underclothes in there, nicely folded – a couple of pairs of knickers and two liberty bodices – and two pairs of white socks. She had another dress – looked like it had been run up out of curtaining. But there was no room for a winter coat or anything like that.'

'Any identification?'

Brenda shook her head. 'Nothing to speak of. Except this.' She pushed a piece of paper towards Maisie.

'Oh dear, I hope she doesn't notice it's missing.'

'She might not have even known it was there. Tucked down in the pocket – I almost missed it.'

Maisie took the paper. The handwriting was in pencil, and difficult to read – the sheet of paper was about three by four inches and had been folded several times, so it seemed no bigger than a sweet wrapper.

'"My name is Anna. I come from London. I will be five years old on October 21st. I can read and write and I can clean myself. I can be a help in the house, and I know how to wash my clothes. I'm a good girl."'

'Needle in a haystack,' said Brenda.

Maisie rubbed her forehead. 'I just don't understand – it's as if she was abandoned. No one could possibly leave a child to her own devices.'

'Plenty have, love. Five years of age was always considered old enough to get on and take care of yourself, and she's no exception. P'raps she was looked after by someone – her mum, or an aunt, or even a father who might have been crippled in the war – and had to do for herself without much help.'

'The handwriting is a bit shaky, as if the note were written by someone who had poor dexterity,' said Maisie. 'It could have been someone elderly – or ill.'

'We've got to report it to the billeting officer in any case,' said Brenda. 'It might give them a clue to who she is, and now they have a birth date to get on with. That'll help.'

Maisie nodded, and turned away.

Later, in the library, Maisie sat for an hour, a notebook on her lap. She heard Frankie and Brenda climb the stairs, their voices low as they made their way to bed. They now slept in Maisie's room, though for a time each day they returned to their own bungalow in the village, and a couple of evenings a week a girl came up from the manor to look after the children, allowing Frankie and Brenda to remain at home – though as Brenda pointed out, Maisie's father had taken to being at the manor again, and setting jobs for the boys after school at the week's end. A bed had been set up in the library for Maisie.

The library had not changed since Maurice was alive, which was a comfort to Maisie, as she leant back in his leather armchair, remembering days past when she would sit in the wing chair opposite his, perhaps sipping a glass of sherry as he savoured a measure or two of single malt whisky. She could just about detect the lingering aroma of his pipe tobacco, mixed with the fragrance of the lavender-and-beeswax polish Brenda used on the table. How many hours had she spent in this room, talking to Maurice, answering his questions, listening to him urge her to heed the voice that counselled her from within? They had discussed so many cases, pulling apart testimonies, passing post-mortem reports back and forth, Maurice encouraging her to look at each word, each phrase, every aspect of evidence from a different perspective. 'Even this room will seem different from each corner – you must make your mind look through a new lens every time you read. And to do that, Maisie, you have to move – go to another room, step out on a walk, or drive to

141

a place fresh to you. Move yourself, and you move your mind. Look at the evidence from different angles.'

But this time it was Frankie's voice that echoed in her mind. It was clear he suspected she might be becoming just a little too fond of Anna. She had seen the way he watched her when Anna was present, as if he were gauging the effect of the child's presence upon her. She had known the time would come when her father would have something to say if he found reason for concern – and it had come that evening, after they'd discussed what could be done to find Anna's family. 'Those evacuees are our own refugees, Maisie, and refugees go home,' he'd said. 'I saw it in the war – foreigners came over, needing help, so our people did their best for them. They opened their homes and even built houses for the refugees. But when the war was over, they wanted them out, back to their own country, their own towns, and their own people. You see love, it's not easy for them, the refugees – because people can turn on a pin. And they especially turn if they think an outsider is doing better than them.'

She wondered if someone had turned on a pin to take the lives of Frederick Addens and Albert Durant, someone who had then murdered Rosemary Hartley-Davies and her housekeeper. And she wondered again about the woman who cared for refugees and for a wounded brother at home – what had she known that had led to her death? Or was it just that she was acquainted with the killer?

CHAPTER NINE

Billy was reading the newspaper when Maisie arrived at the office on Monday morning. 'Morning, Billy,' she said, as she hung her gas mask on a hook behind the door, Billy folded the paper and put it to one side. The country had been at war for one week.

'How're them little nippers getting along down there?' he asked, coming to his feet. He reached for his notebook, ready for their customary meeting to talk about cases in hand and new business.

'Oh, all right, though there have been some ups and downs. I think there was a little panicking last week, which is why Brenda called me down early. But everything's on an even keel now. My father and Brenda are staying at the Dower House to oversee the children, though they get back to their bungalow a couple of days a week and during the day while the children are at school – Lady Rowan has sent up one of her staff to lend a hand.' She shook her head. 'It's a lot for people their age, but they want to help, so they're happy to move for a while.' She turned to Sandra. 'How are you, Sandra?'

'Quite all right, thank you. I've laid out the case map, and I've notes on the other cases ready for us. We're closing up two today, so the invoices are ready for you to check.'

'That's good. And I've a new case too.'

'What's that, miss?' asked Billy.

'A lost child, I suppose you could say. And another murder – well, two, to be exact. But I must make one telephone call before we start. Just give me a minute or two.'

Maisie stepped through to her office, closing the concertina door behind her. She knew that as the door closed, Billy and Sandra would look at each other, raise their eyebrows, and then speculate in a whisper as to what might be happening with what they were now calling 'the refugee case'.

She dialled the number she had been given for Dr Francesca Thomas.

'Yes?' It was a brief one-word invitation to speak. No number recited, no greeting. Just 'Yes'.

'Dr Thomas. Maisie Dobbs. Do you have a few moments?'

'Of course. Is there news?'

'I have news, but not the sort you might want to hear. There has been another murder – two victims – and the circumstances point to a link with the deaths of Frederick Addens and Albert Durant. Let me explain.'

Maisie recounted the events following her visit to Rosemary Hartley-Davies' home in Sussex. She described the work Hartley-Davies had undertaken during the war, and her life since then, which – as far as Maisie knew – had been in the service of her severely wounded brother.

'Why do you think she was killed?' asked Thomas.

'I think it's pretty clear, Francesca.' As she spoke, Maisie realised she had used the other woman's Christian name several times of late, and conceded it still felt as if she were taking a liberty. Even when Thomas referred to her simply as 'Maisie', she had in reply always been respectful of her professional status. A doctorate was, after all, not an easy accomplishment for a woman. 'I believe she was killed because she knew something. She stalled when she found out why I was there, and who the dead men were – she was obviously shocked by the revelation, and played for time in asking me to return the following day. Whilst it would not have surprised me if she had left the premises, I had not expected her to be murdered alongside her housekeeper in the time between my leaving and returning some twenty-four hours later.'

'How would anyone have known you'd been there? Unless she was in the murderer's sights already.'

'I think she alerted her killer. There's no telephone at the house, but there's a kiosk in the village. I suspect she walked to the kiosk and placed the call from there.'

'And someone was able to come down from London to take her life before she said anything to you.'

Maisie allowed a beat of time before replying. 'Of course, they might not have come from London.'

'Yes. Yes, I suppose so. And I take it there were no witnesses – no one saw anyone going into or leaving the property.'

'It's a quiet village, and the house is on the outskirts. I was lucky a policeman came along when he did. This suggests that the man – if it was a man – came on foot, or parked a vehicle at a distance. I checked at the railway station, and the station manager could not recall seeing a stranger, though he said that there's often a visitor or two who comes via train just to see the church – it apparently has the oldest weather vane in the country and an impressive series of misericords. He told me he cannot account for everyone. And our one witness was woken by the gunshots.'

'So there was a witness? What does he know?'

'Not terribly much, I'm afraid, even though he was in the house at the time. He'd sustained rather devastating wounds in the war – he is blind and crippled in his lower legs. I suspect his sister – one of the deceased women – did little to encourage him to be even a little more independent. And I believe it would have been possible for him, though he clearly required assistance. I think it assuaged some level of guilt in her to be his keeper and caregiver.'

'Why would she do such a thing?'

'It could have been because she felt distress at having lived – her husband had been killed at Arras, which is why she immersed herself in helping refugees. That's how she met Addens and Durant. And her guilt deepened when her brother came home from the war wounded.'

'Are you speculating here, Maisie?'

'That's what my job is about. It's like sticking pins into anything I touch, until I hear someone scream 'Ouch'. Only that scream is something I feel in my heart, as if the dead are letting me know I'm on the right path.' Maisie paused, wrapping the telephone cord around her fingers. 'And if that sounds dramatic, let's just say that if I were tracking an animal in the forest, I've only seen a few footprints here and there in different directions. There is no clear path to the killer.' She took another breath. 'However, I have a photograph of Addens and – possibly, now I've had time to think about it – Durant, taken on a farm somewhere in the south-east of England, I would imagine. After all, most of the refugees came through Folkestone, so it was in this region that a good number were able to find work and a home until the war ended. Of course there were settlements in other parts of the country – Elizabethville in the north, and others in the Midlands. The thing is, in the photograph the dead woman, Rosemary Hartley-Davies, is with them, along with two other men. That's why I would like us to meet soon. I want to know if you can identify them.'

'Maisie, I didn't personally know Addens and Durant – I am involved on behalf of the Belgian embassy. I doubt if I'd know anyone in the photograph.'

'I'd like you to look anyway. When and where could you see me?'

Maisie heard Thomas sigh. It was a sigh of forbearance, as if she had no choice but to indulge Maisie.

'Lyons Corner House. Charing Cross. About noon.'

'Right you are. Until then, Francesca.'

Maisie returned the telephone receiver to its cradle and leant back in her chair before standing up and stepping across to the window. She cast a gaze at the terracotta pots in the yard below, wishing she could put her finger on the deep-seated feeling she experienced now whenever she spoke to Dr Francesca Thomas. Shaking her head, she turned, passing the case map pinned on the table on her way to the concertina doors, which she drew back to call Billy and Sandra into the office. It was time to bring her assistants up to date on the events of the past few days.

'I've this photograph, so I'm taking it to Dr Thomas, to see if she can identify the other people.' Maisie placed the photograph she had taken from the home of Rosemary Hartley-Davies on the table and pushed it towards Billy. She tapped the images of two men with her forefinger. 'Those two could be Frederick Addens and Albert Durant, respectively.' She paused, giving him an opportunity to study the photograph. 'At first I'd only concentrated on Addens, but later I thought I recognised a younger Durant alongside him, though I could be wrong about both. And the woman in the middle is Rosemary Hartley-Davies. Billy, could you see if you can find out anything of note about her late husband, Rupert Hartley-Davies? Here are the details of his death – he was an infantry officer.'

Billy passed the photograph to Sandra so she could look, and picked up the paper Maisie handed to him.

'I'll jump to it. And remember, I went over to the City last week, after you left, and I've a few things to report there. What with the banks being closed last Monday on account of war being declared, it was a bit of chaos all week – you'd've thought a bomb had dropped!' He looked at Sandra, as if waiting for a smile, but she did not respond. He turned back at Maisie, his cheeks flushed with embarrassment that his joke had fallen on stony ground. 'Anyway, I went back to St Pancras.'

'And I did some more checking on refugees from the war, when I came in on Thursday,' added Sandra.

'Let's get it all on the map. You first, Billy.'

'Well, I went along to St Pancras Station, as I said, and I saw the woman with the flower stall. She said she knew Addens because he was always one to pass the time of day with her and would buy a bunch of flowers once a week to take home to his wife, on a Friday. She said she knew something was wrong when he didn't come back for the blooms he'd picked out when he came outside for a smoke during his dinner break at twelve o'clock. He'd been at work since about six in the morning, and they stop for a quick smoke and cuppa at nine, if they can, and then at noon they have another break. That's when he asked her to keep the flowers for him to pick up later.'

'Did she say anything about his demeanour?'

Billy sighed and ran his fingers through his hair, pushing an unruly fringe from his eyes. 'Sort of, and not really. She said he appeared a bit worried, but that he'd been like that for a little while, and she thought there might be trouble at home with their son. He'd told her he was wondering what would happen to the boy if war came – and let's face it, miss, we've all been like that, us who've a son of fighting age. Not that you can stop them if they want to go. Hot-headed, they are – like I said before, they come over all mannish and start talking big before they fit their boots.'

Maisie looked at Sandra, who raised her eyebrows. Maisie would speak to Billy about his own worries later.

'So he had been preoccupied, but we don't know why,' she summarised. 'Let's speculate that whoever he met was the reason for his concerns. Did the woman see him leave to meet a friend? The attack seems to have happened as he was taking a breather between the usual end of his working day and starting his overtime.'

'She said she was suddenly very busy, what with it being the end of the day and people rushing home. She saw him step out at about five o'clock – she could not be sure of the time – but only caught sight of him for a second, and didn't think any more of it until she was packing up a couple of hours later and he still hadn't come back for his flowers.'

Maisie tapped the case map, though she had nothing to add. 'I think that to get anywhere on this case, we have to speculate more than in the past. First the easier part – and let's face it, we could be wrong – that the same man or woman killed our victims. What might have caused someone to kill each of these people? Frankly, we can't help but come to the common denominator, that of Belgium. We could assume that something that happened

149

before they reached our shores is at the root of this case.'

'What about the woman in Sussex, and her housekeeper?' asked Sandra.

'If she knew Addens and Durant, then we could posit she knew the killer. But did she know this person *was* a killer? Or did she believe she was speaking to a friend, or someone who should know the other men had died?' Maisie lifted her hand. 'Perhaps we shouldn't try to answer the questions now – let's just note them down. Maurice always said the power in a question is not in the answer, it's in the way the imagination gets busy when the question is at work.'

'I didn't get much joy from anyone who knew Durant over where he worked in the City,' said Billy. 'I think banking types are more up your street when it comes to an investigation, miss. I mean, they hear me, and you can see it on their faces – what with my accent, they think I'm nothing more than a barrow boy in a suit. And I'm not going to start adding me aitches for the likes of them. I reckon they're all blimmin' crooks anyway – let's see how they look when it comes to putting on a uniform.'

'But Billy – coming back to something you said last week, about Addens.' Maisie leant forward, tapping her pen on the paper again. 'You thought Addens had been a soldier, didn't you? Now look at this photograph.' She pushed the photograph taken from Hartley-Davies' home towards Billy. 'What do you see? And what about Durant? This was probably taken not long after he came here as a refugee. I would imagine we were still at war in any case, that it was before the Armistice.' Maisie stood up and went to her desk. She picked up a magnifying glass and passed it to Billy as she returned to the table.

Using the glass, Billy studied each face in turn. 'Miss, there's something about both of them, and you can see it – but even with what I said about Addens being a soldier, I can see a sort of sadness in all of the men. The boy as well. And the woman, come to that.' He shrugged. 'You've got to be careful, haven't you, miss? I mean, if you want, you can see anything in anyone's eyes, and give them feelings they didn't have.'

'I'd like to know who the other men are,' said Sandra. 'Here, I managed to get the name of a woman who worked with Hartley-Davies – perhaps she can help.'

Maisie looked at the paper Sandra passed to her. 'Miss Clarice Littleton,' she read aloud. 'No telephone number, but an address in Maida Vale. Now that's interesting – I wonder if she kept in touch with Addens.'

'I was curious about that too,' said Sandra. She put her hand to her mouth. 'Excuse me—' She ran from the room.

Billy looked back as the outer door slammed, and the sound of footsteps moving in the direction of the lavatory echoed along the corridor outside. He turned back to Maisie.

'Reckon she's going to tell us soon?'

'I don't know, Billy,' said Maisie. 'She'll let us know when she's ready.'

'I mean, it's not as if I don't know a woman with a bun in the oven when I see her – what with my Doreen having had four of 'em, and not one an easy time of it.'

Maisie looked at Billy. He glanced back at her, and sighed.

'I know – you can see something's up with me a mile off. It's probably showing in my eyes, as far as you're concerned.' Billy pressed his lips together before speaking again. 'My eldest has gone and enlisted. I thought he would wait until his call-up papers arrived on the doormat, but no, he went and did it anyway, and of course I could try to stop him, but . . .' He sighed. 'Of all the blimmin' things, he wants to drive a blimmin' tank. A tank! I told him, the only thing he's driving is his mother and me up the wall! Mind you, I suppose if they give him a job like that, at least he's inside something strong – not like I was, when I was over there in the last war. I was under the ground digging tunnels, and half the time I could hear the Germans digging tunnels on top of mine! I tell you, all the money they get, these politicians, and they have nice houses to live in – yet they can't sort out an argument to stop us all ending up at war.'

'Adolf Hitler is a very dangerous man, Billy. I saw more than I can say, when I was in Munich. He has to be stopped – we all know that.'

'Of course he does. I just don't want my boys being the ones out there trying to stop him, I s'pose.'

'Is Doreen holding up?'

'Our little Margaret Rose keeps her from going down. Blimey, if we lost her like we lost our Lizzie, it just doesn't bear thinking about. Her mind just couldn't take the strain. But if the Germans start to bomb us, like they're saying they will, then she'll go down to her aunt, the one who lives in Hampshire. We can't go through that again, in and out of them mental hospitals. And seeing as you've asked, I—'

Billy stopped speaking as Sandra came back into the office holding a glass of water, and took her seat.

'I think it's time I told you, miss – and you, Billy.' Sandra swallowed, and took a sip of the water. 'I'm expecting a baby.' She leant forward and began to weep. Billy reached across and took away the glass before she spilt the water.

'Oh, Sandra, that's wonderful news, just wonderful,' said Maisie, moving to comfort her assistant. She looked at Billy, who nodded and stepped away into the outer office, closing the doors behind him.

'Sandra, whatever is it? This is not a time for sadness – it's a time of great joy for you and Lawrence. A baby – after all you've been through, you'll have a new baby.'

Sandra pulled a handkerchief from her cardigan sleeve and wiped her eyes. 'I know, I know all that – but how can I feel joy, bringing a child into a world like this?' She paused, choking back her tears. 'And do you know what I saw this morning, miss? I was walking down to the tram stop, and a woman was coming towards me with a pram. I'd never seen one like it – it was like a metal box on wheels, with a little window so she could see her baby inside. It was as if the baby was in its own special chamber to protect it from gas. What kind of world will I bring my baby into? What kind of world, when the poor little mite has to have a pram like a metal box to stop it being gassed to death?'

Maisie held on to Sandra as she continued her weeping, allowing the younger woman to cry until she could shed no more tears. But she said nothing. There was nothing she could say about a baby in a metal box to protect it from poison gas.

Francesca Thomas was sitting alone at a table set in the shadows of the busy Lyons Corner House. Maisie joined her, slipping into the chair opposite as Thomas stubbed out a cigarette in the ashtray. A waitress in the distinctive Lyons uniform – black dress with red buttons, white apron, and a black-and-white band with pleated edges across her forehead – had seen Maisie take her seat, and began to weave between the tables towards them.

'You can tell why they call a Lyons waitress a "nippy", can't you?' said Thomas. 'I've been watching them at work – they nip everywhere. They're like little mice, nipping back and forth between the tables.'

The waitress reached the table, and flicked open a notebook to take their order.

'A pot of tea for two and a couple of Eccles cakes, thank you,' said Thomas.

Repeating the order, the waitress said she would be back immediately with the tea and cakes.

'You must have known Eccles cakes are my favourites,' said Maisie.

'Just something I remembered.' Thomas shrugged. 'Do you have the photograph?' She reached into her handbag and brought out a pair of tortoiseshell-rimmed spectacles as Maisie handed her the photograph. 'Ah, that's better,' she said, and began to study the print.

Maisie watched Thomas' eyes move, as if concentrating on one face after another. She saw her gaze linger in two places, but no movement indicating unexpected recognition – except perhaps once, when the ridged skin between her eyebrows crinkled to form a well-worn frown. She shook her head and passed the photograph to Maisie.

'I could pick out Addens and Durant from the photographs I've received since their deaths – I wanted to at least know what they looked like. But no, no one else. And if that woman is the latest victim, Rosemary Hartley-Davies, then I would say she is a bit of a flirt, wouldn't you?'

Maisie looked at the photograph. Without doubt, Hartley-Davies was having a good day despite any observations Billy might have made about her expression in the photograph. Those present in the field – she now thought it must have been during haymaking – seemed sun-kissed, even in the sepia tones of the photograph. They were smiling, and if there were clouds overhead, they weren't apparent. Hartley-Davies seemed at ease among the men, and the boy appeared to be leaning into her, as a child would his mother.

'I wonder who the boy is,' said Maisie.

'Probably a farm worker's child.'

'Yes, probably – country children always work throughout the summer. It's all hands on deck, helping with the harvest, picking fruit and hops.' Maisie slipped the photograph back into her bag. 'Anyway, I wouldn't have taken Hartley-Davies for a flirt – I think she's just at ease. Perhaps her work and the knowledge that she was helping people took the edge off her grief.'

'And we both know what that's like, don't we, Maisie?'

The question, posed as a throwaway comment, felt akin to a fine blade entering Maisie's heart. She opened her mouth to speak, but was grateful when a voice broke in.

'Pot of tea for two, and your Eccles cakes,' said the nippy, unloading her tray onto the table. A cup, saucer, and plate were set before each woman, with the teapot and milk jug between them. Another plate bearing two cakes was placed on the table. 'Would you like anything else?' asked the girl.

Maisie shook her head, still unable to speak. Thomas reached for the teapot. 'Thank you, that will be all.' She poured for both Maisie and herself, and pushed the milk jug towards Maisie. 'I'm trying to take it black and definitely without sugar. Preparing myself in case we can't get any in the days to come.'

'I think we'll be all right for milk,' said Maisie. She cleared her throat, still stung by Thomas' comment. 'Anyway, there's more to discover about Hartley-Davies, and I am sure I will be able to identify the other men in the photograph soon. I'm seeing another woman later – another volunteer who worked with Hartley-Davies to assist refugees.'

'With any luck she's lending a hand again – they've been coming in thick and fast since the Sudetenland was sold to the Nazis by this government, and since Poland was invaded, who knows which sovereign land will be next on the Fuhrer's list?' Thomas sipped her black, bitter tea and winced. She cut a small wedge from her cake, and finished it in one bite. She pushed the plate away.

'Have you had any reports from Scotland Yard?' asked Maisie.

'Your friend Caldwell keeps in touch, but even I can see how difficult this might be – which is why I called you in.'

'I would have liked to be further along, to be perfectly honest.'

'You will be, Maisie.' Thomas took up a paper napkin and dabbed her mouth. 'I have every confidence. Telephone me when you have more news. Now, I must go.' She reached into her bag as if to find her purse.

'No, that's all right – I'll pay for this. You've hardly touched your cake anyway. And I'll telephone you in a day or so unless there's more to report.'

'Right you are,' said Thomas. She scraped back her chair, smiled at Maisie as she pushed it under the table, then turned and left the cafeteria.

Maisie topped up her teacup, and sighed. She had not taken a bite of her cake. She wrapped it in a paper napkin and placed it in her bag, then pulled the remaining cake left by Francesca Thomas towards her and began to eat. What had Thomas seen in the photograph that had unsettled her? What was the emotion she'd experienced that gave rise to a comment that could only disable Maisie's thoughts? She knew the words were akin to Thomas drawing her sword. But why would she reveal herself in such a way? What had led her to be so unguarded in that moment?

'Well, you both enjoyed those Eccles cakes, didn't you, madam? Would you like more tea, or something else?'

'No, I'll just settle up.'

It was later, as Maisie walked to the underground station to catch a train back to Warren Street, that she realised she knew quite well which of those faces had undermined the tight control Thomas was accustomed to exercising over her emotions. And she decided that, at the present time, she would do nothing more about it. Like a fisherman on the bank of a river, she would play out her line, she would watch the fly skim across the water's surface, and she would bide her time. It would serve her to wait.

CHAPTER TEN

With Billy dispatched to speak to Mike Elliot about his friend Frederick Addens, Maisie made her way to Maida Vale to see Clarice Littleton. The address furnished by Sandra – before Maisie sent her home to rest – was that of a flat in a tall terraced house built over one hundred years earlier. Maisie thought it resembled the house where her own home was situated, though she was fortunate to have the ground-floor flat, which offered more space given the doors leading out to the garden. Clarice Littleton lived on the third floor, which entailed climbing several flights of stairs. When Maisie reached her door, a note pinned to the frame informed callers that Miss Littleton would be 'back in five minutes'. She checked her watch – Littleton had left ten minutes ago, according to the time pencilled on the note. But she had not informed the woman of her visit, so she would wait. Maisie thought it interesting that a note had been left at all. Had the woman been expecting a visitor who might arrive early while she was out on an errand? Or was she perhaps lonely, and did not want to miss a friend who had popped by on the off chance of her being at home. Maisie thought it might be the latter, and hoped Miss Littleton would not be disappointed. She checked her watch again, and leant against the bannister.

Two minutes later, she heard the front door to the house slam, then the sound of footsteps coming up the stairs towards her. It sounded as if the woman had been running, for her breathing was laboured. As she reached the last stair bringing her to the third floor, she stopped and put her hand on her chest. Then she saw Maisie.

'Oh my goodness, you made me jump.'

'I'm sorry,' said Maisie. 'I thought you might be expecting someone – you left a note.'

Clarice Littleton waved a hand as if the note were of little significance. 'Oh, I always leave a note – you never know when someone might call, and I wouldn't want to miss a visitor. Not that I get many of those – though I have two letters today!' She smiled, holding up the post she had just collected from a table set inside the front door. It was a welcoming smile, a smile without guile. 'Come on in – if you're waiting here, then it's me you want to see.'

Littleton unlocked the door and led Maisie a few yards along a hallway, dropping the letters on a small table set against the wall as she went. She opened another door on the right, which led – Maisie knew already – into the drawing room. She had anticipated the entire geography of the woman's flat. A door to the right would lead to the drawing room, with big bay windows overlooking the street. If she had proceeded farther, a second door to the right would lead to a bedroom, and that to the left to another bedroom. A bathroom would come next, also on the left, and then there would be a kitchen, with perhaps a small room – possibly used as a dining room – overlooking a brick yard at the back.

Littleton was a tall woman with shoulder-length hair in a mass of black curls, some of them turning grey at her temples. It seemed to Maisie that perhaps in the past the woman had tried to control her hair, but had given up and now allowed the curls to cascade down. She wore a summer linen skirt, a white blouse, and a short black jacket, which she took off and draped across a sofa upholstered in a fabric of geometric designs popular fifteen years earlier. Her black leather sandals were likely worn for comfort, not fashion. As they entered, she ran her hands along the mantelpiece over the fireplace until she found a pencil. Inviting Maisie to take a seat on one of two leather armchairs, she twisted her hair and pinned it into a high chignon, using the pencil.

'That's better. I can't remember a summer when I have felt so sticky all over, even when it rains.' She smiled at Maisie. 'You know, this is terrible of me – I've dragged you in here and I don't know your name or why you were outside my door. I might not even be the person you're looking for. I just hope it's Clarice Littleton, or I'm going to have to show you back out again!'

Maisie returned her smile. 'You're exactly who I've come to see.' She reached into her bag, now set alongside the armchair, and passed a calling card to Littleton.

'Oh my goodness, private investigations. I do hope you don't think I've nabbed someone else's husband.'

Maisie shook her head. 'Not at all. But I think you might be able to help me. May I ask you some questions about an association you volunteered with during the war—'

'Belgian refugees,' Littleton interrupted. 'You're here about Albert Durant, aren't you?'

160

'Yes, I am. I have been retained by the Belgian embassy to look into the case. Of course, Scotland Yard are investigating, but the embassy wishes to conduct its own enquiries, and I have worked with their representatives before.'

'Right, I see.' Littleton nodded. 'He only lived a few streets away. I didn't keep in touch with him – I didn't think it was right, and of course there were so many who came through, and you can't keep tabs on everyone. But I would send a Christmas card, and of course a card of condolence when his wife died. That was terrible, after all he'd been through.'

Maisie nodded. She wavered between asking more questions about Durant and telling Clarice Littleton about the death of Rosemary Hartley-Davies. She didn't want her to lose track of whatever memories she had of the dead man once she'd heard about the murder of her former fellow volunteer, so she would take the chance that holding the information just for a while would not alienate the woman.

'Miss Littleton, could you tell me how you came to volunteer for the Ladies' Refugee Assistance Association, and describe your interactions with the refugees – how well did you come to know them, and how long were you in communication with them?'

'I was roped in by my friend Rosie Miller – well, that was her maiden name, and we'd known each other since school days. She married Rupert Hartley-Davies just before he left for France. Needless to say, she was completely devastated when he was killed – I mean, it was happening to everyone we knew, it seemed, losing a sweetheart or husband, or they were coming home wounded, so you tried not to show how affected you were.' She looked at Maisie. 'I'll be absolutely frank – I became fed up with all that "just get on with it" nonsense pretty fast, you know. I wanted to scream from the rooftops, so to see all these ramrod-straight backs made me rather angry, to tell you the truth.'

Maisie glanced up at the mantelpiece at the photograph of a young man in uniform, alongside a single fresh red rose.

'Anyway, Rosie pulled me in,' continued Littleton. 'She said we both could do something worthwhile, and it would take our minds off everything else, and there were other women involved, so why not just get stuck in? And so we did. We weren't the only association trying to help, but a good number of refugees – women, boys and girls, and the elderly – were being sent to us. When they arrived, we did several things – registered their names and any other pertinent details, then we set about supplying them with what we termed their basic human needs. Many had left with only the clothes they stood up in, so if they needed clothing, we sent them down to our lady who worked in the room with all the unwanted items people had sent along. By the way, I should add, the association managed to get premises for next to nothing for the duration.'

'A generous landlord?'

'Yes – egged on by Rosie's name. She was very well connected socially.' Littleton glanced out of the window as if to gather her thoughts, then brought her attention back to Maisie. 'Where was I? Oh, yes – once they were clothed and fed, we found the refugees lodgings. At first people were very accommodating – we had a good number of names on our list of possible foster families. That's what we called them – "foster families". And during the registration we checked any personal documents refugees brought with them, and helped to get them identification cards. If they could do a job of work, then we would find them a position if we could – seamstress, secretary, plumber, clerk . . . many of our refugees were very able

162

when it came to work, and of course with our boys all over there, and women having to do all manner of jobs, the extra help was needed – and they wanted to work. Within a short time, a lot of the refugees were very self-sufficient. We tried to direct the families to the Belgian villages that had been set up – they even had their own churches and used their own currency in those places.'

'So you became very organised and very efficient very quickly,' said Maisie.

'Miss Dobbs, I think it's fair to say that some of our volunteers were like regimental sergeant majors – they threw themselves into the work and did what had to be done, and the rest of us did the same. It took your mind off your own problems and straight on to another's, and with our men fighting over there, what was it to give up your days to help people? At least we weren't in trenches.'

Maisie nodded. 'Yes, you're right, of course. Did you keep in touch with Mrs Hartley-Davies?'

Littleton shrugged. 'We were quite pally at one point, but when her brother returned home, she became obsessed with being his helpmeet, I suppose you could say – though they were siblings, not husband and wife.' She seemed wistful for a moment. 'Actually, when we were all younger, everyone thought it was going to be me, that because Rosie and I were such good friends, Robert and I would marry. But I met David instead, and that was it, as far as I was concerned.' She looked up at the photograph. 'We were going to be married on his next leave, but he never made it to the next leave. He's buried near Albert – it's a town in Belgium. I've been over there a few times. I was going to go again soon, but not with the war, not now, and travel across the Channel is at a standstill anyway.'

'So were you courting Robert Miller at one point?' asked Maisie.

'Oh, not really. It's just that we got on so well, and we'd known each other for years, so everyone jumped to the conclusion that we would one day throw in our lot with each other. Then at a party, just before the war – we were all there, of course, the Littletons and the Millers – I met David, and my world changed. We fell in love. And there would never be anyone else, not for me.' She sighed. 'Anyway, now I have a job four mornings a week, including Saturdays – very easy, in a dress shop. And I've joined the Women's Voluntary Services too. I can put all that work in the last war to good use. It left me with an ability to organise anyone to do anything, you know.'

'Yes, I am sure it did, Miss Littleton.' Maisie paused. 'Miss Littleton, I am afraid I have some news for you, and it's very bad news. Mrs Hartley-Davies is dead, along with her housekeeper. She was murdered, and it's likely the attack is connected to the death of Albert Durant, and that of another Belgian refugee, Frederick Addens.'

For a few seconds, time seemed to cave in on itself. Clarice Littleton stared at Maisie, her shock registered in the involuntary movement of a muscle under her right cheekbone, which gave the impression that she was trying to stifle a giggle. Her eyes closed, and her breathing quickened.

'Miss Littleton, please put your feet up, go on, lie back. I can guess where the kitchen is – I'll make some tea.'

Clarice Littleton did as instructed, while Maisie plumped a pillow and placed it under her ankles. She pressed two fingers to the woman's forehead and then lifted her wrist and felt her pulse.

'You'll feel more stable in a moment – the shock caused your blood pressure to drop.'

A few minutes later, with a cup of sugared tea clasped between two hands, Clarice Littleton was sitting up, the colour now returned to her face.

'I'm so sorry. You know, since David was killed in action, every time I hear of someone I know dying, it's as if I am falling down a big hole – as if I'm hearing the news of his death all over again.' She sipped her tea. 'And if this war goes the way of the last, I suppose I will hear that news over and over again, only this time it will be the sons of women I knew when I was a girl – those who were lucky enough to be married.'

'I'm sorry, but I must ask you some questions.'

Littleton sighed. 'Yes, I suppose you must. I knew Rosie better than anyone else involved in the association, and I knew one of the dead men. The other doesn't really ring a bell.'

'I wonder if you wouldn't mind looking at this.' Maisie held out the framed photograph taken from Rosemary Hartley-Davies' house. 'It's quite old, from the war, and the faces aren't very distinct. Can you tell me anything about it?'

Littleton set down her cup and saucer on a side table and reached for the photograph. She shook her head.

'No one familiar to you?'

'Oh, no, it's not that. I looked at this photograph, and it was as if time had wrapped her arms around me. Look at the laughter – a sunny day in a hay field, people with broad smiles, and yet so much grief to weather. How could we ever smile in those days?'

'We did, though – and make no mistake, as bad as it was in France and Flanders, and in all those other places where men fought, there were times of laughter. Just because the circumstances might be almost intolerable does not mean there are not moments when the light shines in.' Maisie looked down at her hands and rubbed them together, remembering.

'Anyway, yes, I can tell you about this photograph. And it's simple, really – I was the photographer. Not terribly good, I confess, but I was on the other side of the camera.'

'Then what can you tell me about the young men either side of Rosemary?'

'It's coming back to me now. This one is Albert and this one is Frederick – until I saw his face, the name didn't click, but now it does. Gosh, I wish I could remember the names here – I think that one was Peter and the other Thomas. Or was his surname Thomas? I can't remember the others – it will probably come back to me later. And then there was this little scamp. I can't recall his name at all. He arrived in England alone, but with the older boys. I think his mother died on the walk through Belgium – though I could be mixing him up with someone else. But there were deaths on the journey. If you add malnutrition, thirst – and of course fear – those things could quickly conspire with some disease or another to bring them down.' Littleton looked down at the photograph again. 'This was taken on one of the farms Rosie's father owned. Rosie said they needed extra help with the haymaking, so she arranged for a number of the lads on our books who had either not yet found a job or were only getting piecemeal work to go down to Sussex – they stayed in the old hopper huts, and the farmer provided food and so on. I went down to visit, just for a couple of days. You could see how much good it was doing everyone – their cheeks were rosy, they'd put on weight, and for those lads, it helped to be doing a job of work in the open air. I mean, what were they? Fifteen or sixteen, something of that order. That was the summer of 1917, I think. Or was it 1916? I should remember, shouldn't I, but sometimes I look back and it's all a bit of a blur, with certain moments standing out. David was dead by then, killed at Neuve-Chapelle in early 1915 – so it was after that.'

'Could you find out the names of the other men for me?'

Littleton shook her head. 'Oh dear, I'm not really sure what happened to the records. At the end of the war we were assisting with repatriation, and of course Rosie had left the association by then, as her brother was in a military hospital in Surrey. I left too, to look after my mother – she'd gone down with that terrible flu, as had my father. It didn't kill them, but it certainly shortened their lives. Anyway, you don't want to know all that, do you?' She tapped the photograph against her palm. 'There is a woman who might well know if the files are still available. The association merged with another after the war, and of course when all the repatriation was done, it was disbanded, but the information might be lurking somewhere, though it could well be in several places. You see, we had a card file with basic information on everyone as they came in that we could get to quickly, then we began establishing proper records so we could assist with jobs and – with a bit of luck – refugee repatriation at the end of the war. We knew it had to happen eventually, even though at times we thought it would never end.' Littleton sighed. 'Anyway, you never know, these records might one day be important to someone.'

'They're fairly important to me, Miss Littleton. So if you can find out how I might have access to them, and a name of someone to contact, I would be very much obliged to you.'

'I'll do my best.' Littleton took Maisie's card from her pocket and looked at it again. '"M. Dobbs. Psychologist and investigator". That sounds very good, doesn't it? How does one get to do what you do?'

Maisie smiled and came to her feet. 'A long and arduous training, Miss Littleton.'

Clarice Littleton made as if to stand.

'I can let myself out,' said Maisie. 'You stay there, and I suggest you rest for the remainder of the afternoon.' She paused, wondering if she should add the caution she felt was necessary. 'One thing, Miss Littleton. Do take a measure of extra care – please do not just open the door to anyone, and use the chain on the door if necessary. I don't want you to live in fear, but you must consider your personal security. I believe Rosemary was killed because she knew something about the killer. You might not have the same knowledge – it sounds as if she'd been rather more involved in the lives of a number of the refugees. But your friendship with her and the work you did for the association render you vulnerable.'

'I can take care of myself, Miss Dobbs.'

'Not against a man with a revolver.'

Littleton rubbed her forehead. 'I'll see if I can find out about the files, then perhaps go to stay with an old friend in Norfolk. I can take some time off work.'

'You won't lose your job?'

The woman shrugged. 'It's not for the money – my parents left me well provided for, and I was the fortunate beneficiary of a maiden aunt on my father's side. I suppose it's the sunny side of being the only one left to carry the family name. I go to work to stop the walls drawing in and pressing me into the past.' She looked towards the photograph on the mantelpiece, then back at Maisie. 'But who would have believed it would come to this, twenty-odd years after the Armistice? I don't see how someone could commit murder, not when there's been so much death and going to be more. Goodness, how on earth do you do your job?'

Maisie rested her hand on the door handle, ready to leave. 'I do it for the dead, Miss Littleton, and for those left behind. And when I've done my job, Justice has to carry the weight.'

Maisie did not at once leave the neighbourhood. There was a small park opposite the street where Clarice Littleton lived, so Maisie chose a seat and watched the entrance to the flats. There were several passers-by, none who drew special attention. All were carrying gas masks. A few raindrops fell, and Maisie wished she had brought an umbrella. But she remained in place, partly protected by the canopy of tree fronds overhead. Once again she looked at the barrage balloons bobbing in the sky above the buildings, finding their apparent lightness surprisingly soothing. It was just at the point when Maisie stood up to leave that she saw Clarice Littleton step out of the front door of the converted mansion, carrying a small case, her gas mask in its box with the strap over her shoulder, and a handbag. Littleton hailed a passing taxi-cab and was soon on her way. Maisie suspected the woman had elected to go to Norfolk sooner rather than later, a decision she considered sound. There had been a moment of recognition when Littleton reached the top of the stairs and saw her. Among the letters Littleton held in her hand was one written on stationery Maisie recognised. It was of course not an unusual stationery, but the smooth cream vellum was familiar, and used by at least one office of the Belgian embassy.

Before leaving Maida Vale, Maisie looked up the address of Albert Durant in her notebook and then took out her London map. The street was not far, and overlooked the Regent's Canal. Fortunately, the clouds had all but cleared and showers had passed. The address proved to be that of a grander terrace of mansion flats, not smaller conversions of what was once home to one well-to-do family. The property was significantly larger than the one that housed Clarice Littleton's abode.

The flat she was interested in was on the first floor above ground level, offering a residence of considerable size. Maisie imagined it to be light and airy, comprising a spacious drawing room with doors through to a dining room. Bedrooms would be on the other side of a wide hallway, and in recent years there would have been the addition of a bathroom and perhaps a separate lavatory. There would be a kitchen and even a scullery for the washing of clothes and other heavier chores. Maisie doubted the residents had a live-in housekeeper, though in all likelihood there was a daily, a woman who came in at six in the morning and remained until late afternoon, a woman who would cook and clean, who could wash some laundry and sort the rest to send out. And there would of course have been a nursery, decorated in anticipation of the new arrival. Maisie thought she knew how Durant must have felt following his wife's death in childbirth, for hadn't she returned to a flat in Toronto following the passing of her husband and stillborn child? And hadn't she broken down on the threshold of the nursery, a sweet room painted in shades of shell and sky, with a crib empty, and the counterpane drawn back, as if awaiting the child who would never come home?

And she wondered, now, if the killer had known of his victim's sorrow. Had he known this man might well have welcomed the bullet that took his life, that put an end to the terrible thoughts and nightmares that must have tortured him? Or could she be projecting her own emotions, because she had endured a similar loss? While

Maurice had always encouraged imagination, he had also cautioned against such leaps of creative thought, telling her that just because she would feel a certain way in a given set of circumstances, she must not conclude that her feelings were universal. It was sometimes hard to reconcile his lessons, but in time she had come to understand the importance of grounding intuition and speculation in truths she discovered along the way.

It was clear Durant had some consideration of the future, because he was on his way to deposit funds at another bank – the most efficient means of investment, as he'd informed a colleague. Or could that have just been his training? Perhaps it was second nature for him to move money around as if he were playing a tactical game.

Maisie approached the front door of the building and was poised to ring the bell to summon the caretaker when it was drawn back and a young man emerged, almost bumping into Maisie.

'Oh, Miss Dobbs. What a surprise to see you here.' The man paused. 'Well, perhaps not, considering the work you're undertaking for Dr Thomas and our department.'

'It's Mr Lambert, isn't it?' Maisie held out her hand, in part to watch as Lambert passed a clutch of documents from one hand to the other, enabling him to take her hand. 'And I am surprised to see *you* here, but by the same token, perhaps not, in the circumstances.'

The young man met Maisie's eyes. 'I had to find some paperwork with regard to Mr Durant's period of residence here in Britain, for consular purposes. The police gave permission, and I was provided with a key, which has to go back to the police station.' He paused. 'I would have thought you should've been given leave to inspect the flat, all things considered.' He consulted his watch. 'Shall I show you up? I have time.'

'Thank you – yes, I would appreciate seeing where Mr Durant lived.'

Lambert led the way to the dead man's flat, and opened the door with a key on a fob with a silver lion's head.

'Were those the keys found on the deceased?' asked Maisie.

Lambert nodded. 'Yes. They were at Scotland Yard, and I had to present myself there to receive them. A Sergeant Able helped me.'

'Oh, yes, I know him. Tell me, do you know if there was a guard on the flat at any point following Mr Durant's death?'

'I believe there was for a couple of days while the Murder Squad men did their work, but not since.'

Lambert left the keys on the stand in the hall. It was made of dark wood and comprised a mirror, several hooks for hats, and others at the side for coats. Two umbrellas were poked through a hole in the centre of the stand, with a porcelain bowl on a ledge underneath to catch water, should the umbrella have been brought in wet. Another series of smaller hooks underneath the mirror held a few keys and a clothes brush. Maisie imagined Durant leaving for his job in the City every morning, perhaps checking his tie and brushing off his jacket before leaving the house, or if it was winter, putting on his heavy coat and gloves, taking up his keys, and then opening the door to be on his way. She wondered if his wife used the brush, if she picked specks of lint from his shoulders and drew him towards her for a kiss before seeing him off for his day of work.

The flat was more or less as Maisie imagined, though the kitchen was larger and the dining room less spacious. If one of the bedrooms had been decorated for a new baby, Maisie could not tell which one it was. There was nothing in the flat to indicate that it was the home of anyone other than a man without a wife, though perhaps one who liked a few feminine touches.

In the corner of the dining room a roll-top desk had been left open. 'Was that open when you came in, Mr Lambert?' asked Maisie.

'Yes, it was – fortunately, because I didn't have a key for it, and the identification documents and passport were in there.'

'I'm surprised the police didn't take them,' said Maisie.

Lambert shrugged. 'I'm not, and neither is Dr Thomas. The reason she asked for your assistance is because Scotland Yard have seemed less than willing to work a bit harder on these two cases.'

'In their defence, Mr Lambert, they are somewhat overwhelmed at the present time, and it is a difficult case. Not much in the way of clues.' She stepped towards the desk. 'I'll just have a quick look here.'

Maisie leafed through a series of bills, some receipts, and other items of little interest. A ledger kept in a fine hand offered a precise accounting of household finances and notes on economies and the odd purchase considered extravagant. A small pile of correspondence tied with string revealed cards and letters of condolence. A folder in the top drawer contained various notes in connection with the dead man's deceased wife, and a death certificate confirming her passing was due to an embolism, which also led to the death of the unborn child. Details of the funeral revealed that the woman had been cremated, though there were no notes indicating a final resting place for the ashes. The last item in the folder was a photograph of a woman wearing walking clothes – a pair of long shorts, a short-sleeved blouse, and strong leather lace-up boots. With one hand she was holding back fair, windswept hair, and in the other she held her knapsack. She was standing at the edge of a field, with woods to her left – Maisie could clearly see ridges in the field, carved by a plough. In the background, one had the impression of a hillside.

'Anything of interest?' asked Lambert.

Maisie sighed. 'No, nothing really. Just an old photograph. It might prove to be useful.' She slipped the photograph into her jacket pocket and closed the drawer. She reached down to open the second drawer, but as she pulled it towards her, she heard a rattle. She closed the drawer and opened it again. Once more the rattle sounded.

'That's a very old desk,' said Lambert, looking at his watch.

'Yes, it is. I just don't want the drawer to get stuck on anything – it can take ages to put this sort of thing right.' She knelt down and pulled out the drawer partway, turning back to Lambert. 'Did you look in here?'

He shook his head. 'No, everything I wanted – passport and identification papers – was in that little cubbyhole at the top, so I left the drawers alone. I felt a bit bad touching anything, actually – it's all personal, isn't it? I was just keen to get the things I was asked to find, and get out of the flat.'

'Are you scared?' Maisie asked, turning back to the drawer. She squeezed her hand in, turning it so her palm faced the underside of the drawer above.

'It gives me the shivers, Miss Dobbs. This is the house of three dead people – a man, his wife, and their not-yet-born child. To be perfectly honest, the sooner we leave, the better. I only wanted to fulfil my task and then report back to Dr Thomas.'

Maisie removed her hand, took a clean linen handkerchief from her bag, and reached back into the drawer. 'You're going to have more to report than you expected, Mr Lambert.' She withdrew her hand again and held up a revolver, her linen handkerchief protecting the integrity of any fingerprints remaining on the grip. 'This thing, for a start. It looks like a Browning, but I believe it's known as a Ruby. I think we should take a taxi-cab directly to Scotland Yard. Caldwell is not going to like this at all.'

Lambert stepped back, the colour draining from his face. 'Won't he be pleased you found it?'

Maisie shook her head. 'I doubt it – because either his men missed it when they made their own search, which I concede was probably cursory. Or it was used to kill four people and brought here once the job was done – which means it is as clean as a whistle, because only the most careless criminal would leave his fingerprints all over a murder weapon. And the other scenario is that it was indeed the property of the dead man.'

'Pity he didn't have it with him on the day he died,' said Lambert.

Maisie looked at Lambert. 'Surprisingly, I don't think he was that kind of man, though if it was his revolver, I would like to know why he had possession of it in the first place.'

CHAPTER ELEVEN

'Miss Dobbs, I just knew it the moment you walked in here the other day, that you would start making my life a misery again.' Caldwell held up the revolver, with Maisie's linen handkerchief still wrapped around it, and let it swing back and forth. 'I'll send it down to our weapons man and see what he thinks. You were wise to keep it clean, but my guess is that there is not one dab to be found.' He looked up from the gun. 'Do we still have yours on file?'

'Let's do them again – it was a while ago, so we should make sure.'

'And you didn't see or touch this thing, sonny?' Caldwell looked at Lambert.

Lambert shook his head, his eyes widening. 'Absolutely not, Inspector!'

'No, I wouldn't have thought so.' He sighed. 'Right then, we've got your statement, Mr Lambert, so you're free to go. I hope we haven't breached any consular agreements keeping you here for a bit.'

'I'm sure it's all perfectly all right, Inspector.' Lambert came to his feet, turning to Maisie. 'I'm glad you came along when you did. Thank you.'

Maisie gave a brief nod. Though no words were spoken, she knew Lambert understood the message in her eyes: she would be in touch with his superior later.

Lambert appeared to shuffle out of the small office, as if he were afraid to allow his lanky frame the freedom of a long stride lest he knock over a chair or a pile of papers. He closed the door behind him, and through the glass Maisie saw Sergeant Able approach to lead him out.

Caldwell shook his head. 'They're like two peas in a pod – all arms and feet and a bit dozy with it. Both still going on fifteen, by the looks of them.'

Maisie made no comment on Caldwell's observation. 'Let's get my fingerprints done, shall we? And that gun inspected.'

Caldwell and Maisie stood up at the same time.

'You seem quiet, Miss Dobbs.'

'It's nothing, Inspector. Just thinking.'

'Oh, I wouldn't do that if I were you. Bad for the constitution.'

The revolver was confirmed to be a Ruby, although the 'weapons man' had not yet come to a conclusion about when it was last fired. Maisie did not expect an easy answer. She had known as soon as she looked at the gun that it had been cleaned well and by someone who knew how to look after a revolver. Although it often seemed like yesterday, some eighteen months earlier Maisie had been pressed into work with the Secret Service, which in turn required she learn to use a gun – and part of her training was in understanding the importance of cleaning her weapon to military standards, ensuring that every speck of dust was removed whenever it lay dormant, so that when the time came to use it, she could feel confident her revolver was in full working order. She made her way back to Fitzroy Square, pondering the fact that the same brand of revolver had been discovered twice – one at the scene of Rosemary Hartley-Davies' death, and one in Albert Durant's flat. It had also been implicated in the killing of both Durant and Frederick Addens.

Billy was already at his desk when Maisie entered the office.

'Hallo, miss. Ready for a cuppa? I know you think I do nothing but drink tea all day, but you look all in. A cup would do you the power of good.'

'I'm all right, Billy – perhaps later. Did you find Mike Elliot? And what about the publican at the Crown and Anchor? Come on in and tell me what you've found out.'

Billy followed, notebook in hand. Although he'd loosened his tie, he had kept his jacket on. He took a seat alongside Maisie at the table as she pulled out her own notebook.

'Did you find that woman – the one who worked with Rosemary Hartley-Davies during the war?' asked Billy.

'I did indeed. She's very strong, forthright. And though I don't think she was fearful when I first arrived, by the time I left, she had changed her mind and seemed rather unsettled. Mind you, that's hardly surprising.' Maisie went on to recount the events that followed her visit to see Clarice Littleton.

'And you reckon she's in Norfolk somewhere.'

'I do, and I would like to know where, exactly, she is.'

'I'll see what I can find out, if you like.'

'Thank you, Billy.'

'And what do you make of the Ruby in Albert Durant's flat?'

'I don't know. It could be a weapon he'd had for years – perhaps even before he left Belgium. It begs the questions, why did he have the gun, and how did he obtain it? And who owned the revolver – same type – used to kill Rosemary Hartley-Davies?'

'Well, miss, Durant had it for protection, I would imagine. And if there were a lot of them guns around, it might not have been so hard to get your hands on one.'

'But what if he'd obtained the Ruby since coming here. Why?'

'Again, for protection – possibly.'

'Which brings us back to square one – who was he afraid of? You don't expect a banker to be afraid for his life, do you, Billy?'

Billy frowned. 'You did about ten years ago! But you're right, miss, we need to find out the names of the other men in that photograph. I mean, it's a thread, and you're always saying we have to pick at the fabric until we find a loose thread. They might not have known him that well, but there again, finding one might lead to someone else.'

The telephone rang. Billy stood to answer it at Maisie's desk. He gave the office number, and listened.

'Just a moment, Miss Littleton,' said Billy, before holding out the receiver for Maisie to take.

Maisie looked up and reached for the telephone. She nodded to Billy, indicating that he should remain in the room.

'Miss Littleton. It seems I left you only a short time ago – is everything all right?'

'Yes. Yes, I'm all right. Look, I'm in a telephone kiosk, and I don't have many coins on me. I remembered the names of the two other men – Carl Firmin and Lucas Peters, though I think he spelt it with two e's, so it's P-double-e-t-e-r-s. And he might have changed it by now.'

Maisie pulled a notepad towards her and began to write. 'Yes, I've got that. Have you any idea where I can find them?'

'I know where the records are – from the association. Rosie passed them all on to another refugee association, I think in Greenwich. I can't tell you any more than that – I've tried, but I can't recall the name of the woman who runs it.'

'But about Peeters and Firmin – do you have any idea where I might find them?'

'No, I'm sorry – and I must go n—'

She heard a series of beeps, the telephone signal for more coins to be put into the slot and button 'A' to be pushed. But no more coins were forthcoming, and the line disconnected.

'Anything for us, miss?'

'We have to find two men, a Lucas Peeters' – Maisie pushed her notepad towards Billy so he could see the spelling – 'and Carl Firmin. If they are in the telephone directory, it shouldn't be too hard. On the other hand, if they aren't, then it's back to the drawing board, the lists, and asking a lot of questions.'

'Just a tick,' said Billy. He left his chair and went through to the main office, returning with the London telephone directory. 'Well, Firmin's here. Want me to find him?'

Maisie shook her head. 'I'll go – and I'll not telephone first. I don't want to give anyone a chance to leave. And I'll visit this association in Greenwich – I'm sure it's on Sandra's list.' She made a note of the telephone call on another sheet of paper. 'So, Billy, what about Mike Elliot?'

'Nice bloke. Seems as if he was easy-going – once upon a time, anyway. He works on the railways, but not at St Pancras. I found him at Euston – they'd transferred him up the road there after the business with Addens and him having to identify the body. Turns out he met Frederick Addens when they were both apprentices, and they became pally, you know, had a drink after work every now and again. Mike worked in another part of the station and would wander over to see if Frederick was there and wanted to have a swift half-pint after work, that sort of thing.'

'Anything interesting?'

'This Mike was still sort of shaken about it all. Said he couldn't think why anyone would want to kill Addens – unless it was to steal whatever he had on him at the time, and of course we know now that he had more than a little bit on him, on account of having been given his wages and having overtime paid on top. Elliot said he was a good worker, quiet but not standoffish, and good to his wife and children. Mike said that if he asked Frederick to have a second pint, he would always say no, had to get back to the family.'

'But nothing about any worries or concerns?' said Maisie.

Billy shook his head. 'Not exactly, but he did say that Addens had a cross to bear. He said he put it down to his background – not that he'd spoken much about it to Mike. But Mike said Addens couldn't stand any discord, any argy-bargy at work, and even when they were younger, he would always step in if there was a bit of nastiness between a couple of the blokes they were working with. He said it was always the same, he would say, "Don't argue, because arguments lead to battles and battles become wars and we all know where they lead." Anyway, Mike said he asked him about it once, why he was so touchy about it – I mean, they all knew what war meant, didn't they? – and he just shrugged and said, "I saw too much death, Mikey, to leave it alone."'

Maisie nodded, imagining a younger Frederick Addens pouring oil on troubled waters, smoothing tempers and ironing out disputes. And she wondered about the death he had seen before his escape from occupied Belgium.

'And did you get anything from the landlord at the Crown and Anchor?'

'Oh, good old Smitty, the drinker's friend!'

'Smitty?' said Maisie.

'He was all very chatty, very welcoming. Name of Phil Smith, but the locals all call him Smitty.'

'I knew you'd have better luck than me.'

'And I've saved the juiciest morsel for last, miss.'

'Go on.'

'I showed him that photo of Albert Durant, and he said he's not one hundred per cent sure, but he reckons he might have seen him a week or so before Addens was murdered.'

'That's as near a thread as we've managed to get so far,' said Maisie.

'He wasn't entirely certain, but I reckon there's a good chance. Turns out the man came in after a Sunday darts match, when all the lads were having a drink to celebrate another win. He walks in and taps Addens on the shoulder – Smitty noticed it because, apparently, this bloke was well dressed, looking every inch the City type. Addens turns round, big beaming smile on his face, and then Durant – well, the man we reckon is him – whispers something to him, and they go over to the corner table and sit and talk, heads close together. Smitty said it wouldn't have surprised him if Frederick Addens didn't start to weep, his face was so torn. Said that he assumed the other bloke was an official visitor, bringing news of someone they'd both known who'd died. Frederick didn't say much, according to Smitty – he just plonked money for his shout on the bar, said thank you, and they left.' Billy paused, looking at Maisie. 'What do you think, miss?'

'One part of me believes there is a very strong argument for this visitor being Durant, and that there was a connection between the two that began when they were refugees and continued through their time in England. On the one hand, it's hardly surprising that there was some communication between them, but on the other, I wonder what news he brought that could have led to a reaction so obvious that Smitty remembered it weeks on.'

'I was wondering that too,' said Billy, running his fingers back through his hair.

For a fleeting moment Maisie thought she should tell him to be aware of the habit, for beyond Billy's fringe his hairline was receding, and he might be making it worse. But perhaps the constant running of fingers along his scalp had nothing to do with the loss of hair. It was just Billy getting older. 'I want to know if they knew each other before they came here,' she said, her tone resolute. 'We know they came from the same area, but that doesn't mean they knew each other.'

'This is where you wish they were from over here, then you could just whip to wherever they came from and have a word with the neighbours.'

'Hmmm.' Maisie doodled on the edge of the case map with a red wax crayon, feeling Billy's eyes upon her.

'Miss, what with the train services stopped all over the place, I can tell you right now that you could never get over there. Even for a day. And it's not only the trains and ferries that have stopped going to the Continent – there's no aeroplanes going either, not for us civvies, anyway, as far as I know – so that idea won't work.'

Maisie looked up at Billy. 'You've heard that old phrase, haven't you? "There's more than one way to skin a cat."'

'I never liked that one. I mean, who would want to skin a poor cat anyway?'

Maisie stood up and went to her desk, lifting the telephone receiver as she looked up at Billy. 'I read that it refers to catfish – they're from America somewhere, and the people there call them "cats". It's about skinning a fish. And there's one or two different ways to do it.' She began to dial. 'I could do with that cup of tea now, Billy – I know you're gasping, and you do make the best strong brew.'

Billy gathered his notebook and pen and left the room, knowing Maisie was sending him from her office because the telephone call she was about to make was private – and they both understood why.

Maisie dialled a number known to her by heart.

'Yes!' a voice boomed, its timbre rich and round, with a resonance suggesting weight and strength – and that the man who answered would not suffer a fool gladly.

Maisie held the receiver away from her ear for a second, then brought it back to speak.

'Hello, Robbie,' said Maisie.

'Hello, lassie. And if it's Robbie you're calling me, and not MacFarlane, then you're about to try to butter me up, and this is not a good day to try any buttering.'

'I didn't expect it to be, Robbie. But I need your help.'

'What can I do for you? And please make it easy.'

'I think you owe me one or two favours, don't you?'

'Aye, lass, I do. More than one or two. So go on, tell me what it is.'

Maisie paused, wondering if she wasn't making a great error in taking Robert MacFarlane into her confidence. But on the other hand, it wouldn't be a stretch to assume Robbie knew everything she was working on anyway.

'Hurry up, lassie – I've not got all day. The clock is ticking, the sun is nowhere near the yardarm anywhere in the British Isles, and my patience is being tested.'

'Do you know if I could get on a government aeroplane to Brussels?'

'What do you want in Brussels?'

'I would like to travel on from there – I'll give you more information as soon as I can. I just want to talk to a few people. A day's work at most. I would jump at the chance of a driver if you could get me one, and of course I will pay all costs.'

'No.'

'Robbie, is that "No, there are no aeroplanes leaving for Brussels"? Or "No, you can't get on an aeroplane"? Or is it "No, you don't have to pay because we still owe you money"?'

'It's "No, because I won't let you fly into danger."'

'You didn't mind in 1938, did you?'

'That was different.'

'Yes, it was far more dangerous. This is just to get some answers to questions, and I'm not going there to do business with Nazis.'

There was silence on the line, though Maisie could hear MacFarlane breathing, then turning the pages of a book. He swore in a whisper and returned to the call.

'You don't like flying – in fact, you hate it.'

'I can do it if need be, as we both know. What about it, Robbie?'

'It can be arranged. The aeroplane will not be leaving from Croydon or anywhere fancy now, and it won't be comfortable – you're likely to be in a Lysander normally used for aerial surveillance, and it will be landing in a field, not an airport in Brussels. But I daresay I can get a motor and driver for you, if you're not in the bushes losing your breakfast.'

Maisie shook her head, though she was never surprised at Robert MacFarlane's colourful turn of phrase. 'Thank you, Robbie. When do I leave?'

'I'll let you know, but it won't be immediate. Strings will have to be tugged in a good many places, and I will say here and now it's not without danger, lass. Things might have been quiet since war was declared, and as we know our friends over there in Belgium have again declared their position of "armed neutrality", but the Luftwaffe boys could be out in force any time – any time – and you could be in their sights. A Lysander was never built to go to war, only for reconnaissance and that sort of thing, whatever these boys do.'

'I've been in Luftwaffe sights before, Robbie. I'll be all right.' Maisie took a breath as Billy knocked on the door. 'I'll hear from you soon, then. And thank you.'

'It'll cost you a dram or two, lassie.'

Maisie laughed, and replaced the receiver. She looked up at the door. 'Come in, Billy.'

'Here you are – nice cup of tea, good and strong,' said Billy. 'That'll get us through the war – though they say it'll go on rationing soon enough.'

'Tea?'

'Yes, tea – along with everything else.' Billy set a cup and saucer on the table. Maisie came around from her desk and took her seat once again.

'I don't know why I bother to read the news. I should just wait to get it all from you every day, complete with a running commentary on my personal safety preparations.'

'If I was doing that, I'd tell you not to go,' said Billy.

Maisie reached for her tea and lifted the cup. 'We'd better make the best of this, then – and might as well stockpile a few bags of Brooke Bond, or we'll never get through the war.'

'I just hope you know what you're doing, miss.'

'I'll be all right, Billy. This is important. And I'm only going to Greenwich, and to – where does this Firmin man live?'

'Lewisham.'

'Lewisham – I'll go there first tomorrow morning, then on to Greenwich. Not too bad a journey. And quite safe, don't you think?'

'Unlike Belgium,' said Billy.

Maisie left early the following morning to allow for delays, though traffic diversions put in place to allow for the evacuation of children and movement of troops in the days immediately following the declaration of war had been lifted. It was just before ten o'clock that Maisie knocked on the door of a Victorian terrace house just off Lewisham Way. She waited a moment or two and knocked again. Soon footsteps could be heard, and the door opened. The woman who stood before Maisie had her blonde hair pulled up in a kerchief and wore a blue boiler suit, but no shoes. The boiler suit was cinched at the waist with a belt of a different shade, as if the woman were trying to grasp a last vestige of femininity while wearing men's clothing. She was about thirty-five years of age, and before speaking, she took a cigarette from her mouth and blew smoke upward. She tapped ash to the side, just missing the step.

'Whatever it is, love, I don't want any – I can barely make ends meet as it is.' She stepped back, ready to close the door on Maisie.

'Mrs Firmin? Mrs Firmin, I am not selling anything – I wanted to speak to your husband.'

'I can't pay you back, whatever it was for – and if you want to speak to him, you'd better know how to get to the other side, because he's not on this one any more.'

'I'm so very sorry – and I am not looking to extract money from you. Could you spare me a moment or two?'

'What do you want?'

Maisie looked around at other houses on the street. 'Probably best not to speak on the doorstep.'

The woman sighed, stepping inside and pulling back the door for Maisie to enter. 'You can come in, but you take me as you find me. I don't have time to run around with a duster and broom, and it's all I can do to get a line of washing done these days.'

'Thank you, Mrs Firmin.' Maisie stepped into the passageway, noticing a broom leaning against the wall with a small pile of debris behind it, as if someone had started sweeping the carpet and then abandoned the job.

'Might as well go into the parlour – on the right, first door. Don't breathe in – I think it was last cleaned a month ago, and what with the railway, all you get is dust everywhere. I bet they have dirt from Lewisham landing in snooty Mayfair, the way things are going.'

Maisie stepped into the parlour and took a seat in the armchair nearest the cold fire grate. The armchair was part of a 'three-piece suite' and was probably a good number of years old – not ancient by any means, though the design was very much a hallmark of the previous decade. Faded tapestry upholstery and curved wooden arms reflected an Art Deco styling. A variety of framed family photographs hung from a picture rail, and above the fireplace a mirror was secured with a solid brass hook and a sturdy chain.

Firmin seated herself on the settee, close to the arm. A table next to the settee held a lamp and an ashtray. She pulled the ashtray closer, took a packet of cigarettes and a box of matches from the breast pocket of her boiler suit, and lit up. She shook out the flame of the match and dropped it in the ashtray. 'I'd offer you one, but I can tell you're not the type.' She inhaled deeply on the cigarette and flicked ash on top of the match. 'I don't sit in here much, but my mother liked it. This was her place – rented, of course – but it's only me here now, and I spend more of my time back in the kitchen. Lucky the rent is fixed, or I'd be out on my ear.'

'Mrs Firmin, this is my card.' Maisie passed her calling card to Firmin. 'As you can see, I am an investigator. My client, one who has sympathies with the Belgian people, has asked me to look into the deaths of two former refugees who made new lives for themselves here during the war. And like your husband, they both remained in the country after the Armistice.'

'My husband is dead, Miss Dobbs.' Firmin looked at the card and placed it on the table, next to the ashtray. 'And I doubt there's anything I can help you with.'

'Let's see, shall we? First of all, when did your husband pass away, Mrs Firmin?'

'A year ago. August 1938. Probably best he went, because he couldn't have stood this – barrage balloons, sandbags, armies on the march, and us just waiting for bombs to drop.'

'How did Carl die?'

'Died by his own hand.' Firmin drew on her cigarette and blew a smoke ring. 'Got on a train, went down to Folkestone, and bang!

Put a gun to his noddle and topped himself. Not very pretty, and I had to identify him by a scar on his leg – he copped it in Belgium, when he was coming over. Apparently a group of them made their escape together, though a couple wouldn't leave without their families. Something happened on the way – he wouldn't talk about it – and he was wounded. I never found out how he'd been hurt – would you believe a man could be that close-mouthed with his own wife? It could have been a knife, a bullet, falling over an axe – who knows?'

Maisie made a note in her book. 'He died in Folkestone, August 1938.'

'Better get it all in. The fourth of August, it was.'

Maisie stopped, and looked up at the woman. 'The fourth of August?'

'What – that your birthday or something?' She shrugged. 'He always got a bit on edge that time of year, and I just left him to it. He said it was on account of the memories, of things that happened, you know, in the war. He'd been over there, back to Belgium, for a visit a couple of months earlier. He was only gone about three days. I couldn't go with him – we didn't have the money for that – but I could see he had to go.'

'Did he ever say anything specific about those memories?' said Maisie.

'Not a peep,' said the woman, drawing on her cigarette again. She pressed the stub into the ashtray and leant towards Maisie. 'Is this going to take long? I've been at the factory since the middle of the night, and I don't have a lot of time to myself to get a bit of shut-eye and do something human before I go back there again.'

'I'm so sorry – just one more thing.' Maisie took photographs of

Frederick Addens and Albert Durant from her bag. 'Have you ever seen either of these men?'

Firmin reached for the photographs. She shook her head. 'No, never met either of them. Why?'

Maisie nodded. 'I'm afraid they're both dead, and I believe they were acquainted with your husband. The first died in August, the other a few weeks later.' She replaced the photographs in her bag.

Firmin shook her head, pinched out the cigarette, stood up, and put the remains in her pocket. 'Well, I've never seen them.' She turned towards the door.

Maisie came to her feet and followed Firmin. 'Did Carl keep in touch with any friends from Belgium, others that came to this country?'

'Not as far as I know.' She led Maisie towards the front door. 'The only Belgian I ever met was that woman from the embassy, or consulate, or whatever you call it.'

'Really? Someone came after your husband died?'

'Not that long afterwards. I suppose they had to inform the authorities of his death – the police did that. She came to offer her condolences. Nice woman, very smart, quite sophisticated, like a mannequin, I suppose.' As they reached the front of the house, Firmin turned the lock, opened the door, and stood aside for Maisie to pass. 'Mind you,' she added, 'I saw her reach into her bag – she leant over, just like you did to take out those photographs – and when she did, her scarf slipped. She had a nasty scar right across her neck. At first I thought it looked as if someone had tried to take off her head, but then I thought, no, she must have had a thyroid operation. They say you're left with a very nasty scar if they get in there and mess about with your thyroid.'

'Thank you, Mrs Firmin.' Maisie turned to her and smiled. 'By the way, most remiss of me – may I ask your Christian name?'

'Irma. Irma Firmin. Hard to believe, isn't it? I said to Carl when he proposed, I said, "You couldn't change that name of yours, could you?"' She laughed. 'Anyway, sorry for being rude, but I've got to get some sleep now.'

Maisie thanked her for her time, and made her way down the steps and to her motor car, which now had a gaggle of three boys and a girl gathered around like bees on a rose.

'This your'n, miss?' said a lad with red hair and a peppering of freckles across his nose.

'No, it belongs to my boss – so I hope it's not scratched, or he'll give me the sack and a bag to carry it in,' said Maisie, smiling as she paused to find her key. 'Anyway, why aren't you all evacuated? And shouldn't you be in school?'

The tallest boy laughed. 'Our mum said she missed us and came down to fetch us home. She said there hadn't been any bombs, and it looked like that Mr Hitler had forgotten all about England – he's got more on his plate over there. And when we got back here, there was nowhere to go to school – the army are in our school now. Mind you, the school-board man has been round and said we've got to go back down to the country, but Mum said no.'

Maisie looked at the barrage balloons above, and then at the four children, alone in a street with no other children. She reached into her bag, took out her purse, and handed a coin to each child. 'Here comes the ice-cream man – treat yourselves to a penny dipper each.'

The children's eyes widened as they looked at the coins, uttering a quick 'Thank you' in unison as they turned and ran towards the ice-cream man on his bicycle. Maisie smiled for an instant, but her thoughts were elsewhere. In her mind's eye she could see the scar on Francesca Thomas' neck, a wound sustained while a young woman, and member of the Belgian resistance during the Great War. But Thomas had prevailed in that fight, killing the man responsible for the death of her husband.

CHAPTER TWELVE

The London Overseas Reception Board was only a short walk from Greenwich Market. It was situated on the first floor of a modest Victorian building with a shop on the ground floor and a dwelling above. Maisie had managed to park the Alvis nearby, and waited until the manageress, Miss Golding, could spare her ten minutes. She suspected there were only about three or four staff, all told.

A young woman who introduced herself as Miss Hatcher led Maisie to a room with a table and chairs in the centre, though around the walls were boxes in various stages of leaning to the point where it seemed they might fall at any moment. Golding was standing alongside the table leafing through a file as Maisie entered. At first glance she appeared to be a no-nonsense sort of woman. Her dark brown hair was permed into tight curls, reminding Maisie of winkles, the tiny black shellfish her father favoured with bread and butter and a lettuce, tomato, and cucumber salad for Sunday tea. Her cotton blouse was starched, and she was dressed in a jacket and skirt costume of pale green wool barathea. Her appearance was in stark contrast to her employee, whose blonde hair was so fair it might have been coloured at home, and who had enhanced the silhouette of her fashionable narrow dress with a leather belt that matched her wedge sandals. Golding wore brown shoes that Maisie thought were akin to a style that a school headmistress might have termed 'sensible'.

Golding looked up. 'Thank you, Miss Hatcher, that will be all.' She inclined her head in the direction of a chair, and Maisie took a seat. Without offering a greeting, Golding continued, 'Miss Dobbs. I looked up the names you've furnished us with, and yes, it seems we have records for the men. I just have to lay my hands on them in one of these boxes. As you know, they were passed on to us by the Ladies' Refugee Assistance Association years ago. Normally it would have taken me ages to find them, but we've been having a huge sort out to make more room – and we're moving to larger premises soon, in any case. We weren't at all sure what to do with these records, and then the government stepped in. Most of the men and women who came through our original association – and the one Rosemary Hartley-Davies worked for – returned home after the war, and of those who remained, well, they're here in Britain now, and no one knows any difference, do they?' Golding chattered on as she opened a heavy-duty cardboard box and began pulling out folders. 'Mind you, we've had enquiries here about Belgian citizens, mainly to confirm details provided to the authorities when they arrived – I mean, as far as the population's concerned, some of them could have been deserting Germans who now want to desert back the other way, couldn't they? Personally, I'm worried that this vigilance is all going to get out of control, and anyone with a bit of an accent is going to be reported, or even worse. People start taking matters into their own hands, don't they?'

Maisie was about to respond when Golding resumed her

monologue. 'Ah, here we are, yes, all in one box together.' She put the box to one side and stacked the folders on the desk in front of her, then looked at Maisie, one hand tapping the pile of folders. 'The reason they are in the same place is that they came in on the same day, or thereabouts.' She opened one file after another, studying the first page before moving on. 'And it seems they all lived in roughly the same area.' Golding tapped an open file. 'I don't know much about the geography of Belgium, but there's a line for a comment here regarding place of birth and residence, and name of nearest large town or city, and it seems these men – Peeters, Firmin, Addens, and Durant – all came from the same region, or thereabouts. You will also see that there are other files here too, other boys, women, and children who were on the same boat. Of course, these men would have been too young to join the fighting – they were still boys, for the most part.' She pushed the folders towards Maisie. 'You might as well look through these yourself – I've checked your particulars with Scotland Yard, and in any case, there's nothing there that seems top secret in that lot, so I might as well save myself some time and hand them over to you. You can stay here in this office if you like – but not for long, as I've got a couple of my girls coming in soon to start boxing up files ready for transport up to London.'

'Where will they go?'

'Our instructions are to send them to the Home Office in the first instance, where the information will be catalogued. I've an inkling, though, that they'll be sent to the Belgian consulate – after all, it's their people and it's part of their history now, isn't it?' Golding stepped towards the door. 'Right then – I'll be back in fifteen minutes or so.'

She was gone before Maisie could thank her, so she reached into her bag for her pencil and notebook, which she opened to a blank page.

She laid out the folders and picked up each one in turn. The ages of the young men when they arrived in England were similar – fourteen, fifteen, sixteen. As Golding had observed, little more than boys. And confirming Golding's comment, Maisie could see that they all came from an area not far from Liege. She wrote down the first and last names of each man, along with details of any family members he had travelled with. Death, it seemed, had stalked them on their journey to the coast, for by the time they reached England, several were alone in the world – except, perhaps, for one other.

While there was not much of note in the files, Maisie jotted questions as she read. Did the young men know each other? If so, how? There was nothing to indicate common schooling – only the proximity to Liege – that in itself would have drawn them into a tight group. She had hoped there were at least two who came from the same community, who knew the same people. But then, why would these boys have known each other, apart from managing to find a way onto the same boat for a crossing of the English Channel? Could they have met on the journey, the arduous walk to freedom? Maisie sat back, considering her questions, reaching for each file in turn and reading a second time before stacking them in a pile. She consulted her wristwatch, and could hear voices in the corridor signalling that Golding's 'girls' were on their way to begin preparing the boxes for transit to London. She closed her notebook, but before leaving the room, she pulled the box towards her and leafed through a few remaining files – mainly women and children, a few more boys. She lingered over the final file. Something was amiss, though she could not quite put her finger on what was making her go back and forth, rereading every note on the refugee.

Miss Hatcher entered the room, with another young woman

following her. They both held shorthand notebooks and pencils.

'Sorry, Miss Dobbs, but we have to get to work in here now. I hope you've found everything you've been looking for.'

'Do you happen to know what might have happened to this one?' Maisie passed the folder to Hatcher, who took a cursory look at the information – most of the pages contained only short answers to mundane questions.

Hatcher shrugged. 'Not much information there – he couldn't even write a full name. But as far as I know, some children arrived on their own and couldn't speak or write in English. I would have thought someone of this age would have been situated with a Belgian family who'd already found accommodation, or placed in a children's home. There were also British families of Belgian extraction who took in refugees. There's no forwarding information, so I would imagine this one was sent back to his home country, eventually.' She placed the file in the box and looked at Maisie. 'Anything else we can do?'

Maisie shook her head. 'No, that's all right – I've gathered as much as I can from the notes. I'm obliged to you for your help.'

She returned to the motor car and sat for a while, the engine idling, before putting it into gear and moving off into traffic. She knew it was even more imperative now that she reach Lucas Peeters – perhaps for no other reason than to save his life.

At the office, Maisie read a note from Billy, and another from Sandra, who had come to work after Maisie's departure, and left before her return. Telephone calls had been received, and their messages transcribed in Sandra's neat hand, with time and date recorded, along with a personal note regarding her impression of each call's urgency. There were messages from Lady Rowan Compton regarding the imminent arrival of Rosemary Hartley-Davies' brother. Maisie had arranged for Robert Miller to be brought to Chelstone Manor on Wednesday morning, but just for a fortnight at most, as it transpired that a cousin with whom his family had been in touch only sporadically over the years had offered accommodation at his home in Wiltshire. Miller, it seemed, was not without funds, as both he and his sister had inherited money from their parents, and Rosemary had received a significant legacy from her late husband, a sum that would pass to her brother in due course. Maisie suspected Miller would in time move into a home of his own, though he would always require a companion to assist with everyday needs; but for now he should have a place of rest while he recovered from the death of his sister and Mrs Bolton. Maisie could only agree with Brenda when her stepmother observed, 'Well, at least he's got money tucked away – think of the thousands that haven't. And who's looking after them? I'll tell you who – the poor women they came home to, that's who does the looking after, and with precious little to help them!' Whatever Miller's circumstances, she would at least have the opportunity to question him at Chelstone.

There was a message from Priscilla, and from Brenda, who asked when Maisie would be at Chelstone, and whether she could come early again, instead of waiting until Friday. The note from Billy was by way of an update, informing her that he was trying to find out more about Lucas Peeters, as well as continuing work on another case involving a woman who had not believed her husband when he said he had joined the army. The man had not arrived at the barracks he had stated as his destination, and the army had no record of his enlistment.

She lifted the telephone receiver and placed a call to Priscilla's home.

'Thank goodness – I thought you'd gone off on a ship again, never to return,' said Priscilla. 'You live less than one hundred yards along the road, and it's all I can do to gain the attention of my best friend in my hour of need.'

'Rather dramatic, Pris, don't you think?' offered Maisie. 'Sorry – I've been busy.'

'Well, just so you know everything happening under this roof, I'll start with the good news. Tarquin is staying out of trouble, which is more than I can say for the other two, and even, perhaps, my dear husband.' Priscilla's voice cracked, evidence of her emotional state.

'Start with Thomas – I know he's at the heart of this, Priscilla.'

'He's gone and joined the RAF. We all knew it was coming – he just couldn't resist it, could he? Instead of applying to university, perhaps to study something like, oh, I don't know – let's say something boringly safe, such as philosophy, politics, and economics – he applied to Cranwell, the air force college in Lincolnshire, for officer training. And he's just old enough to be accepted, but thankfully not old enough to fly in a real battle, though we both know how so-called rules are broken, don't we? Anyway, the good news is that he will be there for a while, at least until next summer, I hope! I confess, my mind went a bit blank as soon as he told us, so the details might be woolly.'

Maisie could hear Priscilla's breathing quicken, and suspected the mood in the Partridge household was far more volatile than her friend would reveal in a telephone call.

'I could throttle him, to tell you the truth, Maisie,' continued Priscilla. 'In the meantime, Douglas has been pulled into the Ministry of Information, and Timothy is professing readiness to join the Royal Navy, claiming that a midshipman would have been a boy in

Napoleon's time. And as you know, the trouble with Tim is that he is so very quick with his tongue, you can't argue with him, and I end up shouting at my own beloved son. Tarquin, bless his cotton socks, has stated his intention to join the Peace Pledge Union, clearly a move to rattle the cages of his older brothers – he takes a childish joy at starting them off, as if they were toy motor cars you could wind up with a key and let whizz across the floor. The stupid thing is that my boys would kill anyone who threatened one of them, and yet I sometimes think they'll murder each other when they get going. Tarquin seems to be enjoying walking around with a beatific look on his face, though we both know he still cherishes the aviator's cap that James gave him, and if truth be told, he's only taking his current position because it's in direct opposition to his brothers.' Priscilla paused for half a second. 'Anyway, I'm sure you have better things to do than listen to me. Do come over for a drink after you get home from work. I have some other news for you.'

'That sounds ominous, Pris. I'll walk along around half past six, I would imagine.'

'Stay for supper – please.'

'All right, I'd love to.'

'Maisie—'

'Pris?'

'I'm so terribly scared.'

'I know . . . I know. I'll come as soon as I can.'

In telephone calls to Lady Rowan and Brenda, Maisie assured both women that she would return to Chelstone as soon as possible. Brenda reported that twice already Emma the dog had calmly left the house and walked to the school half a mile away, and was waiting outside when Anna and the boys emerged, ready to escort them home.

Maisie took a deep breath before her next call, which was to Francesca Thomas – who was 'not in the office' according to Lambert, who had answered the telephone.

'May I take a message for when she returns,' he asked.

Maisie hesitated. 'No . . . no, that's all right. Just tell her that I telephoned. She knows both my office and home numbers.'

'Very well, Miss Dobbs. Will there be anything else?'

'That will be all, Mr Lambert. Thank you.'

Lambert bid Maisie good afternoon. She replaced the receiver and leant back in her chair, her gaze cast out towards the window and across the rooftops as she considered the case and the many questions she had asked of those she had met and of herself. At last she reached into her bag and brought out her notebook, going back through details recorded along the way. Taking out her pen, she began to tap it on the desk, as if she wanted to write a certain sentence, but could not bring herself to fashion the words that would without doubt point the finger in one or two directions. She closed the notebook and placed the pen on top.

'Spain was easier than this,' she whispered to herself, before coming to her feet, taking up her bag, her keys, and hat. It was only as she reached the front door that she realised that, once again, she had left the box containing her gas mask behind. She sighed, not bothering to return.

When she reached Priscilla's house, she stopped for a moment to look up at the mansion, which she now knew as the home of a family to whom she was devoted, but when she first crossed its threshold, it had been as a girl still in her teens, nervous about meeting the parents of the young man she loved, Captain Simon Lynch, a doctor with the Royal Army Medical Corps. They had been introduced by Priscilla at a party in the autumn of 1914, when the women were at Girton College. For Maisie and Simon it was a first love, a love forged in wartime, and for the most part in France. Following Maisie's posting to a casualty clearing station, it seemed fate was playing a strong hand in their lives when Simon was sent to work at that same station.

The house where Priscilla and her family lived had once been the home of the Lynch family; Simon's widowed mother had sold the property to Priscilla and Douglas Partridge when she realised she wanted to spend the rest of her days at her country home in Cambridgeshire. But Simon had grown up in this house. Now he was dead, a casualty of the Great War who had succumbed to his wounds years after the Armistice.

'Tante Maisie!'

Maisie looked up to see Thomas bounding down the steps. Priscilla's eldest son bore a broad smile as he held out his arms to the woman he considered a beloved aunt.

'Thomas, I hear you have broken your mother's heart,' said Maisie.

'Oh, I might have known she'd have to tell you.' He stepped back, hands in pockets. 'She just doesn't understand – I thought it best to sign up for the RAF now.' He shrugged, sighing. 'I mean really, Tante Maisie, if she thought about it, Mama would realise that by the time I'm assigned to a squadron, this war will all be over – I'll just be square bashing until then, with the odd training flight, and I'll be earning money! I keep telling her, she really has nothing to worry about. But at least I'll be near an aeroplane or two and, well, doing something important.' Another sigh. 'Do tell her to keep her hair on, won't you? Really, they won't let me take on the Luftwaffe for ages yet.' Thomas reached forward, grinned again, and kissed Maisie on the cheek. 'Got to go now, Tante Maisie.'

She watched as he jumped down the final steps. 'Is she pretty, Tom?'

He turned and laughed. 'Absolutely! Must dash, can't be late!'

And as Maisie looked up, she saw the curtain move: Priscilla, watching her son as he ran towards the underground station. 'Oh, my dear Tom,' she whispered, following Priscilla's line of vision. 'Your mother does understand, that's the trouble – she understands only too well.'

Maisie listened to Priscilla's grievances regarding her sons, and her concern that Elinor – her sons' nanny, not yet thirty years of age – had decided to enlist for service.

'She says that all the years of living in France, first with another family, and then with us, has given her such a fluency in French that she would be useful in any arm of the services. It was those advertisements over the past six months, telling us all to do our national service, that did it – she signed up, and she's in the army auxiliary . . . I think. There are so many services now, one never knows which is which.'

'I take my hat off to her, Priscilla – and let's face it, keeping your boys in order has given her good practise for the army.'

'Oh, very funny, Maisie – but you've got a point there.' Priscilla shook her empty glass. 'Another?'

'I've barely touched mine yet – don't let me stop you, though!'

'Oh, don't worry – you won't.' Priscilla stood up and walked to a chrome trolley laden with an assortment of decanters, an ice bucket, and a soda syphon. The shelf underneath was stocked with glasses and several bottles of Indian tonic water. Eschewing ice tongs in favour of her fingers, she half filled her glass with ice and prepared her second gin and tonic, then returned to the sofa.

'Is Elinor's French that good?' asked Maisie.

'Most definitely,' said Priscilla. 'She picked it up from the locals, but – very clever of her – she took lessons twice a week from a local woman who had decamped from Paris to Biarritz. She said she was aware the accent was different there, so she wanted to learn properly, to "broaden her horizons" when the boys were older and she left us.' Priscilla laughed. 'The trouble is, they've been old enough for a few years – Tarquin is almost fourteen now – but we were loath to let her go. She's become one of the family. But now she's on her way, though we have insisted that this is her home when she is on leave, that sort of thing. Which leaves me to do my bit.'

'What do you mean?'

Priscilla took a sip of her drink, then another. 'I'm sure you saw the newsreel at the cinema, when they were telling us that everyone should do their national service – the same plea that tempted Elinor. You and Tim are always going off to the pictures together, so I would be surprised if you hadn't.'

'Yes, I've seen them,' said Maisie, folding her arms and leaning closer. 'What are you up to, Priscilla?'

'See, it's Priscilla now – you always call me Priscilla when you're worried or you think I'm up to something. I should start calling you Margaret or addressing you as Lady Maisie, or whatever title you're entitled to use.'

'Stop trying to distract me – tell me what you've done.'

'It was the reel about preparations for civilian casualties if – and perhaps I should say when – Hitler's Luftwaffe boys are sent to bomb us that caught my attention. They're recruiting women who can drive to train as ambulance drivers, with extra points if you know some first aid. So I thought to myself, I've done it before and I can damn well do it again. I can drive, I can tend a wound, and I have experience – I'm not a girl any more, but I bet you I'm as fit as a twenty-year-old.' Her eyes widened as she explained. 'That's another thing – you have to attend fitness classes, just to make sure you can run into a building and run out again with a wounded person.'

'Have you signed up?'

'Not yet. They boys were having a row yesterday, the RAF against the navy, with Tarquin saying it was all a waste anyway, and if no one fought, there wouldn't be a war, which got him a semi-friendly pummeling. Anyway' – Priscilla took another sip of her gin and tonic – 'anyway, I thought, that's it, I will not be the only one in this family not doing my bit. Even Cook says she will volunteer with the WVS. So I'm ready, and no one can question my abilities, which I must say are quite considerable – I've driven all over Europe. And I was with the First Aid Nursing Yeomanry for four years during the last war, behind the wheel of something a lot harder to start than any ambulance working today.' She paused, took another sip of her cocktail, then held the glass up as if toasting Maisie. 'You should do it. It'll mainly be night-time work, plus you can drive – and after Spain, especially, you're well placed to tend the wounds of war, now aren't you? And we have to work in pairs, so perhaps we could be a team.'

At that moment, the door to the drawing room opened, and Timothy and Tarquin rushed in with the news that they'd followed their older brother and seen him kissing a girl. Priscilla dismissed her two younger sons, admonishing them for telling tales.

'When does Tom leave, Pris?'

'He has a few weeks' grace. You'll come to our special family supper, won't you? I believe he has to be at Cranwell on October the second, so on the first we'll send him off with a good meal inside him, at the very least. And I do hope he behaves himself with this girl. You know what they're like at that age.' She sighed and finished her drink. 'I wish that were my only worry – it seems so insignificant.'

Maisie nodded, reaching for Priscilla's hand and feeling her friend's tight grasp in return. 'I'll be here for Tom's going-away supper – I wouldn't miss it.'

CHAPTER THIRTEEN

It was dark by the time Maisie arrived home to her garden flat, and she was careful to close the blackout curtains before turning on a light. She knew that if even the slightest chink of a beam from her window were visible from the street, the Air Raid Precautions man would be knocking at her door, admonishing her for risking life and limb, and those of her neighbours, with her carelessness. According to Billy, the blackout had already caused accidents, with pedestrians losing their way or stepping out in front of unseen motor cars, headlamps covered lest they be spotted by an eagle-eyed Luftwaffe pilot intent upon killing anyone, anywhere.

'I tell you,' he had warned, 'the way things are going, the blackout's going to do away with more people than blimmin' Hitler. Never mind a gas mask, they should have given us all a white stick – I mean, Hitler don't need to bomb us, he only has to wait until we've knocked each other out and just wander in with his troops.'

The telephone was ringing by the time she'd picked up her

notebook, ready to review all she had learnt since Francesca Thomas arrived unannounced in her garden.

'Maisie. Francesca Thomas here. I understand you've been trying to get in touch with me.'

'You have an efficient assistant,' said Maisie, twisting the telephone cord around her fingers.

'Taking a message is not efficient, it's expected. But yes, he's efficient.'

Maisie felt her breath catch in her throat. 'Dr Thomas, I wanted to ask you about a man named Carl Firmin. He died last year.' She leafed through her notebook. 'On the fourth of August – exactly one year to the day before Frederick Addens was murdered. I visited Firmin's wife because it came to my attention that he had associated with both Frederick Addens and Albert Durant, and I know he knew Rosemary Hartley-Davies. I understand you visited his wife following his death.'

There was a noticeable pause before Thomas responded. 'Yes, I did. My role here changes all the time, but it fell to me to visit her, given her husband's position as a former Belgian refugee. It was a respectful visit, in consideration of his service to his country – I mean—'

'What service to his country?' asked Maisie. 'According to my findings, he was little more than a lad when he arrived here. His life had been under threat in Belgium, so he left and entered British waters as a refugee. How had he served?'

'Forgive me – an error of speech. He served Belgium only in assisting his fellow countrymen even after arrival in Great Britain. He was known to keep in touch with other refugees. He was loyal, and that was worth my visit.'

'I see. His wife said you were asking for documents that might be of interest to Belgium.'

'If we are to be able to reflect on the Great War – and, indeed, on this war – and learn, then the recollections of the ordinary people will be valuable indeed. I wanted to make sure we had a chance to make a case for preserving any diaries Firmin might have kept, before they were destroyed. The bereaved will either get rid of things indiscriminately in their grief, or keep them very close to hand. If Mrs Firmin was of the former, then we wanted to have her husband's papers before she disposed of them – that's if such papers existed, and it was my job to find out. Most importantly, though, it was my job to collect official documentation belonging to a deceased Belgian national – a passport, a certificate confirming status as a refugee, that sort of thing. We've done the same with papers belonging to Frederick Addens and Albert Durant, as you know. After all, we don't want them falling into the wrong hands and aiding a spy – and let it be said that such things can and do happen.'

'Yes, that makes sense.'

'And your progress on the case, Maisie?'

Maisie unwound the telephone cord from her fingers and let it drop. 'The threads are leading somewhere, Dr Thomas.' She paused, allowing her words to linger in the air, just as microscopic drops of a fragrance might remain long after a woman had used an atomiser to apply perfume to the soft skin under her ears, or to her wrists. 'In fact, I would say that I am close.' Another pause. 'But of course, you have to remember, I must take due care, for if I pointed the finger towards the wrong person, it would lead to a tragedy, so I take my time.'

'Surely there's a risk involved – Maisie, if you have a name, you must tell me.'

'As I said, I am close, Dr Thomas – though not close enough yet.'

'Right you are. I trust you implicitly.'

'One more thing – do you find it interesting that Firmin and Addens died on the same date, one year apart?'

'It's probably just a coincidence, but if not I am sure you will discover the link.'

'Thank you. I'll report again before the week's end.'

'Good enough,' replied Francesca Thomas, ending the call.

With the long tone of disconnection ringing in her ear, Maisie set down the receiver, turned off the light, and opened the French doors to the garden. There was a chill in the mid-September air. She pulled her cardigan around her and sat down in a wicker chair.

It seemed that no matter how many times Francesca Thomas had invited Maisie to address her by her Christian name, she always reverted to 'Dr Thomas'. Sometimes she felt like no more than a girl alongside the other woman, who was, in truth, only a few years older than Maisie. But such feelings were not the aspect of their conversation that troubled her, as she looked up at the night sky, now accustomed to the darker shadows of barrage balloons floating above. Thomas had lied to her. She had slipped up and lied. But was the error deliberate? And could it be that, having asked Maisie to investigate the case of Frederick Addens, she now wished she had left well enough alone? What was the risk that Francesca Thomas was taking? But more to the point – what other risks might she take, and why? Yes, it was true, Maisie did not want to point a finger without all the evidence to hand. Maurice had cautioned her against such a move from the very beginning. 'No matter how loud the wolves bay, no matter how much they want blood to atone for a terrible loss of life, Maisie, you must take your time. Know that the moment you feel pressure bearing down, you are primed to make a mistake. You can never bring back the life of an innocent swinging dead in the hangman's noose.'

Yes, perhaps 'Dr Thomas' was best, thought Maisie. Distance, rather than familiarity, would serve her.

'Morning, hen.' The voice boomed into the receiver as Sandra passed it to Maisie. She had no need to introduce the caller, for Maisie could hear MacFarlane asking for her from a distance of several feet.

'Good morning, Robbie. Do you have some news for me?'

'Not the news you might have wanted – nothing doing this week. But on Monday morning – that would be the eighteenth of September – at five sharp, your transport will be leaving from an airfield in Kent, not far from Bromley. Called Biggin Hill. We've got a Lysander going out of there into Belgium. None of your business what it's up to, but he can take you. Very much on the QT, though. And because I owe you – as you so kindly reminded me – I've arranged a motor and a driver ready to take you on from there – assuming you know where you want to go. That's for my peace of mind, not yours. But – and this is a big but – you must be back at the airfield no later than three in the afternoon, and if you tarry, the driver is instructed to tap his fingers on the steering wheel and make a noise. I do not want to have to get on one of those bloody Lysander things to come and get you. This is all very improper anyway.'

'I want to go to an area close to Liege. And when did you ever worry about what was proper, Robert MacFarlane?'

'Granted. Everything I'm doing now is improper, and I sometimes think a nice cushy desk job at Scotland Yard would have been a better choice, but this is what they pegged me for, so this is what I do. One more thing. Wrap up warm for the journey and bring a flask of tea and one of those buns you like. There'll be no steward offering silver service breakfast on the way. And I want you to get on the blower to me as soon as you return, so I know you're safe and sound.'

'Thank you, Robbie. I appreciate it.'

'I would appreciate it more if I knew what you were up to, but – against my better judgement – I trust you. And speaking of trust, one more thing.'

'Yes?'

'You'll see a lot going on there, at the airfield. You know what the government posters say, don't you? Keep mum.'

As soon as Billy arrived at the office and they were settled, he recounted the results of his enquiries. Apparently, Clarice Littleton owned a cottage just outside Norwich, the property having been left to her by a maiden aunt. As a rule it was rented out during the summer months, providing a means of increasing her income – she would go to Norfolk on the train every two weeks to check the house and to welcome another family who had come to enjoy a rural respite alongside the River Yare. But with the declaration of war, the last two tenants of the summer season had cancelled, and she had decided not to place an advertisement again until the following year. She had informed a local shopkeeper – as a favour to Littleton, every year he would place a card in his window with details of the cottage – that it might be safer altogether if she left London for the duration, she just wasn't sure yet.

'I'm surprised,' said Maisie. 'She seems to have been pretty open with the shopkeeper regarding her plans. The way she moved along the road after I'd visited her suggested a worried woman in a hurry.'

'Yes, but she told him all this last week, before she knew about the murders.'

'You know, Billy, I would place money on her not being at the cottage at all. In all likelihood she has contacts – friends, perhaps – who would put her up for a while. It was easy enough for you to garner this information, which means that if she is at some risk, it would be easy for a killer to know her whereabouts.'

'Are you going out there, miss?'

'To Norfolk? I really don't wish to waste petrol, but I want to talk to her. If anything, I want to know she's all right.' She glanced at her wristwatch. 'It's half past nine now, so if I leave by eleven, I can be there by early afternoon, and then return after I've found her and had a little chat. I'll stay in a local inn overnight if necessary – the last thing I want is to drive in the blackout.'

'Then what?'

'Let's see what she says. But I must also get to Chelstone to speak to Rosemary Hartley-Davies' brother. And then there's this.' Maisie took the ticket for the opera that she'd removed from the home of Rosemary Hartley-Davies. 'It's for the end of next week – I wish it were sooner.'

'Are you going?'

Maisie nodded. 'If only to linger in the shadows, and see who sits in the seat next to the one indicated on this ticket.'

'You think it could be the murderer?'

'It could just be an old friend from school days who bought two tickets and sent one to Hartley-Davies, or the other way around. In any case, I hope the identity of the person who takes that adjacent seat will tell us something.' She returned the ticket to her desk drawer. 'I'll try to get a couple of seats in a box, so I have a good view of the audience. Interested?'

'Me? The opera? Oh, blimey, no – my ears would never take it, miss. You get a bloke singing away in a high voice, with his passion and spittle, and all he's saying is "Let's go down the road for a pint." No, not my cuppa at all. Take Caldwell.'

'No, I don't think so. I'll find someone.'

At that moment, the telephone began to ring. Billy picked up the receiver and answered, as usual giving the number. Maisie watched as he listened to the caller, then smiled at Maisie. He put his hand over the receiver, still grinning. 'Would you believe it? Out of the blue – a Mr Stratton. Asking for you.'

Maisie reached for the telephone receiver with one hand, and pointed to the door. 'Thank you, Billy.'

'I think I'd better nip down to get the post.' Billy winked at Maisie and left, closing the concertina doors behind him.

'Hello, this is Maisie Dobbs,' she said, not knowing quite what else to say. She had not seen Richard Stratton for five or even six years, and while she had once addressed him as 'Richard', she now felt unsure of herself.

'Hello, Maisie. Richard Stratton. I was in London today, and thought I would give you a ring. I – I heard about your . . . your bereavement. I am so terribly sorry.'

Maisie curled the telephone cord around her fingers. 'Thank you, Richard. Yes, thank you. I suppose you understand more than some, having suffered a similar loss.'

'Time, Maisie. It all takes time. I'd heard you were in Spain a couple of years ago – I thought it very brave of you. And now you're back in business, in London.'

'Yes, I'm back in business – and busy, so that counts for something.'

'Of course – I'm sorry, you are most definitely busy. I wasn't thinking.' There was a silence on the line; only a second, though it seemed longer. 'Look, would you like to meet for tea? Or perhaps lunch? I'm in London at the moment, though I'll be working in, well, the country, for the most part.'

Maisie paused, opened the desk drawer, and lifted out the opera ticket. 'Richard, might you be in London towards the end of next week?'

'Let's see, yes, I think so – I'm coming back in on Thursday. Meetings, that sort of thing. I'll be staying at a flat until the Sunday evening.'

'All right. Can you meet for a cup of coffee this morning? I must leave town today by eleven, so it would have to be quick, but I would like to see you.'

'It's work, isn't it?'

'I'm afraid it is – but I mean it . . . it would be lovely to see you, Richard.'

'The usual caff, if it's still there – in about half an hour?'

Maisie laughed. 'Oh, yes, I remember you always said it was "More caff than café." It's still there, still serving tea straight from a big urn, and the toast is still buttered until it's dripping from the crust. I'll see you there – and Richard, thank you.'

'The caff, half an hour, Maisie.'

'But Maisie, you've overlooked something here,' said Stratton, returning his cup to the saucer. 'Everything's closed – this ticket is useless. The theatre performances were suspended last week. Government orders.'

'Oh, for goodness' sake – I cannot believe I missed that.' She looked at the ticket again. 'And it's not even for a big auditorium, but a small theatre just off the Grays Inn Road. It was probably more music hall than opera.'

'Now the Royal Opera House is being converted to a Mecca dance hall, there won't be anything for a while anyway. Not that I'm a fan.' Stratton looked at Maisie. His once-dark hair could now be described as pepper and salt. And yet he seemed more rested, more at ease, as if the strain of the years since his wife died, leaving him to raise his son alone, had been erased. 'You're looking better than I thought you might, Maisie.'

'As you said, Richard – time. It takes time. The pain of loss does not go away, but it takes up a place in your heart. And it nestles there in the corner, another dragon to keep at bay – that's what my friend, Priscilla, said about the war. He took up residence then, that war dragon, and must be mollified, not tempted out of his lair.'

'Your friend has a point.'

'What are you doing now, Richard – can you say?'

'Roped in for war work. My son is now sixteen, and looking at university. I hope he keeps looking at it, to tell you the truth. The last thing I want is any heroics on his part. He says he wants to be a doctor. His mother would have been so very proud of him. At the moment he's with his grandparents – her parents. School will start again in a week.'

'I can't believe you left your job – I'd been told you loved the school and your teaching post.'

'They've given me a leave of absence until January. I don't want to do this for long, and I believe it will only be short term anyway.' He looked around the cafe. 'I doubt our lady of the urn over there is a spy, but just in case.' He lowered his voice. 'There's a move afoot to bring together scientists, mathematicians, those sort of people, to serve the country – it's very unofficial, and will probably remain so. Their task is to keep us one step ahead of the Germans. I can't say more than that, but I was earmarked to work with the War Office on security. The fact that I'm a mathematician at heart and have studied alongside the sort of men they'll be recruiting, together with the fact that I was with both the military police and Scotland Yard, means that – according to the powers that be – I can work with security personnel as well as liaise with the boffins, who are the sort who generally balk at any suggestion that they must follow rules. According to the man who brought me in – and it wasn't as if I was asked, exactly, it was more of an order – they'll have one of their own among them, so we'll know if we've got a bad 'un.'

'Richard, that sounds like more than a short-term job – I think they'll want you for longer than they've given you to believe.'

Stratton sighed. 'Frankly, I would rather be teaching quadratic equations to pimply boys any day. I wanted my policing days to be over.'

'You're doing your service on behalf of the nation.'

'Yes, I suppose so. How about you?'

'Me?' Maisie shook her head, and was quiet before adding, 'I don't know. I might be a liability. You see, I don't know that I have what it takes to do what I was trained to do any more. I've not talked about Spain, but . . . well, let's just say it's another dragon to be mollified.' She looked at her watch.

'What are you going to do about this case? The ticket seemed a pretty important lead.'

'Important, but not the be-all and end-all. I have a feeling it will still come in handy,' said Maisie. She consulted her watch again. 'I really have to be on my way – a long drive ahead.'

Richard Stratton pulled a couple of coins from his jacket pocket and placed them under the saucer, a tip for the waitress. At the door he turned to Maisie.

'You know, I have some time on my hands – I could find this theatre and ask if they kept any record of when the ticket was purchased. There's bound to be someone working in the office I can find to talk to. They might have retained a note of whoever bought the ticket – some of the smaller theatres do that, so they know the next time the person buys a ticket and can acknowledge a regular customer, that sort of thing.'

Maisie hesitated before responding. 'Only if you've time, Richard – and I'm so sorry, I have to run.'

The drive to Norfolk gave Maisie time to think, to consider the morning and ask herself what she wanted in the way of information, so that by the time she returned to London it would be as if she had defined the parameters of the puzzle, and only needed the details, the centre of the picture. The killer knew each of his victims – that, she felt, was without doubt. She believed Rosemary Hartley-Davies was not aware that the person of her acquaintance to whom she'd placed a call was the killer – or was he? Or she? And if not the killer, might the person who received the call have alerted someone else? That the telephone call took place at all was speculation on Maisie's part, but she felt sure that Rosemary Hartley-Davies had been playing for time as soon as she understood the purpose of Maisie's visit. And part of that time would have been spent informing another person that the two men had been killed. What was the connection? And the connection to Firmin, and possibly to Lucas Peeters? – apart from the fact that they stood together in one photograph. She didn't like the direction in which the finger of her investigation was pointing. It was one thing to intuit the killer's identity, but quite another to work out the grievance at the heart of such passion – and what was murder, if not a passionate act? It was an inflamed, yet devastating, immoral deed of destruction. And Maisie suspected that in this case it was a misguided and malevolent undertaking in the name of retribution. More than anything she hoped her undercover journey to Belgium would provide her with the knowledge she needed – that it would establish the why as much as the who behind the killings.

If Clarice Littleton had taken precautions to render herself secure in Norfolk, Maisie had not been hampered by them. A few enquiries of neighbours at the cottage and a pub landlord led Maisie to the home of Miss Phyllida Lorimer, a friend of Littleton's deceased aunt. Clarice Littleton showed no surprise when she came to the door to answer Maisie's knock.

'I might have known you'd find me,' she said. 'Come on – let's go into the garden. Phyllida is having what she calls her "afternoon forty winks" upstairs – she probably won't rise until after four.'

Maisie followed Littleton into the garden, which swept down towards the river. Cast-iron chairs with blue gingham-covered cushions were set around a matching table. Littleton pulled out chairs for herself and Maisie. 'What do you want to know? Frankly, I think I've told you everything I can.'

'You left London for a reason, Miss Littleton. And I don't think it was simply to make your cottage ready for the next holiday let. To my knowledge, both parties have withdrawn their bookings – so it's a surprise you're not staying there, isn't it?'

Littleton shrugged. 'Not really. Phyllida isn't getting any younger, so I thought I would give her a hand until I go back to London.'

'Which is when?'

Littleton sighed. 'Not sure. They say we're pretty much in the line of fire, here in East Anglia – the Germans could whizz across on their way to London and make the most of bombing us at the same time. I wanted to make sure that Phyllida knew what to do in case of a bombing – she hasn't an Anderson shelter, and I can't see her staggering out into the garden anyway. But she should be all right with a Morrison table shelter in the house, though by the time she'd got herself in there, the bombing might be over. But having it there might be a comfort, at the very least – dogs always go under something when they're frightened, so there must be something to it.'

Maisie nodded. 'What do you know, Miss Littleton? There's a missing piece of information you're keeping to yourself.'

'I know only what you told me, and I did my own working out. Two of the men in that photograph of Rosie's are dead – and so is she. That means two are left. And me. The woman behind the camera. I didn't like the odds.'

'Actually, three of the men are dead – Carl Firmin died a year ago. It was decreed a suicide at the time, though his wife seemed to have her doubts regarding the police report.'

'Then there's the other one. Peeters.' Clarice Littleton looked at Maisie, as if anticipating another question.

'There was someone else in the photograph, wasn't there?'

'Just the boy,' replied Littleton.

'What was his name?' asked Maisie.

Littleton shook her head. 'I don't really recall. Rosie just called him her little lamb, because he followed her everywhere. I'm sure he was placed with a family at some point – the refugee families were very tight, and would have taken in an orphan. And you've got to remember, we were only doing administration – it's not as if we were putting up refugees ourselves. It was just that for a few weeks in the summer, Rosie had this work for a few of them, and I think she'd felt sorry for this group, that they'd come over together and had had it pretty rough.' Littleton sighed. 'I mean, we all felt terribly bad for them, which is why we moved heaven and earth to find places for them to live, to work, and so on. But Rosie was a soft touch, one of those people who was a little more involved than she had to be – I think it was her way of dealing with the loss of her husband. That boy was well-cared-for, and those lads looked out for him too.'

'And you're sure he was an orphan,' said Maisie.

'As far as I know, he didn't have anyone. So yes, an orphan.'

Maisie looked into the distance, considering Littleton's response, then turned back to her. 'May I ask one more question?'

'Of course.'

'When I came to your flat, you were holding two letters you'd just received. I noticed one of the envelopes bore a striking resemblance to stationery used by the Belgian embassy. May I ask if they have made contact with you?'

'Very observant,' said Littleton, raising her eyebrows. 'It seemed the sort of letter they'd sent to a dozen people or associations. It mentioned the deceased Frederick Addens and said that it was their duty to collect any information as it was important to the Belgian government, and they thought I might have known him. It was sent from the office of someone called Dr Francesca Thomas. I sent a quick reply that very day – before I left the house. I said I had been acquainted with him when he was a new arrival in England, and that I'd had no contact with him in over twenty years.'

'I see. Yes, I think it might be just a formality, gathering information on someone who's died – but you did well to reply straightaway.'

Maisie once again consulted her watch. 'I must get on the road soon. The last thing I want is to be out in the dark, or even at dusk, with my headlamps off.' She reached across to Clarice Littleton and took her hand. 'Miss Littleton – Clarice – I know you've told me all you can now; however, the killer might think you know more than you do. You are not secure here. Finding you did not present me with a challenge, so I can only assume someone else would have similar fortune, if they were searching for you. Is there anywhere else you can go?'

'Yes, I suppose so – I've an old school chum who lives in Yorkshire. I could go to her.'

'Please pack your belongings and I will drop you at the station in Norwich. I would like you to leave without delay. You can make up a story for Phyllida. Just make it stick – Cornwall would be my suggestion, if you are telling tales. It's lovely at this time of year, and perhaps you can invent a friend who is having trouble with her children now that their father has been called up into the army.'

'I'll be about five minutes – two to pack and three to have a chat with Phyllida.'

As Clarice Littleton ran into the house, Maisie strolled down to the river. The current was calm and steady, appearing to meander with ease as it made its way to the North Sea. In that moment, she felt the passage of time, the flow of the years, and the way in which death had stalked her – even in her choice to join Maurice in his work. Her thoughts returned to the reasons for a premeditated murder. She knew only too well how blame could eat into a soul, and she understood how hard it could be to forgive – hadn't she suffered a lack of compassion towards the woman she'd held responsible for her husband's death? And the path to forgiveness had not been an easy journey for Maisie, but she had come to learn that it was the only way to break free from the dark grief that could grow like bindweed around the heart, pressing into the fibres of her goodness, rendering her unable to feel anything but anger, and precluding any understanding of why events had unfolded in a given way. Forgiveness had been the only way to release herself, because she had not been able to prevent James' death.

An image of the girl Anna came to her. Poor Anna, as homeless and rootless as the boy Rosemary Hartley-Davies had called her 'little lamb'. Children, Maisie believed, could often only see their world in black and white, never shades of grey – which meant the hard-found forgiveness that provides respite from the dark melancholy of blame might never lift from the soul of a wounded child. And Maisie wondered, then, what she could do to bring light into Anna's heart, so that a smile was not just a movement made by her lips because she thought it was expected of her, but an immediate and unlimited response to deep-felt joy and complete contentment. What could she do to help the child feel safe?

CHAPTER FOURTEEN

Sandra looked up from her desk when Maisie arrived, her document case in one hand and her shoulder bag in the other.

'Miss – what happened to your gas mask?'

'Oh, blast! Did I leave it here yesterday?'

'Yes, it's on your desk. Better not do that again – I mean, you never know, do you?'

'You're right – I'll try to remember. But it's such a silly thing – it gets in the way when it's around your neck, and when I'm in a hurry, I always forget. Here, I'm going to get it now and hang it on the back of the door – then I'll see it as I leave.'

Sandra smiled. 'You're not the only one who forgets. Apparently there are shelves upon shelves of them in lost property at the railway stations, and people keep leaving them on the buses and trams. There was a man talking about it at the bus stop this morning – you know, one of those old military types with the handlebar moustache. He said that the army should let off some sort of nasty-smelling bomb, you know, harmless, but one that spreads a stink. He said that would make everyone remember their gas masks a bit sharpish. I don't know if I would care for that.'

'It would make you very sick indeed. I remember when I was—' Maisie stopped, and shook her head. 'Anyway, how are you feeling, Sandra?'

Sandra's complexion was heightened. 'Much better. Much better – I feel a bit more, well, optimistic in myself. Lawrence has been wonderful, very understanding.'

'He's a good man, Sandra. And speaking of good men, any idea what's happened to Billy?' Maisie leafed through the post on Sandra's desk, as if the comment had been offered in passing.

'I think there's trouble at home. He's not said much, but I've had the impression that Doreen is suffering again – not like before, but due to her anxiety about young Billy being in the army. She's seeing the doctor – that nice woman you put them in touch with a few years ago – so I reckon it will be all right. Little Margaret's school hasn't been evacuated yet, but apparently they're off on Monday – personally, I think it would be best if Doreen takes Margaret and goes down to the country to be with family, like Billy said they would. Bobby has his apprenticeship, and he can do for himself, though it'll be only him and his dad in the house – which might not be a bad thing, as it can't be good for the lad, being around his mum when she's that anxious. I think he remembers what it was like when Doreen was so ill. Probably scares the life out of all of them.'

'Thank you for telling me, Sandra. I knew something was wrong. It might help if I offer to put Billy on shorter hours. He's an air-raid warden anyway, so he has his shifts. And what with the war, we don't know how business will go – everything changes in wartime.'

Sandra nodded. 'There was a telephone call from Mrs Dobbs too – she said she thought you would be back at Chelstone today. She sounded anxious.'

'I'll go later, but I have to get some work done before I set off.'

'And another telephone call came in, this one from a young man.'

'A young man? Who?'

'Name of Arthur Addens. Son of Frederick Addens. He's on a short leave, going back on Sunday morning to a barracks in Colchester.' Sandra looked up from the sheet of paper on which she had transcribed the message. 'I don't think he should be telling people that, do you?'

'I daresay he shouldn't – but what else did he say?'

'He was in a telephone kiosk, and said he would come over here at ten, taking a chance on seeing you because you can't telephone him back. And he didn't say why – just said he wants to see you.'

'All right – that sounds promising, and a bit ominous. He might be coming here to harangue me for going to see his mother twice.'

The door opened, banging back on its hinges. 'Miss, I'm really sorry, but—'

'It's all right, Billy, really—'

'I found Lucas Peeters.'

'Oh, well done! How did you do that? – no, wait, catch your breath. Come on in and sit down. Sandra, you too.'

Once seated at the table in Maisie's office, Billy pulled the tin of crayons towards him, ready to add details of his discovery to the case map.

'I got his last-known address from a bloke he used to work for, and I took it from there, wearing out shoe leather until I realised that the man called Leonard Peterson living in a couple of rooms above a cobbler's in Islington must be Lucas Peeters, only he's changed his name. I saw the name next to the door downstairs, matched the initials, and put two and two together.'

'You're sure it's him?'

'I spoke to the cobbler – and I thank my lucky stars, because he made my poor old soles as good as new before I left. Anyway, that Peterson – about thirty-five years of age – apparently doesn't have an accent at all, except on the odd occasion when he's had a rough day at work. According to Jim – the cobbler – the rest of the time you'd think he was a London boy born and bred. Mind you, he said he reckons Peterson has worked at it. And apparently he got married a few weeks ago – out of the blue – to a hairdresser, name of Alice. Neither of them were at home, and Jim said they'd gone down hop-picking – their honeymoon, of all things.'

'Where is the farm?'

'Out Charing way.'

'Do you have the details?'

Billy grinned, leafed through his notebook, and pulled out a page. 'There you are, miss. Got the lot.'

'Excellent! Billy, let's get this map up to date,' said Maisie, looking at her wristwatch. 'Frederick Addens' son is due in about half an hour, so with any luck we can be on our way by eleven. We'll drive down together – should be there easily by one o'clock – and after we've found him and had a chat, I'll drop you at the station and you can go straight back home from there. We've a lot to talk about on the way, in any case.'

'Have you got your motor spirit coupons? I don't want us getting stranded – and I know how fast that jam jar of yours can go, so you bet it drinks up the juice.'

'I have my coupons, and I also have a full tank – plenty of "juice", as you say. And today you might find out exactly how fast my jam jar can go!'

Billy seemed ready to make a game retort when he looked down at the case map and saw the name Maisie had written in red letters, joining the names of the dead.

'You're kidding, miss.'

'I wish I were, Billy. I wish very much that this was a joke.'

Arthur Addens arrived at the office at quarter to ten. He was dressed in his No. 5 Battle Dress serge, with his trousers tucked into heavy black boots polished to a shine. Frederick Addens' son was a tall man. And although there was no requirement for him to take off his cap, he removed it as he entered the office and tucked it into his blouse epaulette. He ran a finger between his collar and neck, revealing a red welt where the fabric had rubbed his skin. Maisie offered him a seat. She explained that both her assistants would remain in the room, and that anything he chose to reveal would be kept in utmost confidence.

'My mum and sister – Dorothy – told me that you'd been to the house to talk to them, and that you were investigating my father's death, on a sort of private basis, not working with the police. I thought I'd come and ask you about it. I want to make sure they're all right. And what with me being gone, and them two women on their own, I thought I should know what's going on.'

'Thank you very much for coming,' said Maisie. She went on to explain her role, and that she had been contacted by a representative of the Belgian government in London to have another look at the case, given that Arthur Addens' father was a Belgian citizen, though a resident of many years standing in London.

'So they reckon the police aren't doing their job, is that it?'

'Not exactly.' Maisie was aware that Billy had raised his eyebrows in response to her comment, then looked away. 'With the tensions of war mounting in recent months, and following the Prime Minister's speech the Sunday before last, they are very . . . busy, let's say. Not that there's more crime, as such, but there is much to do with an influx of new refugees and a great movement of people – soldiers, children, and of course the many arrangements that have to be made to ensure the security of the citizenry.'

'Yeah, well, that's why I'm here in this scratchy, uncomfortable uniform – security and all that.' He looked at his hands, then at Maisie. 'And you still don't know who killed my dad.' It was a statement made with no indication of blame.

Maisie chose her words with care. 'We are coming closer. It's hard to describe how we work, Mr Addens, but it's a bit like making our way into a funnel. At first there are a broad range of possibilities, so we go back and forth, testing our assumptions and questioning each other, making sure we don't eliminate a suspect or motive before time. Then the options narrow, and we find ourselves focusing on one or two possibilities, which is when we have to be absolutely sure we have an understanding of history – of what events might have led to the taking of life.' Maisie could see that Addens was about to interrupt, and gave him no opportunity to do so. 'You were probably about to ask why we don't just alert the police to make an arrest of two or three suspects and whittle it down while they are behind bars, so we don't take the chance that they will strike again. I can only say that it is a very calculated risk – but we must have absolutely no doubt when we make our move.'

'How long will it be before you've got rid of all that doubt?'

'Another five days at most, I would say.' Maisie could see the young man's anger rising. He rubbed his hands up and down along the rough serge of his trouser legs.

'Well, you'd better tell me first, so I can have the bast—'

'Steady, son,' said Billy. 'There are ladies present. You're not in a barracks now. And Miss Dobbs knows what she's doing. When she brings in your dad's killer, no one will have a shred of doubt – there'll be no chance of the beak letting him off on what they call a technicality. Now then, pull your neck in.'

'I'm sorry, Miss Dobbs. I know we're lucky to have someone else and not just the police looking into who shot my dad.' Arthur Addens' eyes filled with tears, and at once he seemed less the soldier ready for battle than a boy in a man's uniform. 'I believe you will find him, now I've heard what you have to say. But I just want to know my mum and Dottie are safe, that's all.'

'Either Mr Beale or I would be more than happy to go round regularly to check on your mother while Dottie is out at work, if you like.'

'I'll go too,' said Sandra.

Addens looked at Maisie, then at Billy and Sandra. 'Would you do that? I mean, I know Smitty goes along sometimes after afternoon closing time, but – would you do that?'

'Of course, son – and I'll have a word with Smitty as well,' added Billy. 'I've met him, so he knows who I am.'

Addens stood up, holding out his hand to Billy, then to Maisie. 'That'll take a weight off my mind. I mean, I know the Belgian people at the consulate – or whatever it is . . . I know they're looking out for us, sending someone around, but—'

Maisie felt both Billy's and Sandra's eyes upon her. 'I beg your pardon, Mr Addens – Arthur – did you say the embassy sent someone around to the house? To see your mother and Dottie?'

'Yeah. I don't know who it was, but apparently it was a courtesy visit to ensure that the family were all right. And the bloke also said he needed documents from us, you know, my dad's papers.' He looked from Maisie to Billy, then back to Maisie. 'Do they usually do this sort of thing?'

'Where former refugees are concerned, yes, I believe so,' said Maisie.

'I don't think Dottie liked it. Since Dad died, she's been a bit like a terrier when it comes to protecting our mum.'

'No one could blame her for that,' said Billy.

Addens stood up. 'Anyway, thank you for your time, Miss Dobbs.' He pulled the beret from his epaulette and pressed it onto his head, flattening the saucer of wool against his right ear. 'Better be off. I said I'd get the garden sorted out today, before I have to go back to barracks.'

As Sandra left the room to escort Arthur Addens to the door, Maisie was aware that Billy was staring at her.

'What's that Dr Thomas playing at, miss?'

Maisie consulted her watch and made a note of Addens' visit. 'I don't know – it's all part of some great circle of secrecy.' She sighed. 'And it seems we could have been given a bit more in the way of information about embassy protocols – if that's what they are. Of course, Francesca Thomas could pull me off the case, but she hasn't – she knows that would spike my curiosity even more. But she can try to deflect my attention.' She looked up at Billy. 'There are elements here that are defying explanation – at the moment. Anyway, we should get on our way. At least the hop dust might give us a good night's sleep.'

'And that's something I could do with,' said Billy.

* * *

232

By the time Maisie pulled onto the chalky track that led to Cherry Tree Farm, it had been arranged that Billy's new hours would be from ten in the morning until half past three in the afternoon. The amount in his wage packet would not change, but it would be left to him to undertake overtime if he saw fit and if the case required it. Maisie advised him to take the following Monday off to go to the country with Doreen and Margaret, as it had been decided they would leave London and Billy should go with them, to make sure they were settled. Apparently Bobby was working late anyway, as so many ordinary motor cars were being altered to do war work. According to Billy, his boy was spending more time welding metal to make ambulances than working on engines, but at this point, as far as Maisie was concerned, having Billy out of the office on Monday would keep him in the dark regarding her own plans.

'And Bobby says these motors he's working on are being given up by ordinary people – obviously people who can afford it – because they reckon this petrol rationing will get worse, and we'll end up seeing private vehicles banned anyway. So this nice motor of yours will end up in a garage somewhere. I can't see it being useful for real work, can you?'

'Thank you, oh prophet of doom,' Maisie teased. 'In any case, I can leave the Alvis in a barn at Chelstone, if it comes to that. I'll make do with trains and buses – it just takes longer and limits me in getting to and from some places, and in this work we don't always have the luxury of the extra time it takes to catch a bus, do we?'

'It's a case of having to make do.'

They drove past tall, just-picked Kentish cherry trees and a field with three ponies, before the farmhouse and oasts came into view.

'I don't know what Mr Dobbs might say about that pony in

there – the little one. She's full of mud and dust, and it looks like she's been picked on a bit – see, she's standing all by herself.'

Maisie glanced at the field, then brought her attention back to the track. 'Yes, Dad would sort them out, of that there's no doubt.'

They pulled up in front of the farmhouse to find out where they might locate Leonard Peterson. Mr Epps, the farmer – a gruff man who Maisie suspected was in his late fifties – pushed back his cap, admired the Alvis, and proceeded to tell Maisie that she would have been better off with a tractor for coming down a farm track.

'I'm surprised you've got an axle on that thing, what with our bumpy old road!' He scratched his almost-bald pate, and after declaring that the Alvis seemed to be 'well up to it' after all, he directed them to the third hop garden on the left along the track. 'And if you're not sure, ask for Harrington – that's the name of the hop garden where he was this morning. Oh, and I'd walk if I were you. Lucky you brought a decent pair of shoes, miss.'

'Are you all right, Billy?' asked Maisie, after the Alvis was parked and they had set off along the track.

'It's these old roads that get the leg a bit, but otherwise, yeah, I'll be all right.' Billy looked across to another hop garden as he stopped to rub his lower leg, where shrapnel shards from his 1917 wounding remained embedded deep in his flesh. 'It's mostly women who come down to do the hopping now, so I reckon any blokes out here are old soldiers like me, and more than a few with a fair bit of shrapnel in them. Best not to moan.'

Maisie slowed to allow for Billy's limp, now more apparent on the uneven ground. They found Harrington hop garden, and after two enquiries, located Leonard Peterson, sitting next to a young woman on a hop bin. He wore faded olive-green corduroy trousers, a collarless shirt with the sleeves rolled up above the elbow, a brown weskit, and a patterned neckerchief. Atop his head he wore a flat cap. Two older women picked alongside them, and a child of no more than three years of age sat on the ground, picking a sprig of hops into a wicker laundry basket.

Maisie established that the man was indeed Leonard Peterson, and asked him if she might have a word in private, regarding an old friend of his.

He shrugged and agreed, pointing across to coppiced woodland flanking the hop garden. Peterson pulled a half-smoked cigarette and a box of matches from his weskit pocket as he walked through a tunnel of hop bines ready to be picked, Maisie and Billy in his wake. When they reached the side of the wood, Peterson lit his cigarette and returned the box of matches to his pocket.

'What can I do for you? You with the police? You look official,' said Peterson.

Maisie looked at Billy. Peterson's accent seemed pure London.

'Mr Peterson, I am grateful for your time. I realise you're a newly-wed and probably want to spend time with your wife, but—'

'Don't worry – it's nice to get away from my mother-in-law and my wife's sister and her boy. Gave me a nice break, you coming along.'

'Oh dear,' said Maisie. 'But just so we don't waste your time, may I ask if you were originally known as Lucas Peeters?'

Peterson's stance changed. He stood more upright, his shoulders drawn back. Maisie knew the doubt he'd shown had been replaced by a readiness to fight – with his fists, if need be.

'We're not from the government, or the police, or from any authorities that might do you harm, Mr Peterson.' She did not take a step back, but tempered her breath so that her body became relaxed. Billy did the same. Peterson's body seemed to soften. He took another draw on the cigarette, blowing smoke to the side as he exhaled.

'What do you want, then?'

'You came here to England when you were, what? Fourteen years of age?'

'About that.'

'And you left your family in Belgium.'

'Yes.'

'And you never wanted to go back.'

Peterson shook his head. 'Got used to it here. Started a little plumbing business a few year ago, and I've done well for meself.' He did not render 'year' into a plural – Maisie thought he sounded even more like a Londoner.

'Do you know Frederick Addens, Albert Durant, and Carl Firmin?'

'Didn't keep in touch, but I knew them. Not well – they were a bit older than me, and it counts at that age.'

'But you came to this country with them.'

'I ended up with them. It's not as if we were a little gang. I was on a boat at the same time as them, and we were placed together for a bit. Worked on a farm the first summer, and then that was it. Not seen them since.' He drew on his cigarette again, pinched off the burning end, and placed the small stub back into his pocket. 'Why? What've they done? Robbed a bank?'

'They're all dead, Mr Peterson.'

Peterson's colour heightened, then drained, and for a brief second, Maisie thought he might faint.

'Dead? What happened? They catch something?'

'Addens and Durant were likely assassinated, and Firmin was

236

possibly also a victim, but it was originally assumed he'd taken his own life.'

Peterson looked from Maisie to Billy. 'You reckon I'm next on the list, don't you?'

'It's a risk, Mr Peterson – I can't deny the possibility. It depends upon what you know.'

'What I know about what?'

Maisie looked at the ground, drew breath, and brought her attention back to Peterson. 'Addens. Durant. Firmin. What do you know about them?'

'Well, they were tight. But what can I say? They knew each other well, I think, but beyond that, we were all scared, tired, fed up, and wondering if we'd be allowed into England. The Germans were marching, and – well, I know those boys had something to worry about, now I come to think about it. I can't remember much, to tell you the truth, but I think it had to do with a bloke called Bertrand.'

'Christian name or surname?' asked Billy.

'Surname. Don't know the Christian name.'

'What happened to Bertrand?'

'He died.' Again Leonard Peterson looked from Maisie to Billy. 'And I don't know how he died. I don't even know if I got the name right. I was just on the – what would you call it? The edge of it all. But they were upset, I knew that.'

'Didn't you get close, that first summer, when you worked on the farm? Weren't you all living in huts?'

'Yeah, a lot of the hoppers had gone home, so we went into the huts. I sort of got on with them, but – as I said – they were tight. That woman was nice to us though – she might have something to say about them, after all, she worked for the association who got us sorted out, right at the beginning. Rosemary something or other – one of those double-barrelled names that seem to mean people can wear tweeds. All very lah-di-dah.'

'I swear you could come out of Shoreditch, the way you're talking,' said Billy.

Peterson shrugged. 'She was all right – good to us.'

Maisie reached into her bag and took out the photograph taken by Clarice Littleton. 'Is there anything you can tell me about this photograph?'

Peterson took the photograph and studied it. 'The two women – Rosemary and her friend – they brought out flagons of lemonade for us, and sandwiches. I can't remember how many people we had out there, helping out, but there was a fair queue for it. Then the other woman got out her camera, and took a snap or two.' He shook his head. 'Yeah, we lined up, the four of us with that Rosemary, and then that little toerag squeezed in.'

'The boy?'

'I can't remember his name – I don't think I ever knew it, to be honest. Far as I remember, he'd lost his mum.' Peterson looked at Maisie. 'You should speak to old Rosemary.'

Maisie held his stare. 'I have spoken to her. It was just before she was murdered.'

Peterson shook his head and took a step. 'I'm bleeding getting out of here. I'm going to get my bride, and we're going away for a week or two. Dorset's supposed to be nice.'

'Mr Peterson, are you sure you don't know anything more – anything you can tell us that might help us identify the killer?'

'I'm sure I don't – but whoever's doing the killing don't know that, does he?' He began to walk back towards the cluster of hop pickers.

'Mind you, could be a she, couldn't it? That other woman, for a start, the one with the camera. They say a woman's temper is worse than a man's – and that's another thing, Dorset is well away from my mother-in-law.'

Maisie and Billy watched as Peterson half ran towards his wife.

'He was a right one, wasn't he?' said Billy.

'Not quite what I expected, I must say,' said Maisie. 'What did you think of him?'

'He's worked on that Cockney turn of phrase. Like one of them actor types.' He squinted towards Peterson in the distance, watching as the man pulled his wife aside and was now speaking close to her ear. 'I can't say I trust him. All that losing his accent and sounding more like me than me – it's another sort of disguise, innit, miss? As good as putting on a wig and face paint. And then there's the business of changing his name. What'd he do that for? No need. If he really wanted to sound a bit more English, he could have called himself Luke Peters. And it's not as if we found out much for our trouble, coming all this way.'

'I'm not too sure about that, Billy. I think he gave us some interesting information. Anyway, let's get you to the station. I'll drop you in Tonbridge,' she said as they walked away from the hop garden and turned onto the farm track. 'Keep an eye on him, Billy. He'll go to his rooms first – find out where he goes after that, and if his wife is still with him.'

'I was going to do that anyway.'

'I know.'

When they reached the motor car, Billy took the passenger seat, closed the door, and wound down the window, but Maisie stopped. 'Give me five minutes, Billy. I just want to have a quick word with the farmer.'

'He didn't seem like someone you could have a quick word with. Bit of a talker, one of them who likes to have a good moan about things, if you ask me.'

'Just five minutes, Billy. Then on to the station.'

As she walked towards the farmhouse, Maisie could feel Billy watching her. There was an item of business she wanted to discuss with the farmer, and it had nothing to do with Billy, and nothing to do with murder.

CHAPTER FIFTEEN

It wasn't a long journey from Tonbridge Station to Chelstone, and soon Maisie was driving through the village on her way to the Dower House. In front of her, along the lane not a quarter of a mile from Chelstone Manor, she saw a woman walking at the side of the road, a babe nestled in one arm, while holding what seemed to be a heavy bag in the opposite hand. Even from behind, Maisie sensed a deep fatigue in the woman, as if she were burdened by a heavier weight upon her shoulders. She slowed the Alvis and came to a stop alongside her, wound down the window and leant across to speak to the woman.

'Excuse me. May I give you a lift somewhere? You have a heavy bag and a baby. Are you visiting?'

The woman nodded, catching her breath. 'I was told this was the way to Chelstone Manor.'

'Come on, let me take you. I'm on my way there now.' Leaving the motor car idling, Maisie stepped out and helped the woman and her baby into the passenger seat, placing her bag on the back seat.

'This is very kind of you. My poor feet were killing me.'

'Do you mind me asking – who are you going to see at the manor?'

'I've to go to the Dower House, to see a Mrs Dobbs.'

'Mrs Brenda Dobbs?'

'Yes, that's the one. She's got my boys staying there, and I've come to take them home.'

'Take them home? Isn't that a bit dangerous? They've only been here a fortnight. And they are doing so very well in the country.'

'A bit too well, if you ask me. I've had letters from them – Mrs Dobbs makes them write, which is all very nice – and it seems to me they're glad to get away from London, and us, their family.' She pulled the baby to her. 'Anyway, I miss them, what with their father away all hours at the docks, and when he's not there, he's in the pub. No, they belong at home, and it's back home I'm taking them. I reckon that Hitler has forgotten all about us anyway.'

'Mrs—I'm sorry, I don't know your name.'

'Preston. Mrs Preston.' She took a deep breath. 'No, they're better off at home. I know all about them being safe, but I'm their mother and I know best, and what's best is us being together.'

'What about school?' said Maisie, pulling into the driveway that led first to the Dower House, then across extensive lawns to the Manor.

'Bloomin' 'eck, look at that. No wonder they think this is a nice gaff.'

'Oh, they're not in that house.' Maisie steered the motor car around to the Dower House's back entrance. 'They're here – it's still a fair size, though.' She did not open the door, but remained in the Alvis. 'My father has a good way with the boys – that's Mr Dobbs.

He's from Lambeth, originally. So was I. My mother died when I was a girl. Brenda was the housekeeper here when my father was the groom – he came down during the war, to look after the horses when the men who worked here enlisted.'

'And how come you got this?' She inclined her head towards the Dower House.

'It's quite a long story. Now then, let's go and find your boys.'

Maisie helped the woman from the motor car, taking her bag and leading her into the kitchen, where Brenda was setting the kitchen table for tea, and the girl from the manor who had been sent to help was preparing vegetables at the sink.

'Brenda, this is the boys' mother, Mrs Preston.'

'How do you do, Mrs Preston? You should have let us know you were coming – we'd have put up a welcome tea for you. It's lovely of you to visit the lads. They're helping Mr Dobbs down at the stables at the moment, but they should be back soon. They'll be very pleased to see you, I'm sure.' Brenda turned her attention to Maisie. 'And Anna is out in the garden, with Emma.'

'You've got a houseful, then. Just as well I've come to take the boys home.'

Brenda raised her eyebrows. 'Take them home?' She paused, as if ready to add vociferous commentary, but thought better of it. 'Before you do anything, sit down, take the weight off your feet – there's no need to rush off, not with a babe in arms. And she's a pet, isn't she? What's her name?'

'Violet. Six months old, she is,' said Preston.

'You must be parched and tired. Look, we can make up another bed downstairs for you. Don't you go hurrying back up there to the Smoke this evening – look at the time already. Have some tea, have a rest. Our young lady here can watch the babe, and then you can decide what to do.'

Maisie nodded at Brenda to signal her approval of the approach, then turned to Preston. 'Come on, let me take you into the drawing room where there are more comfortable chairs. And we'll get you a nice cup of tea.'

Signalling Brenda to follow, Maisie led Mrs Preston into the drawing room, where the woman walked across to the window overlooking the gardens, holding the baby as if to show her the view.

'This is all very nice, isn't it?'

'Yes, it is – very peaceful.'

Preston stepped closer to the window. She frowned as she stared at Anna, who was sitting on the grass reading a book, with Emma by her side, her head on the child's lap.

'Oh, so here's where that little girl ended up,' said Preston, jogging Violet on her hip as she began to fret. 'I wondered about that one – she was at the station.' She turned to Maisie and Brenda. 'I mean, it was teeming – teeming – with children and mothers crying, but I remember her, because it was all rather odd. And I always notice when something's a bit off.'

'What was odd?' asked Maisie.

'We got there late. What with the boys, I'm always late. Everywhere I go, I'm late. We were supposed to leave from the school, all the children walking along in a crocodile, you know, in twos, holding hands. We were right at the end, running to catch up and me with the pram as well. I tell you, it was like a river of children and their mums in front of us, going up Denmark Hill towards the station. My boys were jumping up and down, trying to find their mates, when we got to the station, and that was when I noticed her, that girl. She was with an elderly lady. And the old girl was very poorly too, it looked to me, and you don't want to get a nasty chest at that age. She was coughing – that's what made me look. I remember thinking, I hope that child hasn't caught anything from her nan – it'd struck me that the lady was her nan. I mean, I didn't want my boys getting on a train with a sickly child – all them children squashed in together like sardines, and the weather what it was. If one caught something nasty, it would go through the lot of them like lightning.'

'You'd never seen the woman before?' asked Maisie.

'Never seen either of them before – but there were so many children from different schools, I didn't know half the people there anyway. It was all I could do to get my lads with their class, and I caught a few choice words from their teacher. You'd've thought she was *my* teacher, the way she went on. "Not very good, Mrs Preston," she said. "Not good enough at all." I thought she would give me a black mark in my book!' The woman laughed as if she were indeed a naughty schoolgirl caught misbehaving.

The girl brought in a tray with tea and cake. Brenda thanked her, and began to pour.

'What can you tell me about the old lady?' asked Maisie. 'You see, no one knows anything about the child, except her name: Anna.'

'She wasn't with one of the schools, then?'

'I don't think she'd started school.'

The woman put a sandwich and a slice of cake on her plate. 'Excuse me, but I have to get a bite down me before I collapse.' Maisie and Brenda sipped their tea. Preston swallowed, then began to speak. 'You know what's just occurred to me – I think that old lady was just getting rid of her, the girl. Evacuation came up at the right time,

I reckon. I mean, the woman didn't look well enough to look after a child – and where was the littl'un's mother, anyway? That's what I'd like to know.' She took a cup of tea from Brenda. 'Thank you, Mrs Dobbs.' She sipped, picked up her sandwich again, and turned back to watching Anna in the garden. 'The child was nicely turned out – not anything posh, but you could see she was clean. Had her little coat – probably second-hand and not thick enough for colder weather, when it comes. But it was pressed, and her socks were white. She didn't cry, not like some of them. Mind you, mine had smiles plastered across their faces – you could see it on them. They were glad to get away from home and a smart smack on the legs every time they give me a bit of lip. I mean, their father's never there to chastise them, so it's all down to me.'

'About Anna – could you describe the old lady?'

Mrs Preston shook her head. 'I don't know if I could.' She chewed another bite of the sandwich before continuing. 'Her clothes were older, but looked after, as if she was short of a few bob, but had her standards all the same. You know the sort. She seemed kindly to the girl, talking to her, gave her a kiss and cuddle before she pointed, telling her to join the line. The little girl didn't look back, didn't shed a tear, just did what she was told. I remember – now I come to think of it – that she started sucking on her fingers, so perhaps that was comfort for her. The lady was coughing badly – wouldn't't've surprised me if she'd brought up some blood. I saw her walk off – I think she was having a good cry, if truth be told – and then I had to get after my boys, you know, give them a peck on the cheek and remind them there'd be a clip around the ear if they misbehaved.' She looked at Brenda. 'I hope they haven't been too much of a handful.'

'Not to worry – Mr Dobbs has them under his thumb, and he's enjoying having them here.'

'I'm still taking them back, though. We can catch the London train in Tonbridge and be home by ten, I would imagine.'

'Are you sure you don't want to think about it? You should see the billeting officer, and the children's teacher, at the very least,' offered Maisie.

'They're my sons, and I don't have to get permission from anyone.' She looked out of the window. 'That looks like them now, coming up the hill with the old boy.'

'That's my father, Mrs Preston,' said Maisie. 'And he can handle your lads quite smartly.'

The woman grinned in a sheepish manner, as if to apologise for an error that, in truth, she found quite amusing. 'Could you let me know where I can change the baby? I'll let the boys have a bite of their tea, and we'll be on our way.'

Maisie drew breath to offer an alternative when the woman spoke again.

'You know, it wouldn't surprise me if that old girl hadn't been on her way to a hospital. She had a bag with her, and it crossed my mind that she was going somewhere too. Probably somewhere to die, if the state of that cough was anything to go by.'

'Thank you, Mrs Preston. We might find Anna's family yet. Now then, let me show you to the bathroom – I'll get you a fresh towel, and you can take all the time you need.'

'Thank you, Miss Dobbs – it is Miss, isn't it?' As she followed Maisie, Preston added, 'I wouldn't let that big dog near one of my children. German thing, you never know where its teeth might end up.'

Maisie bit her lip. She had learnt that sometimes it was best to let words die of their own accord, rather than fight them.

'She's out there in the garden with those two dogs now – went out there as soon as she'd had her breakfast. All in her own little world, isn't she? And I know those lads only went last evening, but it's not as if she appears to miss the company of other children.' Brenda joined Maisie and her father at the kitchen table. 'She has a way about her – like a fairy child. What do they call them? She's like a changeling.'

'I think she's probably been used to a quiet life,' said Maisie. 'I'm speculating here, but from what we know, it seems she was brought up by an elderly lady, and therefore the house was probably quite quiet. She hadn't started school, and perhaps the woman kept her in a lot, to save worrying about her playing with other children out on the street.'

'I wouldn't be too concerned,' said Frankie. 'You were a bit like that, as a girl. I mean, you had your little friend around the corner – what was her name? Susie? Yes, that's it, little Susie Acres. But after her people upped and left in a moonlight flit and we never saw her again, you kept to yourself a bit more. Always had your nose in a book.'

Maisie looked out of the window. 'Susie Acres. I haven't thought about her for years.'

Frankie put down his cup. 'Right, this won't do, sitting about of a morning. What time do you want to set off?'

Maisie looked at the clock above the fireplace. 'I'm going over to see Robert Miller now, so let's say about eleven.'

'And you're sure about it, Maisie? You know I don't hold with this cock-eyed plan of yours.'

'I think it might help – both of them, actually.'

* * *

Maisie arrived at the manor house, and was shown into the drawing room by Simmonds, the butler. Simmonds had previously worked for James and Maisie at their Ebury Place house – James had taken over the property when his parents decided they no longer wanted to come into town for the season, and were happy to remain at their country estate. Lady Rowan's most recent butler had left their employ, so it was fortuitous that Simmonds was able to take the position.

'You're looking very well, Your Ladyship,' said Simmonds.

'Thank you – I'm feeling much better these days,' said Maisie. The fact that Simmonds always addressed her by the title bestowed upon her by marriage made her cringe. It had never suited her, and felt like a piece of ill-fitting clothing whenever someone used the form of address. In Canada, James had much preferred to be known as Mr Compton, and Maisie was happy to be plain Mrs Compton. He had told her, 'I can get away with it here – no one pays attention to my title anyway.' Although their life together was far from ordinary, being in Canada seemed to give them a greater sense of freedom to do and be who they pleased. And along with that freedom came such happiness and contentment – until the day James was killed, having broken a promise to Maisie that he would not fly, not with a baby on the way.

'The nurse is bringing Mr Miller into the drawing room. It really was better for him to be accommodated on the ground floor. This is a very old house, and with all the beams, it would have been a struggle to get him up and down the stairs each day.'

'Of course. I am sure he is just glad to be away from any sort of institution,' said Maisie.

'And away from the bloody police too.' Robert Miller wheeled himself into the room, the nurse following behind.

Maisie smiled at the nurse. 'That's all right – I can assist Mr Miller while I'm here. And thank you, Simmonds.'

Simmonds allowed the nurse to leave the room first, and gave a short bow as he closed the door.

'I suppose I should start by thanking you – but I don't feel very polite today.' Miller's voice revealed a bitterness, each word spoken as if it was stuttered from a machine gun.

'That's perfectly understandable, Mr Miller. You have suffered a terrible bereavement, and you were unable to prevent the death of your sister. Then you were left to suffer.'

'I don't understand why he didn't just kill me. Why not shoot me? God knows, he would have done me a great favour. You don't know the number of times I would have liked to shoot myself since the war.' He turned his head away from Maisie. 'I used to do it all, you know. I rode to hounds, played tennis, could give up a good game of rugby. I sailed – Cowes, every year. Then this. Bloody legs won't do a thing, and I can't bloody see.'

Maisie was silent for a moment. She did not counter with suggestions of other activities – not yet. And she did not offer condolences or express her sorrow at Miller's condition. When she spoke, it was with a compassionate, yet matter-of-fact tone.

'Mr Miller – Robert – I know you've answered many questions for the police, but I would like to ask a few this morning. I realise you will have heard most before, but I would like you to bear with me.'

'I suppose it's the least I can do, considering what you've done for me.'

'Yes, we'll talk about your arrangements later, another day. Just get settled in first. In the meantime, I want you to try to clear your mind.'

'Dear Lord above, I hope you're not thinking of hypnotising me.'

'No, of course I'm not,' said Maisie. 'But in the process of trying to clear your mind, you avoid any distractions in this room, or for example thinking about Mr Avis, the gardener, who has just walked past the window stamping his feet, which you can no doubt hear. So, please, do your best to clear away any sounds from around you – except for my voice.'

Miller frowned and raised his chin, as if he were able to look at the ceiling.

'Robert, I want you to cast your mind back to the day of the tragedy. What happened?'

Miller lifted a hand and rubbed his forehead. For a second he covered his sockets, and it occurred to Maisie that he must have been an attractive young man before he fell in battle. 'I know there was a visitor, a woman, earlier – that was probably you. I heard Mrs Bolton answer the door. I heard the back-and-forth of voices, and I heard Mrs Bolton show you – the visitor – into the drawing room, and then leave after Rosemary had come in from the garden to see you. Emma was probably with her – follows her everywhere.' He paused and lifted his hand to his eyes. 'I'm sorry – I mean, *followed* her everywhere.' He let his hand fall and turned to Maisie. 'By the way, I understand you've even rescued Em. You're the perfect little angel of mercy, aren't you?'

Maisie felt her face become flushed.

'I must apologise yet again. It seems every time I open my mouth, nasty words come out. I truly didn't mean that, Miss Dobbs.'

'You're in pain, Mr Miller – it has to come out somewhere. I've found that people in distress, either emotional or physical, often cannot help themselves – as if that which hurts has to be exorcised, and inflicting some sort of harm on another provides an immediate if temporary relief.'

'Well, I'm sorry.' Another pause, another deep breath, and he continued. 'Then you left – I heard the door open and close, voices, footsteps crunching down the driveway, and then a motor car start, and you drove off.'

'Then what?'

'Rosie talking to Mrs Bolton. Then a little while later, I heard her leave the house and run down the drive – I could tell she was running. Crunch-crunch-crunch on that driveway. Then Mrs Bolton came up with a tray – a sandwich and some lemonade. I asked where Rosie had gone, and Mrs Bolton said she had walked down the road to the kiosk to make a telephone call – apparently to a shop in Tunbridge Wells. Mrs Bolton said she was supposed to pick up something and wouldn't be going in after all. So she was going to ask them to deliver.'

'I see. Then what?'

'I lost a sense of time, then I fell asleep. That happens a lot – as if my mind finds it hard trying to be useful, so it just gives up. And it takes me a while to come to – I'm in a netherworld. I sometimes wonder if they put something in my tea, or my food, to make me go to sleep. It's such a burden for them, caring for me.'

Maisie noticed that Miller had slipped into the present tense again when speaking of his sister and Mrs Bolton. She waited. In a moment, he sighed and began again.

'Rosie brought me a cup of tea a bit later, sat with me while I drank it. Then I must have fallen asleep again. At some point I woke up – I think it was dark, because the window was open and the air had that evening feel about it, sort of warm and damp, yet with a chill on the

252

breeze. I hadn't heard a motor car, though I was aware someone was in the house – I've come to realise that you have a different sense of things when you have no sight, and especially if your motions are limited. But Emma hadn't barked, hadn't made a fuss, so I thought it might be someone Rosie knew. Or at least, if Emma had not seen the man before, then she was at ease because Rosie had no reason to be afraid. Em is a funny dog – she's a sweetheart, a real rug dog, and very rarely will she be upset – unless she has due cause. That due cause is invariably associated with those upon whom she has bestowed her affections. I understand she's now the protector in chief of an evacuee child.'

'Yes, a little girl. They make an interesting pair. I'm hoping Emma can get the child to speak – she's said only a couple of words, and only to herself, and that took a lot of effort.'

'Oh, I see. Yes, shock can do that to you – I saw it in the war. One of my men, the battalion chatterbox – he was struck dumb when his best mate was blown up next to him, and he was left holding his arm where he had reached to pull him to safety. They put him in an asylum where the doctors tried electric shock to his tongue, but the last I heard, he was still unable to utter a word. Perhaps he needed an Emma.'

The room began to feel musty, as if there were not enough air. Maisie continued speaking to Miller as she opened the French doors to the lawns. 'Getting back to the events of Rosemary's death, when did you know something was wrong?'

'I was still in that sort of half sleep, but I heard raised voices, then two gunshots. What I can't understand is why Emma ended up locked in the kitchen. Was the killer afraid of dogs, so Rosie put Em away? That's a possibility. And I know that since war was declared, she said she might have to be careful with Em, being a German breed – you never know which way people will turn. Thank heavens for those Rin Tin Tin pictures Rosie told me about – might make people think more kindly towards dogs like Emma. Anyway, I think that's what might have happened – and the other possibility is that Emma took a dislike to the caller, and not knowing quite what to do, Rosie shut her away. One thing's for certain – Rosie or Mrs Bolton were the only ones who could have put the dog anywhere, no one else. Frankly, I would always trust a dog.'

'Mr Miller – Robert – could you describe the shots to me?'

Miller furrowed his brow. 'It was quick. Smartly done. One shot, then another. A revolver. I'm not an expert, but it sounded like a Browning, something like that – the army teaches you a few things, you know. There was no screaming, no pleading on the part of Rosie or Mrs Bolton. Not enough time, I would imagine. Just two shots. Then I heard the footsteps back and forth through the rooms. Drawers being opened. Emma was barking, and something was said to her – again, I'm surprised, really. Why didn't he just shoot her? It was as if he wanted to kill just one person with little other damage – Mrs Bolton was that other damage. Or perhaps he liked dogs. He certainly didn't want to kill me – if I was dispensable in his mind, I would be dead, wouldn't I? In fact, I'd bet it was his intention to shoot me at first, then he saw my sockets – a man can't identify you if he has no eyes with which to see, can he? And of course there was the wheelchair close by, so it was evident I could hardly get after him, or wrestle him to the ground. But I could yell, and he soon put a stop to that.' Robert Miller allowed his head to drop forward, his chin lowered, almost touching his chest. 'You know, I think Rosie put something in my tea after all – I think she wanted me asleep when the visitor came. You see, after she returned to the house – following that walk to the telephone kiosk I have assumed she made – she brought me the cup of tea, insisting I drink every drop. And my sense of taste hasn't been the same since the war, so I wouldn't have known if there was a sleeping powder in there. Upon reflection, while I have every reason to believe she could not have predicted her death, she did not want to risk my hearing the visitor. It was all I could do to hear the things I've recounted to you – and by the time he entered my room, I didn't have the fight in me to resist being tied, being silenced.'

'I suspect you're right about the sleeping powder, though a deep sleep without the help of drugs can have the same effect. But yes, you've probably hit the nail on the head. What happened next? He'd tied you, silenced you – did he speak to you, ask you the whereabouts of anything?'

'He loosened the gag and asked where the files were. I told him I didn't know about any bloody files – what did he think I was? My sister's blind crippled secretary?'

'What about his voice?'

'What about it? Ordinary. No regional accent. I would have put him as a middle-class mister nobody – no dropped aitches, no north country dialect, no southern rolling of the r's – nothing to distinguish him at all. Except that bloody Brylcreem on his hair. He must have plastered the stuff on. Isn't that what they call the RAF now? "The Brylcreem Boys". I was listening to the wireless and heard it the other day. Maybe he's a bloody aviator.'

'He definitely asked for the files, though,' reiterated Maisie.

'Files, records, I can't remember the word he used. I have no idea what he meant.'

'I understand Rosemary passed all the Belgian refugee records on to another association after the war.'

'Probably. I know she had a big sorting-out when we moved to Etchingham. She might have kept something, but that was behind her by a good few years. We all lived a very quiet life, really. Too quiet, I thought. I often asked her why she didn't have company.'

'What do you think prevented her from expanding her social circle?'

Miller turned, as if to look at Maisie. 'Honestly? I think she was trying to keep us in a bubble, the sort of little world we were in as children. There was Rosie, me, and Mrs Bolton – and usually a dog of some sort or another. I think she was comfortable like that. I suppose it felt safe – isn't childhood supposed to be safe?'

Maisie sighed. 'Not for all children, Mr Miller.' She came to her feet. 'Would you recognise that voice again – the man who killed your sister and Mrs Bolton?'

Miller sighed. 'I think I would. Yes. If necessary.'

Maisie nodded, reached for his hand. 'I'll leave you to rest here now. There's a nice breeze coming in from the garden. Is there anything else you need? There's a wireless in here now, so I can turn it on if you like. Or I can take you back to your room.' Miller shook his head. 'Lady Rowan will insist upon your presence at dinner, and I wouldn't cross her if I were you. One of the men – probably Lord Julian's valet – will be along to help you dress for dinner, if you require some assistance. And you can go outside. Here's the bell.' Maisie took Miller's hand and reached it towards a bell pull close to the wall. 'There are stables here. My father was once the groom, and he helps Lady Rowan decide on matters to do with the breeding of racehorses. We could get you down there, you know – just to be around them.'

'I can't bloody ride, though, can I?'

Maisie looked at the man in the wheelchair before her. 'Mr Miller, you still have working arms, and the horse can see. There's a strapping groom, a strong chauffeur, and some very hefty gardeners, so I am sure they can get a man in the saddle.'

A shy smile began to form at the corners of Miller's mouth. 'Do you think—?'

'In your good time, Mr Miller. Now then, I'll allow you a rest before Lord Julian's valet comes for you. I should probably have mentioned – there's no lunch on a tray in your room at Chelstone. Unless you go down with a frightful cold, you're expected in the dining room. Lord Julian has a military attaché from the Canadian embassy here today – troops from Canada are going to be coming over at some point, and will be setting up camp not far away. The officers are to be billeted here.'

'I – I – thank you, Miss Dobbs.' Miller lifted his hand across his brow, brushing back his hair. 'But it isn't Miss Dobbs, is it?'

'It's my maiden name, and the name I use in my work. It makes things easier. Lord Julian and Lady Rowan are my late husband's parents.'

'I'm sorry—'

Maisie interrupted Miller. 'You know, you might be able to do me a favour. Our little evacuee has a – well, I suppose you could call it a surprise – coming her way later on, so I'd like her to be distracted. She's barely uttered a word since she came here, as I explained, though I believe we may make headway today. Might I send her to visit, with Emma?'

'I'm not very good with children – I mean, I haven't even seen one since I was in France. I don't know what I should do.'

257

'Just talk to her, tell her what Emma was like as a puppy – I'm sure you have stories. And if you don't – make them up. I'll ask Mrs Dobbs to bring her across this afternoon. You can sit in the garden with her. It'll make a nice change, following all the war talk you'll have to endure over lunch.'

CHAPTER SIXTEEN

'Ready then? George is up at the gate, waiting.'

    'Just a minute, Dad. I want to telephone Billy.'

'At home?'

'He'll understand.'

Maisie went into the library to place the call.

'Billy – glad I caught you at home.'

''Allo, miss. I was about to give you a ring. I was out doing some work on a couple of our small cases this morning, thought I'd get them cleared up before too long. More to the point, I've been sniffing around and I've got something for you on Peterson.'

'Go on.'

'When I got back to London last evening, I thought I'd wander around to Peterson's gaff. I waited a bit, but no one came along. Then I thought that instead of catching the train that evening, the happy couple might've decided to get the coach the following morning – it's cheaper, and I reckon that mother-in-law of his might've had something to say if they'd left with no notice. So I went along to the bus station, looked up the timetables, and worked out the earliest they would be back home. Nipped round there this morning, and there they were, coming along the road. Couldn't believe my luck! I dropped into a shop doorway so Peterson couldn't see me – tucked myself well in. Anyway, he says to her, "Come on, girl, let's get ourselves sorted out and we'll be on the Penzance train tomorrow morning." His missus asked him when they would be back, and he said, "Let's just give ourselves a nice few days on our own – special treat, like I said yesterday." She asked if his job would be all right, and he said not to worry because he's supposed to be down in Kent anyway.'

'Did he say where they were going?'

'I heard him mention going to Paddington in the morning, and nothing more than catching the Penzance train, so I thought I'd go to the station early, get myself a cup of tea, and keep an eye out for them – shouldn't be too hard to find out where they're going.'

'Good work, Billy. You had a late night and an early start today – you must be tired. Are you sure you don't mind the extra time?'

'It's what you pay me for, miss, and it takes my mind off what's going on in this house. Bobby's at work today, and Doreen and Margaret are out – getting a few bits and pieces ready for the off on Monday. Anyway, it'll be a nightmare here tomorrow morning, what with the packing. I'll be glad to get out of it, and I won't get under Doreen's feet! That way we'll have a peaceful Sunday dinner and a nice evening into the bargain. And now I'm home I'm going to make myself a cuppa before going out and doing a bit in the garden – take my mind off it all, and it'll please Doreen no end.'

'All right, let me know if there's anything to report. And Billy –

look, I won't be in the office on Monday, and I daresay I'll be in late on Tuesday. When you get back to the office Tuesday morning, I'd like you to work on something else for me – and it's a priority, so you'll be busy.'

'Right you are, miss. Fire away.'

'It's about Anna, our evacuee.'

'Said anything yet?'

Maisie shook her head, as if Billy were in the room, watching her. 'Hardly anything, and then only to herself when she thinks no one's listening. But I have a plan, and though my father is most disapproving, I think it might work.'

'Hmmm, knowing your dad, whatever it is, I'm inclined to agree with him.'

'I'm sure you would. Now, Billy, here's the job. It seems Anna might have been spotted with an elderly lady at Denmark Hill Station, on the day of evacuation. It must have been teeming with children, but the mother of the two boys who were with us—'

'Who *were* with you? What happened to them?'

'The mother came to take them home to London.'

'Silly woman – there's a few who've done that. I reckon they'll be back, just give it a month or two, let Hitler sort himself out, and then we'll know there's a war on.'

'Be that as it may, Billy, but I can't do anything about the boys at the moment. Anyway, the mother – Mrs Preston – was here yesterday, and she thought she recognised Anna. In a way, I can see why, given her colouring – she stands out a little – but by the same token, Preston may have been mistaken. In the meantime, it's the only lead we've had.'

'What do you want me to do, miss?'

'Apparently the woman with Anna was very poorly, possibly with a bad chest infection, or in the worst case, she's a consumptive. She had a bag with her, and the boys' mother said that she wouldn't be surprised if the woman was going into hospital. There are a few voluntary hospitals within striking distance by bus or tram, so could you check?'

'King's College Hospital, Guys, St Thomas' – and I'll give the Royal Free a go.'

'Good man. That'll be a lot more shoe leather worn through. If you have any trouble with the staff, see if Caldwell can help you – perhaps a letter confirming who you are, or a call to the registrar will help. Explain the circumstances to him, and I am sure he'll understand.'

'Does he owe you a favour?'

'No, I can't say he does – yet. But he will, by Tuesday or Wednesday, I would imagine.'

'You're going over there, aren't you, miss? To Belgium.'

'Very briefly, yes.'

'Do you think you're close, miss?'

'Sorry to rush, Billy. I've got to go now – Dad and George are waiting.'

'George? The chauffeur?'

'Billy, I'm a good driver, but I don't want to get behind the wheel of Lady Rowan's new horsebox.'

Billy was silent for a couple of seconds before speaking again. 'Oh, now the penny's dropped,' he said. 'I don't like to speak out of turn, miss, but I wouldn't want to see you set yourself up for another upset.'

'The hospitals, Billy. On Tuesday. I'm depending on you.'

'If the old lady exists, I'll find her.'

* * *

'It's not like you, Maisie, to go off and do something on the spur of the moment,' said Frankie Dobbs as he sat beside her in the Bedford-Scammell horsebox, with Lady Rowan's chauffeur driving. 'I mean, it's not as if you know the child, and she could be gone in a day or two. They're bound to find her people – the billeting officer said they were looking, and as she's not been evacuated with children she knows, they're likely to send her somewhere else.'

'I think the billeting officers are underwater, and they're probably just glad enough to have her settled somewhere.'

'And where did you say you saw it?' asked Frankie.

'Just up the road, not far now. It's called Cherry Tree Farm. Here we are, George – along here on the left. It's a bit of a tight turn.'

'I can turn this twelve-tonner around inside a matchbox, don't you worry,' replied the chauffeur.

As the horsebox pulled up in front of the farmhouse, the farmer came to greet them, wearing the same old brown corduroy trousers, a pair of worn leather hobnail boots, and a grey shirt with the sleeves rolled above his elbows. He wore a tweed flat cap, and carried a shepherd's crook. A border collie stood at heel.

'Heard that lorry coming a mile off – not seen one of them yet. She's a beauty. And it's nice to see you again, Miss Dobbs,' said the man, as he began to walk around the horsebox, admiring the vehicle.

'Mr Epps,' Maisie said, drawing his attention back to her. 'This is my father.' She turned to Frankie. 'I had to see Mr Epps on business yesterday, and that's when I made the arrangements to come back today.'

Frankie touched the peak of his flat cap, and the farmer nodded by way of a response.

'My father is the best judge here – I didn't want to make the purchase without his advice.'

'Wish my daughter were like that – you never know what she's going to come home with, and none of it good for a farm,' said Epps. 'Went up to London she did, a year ago in May. Said she was fed up with mud and chickens. She'll be back, mind – yes, she'll be back.' The farmer sighed and shook his head. 'Right, let's get on with it. The lass is this way – brought her up from the field this morning.'

Three quarters of an hour later, Maisie and her father were on their way back to Chelstone. Apart from a conversation with George about what goods might be rationed, and whether the motor cars would be mothballed until after the war, Maisie's father said nothing until they had almost reached Chelstone.

'Well, I hope you know what you're doing, love,' said Frankie, looking out of the window, then back at his daughter.

'But what?'

'I didn't say a but.'

'I heard it, though.'

Frankie was silent. Maisie knew he wanted to speak, but was aware of George's presence. He lowered his voice, though George would have had trouble hearing their conversation over the roar of the engine.

'I think what you've done is very nice and all that, but are you sure you're not trying to make up for something? There, that's what I wanted to say.'

Maisie felt her face redden. She knew what her father was alluding to.

'Not at all. But these evacuee children are a long way from home – it's a long way for a child, anyway. I wanted to do something special for them.'

'Or just for one of them?'

'I didn't know the boys would be leaving – and in any case, I have a feeling Mrs Preston will be back with them in short order. A good number of London's deserted schools have already been requisitioned for army use – for bomb disposal crews, soldier billeting, ambulances, and the like.' Maisie did not want to pursue the subject; instead she asked George if he wanted her to get out and direct him through the manor gates.

'No need to run from your father, Maisie,' said Frankie. 'Unless, of course, you think I'm hitting the nail on the head.' Frankie turned to watch George, who was leaning forward, concentrating on his manoeuvre, then brought his attention back to Maisie. 'Anyway, just as well I went with you – that old boy thought he could pull a fast one. Always the way – but I just let him talk himself into a hole, and then I let him know what I know.'

She smiled at her father and nudged his arm with hers to signal her appreciation. She had a distinct feeling, though, that he had more to say about her decision to buy a pony.

George stopped alongside the Dower House for Maisie to jump down from the cab of the horsebox. She closed the passenger door, waved, and watched as the lorry rumbled along the gravelled driveway. She remained in place until the vehicle turned left just beyond the Groom's Cottage, and on towards the stables. When Maisie entered the Dower House by way of the kitchen, Brenda, having heard the lorry, had already put the kettle on to boil, and was setting out teacups and saucers on the kitchen table.

'Is Anna still with Mr Miller?'

'Best to go and get her now, I would imagine,' said Brenda. 'I took her up there after lunch. Lady Rowan had found some old children's books, in case he could get her to read to him, or describe the pictures.

He said he'd had a think and there were a few stories up his sleeve, if she didn't come out of her shell.'

'I'll go now.' Maisie turned to the door, but stopped when she heard Brenda calling to her.

'Maisie. Maisie, just a minute.'

'What is it, Brenda?' Maisie could see the tension in her stepmother's stance, the way she held on to the table, as if she needed something strong to lean on.

'Maisie, before you go over there, I want to say something. I've come to think of you as my daughter, though I've known you from the days when you worked with Dr Blanche, long before I became your stepmother through marriage to your father. And now I feel I must speak my mind, as one woman to another.'

'I know what I'm doing, Brenda – it's just something to make her feel more at home, perhaps to bring her out of herself.'

'That's all very well, Maisie – but what about when they find her family, and when she has to go home? Then what do we all do? What will you do?'

Maisie looked at Brenda without speaking, just for a second, then she placed her arm around the woman's shoulder. 'You and Dad – don't worry about me. I'll be all right, Brenda. I'm up in London most of the time anyway. It was just to help things along with the children, not just one of them. I told Dad, I didn't know two would be leaving. Anyway, Brenda, I'd better get going – they'll have the pony washed and beautiful and ready for Anna soon.'

Anna was sitting on a chair next to Robert Miller, Emma asleep on the floor between them, when Maisie entered the manor house drawing room. The child looked up at Maisie and gave what now passed for a meaningful smile. Without speaking she clambered down from her chair and looked at Miller, as if he could stare back into her eyes. She picked up the ever-present case and slipped the gas-mask strap over her head, leaving the books in a pile on the chair as she came to take Maisie's hand, with Emma following.

'I suppose that look I can feel is Anna saying thank you,' said Miller, smiling. He turned his face towards Maisie and Anna. 'Thank you, Anna. You're a very good listener.'

Maisie felt the small hand grip harder.

'It was lovely of you to entertain her, Mr Miller. Perhaps Anna will read to you next time – I believe she's a very good reader.'

'Very well,' said Miller. 'Oh, and by the way, I've spoken to Lady Rowan and informed her that I hope very much to cease being a strain upon the household as soon as I can. My cousin has already secured accommodation for me, and will take on a man to assist me with daily needs – so I won't be a nuisance for him either.'

'We'll see a little more of you before you go, then.' Maisie was about to turn to leave the room with Anna, but stopped. 'Would you like to come with us, Mr Miller? We have a little surprise here today.'

'It'll make a change from a shock. Yes, of course. If my chair can get to wherever we're going, it sounds as if it might be rather fun. And I'd like some fun.'

Maisie looked down at Anna, who had reverted to her former seriousness, as if she were trying to guess what a surprise might be, and if she'd ever had one before. Soon Maisie was pushing Miller along a well-worn path from the Dower House to the stables at the back of Chelstone Manor, with Brenda and Anna following behind. In earlier days the stables had housed carriage horses, hunters, and draught horses for the farm beyond the gardens. One retired draught horse remained, his power now replaced by a tractor. The hunters – James' hunters – were still there, for neither Lady Rowan nor Maisie could bear to sell them. They were exercised each day by two sisters who lived in the village. There was also a fine mare in foal, another Derby hopeful to join others owned by Lady Rowan Compton. Miller indicated that it was all right to leave him alongside a hunter, who poked his head over the stable door to be nuzzled. With Anna holding her hand, Maisie walked slowly towards a stable at the end of the row of stalls. She could hear Frankie's voice, and then the groom telling him, 'They're here.'

'Hello, little Anna. And to you, Mr Miller.' He nodded to acknowledge Miller, and turned his attention back to Anna. 'I've got a surprise for you!'

Anna looked up at Maisie. She wavered, as if not sure whether to go to Frankie, but Maisie nodded, and she released her hand.

'Come on, got something special for you. Over here.'

Frankie held out his hand, and as he did so, Maisie felt her throat catch, for in that moment she was a child herself, in Lambeth, on a morning when her father was taking her on his rounds, delivering fruit and vegetables to his customers. Still reticent, Anna walked towards Frankie, tiptoeing as if she were stepping across thin ice.

'There you go, pet. Have a look in there,' said Frankie, his hand on her shoulder.

At once Anna released her hold on her case and pulled off the box containing her gas mask, letting them fall to the ground. Frankie picked them up and handed them to Maisie – and she at once felt caught between laughter and tears, for Anna was embracing the white pony, who had been scrubbed until the deep-caked farm mud was washed away. Her hoofs had been trimmed, and her mane and tail brushed until they shone. Maisie watched as Frankie showed Anna the small child's saddle he had brought from the tack room, and the bridle he would teach her to put on the pony before she went for her first ride the following day.

As dusk began to fall, Maisie took Anna's hand and led her from the stable, whereupon the child looked around as if panicked, remembering her case and mask.

'There you are, Anna,' said Maisie. 'I held on to them while you were with the pony.'

Frankie remained behind to speak to Miller, saying he would be home directly the guest had been safely returned to the manor house. For her part, Anna clutched her belongings to her chest, half stumbling as she walked up the slight incline back to the Dower House, Emma at her side and Maisie and Brenda walking a step behind.

Maisie led Anna to her room and drew back the bedclothes, pulling her pyjamas from under the pillow.

When the child was ready for bed, Maisie tucked in the bedclothes and asked, 'Do you have a name for the pony, Anna?'

Anna nodded.

'What is it?' asked Maisie.

She took a deep breath, as if ready to make a pronouncement. Instead she turned on her side and closed her eyes.

With a hurried supper of ham, eggs, and fried potatoes in front of them, Maisie, Brenda, and Frankie sat down to eat. There was little conversation over the meal, though Maisie knew her father had more to say to her. And she knew it would be better if everything he thought about her purchase of the pony was out in the open.

'What is it, Dad? You've had a sore head since before we set off. You haven't said everything on your mind, have you? I think it's best if you got it all off your chest.'

Brenda looked from father to daughter, scraped back her chair, and collected the plates.

'I'll do that, Brenda,' said Maisie.

'Then I'll go and listen to the news, while you two have a word.'

As Brenda left the kitchen, Frankie Dobbs looked out of the window into the night and folded his arms. He shook his head. 'I know Brenda's said something, and I know I've had a word, but I'll say my piece and then have done with it.' He sighed and looked at Maisie, his eyes meeting hers. She felt herself begin to draw back, as her father's pale blue eyes seemed to drill into her.

'We've not crossed each other many times, my Maisie, though we've had our ups and downs – but no worse than any other father and daughter, I imagine. You've done well, and I'm proud of you.'

'This is the "but" you've been dancing around, isn't it?'

'I'm coming to it, because I've never known you so deaf, and they say there's none so deaf as those that don't want to hear. Now then—' He stopped speaking for some seconds, as if to consider how he might go on. 'I want you to hear me out – and really hear me, Maisie. Brenda and me, we got into a bit of a panic with these children turning up, and fair to be said, it was like a fever around here, what with war being declared and then this business about officers at the manor, these Canadians who're supposed to be coming. We took in the lads because it was what we should do – pull together. And then little Anna came along – not a sound out of her, but the lass has a strong will! I can tell you now, in my opinion it takes more to keep quiet than it does to use your voice. I said to Brenda, "It's Maisie's house, she should know what's going on and come down here," so she got on the telephone, and you know the rest. But I felt it even then, that the girl would pull your heartstrings. And I'm telling you – because you're *my* girl, *my* daughter – that you've got to stand back.'

Maisie opened her mouth to speak, but Frankie silenced her.

'And another thing – you've been looking into this business of refugees. I've heard you on the telephone talking about it to Billy, last time you were here. I told you before – evacuees are our own refugees, and refugees go home, Maisie. I saw it in the war – they came over here, and our people did their best for them. They opened their homes – but when the war was finished, they wanted them out, back to their own country, and with their own people. You see, love, if refugees stay on, well, it's not easy for them – because people who belong here can turn on a pin. Same with these children. The locals here might not like it, but they're doing their bit – yet they'll want them gone as soon as it's safe for the nippers to go home. And their mums and dads won't want them down here for ever either. When outsiders come, there's always someone local with a chip on their shoulder, and when those locals see the outsiders getting what they consider to be better treatment, they make it harder for everyone. Now, then – the pony is here, so the girl might find she has something to say, and that's worth the money because we'll be able to find out where she belongs. We'll do for her what we would do for any evacuee – and let that be the end of it. She didn't come here to go home miserable when the time comes – and mark my words, that's what will happen when she leaves that pony behind. What's of account is the child's feelings, and not yours, Maisie. You're not one of these Lady Bountiful types, trying to make up for the fact that they've got nothing better to do all day by interfering in everyone else's lives. And Anna can't fill the hole that James – and the baby – left behind. I'm sorry, but I see it in your eyes, even if you can't see it for yourself. It's got to stop – for your sake as much as hers.'

271

Silence hung in the kitchen. Her father had scored a knife through Maisie's heart – but she knew he was right.

'I think you know me better than I know myself. I've overstepped my mark, and I did it without thinking. I think I do it all the time. It's my Achilles' heel.' She sighed, tears biting at the corners of her eyes. 'I can't take the pony away now, but we can tell Anna she has to share it, if – when – the boys come back.' She sighed, stood up, and stepped towards her father, who had come to his feet; she reached to him for his embrace. 'Thank you for coming with George to collect the pony. And you brought her up a treat; her coat's shining, and she looks so bright – at least she'll appreciate her new home, so it wasn't such a bad day's work.'

Brenda had come back into the room, and soon they set about doing the washing-up together. When all was done, Maisie kissed her stepmother on the cheek. 'Goodnight, Brenda. And thank you too. I'm tired now, but I've work to do before I turn in. I'm going to the library for a while.' Maisie stepped away towards the door, turning back as she grasped the handle. 'I won't do anything else, I promise. She's an ordinary little girl, and I'm sure Billy's going to find her people very soon, so at least we'll know who she'll go home to, when the time comes.'

Having caught up with her work, and made notes regarding Robert Miller, Maisie felt weary as she made her way up the stairs, reaching for the banister at each step. She walked on tiptoe along the landing as she approached Anna's room, where she had left the door ajar, and peered in to check on the child. Anna was not in her bed, but standing by the window, Emma sitting on her haunches by her side. She was looking down towards the stables, where a night light remained on – the groom was making his final rounds before returning to his cottage. Unaware of Maisie's presence, the child rested a hand on the big Alsatian's head, and brought her face close to the dog's ruff.

'Emma, her name's Lady. We'll call her Lady, and we'll go for walks together. Anna, Emma, and Lady.'

Maisie stepped back and crept downstairs towards the library. She was risking her heart, and she knew Frankie was right – it had to stop, for all their sakes. But she couldn't help thinking today's risk had been worth it.

It was as she drove back into London on Sunday afternoon that Maisie reflected upon the several days she had spent at Chelstone, and the commitment she had made to her father and stepmother. With the Preston boys at home in London – and there was still a consensus that they might well be back at Chelstone in short order – Frankie and Brenda had voiced a desire to return to their own home, yet they did not want to remove Anna from the house she was becoming used to. Indeed, she had been up at dawn to rush down to the stables, where the groom found her curled up on a horse blanket outside the pony's stall, Emma having taken up a place alongside her. Maisie agreed that every Friday afternoon she would return to the Dower House, and would not leave again until early on Monday morning, when the girl from the manor came up to get Anna off to school. Frankie and Brenda would look out for Anna from Monday after school until Friday lunchtime.

However, the events Maisie replayed again and again in her mind were those of the Sunday morning. Word had spread among the staff at Chelstone that the little girl had no suitable clothing for riding a pony. One of the gardeners came to the house with a pair of long trousers that had belonged to his son when he was Anna's age, and the groom found a pair of very old leather boots in a trunk in the tack room that might suit a child, though perhaps thick socks might be required. Brenda suggested that Anna could wear her white blouse until another was found, as it could easily be washed and dried before school the following day. In the same trunk, a small bowler hat had been discovered, leading Maisie to wonder if the clothing had once belonged to James' older sister, the girl who had died so young. By all accounts she had been a fearless rider.

But it was seeing Frankie with Anna that challenged Maisie's composure. Her father's sure hand, his clear instructions, and the way he taught the girl to groom her pony before she even thought about riding, how she should run her hands across the pony's body and down her legs, feeling for heat or something that had not been there before. And Anna was so serious, following his every word, and each and every person present – not only Maisie, but Brenda, Lady Rowan, the groom, and even Robert Miller, who had insisted that he wouldn't miss the event – seemed to react to the moment when Frankie said to the child, 'Do you understand, Anna?'

And the little girl who had seemed so intent in removing her very essence from the world looked up at him and said, in a calm, strangely mature voice, 'Yes, Mr Dobbs.' She patted the pony and rested her head against her neck. 'Can I ride her now?'

'Better get the girl on that fine steed, Mr Dobbs,' said Robert Miller.

Once Anna had learnt how to mount, and to hold the reins, Frankie slipped a lead rope onto the bridle and led his charges out to the paddock. The onlookers dispersed, and only Maisie walked with her father and Anna down to the paddock, flanked by the two dogs. And as Frankie let out the lead rope, and Anna felt the pony move,

274

she began to laugh, to chuckle as if this were the best thing she had ever done in her life.

'Can I go faster, please?' she called to Frankie.

'Not yet, love. Walk before you can run, Anna. Don't get rush-headed – you don't know the pony well enough yet.'

Anna nodded, as if taking in Frankie's words. But now, as Maisie remembered the morning, and the way in which Anna began to rediscover her voice, she knew that soon enough her true identity would be discovered – and then what? Frankie was right – she could well be removed from Chelstone and billeted with children in another area. And she knew why she had assigned Billy the job of finding the woman who'd been seen with Anna. He would be thorough, and if the woman existed, he would find her. Had Maisie taken on the job herself, she would have dragged her feet.

CHAPTER SEVENTEEN

Maisie departed her flat at half past three on Monday morning, enabling her to reach Biggin Hill in good time. MacFarlane had pointed out that the aeroplane would not normally be at this location, and because it was early, most crew would not even see it depart. Driving through deserted streets forming the southern edge of the capital, Maisie met little traffic, for which she was grateful. For years Londoners had been promised a new south circular road. Parts had been completed here and there, but Maisie knew that if her journey were being made later in the day, it would have taken ages. She was soon driving through Crystal Palace, on to Bromley, and from there to Leaves Green and the aerodrome nearby. She pulled up to the main entrance and was asked to show her identification card. The guard was questioning her, grasping a clipboard and checking her name, when a tall, well-built man emerged from the shadows of a breaking dawn. He flicked open a wallet to show his identification.

'It's all right, Sergeant. I can take over here.'

The guard shone his torch on the proffered official documentation, and directed the beam to the man's face. 'Right you are, sir,' he said, opening the gate to allow Maisie onto the aerodrome. Once through, she stopped and allowed MacFarlane to take the passenger seat.

'I always wanted a ride in this beast,' said MacFarlane.

'You should have said, Robbie – you didn't need to go to this trouble.' Maisie slipped the Alvis into gear and began to move the vehicle forward at a slow pace.

MacFarlane pointed to a building set aside from the others. 'Round the back there – park your motor, and we'll have a little chat.'

'Oh dear. When you say the words "little chat", I get worried. Wasn't it a little chat that took me to Munich last year?'

MacFarlane laughed. 'And that, I suppose, is another reminder that this jaunt is payment of a debt I owe you. Fair enough, lass. Fair enough. But I've made some enquiries and a few arrangements that might make your life a little easier.'

Maisie parked the motor car as instructed, turned off the ignition, and turned to MacFarlane. His face was almost indistinguishable in the early-morning light. 'That's handy. What have you arranged, Robbie?'

'This is, of course, all in my own interests. The last thing I want on a Monday – or any day, come to that – is to have to get onto one of those rickety flying machines and go over there on a mission of mercy to bring you home.'

'Rickety?' said Maisie.

'I jest and exaggerate, but you know what I mean.'

'Are you going to tell me, or shall I guess what you've done?'

'I'm getting to it, Maisie.' MacFarlane's tone became more serious. 'You gave me reason to think you might need a hand, so here's the hand. I told you before about the motor car waiting for you in Belgium. One of our men will be there when you land. He'll take you to the town you specified – and yes, it's not far from Liege, but more of a village, I would say, but then I come from Glasgow, so anything less than a city is a village. He will wait to bring you back to the airfield after you've finished your work. A reminder: the thing – and by that, I mean the aircraft – will only take one passenger, and that's you, but do not try to communicate in any way with the pilot. You won't be able to hear yourself think, in any case, let alone have a chat. All I will say is that this aircraft was earmarked for a delivery operation, and it just so happened I could squeeze you in.'

Maisie nodded, knowing MacFarlane had more to say.

'Now, two people know you're coming. The local policeman – I found the most senior man I could, Janssens. And the mayor, very nice chappie. Monsieur' – MacFarlane pronounced the salutation 'mon-sewer' – 'Martin. He might not spell it like you or I spell it, though. Both speak English very well, so you won't have to embarrass your country in the attempt.' MacFarlane paused.

'I think I did pretty well when I managed to outrun Huntley a few years ago.'

'I don't believe you actually outran him, Maisie. I understand he caught up with you in Paris.'

'But I take your point. Speak in English. And I suppose I can't speak to anyone else.'

'Our man there is under instructions to get you out directly you've had your second little chat. We are allies of our friends the Belgians, but it's always best to take precautions just in case old Mr Hitler has eyes and ears on the ground and no one knows those eyes and ears belong to a German.' MacFarlane sighed. 'Not that you have anything of interest to them, but by now they might be a bit put out by the stunt you pulled in Munich last year. In any case, to try to keep you safe and sound and not having to go up in a kite in the first place, I thought I might try to get Janssens and Martin to agree to a tête-à-tête over the telephone, but neither of them went for the bait on that one – so you're right, you should get over there if you're looking for the confirmation you want. So long as the delay while you're there is worth the risk.'

'There won't be another murder,' said Maisie. 'That's why I have just a little time to make sure.'

In the distance an aircraft could be heard approaching.

'That'll be the five o'clock from Newmarket to a field in Belgium, via Biggin Hill,' said MacFarlane, mimicking a railway stationmaster. 'Newmarket is home to this particular Lysander. Come on, Maisie, we'd better get over there.'

It was, as Maisie had expected, a cramped journey in the only passenger seat on an aircraft hailed for manoeuvrability. But it could do the job – the Lysander was known to be able to land or take off on almost anything, including, in this instance, Flanders farmland. Maisie had kept her eyes closed for most of the short journey, gripping the seat for support. She was a nervous flyer, and was glad to have foregone the opportunity to eat, and now, upon landing, felt her legs almost give way as she jumped to the ground, aided by the man waiting for her. He escorted her to an idling motor car, and returned to the aircraft to speak to the pilot, who handed him a large package. She saw the two men look at their watches, and the pilot nod before taking his seat once again. The man returned to the vehicle, placed the package in the back of the motor car, and covered it with a blanket. He turned to Maisie and shook her hand before opening the passenger door for her. 'Lawrence,' he said.

Maisie was about to ask whether that was a Christian name or surname, but held back. She was not meant to know. Lawrence was about forty years of age; he wore trousers of dark beige and a tweed jacket. His pale green shirt was complemented by a green and yellow cravat at his neck. His hair had been combed back and oiled to keep it in place. As he began to drive out on to the country road, Maisie looked at his hands on the steering wheel. They were broad hands, the hands of someone who had done manual labour, but it was as if they had been freshly manicured in an attempt to render them less rough and ready. They were, thought Maisie, the hands of someone who could very well use them to kill.

'We'll be in the motor for about three quarters of an hour.' With his right hand Lawrence pulled a packet of cigarettes from his inside pocket, shook one out, and offered it to Maisie.

'No, thank you,' Maisie said.

He held the packet close to his mouth and clasped the most prominent cigarette between his lips. Having returned the packet to his pocket, he took a lighter from another pocket – it did not appear to concern him that the motor swerved every time he moved – and lit the cigarette. Lawrence snapped the lighter shut, put it back into his pocket, and inhaled on the cigarette. He removed the cigarette with the V between the first two fingers of his right hand, and blew smoke out of the open window. Flicking ash into a tray close to the gear stick, he began to speak.

'Your first appointment is at half past eight, with the police chief. No need for correct salutations – a simple "M'sieur" will do. Same with the mayor. Both nice chaps, though you mightn't get much joy with either of them. Close-lipped about the war – most people just want to forget.'

'We'll see,' said Maisie, looking out of the window across the flat land of Belgium. More than once they had passed cemeteries and memorials to war dead. 'I believe they know something that will prove of use – I wouldn't have made the journey had it not been important.'

'Fair enough. The Lysander wouldn't have landed if you hadn't been important. That thing can swoop down low and drop anything for me; I sometimes wonder if I couldn't just reach up and take it from the pilot's hands before he goes up again.' Lawrence sighed and pointed in the direction of fields alongside the road, and then at two cemeteries for war dead in the distance. 'Hard to believe how churned up this was after the war. They've done a marvellous job of rebuilding their towns and villages, the Belgians. If you hadn't seen those cemeteries – and keeping them up is down to the British – you wouldn't know a war had been fought here.'

'I think I would,' said Maisie. 'Not only can you feel it, but you can see the ridges across the landscape. Those scars there, as if something had scraped the topsoil – it's where the trenches were. You can't just fill in that amount of earth and expect it not to show.' She kept her gaze trained on the fields as they seemed to flash past. 'War has left its scars here, Lawrence. And those scars might never heal.'

Conversation between Lawrence and Maisie sputtered, started, ended, and started again throughout the journey, as they each avoided questions that might reveal more than they wanted the other to know. They spoke about the local food, the beautiful lace from Bruges, paintings Lawrence had seen in the museums in different Belgian towns – he admired Bruegel, and wondered aloud what Hieronymus Bosch would have done with scenes from the Great War. Having mentioned the war again, he veered away from the topic and asked if

Maisie was hungry, if she needed a cup of coffee. She declined, though she said she would like something to drink when they arrived, but felt it might be best to keep her stomach empty given the possibility of another bumpy flight in just a few hours.

They passed through several small towns and villages, and soon entered the town of their destination. Neither acknowledged the fact, though it was not long before Lawrence parked outside a house that was grander than the others. Maisie was aware that she had reached the home of the *bourgmestre*, the mayor.

A man in uniform answered the door and addressed Maisie by name. She was relieved to be addressed as 'Madame Dobbs' as she feared MacFarlane's string-pulling had included using her title by marriage.

'M'sieur Martin will see you in the library,' said the uniformed man.

With their tall ceilings and ostentatious mouldings, the rooms they passed through might have seemed overwhelming, but curtains of soft velvet and the way light fell across the rich, textured carpets rendered the mayor's official residence welcoming.

'Madame Dobbs, it is my pleasure.' Martin's hand was outstretched almost as soon as Maisie entered. He took her hand, then waved to the soldier – if the man was indeed a soldier – and with the same hand indicated a chair next to an unlit fireplace. Every movement seemed to be executed with a flourish. The chair faced another of the same type – its frame carved and gilded, upholstered in rich red and yellow. The coat of arms of the municipality of Liege had been embroidered into the back of each chair.

'Mr MacFarlane explained that I might be of help to you – you are investigating the unfortunate deaths of former Belgian refugees who remained in England following the war.'

'Yes,' said Maisie. 'I thought you might be able to assist me. You see, I know at least two came from this town, and the others from nearby, perhaps a neighbouring village. I believe – I suppose I should confess it is more of a guess, at this point – that their connection here is the common denominator and that something happened in the war that has now, years later, triggered the killings.'

'I see. As you know, there was enough death throughout Belgium to affect an impressionable young man or woman, and of course you know our immediate region, along the Meuse, was the scene of some of the most terrible battles. We were particularly vulnerable, given our proximity to Germany.'

'The men concerned were not old enough to fight, they were too young to enlist or be conscripted. I know at least two who left were with family members who perished, either on the journey to the coast, or soon after arrival in England.'

Martin sat back, one leg extended in front of him. He leant an elbow on the arm of the chair, and rubbed his chin. Maisie suspected he was a veteran of the war, that he had suffered leg wounds – she hadn't noticed a limp, but she was sure there had been an injury to the limb he was unable to bend.

'When the Kaiser's army invaded, there was a certain amount of chaos – war is always chaos. Boys who had not enlisted were rounded up – those young enough to still be clutching their mother's skirts were allowed to return. Older boys, those who would have been in uniform within a year or two, were taken away. Some as prisoners of war, some to be killed. Murdered.'

Maisie nodded. 'Yes, I have heard this.'

'But we knew what was coming, and many of those boys, though they did not fight in our uniform, they fought in any other way they could – joining women in acts of sabotage, gathering vital information on the passage of the enemy, and of course, if need be, they were also assassins, though that was rare. We had an invader in our midst and we did all we could to stop him. The Germans had marched into a sovereign nation and tried to take her – it was rape by any other name.'

Maisie watched Martin as he spoke, saw the anger rising. 'You must be very worried, M'sieur Martin.'

'We are neutral now. Armed but neutral.'

'Do you think you're safe?'

'I think we're safer than the British.'

Maisie moistened her lips with her tongue and spoke again. 'The young men who left, I wonder, did you know them? Or, I should say, know *of* them? Their names were Frederick Addens and Albert Durant.'

Martin looked down at his hands, now clasped together, and ran his thumbs around each other, as if creating a small wheel that might drive his thoughts. Maisie knew he was debating how much he should tell her. At last he placed both hands on the arms of the chair and rose to his feet. As he walked closer to the fireplace, his limp was quite distinct. This man had fought in the war.

'Addens and Durant left because they had to leave. If the Germans had caught them, they would have killed them – and the Germans were looking. Addens and Durant were engaged in resistance work – all those things I mentioned. Addens, especially, showed a talent for anything mechanical, and taught himself to make explosives. They were responsible for actions that led to the deaths of German soldiers and the destruction of a significant amount of ordinance. They left because they had to – there would have been more death.'

'They were very brave.'

'Very brave – they were little more than children when they began. And know this – our women fought too.'

'La Dame Blanche,' said Maisie.

'Yes – that came later. You know, then.'

'Yes, I know.'

Maisie broke the silence with another question. 'Do you recognise the names Carl Firmin and Lucas Peeters?'

Martin looked at Maisie. 'These men are both dead too?'

'One of them.'

'Do you think they were known to Addens and Durant?'

Maisie nodded. 'I do. I believe they might have been involved in the resistance efforts together, or might have met each other on the journey to the coast, and then on to England.'

'Yes, I suppose it's possible.'

'But what I want to know is why a killer targeted these men.'

Martin shrugged. 'I cannot help you, Madame Dobbs. They were our heroes. All our townspeople – men, women, boys, and girls – they were all heroes. I hope they don't have to become martyrs again.'

Maisie came to her feet and walked towards Martin. 'Thank you for your time, M'sieur Martin. I am grateful for your assistance.'

The man shrugged. 'It was only a little information, for you to have come so far to receive.'

'It was enough.'

'You know, there was another lad, the same age as Frederick. His name was Xavier Bertrand. He was one of those who had to leave with his family. The Germans were after him too.'

Maisie shook her head. 'No, that's not a familiar name. I'm sorry.'

Martin took her outstretched hand. 'I wish you a safe journey home, madame.'

'And I wish you well in the months to come.'

As Maisie left the residence and descended the steps towards Lawrence in the motor car, she knew she was closer. There had been a sensation in her body, almost a shiver, though she had given away nothing in the meeting with the mayor. If she were with Maurice, she would have described a feeling that began in the centre of her being, and flooded out from there. And he would have said, 'Go on, Maisie. Trust your instinct. And then prove it. Always, you must have your proof.' *Xavier Bertrand.* Now she had to find out how, exactly, this name would fit into the puzzle. But she knew, as if by instinct, that she was already halfway there.

Lawrence drew the motor car alongside a dour grey-stone building that Maisie thought she could have easily picked out as the police station. The man known only as Janssens came to meet her, inviting her into a small square office, with a single window offering light but no view.

'Please sit down, madame. May I offer you refreshment?' Janssens remained standing.

'Just a glass of water, please.'

The police officer gave a brief nod, turned to a tray on a sideboard behind his desk, and poured water from a carafe into a fresh glass. He placed it in front of Maisie, who thanked him. Janssens sat down, pulled his chair in close to the desk, and clasped his hands on top of a file of papers before him.

'You are interested in men who were boys when they left for England due to the occupation of our town.'

'Yes,' said Maisie.

Janssens nodded. 'It would have been better had they returned, instead of remaining in a foreign country. We could have done with their help.'

'They were all at that age, I suppose, when it's easier to put down roots, and by the time the war ended, they had become entrenched in life in England.'

Janssens nodded. 'Yes, that's true. And they were all brave young men.'

Maisie leant forward. 'I believe Frederick Addens and Albert Durant belonged to a resistance group, and were being sought by the German army, given the success of their work.'

Janssens chuckled. 'Oh, they were a success indeed.' He became serious. 'And it wasn't just those boys either – their sisters, mothers, and grandmothers helped. The Germans couldn't believe old women could cause much trouble, and only looked for the boys – but in some cases the women and children still had to leave in haste, because they would have been murdered in the attempt to gain information from them.'

'The name Xavier Bertrand has come to my attention, yet he is not known to me or, I believe, to the British authorities – though I can check again when I return to England.'

'Xavier Bertrand, Frederick Addens, and Albert Durant were as thick as thieves. The Three Musketeers. Then there was another boy, from a village along the Meuse – name of Firmin. Younger, I think . . . though perhaps not. He became part of their little gang.'

'Were you here then? Or away fighting?'

'I was here for longer than I wanted – my eyesight. But then the eyesight wasn't a problem any more – getting men in uniform to replace those who had perished, that was the problem.'

'Did Xavier Bertrand have family? Are they still here – mother, sister, brother?'

Janssens frowned, pushed back his cap, and scratched his head. 'A mother who wasn't well – she hadn't been well since the youngest was born – Xavier persuaded her to go with them. There was a sister who had died before the war, and the younger brother – I think he was a much younger brother.'

'Do you remember his name?'

Janssens closed his eyes. 'It's right there, on the tip of my tongue. B-B-B . . . no, no.' He opened his eyes and shook his head. 'I am so sorry – I cannot remember.'

'Do you have a registry of births? Would I be able to see it in the church?'

'That is a possibility. You'll find the church just along the road. There is a ledger held there, a record of all marriages, funerals, and baptisms. You could ask the priest, Father Bonhomme. Otherwise, to obtain that information would take longer than you have at present. There are procedures, and even I cannot make them go faster.'

Maisie came to her feet. 'Yes, of course. I understand.' She took up her glass of water and drained it, then held out her hand.

'Would you like another glass?' said Janssens, shaking her hand.

'No, thank you – I have to run now. I don't have much time.'

'Good luck, madame.'

'And good luck to you too.'

Janssens smiled. 'God willing, we will never see war again here.'

Maisie nodded. 'Yes. God willing.'

Lawrence looked at his watch. 'My instructions were to get you straight back to the airfield.'

'I think just "field" would be enough of a description, don't you?

288

Look, both those meetings were not as long as anticipated, so we have a little time. Please, I must go to that church, and it's just along the road.'

Lawrence wound down his window and threw out a half-smoked cigarette. 'This could lose me my job, you know.' He steered the motor car out on the road towards the church.

'Oh, come on, Lawrence – don't let's be dramatic, just when we're getting along so well. Take me to that church, and then we can go. I will be five minutes. And you would not lose your job just because I might be a minute late to get onto that aeroplane.'

'We have the authority, but not exactly the permission, with regard to a given field.'

'So you're worried a farmer with a pitchfork might come out steaming with anger and an intent to kill because you've ploughed down his sugar beet.' She had not intended to be so curt, but did not want to be tripped up by her driver at a crucial moment.

Lawrence seemed to glare at the road ahead. 'Here's your church. Five minutes.'

Maisie ran into the church, which was still, silent, and enveloped her in chill air, a counter to the warm late-morning weather outside. Walking along the aisle, she noticed a place in the roof above the altar where repairs appeared to have taken place in recent years – and she imagined the unholy scene when a shell – for surely it had been a shell – had ripped through the building. As she approached the altar, a priest emerged from behind a rich velvet drape, beyond which Maisie suspected church records were kept.

He smiled at Maisie, and she stopped, lowered her head before a carved wood depiction of Christ on the cross, and looked up again towards the priest.

'Excuse me . . . Father Bonhomme?' Unfamiliar with the protocols of the Catholic church, Maisie hoped this man spoke her language, even a few words. 'Do you speak English?'

The man smiled. 'I studied theology at Cambridge, madame. Before the war. I'm a little . . . a little rusty, as you might say.'

'Oh, thank heavens! I mean – I'm glad. Father – I am in need of your help.'

He gestured towards the confessional.

'No, no – no, that's very kind of you, but not that kind of help.' Maisie explained her need to view the church records of baptisms.

'Come this way. I can see this is very urgent. How far into the past do you want to go?'

'Let me see – to about 1910, so let's say a year or two either side.'

Father Bonhomme led Maisie to a wood-lined room that was small, cold, and smelt of dust and foxed papers. He opened a tall cupboard and took down a substantial leather-bound ledger, some three inches thick – Maisie could see him strain to lift it. It must contain a record of births from the parish and beyond extending at least a century into the past, she thought. The priest let it half fall onto the table, leant forward to locate the red ribbon marker, and opened it to the most recent page. Each birth had been entered in a fine Italic script, naming the child, the date of birth and of baptism, along with names of the parents, grandparents, and godparents. He leafed back through the pages.

'Here we are. Nineteen hundred and eight. You can start there.'

Father Bonhomme stood next to Maisie as she ran her fingers down the list of names, until she reached the surname she was looking for. She held her breath, looked away from the ledger, and closed her eyes.

'You do not want to see what you came to see. Is that it?' asked the priest.

'Yes. I'm afraid it is.' She met his eyes. 'Father, I am an investigator. I am searching for someone I believe has taken the lives of others. This is always a troubling moment for me, when I am close to the perpetrator of a terrible crime, yet in possession of the knowledge that something equally dreadful must have happened to that person – and I must know what it is, otherwise I cannot draw my work to a satisfactory conclusion.'

Bonhomme nodded. 'And you are seeking your own absolution, for in revealing a man who has taken life, you might also send him to his death.'

'I have to know everything. And though I can see a name here, and I have my finger on it at this very moment – not quite the name I want, but I know what I am looking at – I have much more to do. I have to discover the why. I have to find out what leads a person to do such a thing.' Maisie felt hot tears of frustration rise up, flooding her eyes.

Bonhomme was silent, then spoke in a low voice. 'The confessional is a sacred place—'

Maisie shook her head, pulling a handkerchief from her pocket and pressing it against the corners of her eyes. 'I don't believe it – surely you are not going to hide what you know behind the secrecy of the confessional.'

The priest sighed, then looked up towards the ceiling, as if his God were sitting ready to judge. 'I have information I was given outside, away from the confessional, though it has been argued that any confession made to a priest is sacrosanct.' He brought his attention back to Maisie. 'It would have been over a year ago – perhaps a year and a half. I came out of my church and was met on the steps by a man I had never seen, not one of my parishioners. He did not want to

291

come in, but it seemed to me he wanted to talk – so we passed the time of day, commented on the weather, and he asked about the repairs. The church was shelled in the war, and we had spent many years gathering funds to rebuild – that part of the church was covered with scaffolding on the day the visitor came. His name was Carl Firmin, and he had been baptised in the church, though he said he had lost his faith, that he had seen too much in life.'

'I can understand that,' said Maisie.

'And though I am a man of God, so can I. I knew I could not, at that moment, bring him back into the arms of the Lord, but I also knew that as a man, I had to listen to him.'

The priest had drawn breath to continue when Lawrence entered the room, pulling back the curtain with an energy that Maisie thought might bring down the brass rail holding it up.

'Excuse me, I don't want to get blasphemous or anything, but you've been far longer than the promised five minutes.'

'I beg your pardon. Lawrence, I will be another two minutes. Please leave, and I will be out.' Maisie felt herself biting back her frustration. She was so close.

Lawrence held up his wrist, pointed to his watch, and said, 'Two minutes, or God knows how I will get you back to England.' He turned to the priest. 'Sorry about taking his name in vain, and all that.'

Another five minutes later, Maisie ran from the church, and took her seat in the motor car. Lawrence pushed down on the accelerator, and was soon driving at speed. He never said another word to Maisie, and she said nothing to him. At the landing field, the Lysander's engine was already running. Maisie leapt from the motor car, followed by Lawrence, who helped her clamber on board. She did not look back, did not offer thanks, but as the aircraft took off into the air, she looked down and waved before the Lysander merged into the clouds.

It was on that flight home to England, as the coastline came into view, that Maisie wondered whether Father Bonhomme's very name had dictated his path into the church. Bonhomme – good man. As far as Maisie was concerned, in a moment of difficult choice, he had been a very good man.

CHAPTER EIGHTEEN

'I'm glad to see you, miss – I was worried sick. I mean, I guessed you were going over there on the QT, but all the same, I've been on the edge of my seat.' Billy looked at his watch. 'You're later than I expected.'

'I'm back now, and I've an important telephone call or two to make,' said Maisie.

Billy pushed back his chair and stood up, grasping his notebook. 'Miss, I think I've found her – the old lady who was with the little girl.'

Maisie stopped at the threshold of her office, endeavouring to compose her features to reflect excitement, and not the dread she felt upon hearing Billy's words. She turned to Billy. 'That's wonderful news. Well done. Come in, tell me what you've discovered.'

The case map was already laid out, but neither Maisie nor Billy looked at it. They took their usual chairs alongside the table. Maisie turned to Billy.

'I reckon she's the one,' said Billy. 'I went to all the hospitals she could possibly have gone to, though I think she's a woman in St Giles' Hospital. Apparently when she came in, she gave her name as Louisa Mason, from an address in Camberwell – more about that in a minute. Gave her age as sixty years old, and widowed. She said she had no dependents – and I'll come back to that too, in a minute. She's in a special ward, as she's got some sort of lung disease. It's not consumption, but it's serious – very serious – all the same. She hasn't got long. I asked the nurse what "not long" meant, because it's not exactly a medical term, now is it? She said, "Weeks, not months." I said to her, "So about three weeks, then?" and she said it was hard to say, but three weeks sounded about right, perhaps a bit longer or shorter. I managed to get Mrs Mason's address – they weren't going to let me have it, but I just told them the truth, that I was looking for an elderly lady who'd been seen putting a little girl on an evacuee train, and the child is in a bit of a state, and we need to find the woman. All right, so I over-egged the puddin' when it came to describing Anna's distress, but it did the job. The nurse in charge let me peer over the notes, and I caught the address straight off. So I went down there, to Rye Grove – she had two rooms and a scullery in a terrace house there, with the WC outside, like they all have.'

Billy paused, in case Maisie had questions, but she nodded for him to continue.

'It's not exactly London in its prime, if you know what I mean. But I spoke to a neighbour who saw me looking and called me over – she thought I might be from the Ministry of Health or something like that.' Billy raked his hands through his hair as he studied his notes. 'Here's what I got from the neighbour, a Mrs Headley. The old lady lived in the house – her rooms, that is – with the little girl. It used to be just her and her daughter, Mary. The father died when Mary was about thirteen – and already looking twenty, by the sound of it. And I say "died", but apparently the father topped himself – hadn't been right since he came home, after the war.' Billy paused. 'Are you sure you haven't got any questions yet, miss?'

'No, I'm just listening and thinking. Go on, Billy.'

'Now, there was also a son, older than Mary. But instead of looking after his mum and sister, like you'd think he would, he went off to Africa somewhere as soon as he could get on a ship. This neighbour said he worked his passage, and went to Cape Town – as far as she knew. Apparently there was work in the mines there, and he wanted to earn his fortune. She said he'd sent some decent money home for a time, and then it stopped, and so did the letters. Louisa had a factory job for a good while, and when they first lived in the street, the family rented the whole house, but then Louisa had to take in lodgers, which is why she ended up in the two rooms – and it's not as if they're big houses in a posh area. And from the time she was thirteen, this Mary went off the rails – that's what the woman said. Went from one job to another and out all hours. There were rows, and the neighbours heard every word, by all accounts. Then Mary fell for a baby. They don't know who the father was, but he never came round to the house, never put in an appearance. Louisa had told the neighbour that he was a sailor from Malta, and Mary was swept off her feet by him. Mary would only ever say his name was Marco. The neighbour said that a couple of adoption societies came calling, but Mary said no, she would keep her baby – brave girl, if you ask me.' Billy looked up. 'I've been reading about the new adoption act – about time too, if you ask me. I mean, anyone can just go in and take a baby and go home with it. It's not as bad as it was twenty-odd years ago, but it's been harder to bring home an animal from Battersea Dogs and Cats Home than it is to get a new baby, soon as it's born.' He shook his head and sighed. 'So Mary kept the baby – sounds religious, doesn't it? Louisa had to leave the factory work on account of her chest, so she took in washing, went out cleaning, that sort of thing – and she looked after the baby while Mary was at work. Then Mary went back to her old ways. Didn't want to be a mum. Ended up being knocked about by a bloke one night, and died hitting her head on the pavement. He's in clink for life – the defence persuaded the jury it wasn't an intended death, so he didn't swing for it – and the little girl's an orphan, aside from her nan. And I take my hat off to Louisa – she didn't put Anna into a Dr Barnardo's Home, not like some would. She kept her – but I suppose her chest kept playing up, which must have been terrible for the woman.' He sighed again, closed his notebook, and looked out the window, then at Maisie. 'Once I started on this, I couldn't stop. I thought, I've got to get to the bottom of this, for the little girl, for little Anna. I don't know what that poor old lady went through, not knowing what would happen to her granddaughter – the only family she had left. Then came evacuation – it must have been like a rope thrown out to her before the ship went down. Mind you, I doubt she was thinking straight.'

'Did this neighbour say anything about Anna?'

'Just that she was a very polite child, that the grandmother made sure she was always nicely turned out, that she knew her pleases and thank-yous, and she used to take her to the library all the time – it was somewhere for them to go, I suppose. The neighbour said she thought Louisa was a bit scared that the child might be bullied, called names, on account of her colouring – but no one did any of that, because she was such a good girl. I wouldn't have banked on it staying that way when she started school.'

'She's been all right so far,' said Maisie. 'And Brenda's been keeping an ear out for any trouble. With a big dog following her everywhere, I don't know that anyone would dare, to tell you the truth.'

They sat in silence for a moment, until Maisie spoke again. 'That's a lot to consider, Billy. It would be best if I went to see Anna's grandmother. I might be able to go later in the day. I believe we will be busy this morning.'

'I've got some information on Peterson too, miss.' Billy paused, as if unsure to go on, but continued when Maisie nodded. 'I got there to Paddington, saw him and the wife buy their tickets, and went to the platform – the train was on its way down to Penzance, but they could have been stopping anywhere along the line. Once they'd gone, I went along to the ticket office and gave up a couple of bob – the bloke remembered them and said they'd bought two third-class returns to Exeter. Planning on coming back in a week.' Billy paused again. 'Is it time, miss?'

Maisie nodded. 'It is. Yes, it's time.'

She stood up and walked around to the chair on the other side of her desk, picked up the telephone receiver, and placed a call to the office telephone number provided by Francesca Thomas. Gervase Lambert answered.

'May I speak to Dr Thomas? It's Miss Maisie Dobbs here. She is expecting my telephone call.'

'I am afraid she is not in the office, Miss Dobbs. May I take a message?'

'I see. I wonder, could you tell me when she might be back?'

'I believe it was her intention to go straight home following a meeting this morning.'

'Right you are. Do you have her address, Mr Lambert?'

'I'm afraid I'm not at liberty to divulge that information, Miss Dobbs. I am terribly sorry. But I will ensure she calls you.'

'Of course – I understand. Thank you very much. Good day, Mr Lambert.'

Maisie replaced the receiver, though she did not take her hand away. She looked up. Billy was staring at her, already putting on his jacket. She lifted the receiver again and dialled the same number. A young woman answered in heavily accented English.

'May I speak to Mr Lambert, please?' asked Maisie.

'I am very sorry, but you have just missed him. He left the office a minute ago – may I take a message?'

'No, thank you, that's quite all right. I'll call back later.' Maisie replaced the receiver to disconnect the call, picked it up again, and placed another call.

'Yes!' The answer was as intemperate as Maisie expected, but she was in no mood to banter.

'MacFarlane – Robbie – I need your help. Dr Francesca Thomas – her address.'

'Maisie, you know very well we cannot allow anyone – even you – to have her address. She works on behalf of two governments in a highly confidential realm, and her living arrangements—'

'I know all that, Robbie, but we are on thin ice here – very thin ice. If you don't let me have that address, I will not be able to prevent a murder.'

MacFarlane allowed a second's silence to elapse. 'Here it is – government property. 16 Aldred Mews, Kensington.' He proceeded to give directions, and then added. 'I'll see you there.'

'I'm on my way with Billy.'

'One more thing.'

'MacFarlane, I must go.'

'It's important. Remember there are agreements between allies. It's to do with diplomatic immunity, Maisie. Don't put a foot wrong – we don't want trouble, and we don't need any more enemies.'

'See you there. And hurry.'

Billy hung on to the leather strap above the passenger seat as Maisie negotiated the London streets at speed. He was silent as Maisie swerved around vehicles, sounded her horn when approaching a junction, and raced past lagging traffic. At last, Maisie slowed the Alvis.

'I can't risk driving into the mews – the sound will attract too much attention,' she said. 'This will do – the mews is just around the corner.'

Having parked on Cromwell Road, Maisie and Billy alighted from the motor car and ran into Aldred Mews.

'It's this one,' said Maisie. 'Oh dear—'

The door was ajar. Had Francesca Thomas answered the door and deliberately left it unlatched, so the breeze might push it open? Or had a caller come to the house and inadvertently left the door open? Or was it a deliberate invitation to witness a murder?

'I'll go first, miss,' said Billy.

'No,' said Maisie, her voice low. 'No, you won't. I want you to stay here, at the bottom of the step. You've been gravely injured before, and I cannot face Doreen if you're hurt on my time again. Do not confront anyone who comes – and if there is someone, just pray it's MacFarlane.'

'I don't know—'

'No time to argue.' Maisie turned away and began to make her way up the carpeted staircase.

She had been in mews houses before, and knew there were limitations as to the possible design of a home converted from stabling for horses. At the top of the staircase, the door to the right was closed. One of the two voices inside was raised, the other lower, as if calming, playing for time. She listened for just a moment.

'It was your fault – you were to blame.'

'It was wartime. Xavier chose his path – we all chose our paths. And he knew the price and what the outcome might—'

'Stay down there – stay there with your hands behind your head. Do not move, or I swear I will use this.'

'What do you want from me? I cannot atone for something that happened so many years ago, and of which I was not a part.'

'But you were – you knew!'

'Not these boys, not Xavier. Not Frederick, or Albert. They were not my people.'

'You brought in others like them, though – and you'll do it again, if I don't stop you. The others paid for what they did – but you, you have to be stopped.'

Maisie knew she had little time. She placed her hands on her heart as if to modulate the rhythm, and having taken a deep breath, she placed one hand on the door handle. She opened the door and entered.

Francesca Thomas was kneeling on the floor, her hands clasped behind her head. Gervase Lambert was standing over her, his right hand holding a revolver. It looked like a Browning, but Maisie knew it was the very similar Ruby.

'Maisie, you'd better—'

Maisie held up her hand to stop Thomas from saying more. She looked at Lambert.

'Hello, Gervase. I'm sorry if my telephone call caused you to panic.

It seems you had to leave the office to finish your job in case I was in contact with Dr Thomas first.'

'You do not understand what has gone on – I will kill you if you take another step. I don't want to kill an innocent woman, so just leave. It will all be over soon.'

'It can be over immediately. You can put down the gun, and you can stop this now.'

'I'll go to the gallows anyway – but I'm not scared. They deserved it, all of them, for what they did. You have no idea.'

'In fact I do have an idea.' Maisie kept talking. 'Your name is Gervase Bertrand. You came here as a small boy. You left Belgium with your brother, Xavier, and your mother, though she died on the journey from your home near Liege. But Xavier kept going – because he had to. And you were among others – his friends, the friends he fought alongside: Frederick Addens, Albert Durant, Carl Firmin. They were the main ones, weren't they? All in the snaking line of people making their way to the coast, and – everyone hoped – to safety in England.'

Francesca Thomas lifted her chin just enough for Maisie to see. *Keep going.*

'Your brother and his cohorts were all wanted by the enemy, were all being sought by the Germans – they were fierce resistance fighters, weren't they? Your mother was both fearful for her boys, and so proud of Xavier. And of course you looked up to him – he was your hero.'

Tears welled up in the young man's eyes. He pressed his lips together; beads of perspiration stood out on his forehead and cheeks, and ran down his temples. His now-Brylcreemed hair was slicked back, the smell beginning to pervade the room.

'But here's what happened – what no one believed would happen. You and the other refugees were strafed by a German aircraft. They believed resistance fighters were there among the stumbling line of people, and they took aim. One of the people brought down was Xavier – and he was hit trying to save you. He was a hero, Gervase – a true hero.'

'But they killed him – they killed him!'

'He was mortally wounded – he was in terrible pain, and there was no means of stopping his agony, his terror. And what did he say to them, his friends? If you remember what happened, what did he say?'

'I don't remember. I don't remember any of it. I don't remember . . . I don't even know if I was there.' Gervase Bertrand was weeping now.

'But you know what happened, don't you? He asked them to kill him, didn't he? He asked them to kill him because he knew he would die, and he knew they would never abandon him all the time he was alive – he wanted to die to save his friends.' Maisie put her hand to her mouth, the story catching in her throat, but saw the panic in Francesca Thomas' eyes and went on. 'So, here's what happened. Each of the boys had a Ruby revolver. They'd been manufactured cheaply, were not in short supply, and they had been issued to the boys by whoever was instructing them in their – let's call them "assignments". They took their identical revolvers, put one bullet into each revolver, and then placed those revolvers under a coat. With Xavier screaming in pain, screaming at them to get on with it, they each took one revolver, and having expressed their love of him, their admiration, and having made a promise to look out for you until you reached manhood, they stood back and they took aim. Xavier was released from his pain instantly. No individual boy would ever bear the guilt of killing Xavier – by swapping the revolvers, perhaps, they could try to disassociate themselves from an act they abhorred. They buried Xavier and, because they believed marking the spot with a cross and a name was a risk, drew up a map and notes so that his grave could be found again. That map was held by the young man they all considered to be the one best suited to keeping a document safe – Albert Durant. And they agreed that the only truth you should ever know was that your brother was a hero. They saw you to the cusp of manhood, but by then you were on to greater things – an education paid for by someone else. And at some point they decided you should have Xavier's weapon, something of his, to keep in a drawer, a memento.'

Gervase Bertrand began to weep, and as he seemed to falter, Francesca Thomas came to her feet and knocked the revolver free with her knee, pushing Bertrand backward and slamming him into the wall.

At the same time, Maisie picked up the revolver, aiming it at Thomas and her assistant.

'Now stop, or so help me, I will shoot both of you.' She looked at Thomas. 'And you of all people know I can use a gun.'

'Maisie, what did I say about diplomatic immunity?' MacFarlane's heavy frame seemed to fill the doorway as he turned and beckoned in two men, one in plain clothes – Maisie assumed he was with the Secret Service. The other was Billy. 'Put that down, lass – I'm here now.'

'You took your time,' said Maisie.

'Traffic.' MacFarlane turned to the man who was now locking handcuffs on Bertrand's wrists. 'Go easy on the lad. We know what he's done, but treat him with respect anyway.'

'What about me? Make this oaf of yours let go of me, MacFarlane,' said Francesca Thomas.

MacFarlane shook his head. 'Dr Thomas, my esteemed colleague, who has so little time for our police – not that I am of them any more, but you know what they say, "Once a copper, always a copper" – first of all, that is Miss Dobbs' very efficient assistant. Secondly, I think you and I should have a little chat about which secrets should be kept close to the individual heart, and which shouldn't. This kind gentleman will take you downstairs and make sure you're comfortable in my motor car until I'm ready to join you.' He gave a rueful smile. 'And don't run anywhere, Francesca – I mean, where would you go anyway? We need you. Both your countries need you.'

When only MacFarlane and Maisie remained in the room, MacFarlane sighed. 'Now, where were we? I think you'd got to the part where that tyke's brother was a hero.'

'They were just boys, Robbie – just boys. And they were fighting for their country. Of course his brother was a hero.' She sighed and rubbed her eyes with one hand, her other still holding the Ruby.

'I think I'd better take that,' said MacFarlane, reaching for the revolver. 'Seem to be a few too many about these days.'

'You'd better hear the rest now,' said Maisie. 'Because I can't come back to your office for any little tête-à-têtes today.' She took a deep breath and allowed half a minute before continuing. 'The boys – Addens, Durant, Firmin, and another who palled up with them along the way, by the name of Lucas Peeters – came to England and registered as refugees together. They kept Gervase Bertrand with them – he was so young, and they wanted to look out for him. As soon as they arrived, they were taken under the wing of Rosemary Hartley-Davies, who was one of the organisers of a refugee association. As I've said, Gervase was just a little boy, and she encouraged him to be a child whenever she saw him, which was frequently. It was as if he were *her* boy, in some ways. She called him her little lamb, and in time that's what he called himself. He changed his name to Lambert – keeping his nickname from her and adding it to the first part of Bertrand. Why didn't he retain his true name? I don't know, but it might be to do with a sort of reinvention of himself. Only initials had been written on his first registration card – GB. He had not given a full name at that point – perhaps he could not spell his name, or had learnt to be careful – and the older boys had not revealed anything else about him at that stage. Rosemary Hartley-Davies could not keep the boy, but I believe that in time she made arrangements for his care so that they could remain in touch. Xavier's friends also remained in communication with him – I think you will find he saw a lot of them initially, but the boys became men and grew apart, and it appears their families were never told. Perhaps they were afraid of what might happen if the truth emerged. Then Gervase grew up. He'd rekindled his language skills, he had an education that clearly served him well – likely paid for by Rosemary Hartley-Davies – and he was taken on by Francesca Thomas. And why, you may ask, did that happen?'

Maisie paced to the window, and watched as a black motor car drove away with Gervase Lambert in the back seat, flanked by two men. Billy was leaning against another official black vehicle, speaking to the driver. Smoke spiralled up from the rear window; Francesca Thomas lighting up a cigarette, waiting for MacFarlane to emerge. Maisie turned back to MacFarlane.

'I think she might well have had some dealings with Addens, Durant, and Firmin, as well as Xavier Bertrand, while in Belgium. Perhaps she recruited them. She was working for resistance groups even before La Dame Blanche, so I believe earmarking good and willing fighters was one of her specialties – a young woman, praising those boys, who might well have wanted to impress her. I do not believe she knew Gervase Bertrand – Lambert, as he'd presented himself to her – was connected to those boys. His surname had been changed, and he seemed a good candidate for a job at the Belgian embassy. And I don't think she knew he was the killer. But I have every confidence that she knew, the moment she came to speak to me about the case, that there was a connection between Addens and one of her earlier recruits – she just didn't know what it was, and how the threads of evidence were woven together. And I believe she was quite happy that the police had hit a dead end – excuse the pun, if you will. She wanted the killer found before he caused any more damage, but she didn't want the police to find him. She wanted to get there first, probably for reasons of security.'

MacFarlane sighed. 'Don't think poorly of her. She had a tough job – a very hard job, and it isn't going to get any easier. She's loyal to Britain and to Belgium, and I have to work with her.'

'She could have been honest with me.'

'And that's exactly what a certain Detective Inspector Caldwell is going to say to *you*, Maisie.'

'I know.' Maisie looked at her hand, rubbing a ridge mark on her skin where she had clutched the Ruby.

'One or two more things, Maisie, and then we'll be off. How do you know all this – and what happened to Gervase Bertrand to spark this stream of murders? You can't tell me he was planning this from the time he was six years old.'

She shook her head. 'No, though he might have known by the time he applied to work with Dr Thomas. I found out most of this from a man named Father Bonhomme, a priest in Belgium. It upset your man that I took time to see him, but it was worth it.'

307

'He mentioned that. I told him I had to trust you.'

'Anyway, I learnt that Carl Firmin had been to see him about eighteen months ago. He had returned to Belgium, a sort of pilgrimage, I suppose – possibly a journey of atonement. The man was clearly in distress; memories had returned in sharp relief as he journeyed through his home country. The priest encouraged him to speak of what ailed him.'

'Nice priest – what about the confessional?'

'Father Bonhomme told me he met Firmin outside the church, and though by dint of being a priest, it was a confessional of sorts, he knew I was in great need of discovering the truth. And one thing more – Bonhomme told me he had received a letter from Firmin not long after the exchange. It seems he was filled with gratitude because he had been given sufficient courage to find and then to confess to Xavier's brother. Now, did Gervase remember anything of the actual event? I believe not, because he was taken away by a woman, out of sight of Xavier's final minutes, and far from the sound. However, when you question him, I think you will come to believe, as I do, that once he'd heard from Firmin – who had told Father Bonhomme he would recount the exact chain of events to Xavier's brother – the story grew and grew in Gervase's imagination to the extent that the truth was twisted beyond all proportion.' She rubbed her forehead. 'When I think of the damaging thoughts that must have crossed his mind, it's all so very sad. I believe Gervase wanted to be his brother's hero – after all, hadn't he been told by the others that Xavier was a hero to them all? If Maurice were here, he might well argue that Gervase Bertrand's experiences as a child had left him with a dormant imbalance of the mind. He would suggest that those experiences of loss and dislocation had impaired his thinking – despite the fact that there were people who cared enough to give him a good chance in life. If – as I suspect was the case – those damaging thoughts flourished, he would have been increasingly tormented by Firmin's confession as he went over it again and again in his mind. I believe he reached a point where he believed there was only one avenue available to him – to avenge Xavier's death by taking the lives of the men who had ended his brother's life.' Maisie looked up at MacFarlane. 'Remember, even though they were all so young when this happened, to Gervase they were always grown men. And somewhere inside he was the child who had lost his brother, his hero. If this is how it happened, then all the persuading in the world would not have convinced Gervase that bringing Xavier's life and suffering to an end was an act of love.' Maisie felt her breath catch. 'Those boys shouldered an unfathomable weight. And Gervase was blinded by grief, loss, and the lingering vision of a child.'

They stood for a moment, then MacFarlane broke the silence.

'It's a bloody shame. A bloody shame. The suffering of war, that's what it is – and it goes far beyond the trenches.' He blew out his cheeks. 'Anyway, we'd better get along. I've to report to every bloody government office you can think of this afternoon.'

MacFarlane stood back, allowing Maisie to depart first, but stopped and sniffed the air.

'I've been meaning to ask – what's that terrible smell? It's like the air-force mess in here, with a load of lads having a drink and ready to go out on the make.'

'It's Brylcreem. Lambert – Bertrand – wore it when he was going about this terrible business of killing. It's almost as if he were creating another person to be the murderer, or a stamp that could be left behind, and the stamp was this fragrance. You might find that his brother, Xavier, experimented with using brilliantine, or some sort of hair pomade – you know how boys do these things. But it's also something that could put an investigator off the scent.'

'Scent? Oh dear, I think you should go home and rest, Maisie.'

'I can't – I've important work to do. This isn't my only urgent case.'

CHAPTER NINETEEN

Maisie reclaimed her motor car, and with Billy by her side in the passenger seat, she made her way through London traffic to St Giles' Hospital in Camberwell.

'You know why she went there, don't you?' said Billy.

'Why who went where?'

'Why the old girl went to St Giles' – she could have gone to a couple of other hospitals. I reckon she went there because it used to be the workhouse infirmary – it was where the poor went and they knew they would get help.'

'I wonder if she knew about the other voluntary hospitals,' said Maisie.

'P'raps.' Billy was quiet for a moment. 'You know, miss, that Gervase Lambert – Bertrand, whatever his name is – I reckon Dr Thomas knew he was the one. P'raps not – what's the word – *consciously*. But I bet she had an inkling.'

'I believe she had her suspicions quite early on, when I was giving her reports on our progress.'

'Why didn't she do anything about it?'

'Even the sharpest knife, someone such as Francesca Thomas, makes mistakes. Like me, she was probably waiting for proof.' Maisie paused, weaving around a horse and cart as they approached Vauxhall Bridge. 'It's this business of knowing the who, but not the why. Maurice always said that sometimes we instinctively know the identification of the perpetrator of a crime, but we don't trust ourselves – or perhaps we cannot be trusted, in the circumstances. Which is why the "why" is so important.'

'And you can't wait too long before you move on the why, once you've found it.'

Maisie felt Billy looking at her. 'I cut it fine, I know – probably when I wanted to completely rule out Peeters. At first I couldn't see why Gervase might want to kill Dr Thomas – but then it was evident. She stood for everything he'd lost. Now, it begs the question – did he know about her before he became her employee? My guess is that he made his application to the Belgian government in London to use his skill in language, and of course he was born in Belgium. I doubt he knew exactly who Thomas was, but it soon became evident. It might only have been a passing comment made by Thomas herself. As far as I know, Thomas was not working in a government-sanctioned resistance capacity until 1916, but my guess is she was active before that, though of course she was working in England at the start of the war.' Maisie shook her head. 'It might only have been a slip of the tongue, perhaps during Firmin's confession, that linked her to the boys, and by association, to the death of Xavier Bertrand. And of course, once Gervase knew she was with the resistance in Belgium during the war, he found another victim anyway. I believe any combination of these possibilities could be revealed when both Gervase Bertrand and Dr Thomas have been questioned.'

'And what about this map – what about the place where his brother was shot?'

Maisie slowed the motor car as she came alongside St Giles' Hospital, manoeuvring the Alvis parallel to the kerb in front of the red-brick building with its distinctive white trim around the windows. A red-brick wall separating the hospital from the road had been designed to resemble a long garland hung from pillar to pillar.

Maisie turned to Billy as she turned off the engine and held the ignition key. 'I believe Durant had it, and left it in a place of safety. I think that's what Bertrand was searching for in his flat.'

'That'll be like finding a needle in a haystack.'

'I don't think so,' said Maisie. She looked at her watch. 'Anyway, we'd better get going. If we miss visiting hours, they won't let us in.'

It was clear that beds positioned on either side of the long ward and perpendicular to the wall had been spaced according to an exact measurement – it was a measurement checked by the ward sister every day, and quite possibly by the matron during her rounds. Each cast-iron bed had been allocated two pillows, a top sheet, a bottom sheet, and one blanket. In the centre aisle a desk was used by the staff nurse, with ancillary rooms at either end of the ward for the use of the sister, the doctors, and the nurses. The sterilising room held an autoclave, bottles, bedpans, and various other equipment. Maisie thought she could wander blindfolded into the equipment room and find everything she might need – every item had its designated place, and woe betide the young nurse who made an error.

Having asked for Mrs Louisa Mason, they were directed to a bed at the far end of the ward. A screen had been pulled around the bed.

'Are you family?' asked the staff nurse.

Maisie shook her head. 'Mrs Mason's granddaughter has been billeted with us, in Kent. I wanted to see her, to tell her that the little girl is well. Mrs Mason is the only parent the child has ever known, as her mother died several years ago.'

'Oh, poor little lamb – I suppose I daren't even ask about the father.' The nurse placed a hand on the screen, but did not pull it back. 'She's very poorly,' she whispered. 'The doctor says she has a respiratory disease, but she's not up for even an exploratory operation. She's very weak. She'll come to for long enough to take some soup, or a cup of tea, but then she sleeps again. We keep them at this end, when it gets to this stage.'

'How long does she have?' said Maisie, her voice low.

'I'd be surprised if she's still with us this time next week,' said the nurse. 'A few days ago, I thought it would be more, but she goes downhill every day. We do all we can for her – we'll drain her lungs tomorrow morning, and she'll be more wakeful and be able to take more food. We're just trying to keep her comfortable. Doctor wondered why on earth she didn't come in sooner – he said more could have been done if she hadn't left it to the last minute.'

'She had the child to consider. I daresay it was easy to put it out of her mind, perhaps thinking she would get better if she ignored it.'

'That's what a lot of people do. Anyway, she might wake up – give her arm a little squeeze and tell her you're here.' The nurse pulled back the screen to enable Maisie and Billy to approach Louisa Mason's bedside. 'There's one chair – and don't sit on the bed, sir. Sister will have you thrown out.'

Billy positioned the wooden chair for Maisie to sit next to Anna's grandmother. He stood behind her.

Maisie leant forward and laid a hand on Louisa Mason's arm. The limb was thin and blue-veined, the bones at her wrists and along her knuckles sharp and prominent, as if she were no more than a skeleton wrapped in grey tissue paper.

'Mrs Mason. Mrs Mason, can you hear me?' Maisie took the woman's hand in both her own, rubbing her fingers back and forth as if to encourage the flow of blood through her veins. 'Mrs Mason.'

The woman's lids flickered, as if she wanted very much to open her eyes, but the effort was too much for her.

'Take your time, I'm not going away,' said Maisie.

At last the eyes opened. Maisie reached for a water pot, its long spout designed to assist a patient to drink without sitting up. 'Are you thirsty?'

The woman nodded, so Maisie stood up, placed a hand behind the woman's head to support her, and steered the spout into her mouth. The woman sucked in three mouthfuls, and nodded again. *Enough*. She smiled, and Maisie at once saw something of Anna in her grandmother.

'Who are you?' Mason's voice was rough, as if her throat were sore and inflamed.

'My name is Maisie Dobbs. This man works with me. We're not from the authorities, but he helped me to find you. Your granddaughter, Anna, has been billeted with my family in Kent. I came to find out more about you – and her. And to tell you she is doing well.'

Tears welled up in the woman's eyes. Maisie took a clean handkerchief from her pocket and with a gentle, light hand pressed away the drops of moisture.

'She's a gem,' said Mason. She began to cough again, then tried to catch her breath, which came in an urgent, rasping wheeze. 'A gem. I didn't know what else to do – I knew I couldn't take care of her any more. She was the one doing the caring, not me. So I had to get her away.'

'Mrs Mason, had she started school?'

The woman shook her head. 'I taught her to read at home. I taught Anna her letters and her numbers. She's a bright little girl. But I didn't want them taking her away from me. And I didn't want her at school, to be bullied.' Each word was uttered as if the next would never follow, but her determination to speak now was fierce.

'She's a very beautiful child,' said Maisie.

'But she's not quite like the other children.'

Maisie looked at Billy, and he shook his head.

'She's doing well now, you know. We have a dog who doesn't leave her side – the dog's owner died, so we brought her home, and she has really taken to Anna.'

Mason closed her eyes and swallowed, then opened her eyes again. 'Mary wouldn't give her up, and I wouldn't send her to the orphanage. We had people round from the adoption societies, but you never know what's going to happen to the baby, do you? You hear terrible things.'

'That's in the past now, Mrs Mason. But I have to know – do you have her birth certificate? It's important to know where it is.'

'Are you sending her away?'

'No, she's staying until the war's over, then we'll have to see. But the billeting officer was talking about finding a birth certificate.'

The woman shook her head. 'Mary had the baby at home. Only a local woman came in to her – she delivered all the babies around

316

our way. And Mary never registered the baby. She didn't want it to be seen that Anna didn't have a father.'

Maisie regarded the woman's countenance, her brow furrowed with worry. And as she held her hand, she felt the weight of a lifetime's hard work in her bones.

'Let's not worry about that,' said Maisie. 'I am sure it can be rectified.'

'I wish I'd not let her go now – I was panicking. I was bringing up blood, and I didn't want her to see it. I knew the evacuation was coming, so I thought I'd take her down and perhaps she'd end up with children she would've known at school. And I was going to send her to school, really I was, but I wanted her to get ahead before she got there – you know, because the teachers might not have paid attention to her. I wouldn't have kept her away for ever – after all, I didn't want the school-board man coming round.'

'I understand, and I promise you Anna's all right. Would you like me to bring her in to see you, Mrs Mason? I can talk to the staff nurse. They'll give you something to make you feel better when she visits.'

'I – I don't have time. There's not enough time in me.'

'You have enough, Mrs Mason. I can bring her tomorrow afternoon, if you like.'

As Louisa Mason began to weep, Maisie encircled her bird-like shoulders in her arms, and felt her give in to the grief of relinquishing Anna. In time the tears subsided, and the woman looked up at Maisie.

'I'll smarten myself up. I'll not let her see me like this.'

The tinkling of a small handbell coming closer signalled the end of visiting time.

Maisie settled Louisa Mason, ensuring she was comfortable. She gave her another few sips of water and pulled up the sheet and blanket so she was warm.

'Tomorrow, Mrs Mason – I'll be back with Anna then.'

But Anna's grandmother was already asleep by the time Maisie had spoken her name.

Having had a word with the staff nurse, Maisie and Billy left the hospital and began the journey back towards Fitzroy Square.

'How're you going to get her here, miss?'

'Frankie and Brenda – they can come up on the train, and I'll take them back afterwards. I'll make the telephone call as soon as I get to the office.'

'Not enough hours in the day, eh, miss? I reckon MacFarlane will be on the blower soon enough, calling you over there to Whitehall.'

'My guess is he won't, Billy. This is a delicate issue. Dr Thomas will be all right – they all need her too much, and she hasn't really done anything wrong.'

'Withholding information.'

'It could be argued that she wasn't sure of the facts – and I don't think she was sure. The Gervase Lambert she knew was a very amenable young man. As I've already said, I think we will find that Rosemary Hartley-Davies contributed financially to his education, and she might well have kept it a secret from her brother – given his condition, that wouldn't be too hard. If Lambert had seen Hartley-Davies on occasion, then Emma knew him, and so did Mrs Bolton.'

'They'd've known him all right, with that stuff he put on his hair – all done up like two penn'orth of hambone.'

'He only used the hair cream when he intended to take a life.

Perhaps the disguise was all a part of showing that he was a man now, and not the boy they saw in him.'

'Yeah, I know what you mean – I don't see men when I look at my boys. I feel like I was putting bandages on their scraped knees only last week.'

Almost as soon as Maisie drew the Alvis into Fitzroy Street, she saw an official vehicle waiting outside the office.

'He's not supposed to stop there,' said Billy.

'He can stop anywhere he wants. That's Caldwell.'

'Blimey – he chooses his moments.'

'Nothing I can't deal with.' Maisie parked the Alvis and began to walk towards Caldwell, who was waiting at the bottom of the step, Sergeant Able at his side.

'Good afternoon, Detective Inspector Caldwell.'

'I wish it was, Miss Dobbs. I truly wish it was.'

'Would you like to come up to the office?'

'And have you butter me up with tea? No, not this time.' He gave a theatrical sigh, looked around to ensure there were no passers-by, and turned back to Maisie. 'What happened to "share and share alike"?'

'Inspector Caldwell, I am sure you know my hands were tied. There was a point when there was absolutely nothing to tell. So I decided to take a chance and go to Belgium just for a day. As soon as I returned, I had to move very quickly through official Foreign Office channels. Inspector – we both hit the wall called diplomatic immunity.'

'That means the bugger will get away with it,' said Caldwell.

'Language,' said Billy, stepping forward. 'There's a lady present.'

'You're telling me to mind my language in this business? She's heard it all and talk more ripe than that into the bargain, I'm sure.'

'I don't think he will get away with anything, Inspector Caldwell,' said Maisie. 'We might not know the outcome – that depends upon the government's stance at this point, given Belgium's situation as our ally. Releasing details of the killer might give an indication of resistance operations in the last war – which will in turn provide the Nazis with a clue as to Secret Service plans in this one.'

'Nothing's been happening in this one so far,' said Caldwell.

'Something will happen. We both know it will.'

As soon as they reached the office, Maisie asked Billy to find out what Albert Durant had done with his wife's remains. Had she been buried or cremated? And if she had been cremated, were the ashes interred, or had he chosen to keep them? She could not recall seeing an urn when she visited the flat he had shared with his late wife. For her part, Maisie placed several telephone calls – the first to the Dower House, to ask Brenda to bring Anna up to London to see her grandmother the following day. Next she telephoned Priscilla with an urgent request, and also her solicitor, Bernard Klein, who made room in his busy day to see her before he left his office.

After Billy had left Fitzroy Square, as Maisie once again wove her way through London traffic, she reflected on her father's frustration on those occasions when she tried to do more than perhaps she should for little Anna Mason. She wondered – again – if she were doing the right thing, though, as Klein had pointed out, there were few laws to protect children in Anna's position. He'd also drawn her attention to a proposed law that might affect Anna, though debate about it would now be delayed until after the war. She hoped that by circumventing any action by the authorities, she would be standing up for the child, even if she might again incur her father's disapproval.

* * *

Frankie and Brenda did not at first see Maisie on the other side of the gate where a guard checked tickets. Anna was walking between Maisie's father and her stepmother, her gas mask bobbing up and down on her hip when she gave a little skip as she walked. Frankie said something to her, and she looked up at him and chuckled, turning to Brenda as if to check that she was laughing along with them. Maisie felt her heart leap. How would she ever find the right home for this little girl when the end of the war came, and it was time for her to leave?

'I'm here!' Maisie called out to the trio, standing on tiptoe and waving.

Brenda leant down and spoke to Anna, pointing to Maisie in the distance. Frankie released her hand at the same time as Brenda, and after a second's hesitation, Anna began to run towards Maisie.

'I've trotted on Lady. I've trot-trot-trotted!' Anna's excitement seemed to bubble up and overflow as she threw her arms around Maisie's legs. Maisie looked down, ran her hand across the child's dark hair, and without thinking reached out and picked her up.

'Are you ready to see your nan, Anna?'

Anna nodded, burrowing her head into Maisie's neck before looking up again. 'I'll tell her I trotted on Lady. And I drew pictures for her – Auntie Brenda's got them.'

'Auntie Brenda? Good, that's wonderful – come on then, let's be on our way. Nan's waiting for you.'

'She does look lovely,' said the staff nurse, leading Maisie, Anna, Frankie, and Brenda to the end of the ward, where Louisa Mason lay in her bed. 'Your friend's a bit pushy though – I dreaded Matron coming in, because I'm sure they would have had a bit of a barny, if you know what I mean.'

'Oh, yes, I know very well what you mean,' said Maisie. 'Mrs Partridge is nothing if not forthright – but she acts quickly when required to do so.'

'She brought a lovely nightdress, with Chantilly lace at the neck and wrist – from Harrods, no less. Must've cost a packet, that. And a quilted bed jacket – beautiful peachy colour, it is. Anyway, I'm not supposed to let you all in at once, but Sister is turning a blind eye in the circumstances, and if the child wants to get on the bed, just remember to take off her shoes.'

Maisie thanked the nurse, who pulled back the screen so the group could cluster around the bed, then replaced it to give a modicum of privacy.

Anna clambered onto the bed, aided by Frankie, with Brenda unbuckling her shoes just in time.

'Oh, my lovely one, my lovely girl.' Louisa held Anna's face in her two hands and looked at her with intensity, as if to commit the child's image to memory.

Anna reached out and with her small fingers began to trace around her grandmother's mouth and across her eyes before leaning in so that their foreheads touched. Frankie glanced at Maisie, then Brenda, and they stepped out behind the screen. In time they heard Anna telling her grandmother about her pony, and about Emma and Jook, and about living at the Dower House. When she could hear the deep fatigue returning to Louisa's responses, Maisie drew back the screen and joined Anna.

'Is it time to go, Anna?' asked Maisie.

'Yes, Nan's tired now.'

Maisie watched as the elderly woman and her granddaughter held each other. She helped the child off the bed, and as she was about to join Frankie and Brenda, Anna looked up at Louisa and said, 'I'll see you in heaven, Nan.'

'See you in heaven, my lovely one.'

Maisie remained at the woman's bedside, and did not speak until she heard Frankie and Brenda taking Anna from the ward, the echo of their footsteps diminishing as they walked away.

'Mrs Mason, I know you are so very tired, but there's something we should discuss, and I don't think it can wait.'

'Right you are. Is it about Anna?'

'Yes, it is. I've spoken to my solicitor about your situation – Anna not having a birth certificate, and your desire that a good home should be found for her, after the war – if not before.' She stopped speaking, gauging whether Mason had heard and understood her. The woman lifted her hand, indicating that Maisie should continue.

'I have a couple of documents here. Both have been drawn up to protect Anna. One is an application for a birth certificate. We don't know the father, but we do know the mother, your daughter, who is now sadly deceased. I would need your signature here to that effect. But wait a moment.' Maisie moved the screen to look at the ward. She waved, catching the attention of the staff nurse, who was just leaving another patient's bedside. 'I need a witness.'

She explained the situation and handed the documents to the nurse to peruse while she continued to speak to Louisa.

'This other document is "To Whom It May Concern" and allows my solicitor to protect Anna's best interests, especially when it comes to placing her with a family. I can read it all to you, and I am sure the staff nurse will tell you if anything sounds wrong.'

'I trust you,' said Louisa Mason. 'You brought her to me, and I trust you.'

'This looks perfectly all right, Mrs Mason,' said the staff nurse, handing the documents back to Maisie. 'It means Anna is fully protected.'

In her spidery hand, Louisa Mason signed the documents, which Maisie then passed to the nurse to countersign as witness. She thanked the staff nurse, who reminded her not to be too long.

'Thank you, Miss Dobbs,' said Louisa. 'Thank you for bringing her. I never thought I would see her again.'

'We were worried about her for a while. She was completely silent.'

'No, she wasn't. Anna's never silent when she's not talking. That's how I knew in my heart she was really all right – she was talking to me.'

Maisie was about to reply when the old woman's eyes closed, and her breathing slowed, as if she had slipped into a deep sleep. For a few moments Maisie watched the troubled rise and fall of Louisa's chest, and felt, then, as if she were lingering in a place between one world and the next. It was time for her to leave.

As Maisie departed the ward, she stopped to thank the staff nurse again.

'It's all rules in a hospital – it's nice to break them every so often, I must say.' The nurse giggled. 'And I'm glad the little girl saw her nan before she passes on. Funny little thing, isn't she?' She picked up a thermometer, ready to check a patient. 'But I think you'll have trouble finding her a home. She doesn't look English, does she?'

'She has a lovely heart, that's the main thing.'

'Yes, but people wanting to adopt don't always look at the inside, do they? They want a child who looks like them, so no one asks questions later.'

* * *

324

Maisie drew the motor car to a halt outside London Bridge Station, and opened the rear passenger door for Anna to alight, as Frankie helped Brenda on the other side. The four stepped onto the pavement to say their goodbyes, with Maisie confirming that she would be at Chelstone on Friday. She knelt down to Anna's height.

'Nan told me she would be in heaven tomorrow,' said Anna.

Maisie could feel Frankie and Brenda's attention on her, waiting to hear her response.

'When did she tell you that, Anna? I don't think I heard her.'

'Oh, no, she didn't say it out loud. She told me here.' Anna touched her forehead. 'We talk like that sometimes, when we don't want anyone else to hear.' She stared away from Maisie, as if into a distance only she could see. 'And she told me she would see me in heaven. It would be a lot of years in my life, but not a lot of years in hers. Heaven's different.'

Maisie reached out and stroked Anna's hair, feeling its softness under her fingers. Thick and strong, yet soft jet-black hair.

EPILOGUE

'She was cremated,' said Billy. 'I spoke to Mrs Durant's father – very nice man, devastated at losing his daughter and then his son-in-law. He was widowed, so I felt sorry for the old boy. But he has another daughter, and apparently he sees a lot of her.'

'And the ashes?'

'He said Durant couldn't let go of them, not straightaway, anyway. He'd asked him – Durant – if he would have them interred, and apparently Durant said he was going to take them somewhere special, somewhere that was loved by his wife.' Billy frowned. 'Miss, why are you interested in the ashes?'

'It's just an idea, Billy,' said Maisie. 'Look, I'll be away all day tomorrow – I'm making a little detour on the way down to Chelstone.'

'All right, miss – but I always worry about your little detours. I never know what might happen next. Anyway, Sandra here said we've had two enquiries for assistance. One's a missing person, and the other is a man over in Belgravia who wants someone to look at his house to see if it's secure enough.'

'Secure enough for what?'

Billy shrugged. 'Blessed if I know.'

'All right – Billy, start the initial interview for the missing person case, and then take the Belgravia job on your own. Checking windows before they've been broken is not my bailiwick. But it's an unusual request, I must say.'

'No, it isn't,' said Sandra. 'We've two more of those come in.' She held up the just-opened letters. 'I suppose they're worried about the number of people coming in – soldiers, refugees, and so on – and they think they're all going to go on a burglary rampage.'

'Billy,' said Maisie, 'you've got your work cut out for you. You're now our expert on domestic security.'

Parking the motor car just outside Reigate on the Dorking road, Maisie hoped she had found the place where Albert Durant and his wife had taken their Saturday walks. She had dressed for a ramble across fields and along old footpaths, and was wearing trousers and a light cardigan over a cotton blouse, and carried a mackintosh in her knapsack, along with a flask of water and a sandwich. She had also brought the recent photograph of Albert Durant. Before locking the motor car, she swapped her footwear, and was now wearing a pair of stout walking shoes in well-worn brown leather. She looked around, crossed the road, and set off along a narrow path that flanked farmland leading farther up the hill, where she turned left along the edge of a field of golden stubble. Hay bales were strewn across the landscape, gleaming in the sun. Maisie thought they looked like nature's ingots awaiting collection.

Every so often, she stopped and stared across the fields. At one point she watched a hawk hovering in the morning sunlight before swooping down to claim its prey. She had been walking for over an hour when she came to a stile and was presented with a choice of two routes – the first across the top of the field, so she would remain in the lee of the hill if she chose that way, or she could embark upon the path running perpendicular to the hill, which she thought would lead back down to the road. An area of woodland lay in the distance. Which of the two rustic paths should she take? She sat on the stile, pulled the flask from her knapsack, drank some water, and ran the back of her hand across her forehead before combing her fingers through her short hair – though it was not as short as it had been in Spain, when she had cropped it herself with nail scissors. Taking another sip of water, she set off on the route to the left, down the hill, returning the flask to the knapsack as she walked towards the woodland.

She was about one hundred yards from the cluster of trees when she saw a woman walking towards her with a dog, a spaniel that ran ahead, snuffling around along the verge, until he was called back when he ventured into the wood.

Maisie raised her hand, and the woman returned her greeting. 'Lovely morning, isn't it?'

'It certainly is.' Maisie stooped to stroke the spaniel, who had scampered along the verge to greet her. 'Do you come here every day with your dog?'

'Yes, I do – well, almost every day. My cottage is down there, close to the road.' The woman turned to point farther along the path.

'So you see a number of walkers, then, people coming out for the day.'

'You see some regulars. People who aren't country folk don't come this way – they go to the town instead. But you're right – I always see a good few people walking, and there's been more ever since the government started putting up posters telling us all we should get out and start "hiking for health". I suppose I've seen more faces I'd not seen before, but I know the regulars.'

Maisie reached into her knapsack and brought out the photograph of Albert Durant. 'Did you ever see this man?'

The woman took the photograph and nodded, handing it back to Maisie. 'I used to see him on Saturdays or Sundays. He walked here with his wife. Younger than him, she seemed – and I was worried when I saw her walking when she was expecting. I mean, along the flat is one thing, but she was striding out up and down these hills.' She shook her head and looked down at her feet. 'I remember seeing him once more. He was on his own, and he told me she'd died.' She brought her attention back to Maisie. 'I was very sad for him – he was quite distraught, and seemed so lonely. He asked me if I thought anyone would mind if he scattered her ashes in their favourite place, and I told him I didn't think anyone would know. After all, people can be afraid of that sort of thing – ashes of the deceased – but it's not the dead who can hurt you, is it? It's the living.'

Maisie sighed. 'My father has always said the same thing.'

The woman pointed across to the neighbouring patch of woodland, and described a clearing beyond the fence, with a small pond surrounded by trees. 'They would sit by the pond to have their lunch. It was secluded and it gave a bit of shade from the sun or – more likely – the drizzle. I can't say for definite because I'd walked on by then to give him some peace, but I would imagine he scattered the ashes in there.'

'Thank you,' said Maisie. 'I just wanted to know.'

'Do you know how he is?' asked the woman. 'I wonder about him sometimes, when I come this way with the dog.'

'I'm afraid he passed away.'

The woman turned her head, as if to hide her tears. 'Doesn't surprise me. A broken heart took him. You could see it in his face. I thought then, no matter how old he is, he won't see out another year. Happens more to men, you know.' She paused and sighed, adding, 'I'd better get on. Very nice to have met you.'

Maisie thanked the woman and stood for a while at the edge of the field, watching her continue on her way, the spaniel running back and forth, as if hoping to flush a pheasant or a rabbit out of the tall grasses along the verge. When the woman was almost out of sight, Maisie climbed over the fence and into the woodland. Human ashes, she knew, never composted in the same way as ashes from a wood fire might.

There was nothing of note around the pond, so Maisie continued to spiral out towards the line of trees encircling the water. She kept her head down, and on occasion used a stick to prod away leaves. When she reached the trees, she began scrutinising each trunk from her own height down to the ground. It was clear this was a place for lovers: there were hearts carved into the wood with pairs of names, one either side or etched into an arrow. Iris and Tom had been to the clearing; so had Peter and Millie. Alice and Sid had lingered, and B and E. Time had stretched some of the names as the trunk grew and widened. Maisie wondered if those couples were now married, and if time had given them children and perhaps grandchildren.

She moved on and, feeling hungry, looked for a place to settle for lunch. Beyond the main cluster of trees stood a large beech, its branches outspread as if they were wings. She chose her spot in the curve of its trunk where it reached the ground; it was as if nature had provided her with a seat and a place to lean back. Taking a bite of her cheese and tomato sandwich, she cast her gaze around, down past other trees to the pond, and from side to side. It was at that moment she noticed the words carved into the wood where the trunk seemed to curve around her: Albert, Elizabeth, and Baby, encircled by a heart. Maisie put down her sandwich and leapt to her feet. She began brushing back the carpet of leaves with the stick as she walked around the tree, and then stopped. Ashes. White ashes had been distributed around the tree. Then she saw it – a hollow in the trunk.

She always kept a pair of gloves in the knapsack. She put them on and reached into the hollow, pulling out a broken earthenware cream soda bottle. An empty wallet. A cricket ball. Then her hand touched something else – a cylinder of some sort. As she brought it out, she saw it was a tall, narrow urn of tarnished, greening copper. She knelt on the ground and shook the urn close to her ear. Nothing. The urn was light – if it had contained the ashes, then all were now laid to rest under the tree. She sat back on her haunches, closed her eyes, and prayed the urn contained what she had set out to find. She unscrewed the lid and looked in: a cone of rolled paper. She pulled it out, put the urn to one side, and flattened the paper before her. There was no doubt. She had found the map indicating Xavier Bertrand's resting place.

Maisie lingered in the clearing, the map in her knapsack, the urn again in the hollow part of the tree, though now it contained a photograph of Albert Durant and another of his wife, taken while standing alongside their woodland secret place on a fine day. She listened as a quickening breeze rustled through the tree canopy, and watched dragonflies skim across the pond beyond. In time she came to her feet, ready to be on her way, though she felt compelled to speak aloud.

'I will bring him to you, Elizabeth.' She placed her hand on the inscription Albert and Elizabeth Durant had left in their secret place. 'I promise.'

Maisie and Anna were rarely apart from the time Maisie arrived late Friday afternoon, until Sunday evening, or Monday morning, when Frankie and Brenda returned to the Dower House. They visited Robert Miller, who had accepted an invitation from Lord Julian to remain longer at Chelstone Manor, and Lady Rowan, who delighted in having the child in her midst. Maisie watched as Anna rode her pony, and though Frankie was not present, Robert Miller was in his wheelchair at the side of the paddock.

'I might not be able to see you, young lady, but I can hear that trot – come on, make her step out. One-two-one-two – count as she makes her strides.'

In a quiet moment, while Anna was attending to the pony, Maisie asked Miller if he knew Gervase Lambert. 'No,' he said, 'can't say that the name rings a bell. But then, Rosie had friends I was not aware of. At first – when I was feeling sorry for myself – I thought she was embarrassed about me. Then I realised she wanted to keep certain liaisons secret, though I bet Mrs Bolton knew.'

In time she would tell him the truth.

While working with Maurice Blanche as a green young assistant, Maisie had followed a certain routine when closing a significant case where lives had been lost. There was always a point where her work was done, and it was time to conduct what she referred to as her final accounting. Maurice had instructed her that in visiting places and people pertinent to the case, as an investigator she was doing something akin to washing the laundry, then airing and pressing the linen before putting it away. The final accounting allowed her to immerse herself in the next case with renewed energy. It was time, now, to draw a line under the case Dr Francesca Thomas had entrusted her with on the day war was declared.

During a visit to their home, she explained to Enid Addens and her daughter, Dorothy, that Frederick had been a hero, that he had undertaken resistance work before leaving Belgium, and that while he had not fought with an army, he had served his country with the heart of a soldier. And she had added that she could not reveal any more details, given the nature of Frederick Addens' involvement in actions against the invading army, as the current state of war with Germany had placed Belgium once again in a vulnerable position. However, she informed them that the person responsible for the murder of a good husband and father had been found, and would pay the price for his crime. 'Frederick Addens was a hero,' she reminded them again. 'In that you can – I hope – take some comfort.'

'He was always our hero, Miss Dobbs,' said Dottie Addens, standing behind her mother, her hands on the older woman's shoulders. 'But thank you all the same.'

Frederick Addens' daughter accompanied Maisie to the door, where she repeated her thanks, but added a comment that Maisie had been half expecting.

'I knew it was something to do with the war. He never spoke about it, and Mum didn't know, but it was something he said once, when we – Arthur and me – were younger.' She looked over her shoulder into the house, as if to ensure her mother could not hear. 'My brother was a bit of a lazy one when he first left school. Couldn't get a job, didn't really look for one. It didn't last long, but I remember Dad giving him an earful, and then watching Arthur walk up the road, kicking a stone along. Dad shook his head and said, 'Look at him. When I was that age, I was fighting for my country – I was taking my life in my hands for freedom.' Dad never mentioned it again, and I never said anything, but I knew he hadn't been in the army, so he must've been doing something else. Then as soon as you came along, I reckoned the something else had caught up with him.'

'He was extraordinarily brave, your dad,' said Maisie.

'I know,' she said, wiping a hand across her eyes. 'Anyway, thank you – I've got to go to Mum now.'

As the door closed behind her, Maisie could hear Enid Addens speaking to her daughter.

'I bet she doesn't know who killed him. She was just letting us think she did.'

'I don't think it's that simple, Mum. I think it's because it's a secret – you know how these people are.'

Maisie passed the Crown and Anchor, but did not enter. While she could not prove it, she suspected that Albert Durant had visited the pub to speak to Frederick Addens when he discovered that Carl Firmin had died, which was some time after the event. While there had been questions regarding the fact that both men had been murdered while in possession of more than a small amount of money, as Maisie informed Billy, it was a coincidence that had no other truth deeper than facts on the surface: one man was doing his job as a banker, and the other had received his wages. But, Maisie thought later, perhaps there was a deeper truth after all, in that both men had committed themselves to life in their adopted country, and each in his own way had done well.

She moved on to the flat where Albert Durant and his wife had prepared for the birth of their child. She was not allowed access to the flat, but had already spoken to Caldwell, who – when she explained the reason for her call – promised he would be in contact as soon as he had spoken to Durant's in-laws regarding the disposal of his remains.

Maisie visited Carl Firmin's widow and Leonard Peterson – formerly Lucas Peeters – on each occasion informing them that she was not at liberty to reveal the name of the killer, adding that, because the perpetrator was of foreign nationality, there were other considerations, including the penalty to be levied by the judicial system of another country. She hated the lie. To Irma Firmin, she explained that the scar on her husband's leg had been caused by a wound sustained when the line of refugees was strafed by enemy fire. The widow shook her head and sighed. 'I knew it was something like that – he had a rough time of it, poor sod.'

A drive to Norfolk on a fine day took Maisie to the home of Clarice Littleton, to whom she gave more information, having received a promise to keep all details confidential.

'Gervase Lambert – really, Bertrand? I never would have thought it. He was a good boy – a bit of a scamp when he liked, but he was a boy. He made people laugh. I know Rosie took him under her wing, but . . . what on earth made him do it? After all this time?'

'Possibly the shock of learning the truth about his brother's death – and finding out that the men who had been as good as brothers to him had borne the ultimate responsibility. It must have been a staggering blow to his mind and soul. It seems he went on to convince himself that his brother could have been saved, that instead of collectively ending Xavier's pain and terror, the friends could have worked together to bring him through. Gervase felt betrayed, and betrayal by ones we love is a dreadful thing. Gervase had placed these men on a pedestal. They had been so young and brave when they escaped Belgium, yet one by one he took them down.'

Littleton was quiet before speaking again. 'One thing – I hope they let Gervase see that grave, so he can pray over his brother's last resting place before they exhume the remains. If he has to go to his death, it's the most honest thing they can do for him.'

'Yes, it is the most honest thing, Clarice.'

And when it came time for Maisie to leave, she pressed a card into Clarice Littleton's hand. 'It's Robert Miller's new address. I'm sure he'd love to hear from you – if you've time.'

Louisa Mason passed away with Maisie and Billy at her side. She had not wanted to see Anna again, nor Anna her grandmother – it was as if they were both complete in their communication with each other. Louisa asked Maisie once more to make sure Anna had good people to raise her. As Maisie said 'I promise,' she felt the woman's fingers become heavy in her hand, and the cold begin to reach up from her fingertips.

'I hope she's at peace,' said Billy, running the edge of his cap through his hands.

'Me too, Billy. Me too,' said Maisie.

On a showery afternoon in London, Maisie met Richard Stratton for a cup of strong urn tea and a plate of toast and jam at the cafe where they had met so many times. Maisie felt comfortable there in the ordinariness of the place, where the clattering of cups and saucers and the coming and going of other patrons offered a sense of being cocooned in the warmth of humanity, rather than the cold edge of conflict.

'Another job done then, Maisie,' said Stratton, setting the heavy white cup onto its saucer.

'We have others on the go, which means I'm still in business. But I'm glad the jobs involving death – and by that I mean "murder" – don't come along every week. Luckily, they usually bring in more money, so that tides us over and pays the wages.' Maisie sipped her tea. 'And what about you – how are you doing with your new job?'

'So far, so good, but I wasn't sorry to leave police work, and I won't be sorry to leave this, when they let me go.' He looked around the cafe, then returned his attention to Maisie. 'I mean, it's not as if I was strong-armed into it, but there was an element of pressure.'

'I'm sure there was.' Maisie lifted her sleeve to check her watch.

'Do you have to rush off?' asked Stratton.

'Soon. Not yet though.'

'Good. Let's have another cup of that dreadful tea before we leave.'

The final task for Maisie to complete concerned the ashes of Albert Durant. She explained to Caldwell that she had discovered where Durant had scattered his wife's ashes, and that she would like to take possession of Durant's, so she could ensure they were left in the same resting place.

'I'll do my best. The body's not required now, and there's never enough room for the dead, so they'll be cremating him soon, seeing as there aren't any relatives waiting to take him home. The father-in-law doesn't want the ashes, though he said he would've taken them if he'd had his daughter's, as it would have been right to keep them together.'

Caldwell was as good as his word, personally delivering the ashes to Maisie's office. She lost no time in making another journey to Reigate. The weather seemed less than inclined to favour her on the day she walked down towards the woodland Albert and Elizabeth Durant had designated their secret place, yet despite a steady fine rain, the ground underfoot was quite dry, protected by branches thick with leaves above. Close to what she now thought of as the grandmother beech tree, Maisie pushed back fallen leaves until she could see Elizabeth Durant's ashes, spread on the loamy ground by her husband. She tipped the urn, watching as the breeze stilled and the ashes floated down to a gentle landing. Once all were distributed around the base of the tree, she covered them with leaves and placed the urn in the beech tree's cavernous trunk. And before leaving, with her forefinger she traced the names carved on the trunk: Albert, Elizabeth, and Baby.

'May you now all rest in peace,' she whispered, before walking to the edge of the woodland. There, she looked back once, then went on her way, back to the Alvis. Her final accounting was complete.

The party to see Thomas Partridge on his way to Cranwell for the commencement of his Royal Air Force training was an intimate event, with just Priscilla's husband and boys, along with Lady Rowan and Lord Julian, whom Priscilla had come to know quite well over the years. Thomas had also invited a young woman of about eighteen years of age, who – Maisie thought – conducted herself very well, considering the scrutiny she was receiving from Priscilla. Jokes were made back and forth across the table, and guests laughed at stories of Thomas' childhood, including how he broke his wrist jumping from the top of the stairs, his arms wrapped in a sheet to simulate the wings of a Tiger Moth. Douglas made a speech, Thomas thanked everyone present and raised a glass of champagne to his parents, and soon Priscilla – possibly having had one gin and tonic too many, thought Maisie – came to her feet.

'This is my toast to my son, to the leader of our pack of toads. You took your first breath and I was given you to hold, and I have been holding you ever since – when you grew too much of a man for my arms, the muscle of my heart did the holding.' Laughter accompanied her pause. 'I know it will be a few weeks before you achieve your dream to fly, but I insist you never, ever repeat the landing you made on the tiles in the entrance hall.' More laughter. 'And may you come home every chance you get.'

Thomas blew a kiss to his mother, but instead of sitting down, Priscilla continued speaking. 'And tomorrow your beloved Tante Maisie and I will have a surprise for you. After all, it's not only you boys who have to do your bit. But it's a secret until tomorrow, so you'll have to read your letters, Tom.' Another round of laughter ensued, though there were glances back and forth between Priscilla and Maisie. Priscilla lifted her champagne glass and looked at her husband, who came to his feet. Their guests followed suit.

'To Thomas Philip Partridge.'

Voices echoed the toast.

'Thomas Philip Partridge.'

Maisie made her way home from the party, escorted by Timothy and Tarquin. She bid them goodnight as she reached the house, giving each a kiss on both cheeks, then watched as they ambled back along the road towards their home. At one point Tim pushed Tarquin, who pushed back, and then they raced down the street until she could see only shadows in the grainy light of a late Sunday evening.

As she walked to the flat's garden entrance, she was aware of cigarette smoke curling up into the air, and was not surprised to see the silhouette of a visitor seated in one of her wicker chairs outside the French doors leading into her home.

'You could telephone first, you know,' said Maisie.

'I didn't break in this time – I thought I'd just wait for you.' Francesca Thomas took another draw of her cigarette. 'A good send-off for Tom?'

'Yes, it was a lovely evening.' Maisie joined her on the terrace, taking a seat in a wicker chair. 'I have something for you,' she added.

'A report? I dread to think what you've concluded about me.'

'I have a report – with no criticism, just the facts as they emerged since the last time you were here.'

'Good. I think I'm under a big enough microscope already.'

'You didn't know who Gervase Lambert was when you took him on, did you?'

'He was simply a qualified applicant with a superb grasp of English and also French as it is spoken in Belgium. I had no reason to suspect him.'

'Until you did – and even then you didn't believe it.'

'He was a mild-mannered young man, with good references. He was considered trustworthy with delicate information – he had none of the hallmarks of a killer.'

'Dr Thomas – Francesca – I don't know what you consider to be the hallmarks of a killer, but a somewhat common one is that of a person terribly wounded by circumstance, and your assistant fell into that category. He was not a man who killed for the sheer joy of the chase and the final surrender, but a person who was trying to vanquish ghosts he never knew existed until Carl Firmin came to make his confession.'

'Firmin should have stopped at the priest.'

'It would have saved lives had Gervase never known the truth, but truth has a certain buoyancy – it makes its way to the surface, in time.' Maisie sighed. 'What will happen to him?'

'He is currently imprisoned – I cannot say where. He is awaiting certain . . . certain judgements from the British government. It is a highly confidential, delicate matter; however, we are endeavouring to get him transferred to a prison in Belgium. His life – or death – will be no easier, wherever he is.'

Without looking at her guest, Maisie asked another question. 'When you came to me on the day war was declared, why weren't you honest with me? Why didn't you tell me about Addens, about his role in the resistance, and that there were others in the same group who'd remained in England? Why was I left to waste precious time fumbling in the dark, when you suspected Addens was not the killer's first victim? You knew about Firmin's death, after all.'

Thomas was silent for a minute, then sighed. 'In a nutshell, I suppose it's the habit of keeping secrets, Maisie – to the extent that even talking in this way with you is difficult.' She lowered her voice and turned her head as if to detect the presence of another. 'I deal with highly confidential information all the time, and I'm used to protecting people, keeping *their* secrets. That is my world. I have to take utmost care when I provide or receive information.

And I made an error, I know that now. My training, almost my entire adulthood, has required me to live a life apart – and if I am brutally honest with myself, in this instance it was to the extent that I had detached in such a way that I did not suspect Gervase. Add to that the obvious issue of keeping details of our resistance work under wraps as far as possible, and certainly not allowing it to become part of a reported crime and fodder for the press. Suffice it to say, we know – as do you – there are German infiltrators in Britain, and we cannot afford even the slightest hint at our plans for future intelligence efforts.'

Maisie allowed more time to elapse before she spoke again. 'I have something of importance to the case.'

Thomas drew on her cigarette. 'No more shocks, please.'

'It's a map indicating the location of Xavier Bertrand's remains. At the very least, perhaps Gervase could be allowed a visit to pay his respects.'

'I doubt that, but I will take the map now, and be on my way.'

Maisie took a key from her pocket, let herself into the flat, and returned with an envelope, which she handed to Thomas.

'Thank you, Maisie. I suppose all that remains is for you to send me your bill.'

'It's in the envelope,' said Maisie.

Thomas gave a half smile and began to walk towards the side gate. Maisie accompanied her to the front of the property.

'I don't know much about your work, Maisie, but I would imagine that this was not an easy case.'

Maisie looked up into the night sky, at the stars visible between barrage balloons. 'Death is never an easy case, Francesca.'

* * *

The following afternoon, Priscilla arrived at Maisie's office at four o'clock. Sandra had left early, and Billy was visiting a new client, and would not return until Tuesday.

'Are you ready?' asked Priscilla.

'You certainly look the part,' said Maisie. 'Very sensible.'

Priscilla was dressed in a plain costume of navy blue jacket and skirt, brown shoes, and matching brown leather bag. Her hair was pulled back in a chignon, and she wore a brown Robin-Hood-style hat with a blue band.

'You too – but then you always look sensible when you're at work. Bit too sensible after work too.'

'Let's go, then,' said Maisie, ignoring the jibe. 'I'm glad one of us brought a motor car – at least we can prove we can drive. Did you remember your papers from the war?'

Priscilla took a sheaf of documents from her bag and held them up for Maisie's inspection. 'I think we're more than qualified.'

'Are you sure about this?'

'Positive. And you? What about your work, and little Anna?'

'It won't be every day. When I asked, they said the shifts would be mainly at night. I'll tell them I've responsibilities from Friday to Sunday evening.'

Priscilla looked at Maisie, as if gauging her response. 'Might be best all around, when she can join a family to settle into.'

Maisie nodded.

'Well, then, what are we waiting for? Come on, Maisie – let's hold hands and jump into the deep end together.'

Maisie steered the motor car into Tottenham Court Road traffic. The journey was short, taking them to a West End depot of the new London Auxiliary Ambulance Service. Maisie left the Alvis outside the building. They entered together, joining a queue of women waiting to place their applications. Finally it was Maisie's turn.

'You're at work during the day, and you finish at about five or six, you say?' said the man, his eyes moving down the list of responses Maisie had made to a series of questions.

'Yes, but I'm flexible, due to the nature of my work. I can meet the demands of your shifts.'

The man looked up at Maisie and seemed about to question the type of work she was engaged in, before thinking better of it. He looked down at her application again. 'Trained nurse – yes, good. Casualty clearing station over in France during the last war.' He looked up at Maisie. 'S'pose we're all getting used to calling it the last war now, aren't we?' He went back to the page. 'Right, that's good. And Spain too?' Once again he looked up from the pages into Maisie's eyes, this time grinning. 'What's the matter, don't you like it at home?'

Maisie met the joke with a smile. 'I want to volunteer to serve my country. I can drive. I know I can tend the sick and wounded, so I have the right experience.'

He nodded towards Priscilla, waiting by the door. 'She your friend?'

'Yes, we came together.'

'Then you two'd better get busy – ambulance drivers need to be fighting fit, and you've got a few years on the other women in that line. It creeps up on you, does age. Anyway, here are your instructions. Report here tomorrow evening, for the start of your training – it'll mainly be uniform distribution and general rules, though you'll be back Tuesday, Wednesday, and Thursday, and we'll need you for a few weeks' worth of more training – not all day though, again, mainly evenings. We'll tell you more tomorrow. And we'll try to roster you two together, but we can't promise. You both know what we're in for, so we might need you to go out with a girl who's still a bit wet behind the ears – at least you know what death can look like.'

The man's words lingered in the air as Maisie stood up and gathered her bag. 'I'll see you tomorrow then.'

'Ready to do your bit?' He smiled as he came to his feet, shuffled her application papers, and added them to a folder.

Maisie smiled in return. 'Yes, I'm ready.'

AUTHOR'S NOTE

Those familiar with the events of 3rd September 1939 will know that the first air-raid sirens were sounded very shortly after the broadcast of Neville Chamberlain's speech in which he announced that Britain was at war with Germany. In this novel the sirens are heard some twenty minutes after the broadcast ends – I added the lapse in support of the story at that point. Though preparations for war had been in progress for months – the sandbagging of Tube stations and shops, barrage balloons overhead, postboxes painted in a yellow paint that would change colour to signify the presence of poison gas, and trenches prepared in London's parks, for example – the first air-raid siren was a terrible shock to a populace on tenterhooks, many hoping war could be avoided. It was, however, months before the Luftwaffe mounted a full-on air raid on London and other British cities, leading to the hiatus being known as the 'phoney war'.

ALSO IN THE MAISIE DOBBS SERIES

JACQUELINE WINSPEAR

'WRY AND IMMENSELY READABLE' *DAILY MAIL*

LEAVING EVERYTHING MOST LOVED

London, 1933. Two months after Usha Pramal is found murdered in a South London canal, her brother turns to Maisie Dobbs to find the truth about her death, as Scotland Yard have failed to conduct a proper investigation.

Before her murder, Usha was staying at an ayah's hostel, a refuge for Indian women whose British employers had turned them out. But nothing is as it seems and soon another Indian woman is killed before she can speak out. As Maisie is pulled deeper into an unfamiliar yet alluring subculture, her investigation becomes clouded by the unfinished business of a previous case. And at the same time her lover, James Compton, gives her an ultimatum she cannot ignore . . .

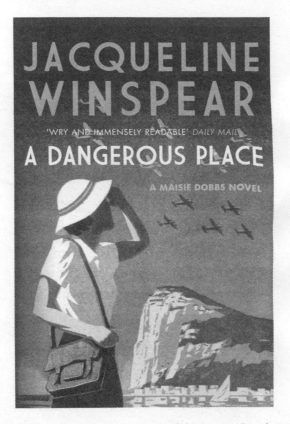

JACQUELINE
WINSPEAR

'WRY AND IMMENSELY READABLE' *DAILY MAIL*

A DANGEROUS PLACE

A MAISIE DOBBS NOVEL

Spring, 1937. Four years after she set sail from England, Maisie Dobbs is making her way home, only to find herself in a dangerous place. She was seeking peace in the hills of Darjeeling, but her sojourn is cut short when her stepmother summons her back to England. But on a ship bound for Southampton, Maisie realises she isn't ready to return.

Against the wishes of the captain she disembarks in Gibraltar – the British garrison town is teeming with refugees fleeing a brutal civil war across the border in Spain. Days after Maisie's arrival, a photographer is murdered, and Maisie becomes entangled in the case, drawing the attention of the British Secret Service as she is pulled deeper into political intrigue on 'the Rock' . . .

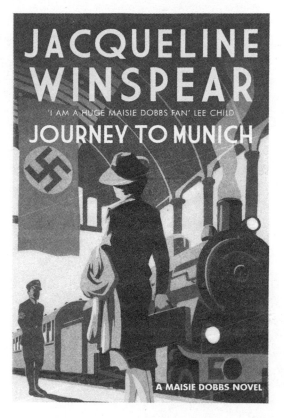

Early 1938. The German government has agreed to release a British subject from prison, but only if he is handed over to a family member. Because the man's wife is dead and his daughter ailing, the Secret Service wants Maisie Dobbs – who bears a striking resemblance to the daughter – to retrieve the man from Dachau Prison, on the outskirts of Munich.

Travelling into the heart of Nazi Germany, Maisie encounters unexpected dangers and finds herself questioning whether it's time to return to the work she loved. But the Secret Service may have other ideas . . .